## DEDICATION

"On a blue Aegean night, when all the gods and nymphs
have said adieu, your muse will find new life."
– Jack McGrath

It did indeed. Thank you, Mr. McGrath.

# TASK FORCE:
# GAEA

## FINDING BALANCE

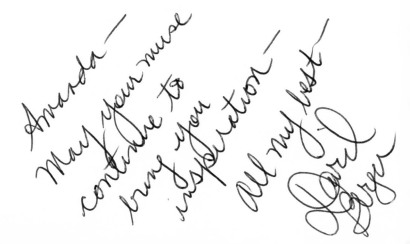

Amanda —
May your muse
continue to
bring you
inspiration —
All my best —

Email: tchrofengl@gmail.com

First Edition

Task Force: Gaea—Finding Balance / Written by David Berger, Land O Lakes, FL 34638

Summary: Four super-powered mortals must save the world from a mistake made by the Olympian gods.

ISBN-13: 978-0615596129 (Custom Universal)
ISBN-10: 0615596126

Printed in the United States of America. Layout by David Berger. Illustrations by Michael Hamlett.

# ACKNOWLEDGMENTS

To my parents, sisters, friends, and my partner Gavi—thank you for all your love and support. This journey has finally come to fruition, and I'm glad you've been there with me.

To my former students—thank you for your interest in reading this labor of love. And to Jason Pioli: I think your people and my people are finally on the same page.

I developed the idea for this novel to express my childhood love of Greek mythology and comic books. From that, grew an adoration for *Wonder Woman*—a comic book character born of myth, the best of both worlds. Thank you, William Moulton Marston, for bringing her into the world, ultimately providing me with endless inspiration. I also want to thank his son, Pete, and granddaughter, Christie: your friendship has connected me to something wonderful (pun intended), and you will always hold a special place in my heart.

To Randy Ham, Brian Sheperd, Brett Crawford, and Cullan Hudson—you have my undying gratitude for helping me bring my dream into reality.

To Michael Hamlett—without your artwork, I couldn't have finished this story. Thank you for being my muse.

# CONTENTS

# PART ONE: OF THE GODS

## 1—FOUNDATIONS

"**B**y Gaea... what have you done!"
Zeus stared at the rubble of the stone door that once sealed Gaea's adyton, a sanctum impenetrable even to the gods, and only the Earth Mother could sanction who entered. Gaea had informed Hermes so he could bring Zeus. He could see the writhing darkness of Gaea's sister scorn him even though she had no face. Zeus could only hear her in his mind for she had no need to be vocal as a *Protogenos*, a primordial being.

"What do you mean I ignored you? And how did you enter this place? Only Gaea can sanction..."

Amorphous and ever changing, her tendrils of darkness curled around the Olympian king. Cloudlike, much like her mother, she roiled throughout the stony chamber, seeming to laugh, if a *Protogenos* could. Zeus, still aghast, examined the wreckage of what once was a set of scales, those that kept the balance of Order and Chaos in this world and the one beyond. Swimming through the dusty air, she smirked at him, or he sensed she did. He, however, was on the verge of tears for the first time in his existence.

"You destroyed the *Hieros Zugos*, O Dark One. Shattered the Sacred Scales as if they were…"

Her voice entered his mind in a language almost forgotten by the gods.

"Yes, *mortal.*"

The vast tenebrosity pervaded the cavern, filling each cavity. Cloudlike wasn't even an appropriate description for her; she was a living, gurgling mass of nothingness, darker than even the sky devoid of stars. For her to destroy something so powerful, so vital… he did not have the words. Or did he.

"Nyx, dark Night, how did I ignore you that you should do *this*? Not even the *Moirae* know the consequences of such an act! Keeping the tenuous balance is what fastens the cosmos together. I do not understand…" His voice trailed off, trembling before this daughter of Khaos, as he knelt by the debris. It was a good thing Hermes had told only him of this tragedy and not the other gods. The winged messenger, the only other witness to the catastrophe, flitted in the shadows. Nyx's silent words brought ire to the Olympian king.

"What do you mean you are not as detached from the gods as I think you are? We felt your detachment, despite what you say, and one would think that a *Protogenos* would have a deeper understanding of the gods.

"Aye, you are correct. I did indeed seek counsel from Erebos, Aether, Thalassa…

"Aye, I sought the same from Eros, Phusis, and even Gaea… and I deeply regret not approaching you. But, this? To have taken the Scales from us? That, O Dark One, seems petty…"

Petty? Filaments of dark, serpents of shadow, made their way toward Zeus—an attack for his disrespect. With clenched fist, he summoned his own filaments, of lightning, and protected himself from her assault. The fires of the sky were enough to repulse Nyx, but Zeus knew well she didn't want to destroy him, simply to scare him for his insolence. He had certainly done as she said. In his pride, he had failed to consult her in the new order after he defeated Kronos and the Titans. Plus, there was one other indignity. How could he now face the gods? No matter. He was King of Olympos, of the Skies, and could wield the thunderbolts forged by the Cyclopes. He would find a way to deal with this. Holding a chunk of one of the scales in his hands, he closed his eyes for a moment and breathed deeply, if gods do indeed breathe. *What to do now*, he mused. Nyx began to reply.

"No, I do not speak with you," he muttered, "And stay out of my thoughts."

He had to tell the other gods. The repercussions of this would resonate throughout time, forward as well as backward, since the scales were not of this world, but merely in it. Even creation itself might change, and he would have to wait to see. Patience was not a godly virtue, however. As he left the bowels of the earth beneath the great mountain, he turned back to see the shifting form of Night vanish into the darkness once more, and he heard what he thought was laughter. The shards of the scales vanished, as well. There was no telling what she had done with them. But, it didn't matter now. The gods needed to know. There was something else, however, that they didn't need to know, and he wouldn't tell them.

He had not walked more than twenty paces when he saw them.

Five immortals stood before him, Hera in front. His sister queen had led them down into Gaea's innards with her consent. Hermes, guilty of letting the others know where Zeus had gone but not why, darted about in the shadows. Indeed, Zeus would be annoyed, but he would overcome that soon enough. When she saw his pallid, angry face, Hera reached for Zeus' cheek.

"Do not be upset at the messenger, my husband. Hermes told us where you were out of necessity. What is wrong? You have been crying?" She had never seen him cry, ever.

Shifting his eyes away, he pointed toward the inner sanctum. As the remaining Olympians witnessed the destruction, disbelief echoed, and the lord of Olympos made his way back to the scene, now devoid of the perpetrator who had undoubtedly skulked back into the depths of the underworld until Helios' sun would set. Only light from a lone torch held by Hesteia shone down on where the debris once sat, and Poseidon knelt and hung his head. He, too, knew the consequence of such an act. Creation's doom, he thought. Hades kept his stoic gaze on emptiness where once sat the keystone of the world, now splintered beyond recognition, its pieces expunged. Unable to remain, Hesteia disappeared in a fiery cloud back to Olympos, ashamed to be in that foul place now. The eldest god, she felt wrenching guilt for not being aware that something like this could happen, or would happen. Deep down, she recognized her own impotence.

Hera touched Zeus' shoulder and radiant eyes spoke words she need not convey, but he understood nonetheless. They had had their differences, to be sure, with all of his dalliances with mortals and immortals alike, but now—at this nadir of their existence—she knew her allegiance was not only necessary, but also required. What do gods do when they despair?

# 2—PERSPECTIVES

Zeus's brethren, after witnessing Nyx's handiwork and realizing how it might threaten their entire being, took a simultaneous moment to reflect upon that day *after* Kronos' defeat during the *Titanomachia*, the day when each took dominion over his or her province of power. Unlike them, Zeus slumped in his throne, the responsibility of Nyx's actions weighing most heavily upon him specifically. He knew all too well why, and he wasn't convinced of her reason either. The gods would look to him for leadership, for strength. How could one who had had prevailed over Kronos now sit, wounded, sulking like a child. His memory of the day after would remain his deep memory, not brought to the nostalgic surface. His ascendance took place the moment the scythe pierced his father's heart, not when he—later—received the blessings of Aeolos, sovereign of the winds, who pledged his offspring into the Olympian's service. Having stretched his hand toward the skies, the newly crowned king of the gods summoned a thunderbolt as his scepter, and thanked Aeolos for his service. The prophecy fulfilled, Zeus had plans to bring Mount Olympos to greater glory than the Titans had. For Humankind, he had much in store, punctuated by lightning that streaked across the bloodstained heavens, a fading reminder of Ouranos' defeat by Kronos that still lingered, but would disappear in time.

Now came his greatest challenge—moving forward and keeping his goals of making the sacred mountain of Olympos the glory of Gaea's earthly crown. So said Zeus, king of the almighty gods.

Almighty indeed.

While he brooded, a conflagration rose in the hearth, its flames erupting, scorching the ceiling. A voice stemmed from the flames, no... three voices, in unison. Not since their birth had they spoken directly with any god, so hearing this made Zeus stand at attention, his fist clenched around a writhing thunderbolt.

"Who speaks to me now? Show yourself!"

The voices of three replied, and Zeus at once knew in whose company he stood.

"Kneel, O Wrathful One, kneel before those who weave thy aftertime!"

Normally, Zeus would refuse such a command, and would kill the one who demanded such for his impertinence, but in this moment, he genuflected, extinguishing the scepter of lightning.

"Summon thy siblings, son of Kronos, for our words have urgency and purpose."

Normally, he would call for Hermes to deliver such a message, but in this instance, thunder would do just as well. Each Olympian appeared instantly; apparently, Zeus' thunder conveyed such urgency, as well as the identity of those for whom he called them: the *Moirae*, the Fates.

"As the Scales kept the balance, they also provided us the thread from which we weave the aftertime of all, mortal and immortal alike. Without such an instrument of equilibrium, our loom is lost, and a new one has taken its place, and threads of unknown origin entwine and braid with new direction." The voices paused. "We know not what the aftertime brings, nor do we know what the beforetime has been. As such, new prophecies unfold and will set forth new paths for mortals... and the gods."

Eyes darted around the chamber, from one god to the other, expressing disbelief mostly, but also, perhaps, fear.

"Take heed of these words, Olympians, if thou hast any yearning to repair what one among has brought.

*"Four not born of godly word*
*Two of vessel, two of sword,*
*Keep vigil over Gaea's kin*
*From Keto's progeny within.*
*Lead day's darkness to finds its path*
*Let spirit restore balance without wrath.*
*Four for Gaea, four must be,*
*For being lacks uncertainty."*

With that, the voices departed, leaving behind simply glowing embers in the hearth, and only the bewilderment on the faces of the gods marked the *Moirae*'s presence, and they had questions. Fate never gave a straight answer.

Gods begat gods, and Olympos grew strong, overshadowing what remained of the Titans' tyrannical rule, the promise of a bright future, perhaps, but only the threads of Fate would truly know.

Nyx's rash act, the ripples of which would crash upon the world, however, would change that which should have happened into what might yet be... or not.

# 3—AFTERMATH

*"A ripple destroys worlds; a wave, yet creates."*

"What troubles you, oracle?"

Stroking his hoary beard, the robed seer aimed his blind eyes skyward. "The Heavens are troubled, Your Majesty. A great tumult challenges the gods, and I fear it shall affect us as well."

Closing the distance to the window, the sovereign looked toward the skies. With a conglomeration of islands under his rule, hundreds of thousands of subjects devoted to him and the Royal House, as well as an army of warriors trained by Athene's guidance, he could easily have grown vain and arrogant. Knowing in the end who ruled whom, he reverently gazed at the white, wispy clouds. Euenor towered over his seer and had become a warrior with whom none would oppugn. However, would it be enough to withstand whatever impinges on the gods? He knew better than most that when something affected Olympos, Humankind's torment wasn't far behind.

"Can you elaborate on this 'tumult'?"

Although he was adept at speaking in vagaries and did so quite often, the ancient prophet simply placed his hood over his head and left the chamber in a prophetic fog, his sad words trailing behind him, "Your Majesty, quite plainly, I fear the destruction of your kingdom will result from the folly of the gods."

Normally, Euenor would question his seer with such an abrupt pronouncement, but he had already intuited the man was correct, and he didn't even possess the gift of second sight. He had not slept in days, or was it weeks—something he learned as a child that meant the world around him was askew. He looked down at the ring on his left hand—the gold ring given to him upon his coronation by Poseidon. Four gemstones in a gold setting, forged in the First Fires, glistened in the daylight. Euenor probed his mind for any reason Olympos might have for destroying his kingdom, if even the gods needed a reason at all. Folly and whim were synonymous with the gods. Could Agisthos be mistaken, he asked himself, knowing that the soothsayer had grown addled since Euenor's father reigned, and that he might be losing his prophetic gift. In all the centuries his kingdom had stood, serenity prevailed, much to the chagrin of Euenor's mainland adversaries for the throne. With the death of his brothers who had ruled beside him, it remained to him to save the majesty and splendor of his world—the lush forests and countryside, the iridescent lakes and rivers which nourished the people, and the self-sustaining system of commerce which had existed years before most lands on the mainland. Only Arkadeia and Themiskyra equaled his monarchy in such beauty and strength. The ring not only symbolized his bond with the gods, having sanctioned his rule, but it also meant he had an obligation to his people to protect them from the capriciousness of the same gods. Euenor would risk eternal castigation in Tartaros to protect his people and his realm.

Three weeks passed.

Olympian time and mortal time do not pass at the same rate, so that which happened on Olympos, or another otherworldly realm, might not show repercussions in the mortal world for weeks, months, or even years. Gold, red, and purple streaked the skies one morning, announcing Helios' chariot's arrival to Gaea, the sun-wheel peering slightly over the horizon. While most of his kingdom slept, Euenor finished reviewing a trade agreement with two heads of state, one from Arkadeia and one from Sparta. Such an accord would be mutually beneficial for all three sovereignties, especially the island monarchy to which Euenor owed his allegiance. Only with his diligence had he managed to keep peace with mainlanders; it was a tenuous peace at best, but Arkadeia and Sparta pledged their fealty to the trade accords, with Athens soon to follow. Euenor's kingdom pledged to send its sea-croppers to show the landlocked regions the benefits of establishing offshore farms to raise fish, ones that his soldiers would protect. In exchange, the mainlanders would deliver ships of crops every few weeks, since not much actually grew on this atoll, except the Royal Garden. Fear and distrust of the unknown could bring this relationship to an abrupt end, but Euenor trusted his advisors, and the delegates, to make this work.

With affairs of state finished for the moment, Euenor walked the gardens to see how Demeter had seen fit to bless his lands, a pastime he grew to love, since the islands bore a limited variety of plants. His people were always welcome to enjoy the vast garden, taking their families to spend the day among the manicured pathways and flowerbeds. Wildflowers sprung up in ornate urns that lined the gravel path, and roses perfumed the air. Some citizens took to the shadow of oak trees beneath which they would share food and wine, gazing out across the cerulean seas. Having Poseidon's favor was advantageous, to be sure, and many of the gods shared the sea god's affinity for the island kingdom. Euenor's sleeplessness continued to weigh upon him as the heavens to Atlas, and his distraction kept him from delighting in the natural wonders. He had hoped to solve the conundrum brought to light a few weeks earlier by his trusted sage, but he had no power among the gods. In the midst of his musings, Zeus' thunder grumbled in the distance and black clouds, moving like angry serpents, overwhelmed the sky while impetuous lightning striated the heavens. Storms were common for islands, but somehow this one seemed different. Stronger. Malevolent. He had wanted to dismiss it as a typical storm, but Euenor then turned to see Agisthos standing in the archway, sweat cascading from his brow while he leaned breathless on a column.

"What ails you?" demanded the king.

A rising gust of wind extinguished the braziers along the path so that only the occasional flash of lightning illuminated them. Echoes of percussive thunder quickened Euenor's warrior heart; he now feared the answers to his inquiries.

"Your Majesty," Agisthos started, catching his breath, "The scrying pool revealed more to me about the heinous misdeed committed against the gods and Humankind."

Euenor escorted the old man back inside and headed for the Hall of Tribunals at the center of the palace to escape the imminent storm.

"Sire…"

Euenor knew that tone. Nothing beginning that way would be good. "Speak."

"I can only see pieces of visions, as if the truth does not want to be known, but this storm is not a sign of Zeus' anger, my king, but rather a consequence of something the sky god has done. Nyx, the blessed *Protogenos*, punished him for disrespect, and now all of Gaea will withstand the worst of this crime. But…"

Euenor fell into his throne, unsure how to respond. His faith for the gods had never wavered, not once, but even Zeus shared similar emotions that oftentimes plagued Humankind.

"…the worst has yet to come," continued Agisthos, "I have consulted with the high priests of Poseidon. Our destruction is forthcoming. I know not how exactly, but I do know that your kingdom will suffer for Zeus' crime. All of Gaea will suffer…"

"Toy with me not, old man…"

"I do not, sire! The signs are clear: in three days, your kingdom will cease to exist. We must evacuate the island now!"

Agisthos fell to the floor, his eyes clenched shut. "O Blessed Olympos, I can see them… drowning… crying out to Poseidon for salvation, but he chooses to answer them not, or cannot."

The king called for servants to bring the soothsayer to his chambers while he sought out the only one who could possibly help him—Poseidon. Standing before the altar, Euenor pleaded for help, not even sure if the god would reply, although he had been favored in the past. He dropped to his knees. Silence crashed down upon him as he prostrated himself before a copper likeness of the sea god. Would the Earth-Shaker come to him? Losing his kingdom like this was unacceptable. Iron braziers shot forth with flames and a voice entered Euenor's mind, but the words didn't bring the comfort he needed.

"I understand, Lord Poseidon," he whispered.

The god's voice trailed off, covered by the ear-splitting thunder. They needed to abandon their home. That was Poseidon's only help, but he did promise safe passage to Akhæa, the Greek mainland, so that Euenor's people could be spared. It would take days to sail to the mainland, more days than those allotted to him. Dear gods, he thought, how could everything he worked for come crumbling down? Moreover, why was Poseidon unable to aid him further? Was Olympos so affected by this that even the gods were afraid?

He returned to the Hall of Tribunals and summoned the captain of the guard. A burly, armor-clad man replied to the summons, his heavy footfalls echoing throughout the corridor, and he saluted his sovereign.

"Diomedes, fill as many ships with our people and send them toward the mainland. Even the gods dare not help us, but Poseidon has promised safe passage to Akhæa. Tell the people to take nothing but themselves and leave immediately!"

"As you wish, King Euenor!" replied the soldier, and he left, not even questioning the strange order.

Over the days that followed, hammering rain and wind ravaged the island while its inhabitants scurried for safety. Women carried their children while the men gathered food and other provisions for the journey. Tremors like those that they had never seen shook the island, bringing down the taller structures first, killing some citizens and seriously injuring others. The living took the wounded aboard the ships while they abandoned the dead. Some of those who perished were children, and soldiers needed to tear grieving parents from their children's bodies as they placed an *obolos* beneath their tongues for Charon. Late into the night, the islanders scurried for the harbor, fear of oblivion motivating them. More dead accumulated on the streets, some trampled while others perished beneath crumbling columns, unable to be buried or properly sent to the underworld. *Hermes Psychopompos* would indeed be busy this day, with no time to shed one tear for the fallen, his only hope that Hades would find them all places in Elysium, where the souls of the good spend eternity. Overcrowded ships left the harbor for the mainland, and some inhabitants simply dove into the ocean hoping to swim the distance.

Euenor helped the infirmed and the young to the ships, knowing his legs would move much more quickly. His royal robes were tattered and dirty, and he had lost his crown in the chaos. Nothing of his regalia mattered. Just before dawn of the second day, the last few ships were leaving the harbor for the *Mesogeios*, or Mediterranean Sea. A handful of soldiers remained, those closest to the king and the Royal House. After the ships had all departed, Euenor returned to the palace to await oblivion. His wife, Queen Syra, now the bearer of the ring, and his two daughters were safe, guaranteed safe passage to the mainland. His lineage would continue. Dozens of faithful soldiers gathered around their sovereign, choosing to spend their final moments in his presence.

• • •

Standing on the beach, the surf crashing around her while her daughters clinged to her, Queen Syra watched the storm's fury grow as small boats came ashore, depositing more and more of her homeless people. Clutching all she had left, her two treasures who were too young to understand, she stood tall against the natural forces determined to destroy her home. Simultaneously cursing the gods for their whims yet praying for her husband's safe arrival, she didn't know that this was the result of a *Protogenos*. All she knew was that the man who had built a kingdom with her would meet whatever the *Moirae* had planned without his family around him.

With a deafening scream from the skies, a fireball—a piece of the *Hieros Zugos*—plummeted toward the island. Upon impact, the earth cracked and Gaea wailed. Crevices split the island, seawater from both sides filling the gaps. At the bottom of the ocean, the sea floor disintegrated beneath the island and the remaining pieces of the once-great kingdom vanished beneath the waves.

Dropping to her knees, shrieking at the horror she had just witnessed, she swore to all who might hear the thoughts of a widowed queen that she would lead her people to survival, and she wrapped her arms tightly around her daughters.

All of Olympos wept, even Zeus, although his act would continue to befoul Gaea's glory. Atlantis was merely the first to fall.

# 4—PENANCE

The Fates' intricate tapestry grew, and time staggered forward; god and mortal remembered the destruction of Atlantis as a twisted, sad tale of the accidental revenge of an angry goddess. Corruption pervaded much of Humankind, and cities propagated like weeds, and fell just as easily. Akhæa became staunchly divided, with many civilizations either seeking to cannibalize one another or withdrawing from the world, many times doing so on a whim—the consequence of no true balance. Order and Chaos fluctuated so much that even Olympos had difficulty determining what was happening, and the gods chose to withdraw more from the world of Man. All but one kept distance from mortals, and the *Moirae* knew who and why.

• • •

When Zeus raged, not only did Olympos know, but also the rest of the mortal world, as the very bowels of the sacred mountain shook with such fervor, even Gaea took note. On this day, he aimed his wrath at a puerile Apollo who had pushed his father to limits even an immortal didn't know he had. *Zeus Maimaktes*—the Agitated One—

tightened his grip on a wriggling thunderbolt, bearing his contempt for disobedience, disdaining the youth. Not since his childhood had Apollo seen such rage that his father's own eyes bore through him so. To whom do the gods pray for mercy?

*"I know why I am here, Father,"* Apollo thought, *"and it is not the reason you shall use to defame me. But, Lord Zeus, I will play your game because not doing so would do much harm."*

His outward demeanor did not betray him, and the god of reason knew Zeus's anger would cloud his ability to discern the truth.

"Your dishonor, Phoebos Apollo, has brought shame not only to me, but also to every immortal on Olympos. How dare you defy me!" Zeus pounded his fist against the arm of the throne. Continents shook.

The young god had entered the chamber a smug, swaggering immortal, his smirk revealing all. What words could he possibly utter that would ameliorate what he had done without revealing that which must remain hidden? None must disobey an edict from Zeus—ever. Apollo had always been the favored son; he was the Phoebos, the Shining One, for his radiance brought such joy to the halls of Zeus' palace, and the king of the gods could ignore many of his son's indiscretions. For so many years, Zeus had sought the company of women and goddess, fathering more offspring than stars in the heavens. When that grew tiresome, some handsome youth would turn Zeus' head; he had had such fond memories of Ganymede. Just after the destruction of the Scales, he immediately wished for a change, forsaking all others and pledging loyalty to Hera, his sister wife and queen. By Olympian decree, witnessed by all the gods, all immortals were to abandon promiscuity for monogamy, which did not sit well with satyrs and fauns especially. Despite objection, they were bound to obey. Some believed Zeus would eventually abandon this folly, and then they could all return to lewdness and debauchery, for those who desired. Of all the gods, haughty Apollo had dallied more than any other had, especially with mortals. If Humankind sought to become more godlike, then it would be the gods who would have to set the example.

Apollo turned his face away from his father. Where he would normally stand, chest inflated, ready to deflect an accusation, now seeing Zeus' ire, all he could muster was, "Father, I deeply regret—"

"Silence!" Zeus' thunderbolt flared. "I will not tolerate your insincerity, so an example must be set. Your impetuousness shall not be ignored."

Zeus' storm-laden eyes would eventually forgive, but not for some time. Eons, perhaps. Portentous clouds churned in the skies above the Hall of Tribunals, and heaven's roaring made the columns vibrate. No other god present dared to support Apollo, not even Hera, or his sister, Artemis. The queen of the gods had not had much affinity for the son of Leto, but even she felt pity for him, and trepidation about how Zeus would handle this. *If she only knew the truth*, Apollo mused.

"To Gaea you will be banished. When you fully understand how you brought such ignominy, then I will allow you to return!" The thunderbolt in his grip flailed like an animal caught in a trap. "And seek not to deceive me, for I shall know if you try," he added.

*Apollo Pythios*, who once slew the serpent Python at Delphi, shook like a storm-blown leaf, knowing that the worst was not over. It had indeed just begun.

"Henceforth, you will be mortal!"

No sooner had that last word left Zeus' mouth than did Apollo gasp, feeling the divine ichor in his veins turn to mortal blood. As his godhood slipped from him, he quavered and lost his balance. No one went to his aid as he almost crashed to the floor.

Zeus continued his pronouncement. "You will wear mortal trappings, and take nothing from Olympos!" Apollo's raiment of silk edged with gold transformed with another thunderbolt to that of common linen, and his feet bore rawhide sandals. Replacing his simple golden circlet that emanated the sun's rays was a leather strap. He touched his face; in just the few moments of being mortal, he felt what he thought was facial hair. Mortality felt limiting and, for the first time in his existence, he was actually aware of his physical self. He had never known what gravity felt like, nor did he understand the physics of walking, bearing his true weight on the ground. Gods manifest themselves as humans for sport, since they are pure energy and need no actual form, but now Apollo was physically human. Athene, wisdom's keeper, whispered something to her father who nodded.

"Aye," he continued, "Rise. Mortals do possess knowledge of healing arts, although in a limited fashion, as well as a bowman's skill. You may keep those abilities, but you must find your own bow. Take nothing from the sacred armory." The word 'nothing' actually brought pain to Apollo.

Once the brazen, arrogant son of the Thunderer, he was now shamed before the assembly of gods and did not belong. *Zeus should suffer this ignominy*, he thought. He had not even started his punishment on Gaea and already felt subconscious twinges of repentance, or what he assumed was such, despising his mortal self more than he had even despised other mortals. Zeus told him to visit Hephæstos in the forge; he would understand when he arrived. Hermes, summoned by Zeus, would have to escort him since he lacked the power to go himself. Before Apollo and his brother departed, the storm god made one more decision.

"Choose another name before you set foot on Gaea, or one will be chosen for you. Apollo is the name of a god."

Apollo, after a few moments, replied, "I will find a name suitable, father. Worry not. There is only so much you can take from me." Disbelief had quickly become resentment. Hermes escorted his brother from Olympos, afraid even to make eye contact.

At an entrance only known to gods and other immortals, they stood before the gaping maw in the base of Olympos, sooty clouds having stained the mouth of the cave. Hermes instructed Apollo to enter the forge and seek out Hephæstos and then the winged messenger flew back to Olympos. Apollo cautiously entered, not knowing how his brother would receive him; so this is what fear felt like, he thought. Scattered torches held in the wall with iron rings illuminated the path through the maze of passageways. Hot, stale air made it hard for him to breathe—another new sensation—but he eventually spied his ash-covered brother sitting on an iron stool, his hammer pounding away on a small object. Not as striking as Ares or Apollo, Hephæstos was a comely god whose upper body rivaled Herakles from centuries of working metal for the gods. Leather straps crossed over his torso, connected in the middle by an iron medallion emblazoned with a fiery garnet the size of an apple; leather pteruges covered his lower half. As the forge god raised his hammer and struck the object on the anvil, the leather straps creaked and stretched against his bulging pectoral muscles. A trimmed beard outlined his square jaw line, and a smudged strap of cloth kept the sweat from his eyes. Hephæstos' legs, although developed from carrying thrones, chariots, and armor, were almost useless for walking—a consequence of being flung from Olympos by Zeus—so he had two bronze automatons that helped him with the heavier pieces.

"I am almost finished," Hephæstos announced, his voice interrupting the clangs of the final hammering. Apollo saw an armband on the anvil and his mortal heart skipped a beat. Perhaps Zeus had relented and this punishment had ended. Unfortunately for Apollo, he began to discern the truth.

Sparks escaped the hammer as it came down on the living metal, a metal only workable in this mystic forge. Centuries of craftsmanship and blacksmithing had honed Hephæstos' ability to shape any metal to his whim, and once worked with his hammer, it could neither be broken nor scratched. Such was the gift of Gaea's fire, the same fires that created Ouranos, the same fires from which burst forth the mountains and valleys, the fields and the deserts. Of all the gods, only Hephæstos had the Earth Mother's approbation to use her sacred fire. He knew his brother had entered, but he kept working on his project, something Zeus gave first priority. Etching god-forged Earthsteel required a swage, and this part demanded his complete attention: one mistake and the binding spell wouldn't work. Having no need for a formal language or symbology, the gods developed a set of glyphs they used for marking sacred relics or, in this case, binding agents. One glyph stood for Olympos, another for Zeus, and a third, for *metemeleia*, or penance. Zeus' high priests would know what these three pictograms meant, but priests of such high honor rarely left the shrine of the Olympian king. If it were not for the paralyzing trepidation he felt in his gut, Apollo would actually admire his brother's handiwork.

"There, 'tis done. Come closer, brother, and see that which restrains you in the world of Man," retorted Hephæstos.

"You still disdain me, eh, brother? I am no longer the Shining One, so you should be pleased. Regardless, Zeus will still not look better upon you now."

Hephæstos smirked, realizing that while his brother was correct, he would still at least have his place as an Olympian.

21

Apollo examined the metalwork, his fingers brushing the symbols. As a mortal, his ability to read such symbols would fade, a frustrating circumstance for someone who had read Olympian glyphs since birth. Yet one more aspect of his godhood denied him. Watching the final adjustments enhanced Apollo's discomfort, and Hephæstos thrust the manacle into the fire one last time. Doused in a marble basin, wisps of serpentine steam ascended and vanished, just like his immortality.

"Being human suits you," sniggered Hephæstos. "I knew your dalliance with mortals would be your undoing."

"Suppress the sarcasm," Apollo replied, wiping the sweat off his face.

"Get used to that, brother, for you will be toiling for sustenance and shelter. Like an animal, you will forage, and like a thief, you will purloin. Give me your wrists."

Glaring, Apollo extended his arms. The blacksmith hammered into Apollo's other wristbands and removed them, but nicked the skin a little. Blood. Red blood. Something else Apollo had never experienced. He didn't care, which surprised him; he knew it would heal, and it wasn't a large wound. He just wanted this moment to end to get on with his humiliation. On his left wrist, Hephæstos placed the freshly forged cuff, the seam sealing itself; such was the nature of god-made metal.

"Be thankful I am human. If I thought for one moment you enjoyed this, I would cripple your arms as well."

"Take heed. As a human, threatening a god is punishable by death." He enjoyed toying with Apollo, since he rarely had the chance to be the antagonist. Joy was not the feeling he had, but rather satisfaction, simply because he was jealous of everything the god Apollo possessed.

The former sun god tightened his fist, the warm metal constricting his wrist; surely, a badge of shame, he thought. Hermes was waiting for him at the entrance to the forge, and he glanced at the metalwork but said nothing. Despite the pranks he enjoyed playing on his brother, he would not instigate since he knew that Apollo would once more wear the mantle of a god, and wanted to avoid his brother seeking him out for revenge, as he could be spiteful and cruel. Apollo asked if he could say goodbye to his steeds, the horses that drew his chariot of the sun across the heavens, but Hermes declined since the horses were beasts of fire and would incinerate him. He agreed to wish the horses farewell for his brother and that seemed to appease Apollo a little, although he was heartbroken knowing he would not see them again for a time. With a whisk of his caduceus, the messenger of Olympos returned them to the throne hall where Apollo could make his farewells. Once again, Helios would take on the responsibility he had bestowed upon Apollo since the sun must rise and fall at the set times.

Awaiting them were Athene and Aphrodite, whose melancholy faces dismayed Apollo. His sister, Artemis, was not with them; he wondered if he would see her at all before he left. Aphrodite embraced her brother, as did Athene, wishing him well and whispering they would always watch over him even if they could not directly aid him. The gods often favored mortals, but under these circumstances, Zeus wanted Apollo to experience mortal life without Olympos. Athene and her brother exchanged a few more words, and then a smile came to Apollo's face as he saw a red-haired goddess materialize right in front of him.

"I almost did not come, but not because of anger. You are my twin, and we have shared much," Artemis uttered. "I cannot bear to say farewell, even though I have faith you will return." A firm embrace followed her words, and he clenched his eyes closed, hoping to keep the tears from falling. A sacred bond they shared, and he would miss his sister more than any other. She whispered, "Despite Zeus,

I will aid you if I can." He wished he could tell her all he knew.

The triad of goddesses escorted him to where the Olympian monarchs sat, but Apollo walked closer, bowing his head toward each instinctively. Zeus noticed the armband, commenting to Hera that their son's handiwork surpassed any mortal blacksmith. He looked beyond Apollo to the three goddesses, and they evaporated into mist; he did not wish them to see this moment, a first in the history of Mount Olympos. Thunder rumbled beyond the marble halls, storm clouds roiling above them. Zeus clenched a squirming thunderbolt, ready to do its lord's bidding. Perhaps it was the moment, or maybe it was his mortality, but Apollo feared his father's power where before he admired it.

"Fare thee well, my son," murmured the sky god. "Before I cast you to a mortal life, tell me the name you have chosen so that I might be able to speak of you to the gods." One more indignity.

Apollo answered. "As the island of my birth had once floated on the seas before it attached to the sea floor, so will I drift in the world of mortals. *And scorn you for my alleged crime against the gods*, he thought, *and my silent accusations toward you.* "I shall be... Delos."

A crack of thunder, and Gaea would soon receive her newest mortal. Zeus hid his smirk well, and his secret would be safe. For now.

• • •

By the wave-battered shores of the Euxine Sea, Delos descended just as the sun-chariot ascended. Helios would tend to it as he had ages past. Delos would no longer concern himself with such issues. He walked westward, not even noticing the cool wavelets creeping up the sand to kiss his feet, as if Gaea bid him welcome to her realm. Earth Mother she would always be, and he would never need to know she watched over him, this wayward great-grandson. If she bore his secret knowledge, she said nothing.

He followed the meandering shoreline, feeling the soft, damp sand. He had never felt the coarse grains between his toes, or the waves gliding over his ankles, so he stopped momentarily to enjoy this. As a god, noticing the details of a beach had no interest for him, but as Delos, he took the time to crouch down and drag his fingers through the wet sand, feeling how it gently abraded his skin.

Ambling onward a mile or so from where he began his journey, he noticed a weathered pillar jutting from the sand supporting an icon of a Nereid. Farther down the beach, he made out the shape of an elderly man standing in the surf trying to maintain his balance as he reeled in his fishnets, full from the morning's efforts. Despite the man's size and age, he had enough strength to pull the nets onto the sand. He reminded Delos of Zeus in a way, strong yet bearing a silver beard, and his weathered countenance laid bare his fisherman's life, always in the sun. Having dealt with mortals only as a god, he wasn't sure how actually to hold a conversation with this man, should it become an issue, but he would make an attempt.

"Are you in need of help, old man?" Delos asked.

Concentrating on casting the net at the precise moment, the old man did not hear the question. Delos asked again.

"Nay, stranger. This old body has many years left, and the day I can't pull in a net of fish is the day Hades takes my soul," replied the man. "I've been here since before sunrise."

Delos, not knowing what else to do, sat down and watched the man fish. The man glanced over at Delos long enough to notice his unsoiled clothes and the unblemished armband. Surely, this man was a dignitary or emissary from a foreign land, the old man thought.

"You are not from this village," he observed. Fish flopped around within the confines of the net, a few making their way back to the sea successfully.

"From a village in the Piereia province, in Macedoneia. You most likely would never have heard of it," Delos answered, trying to be as vague as possible. In reality, Olympos was in the Piereia province, so he was not lying.

The fisherman, his muscles straining, pulled in his last net, emptying it into a damp burlap sack.

"What is your name, stranger? I am Ios, of Trapæzos. My village is yonder," he said, gesturing toward the weathered column Delos had seen earlier.

"I am Delos," he replied, hoping that Ios would not ask many questions, but the conversation took his mind off the events of the morning.

Tying hemp around the burlap sacks, Ios loaded them into a wooden cart along with the nets and gathered the rest of his belongings. Delos noticed a bow and quiver in the cart, not quite the quality of that which is in the Olympian armory. Apparently, Ios was more than he seemed. They apparently had much in common already.

"If you're looking for a place to stay, you can accompany me back to my village," Ios said.

Delos followed Ios toward the path worn in the sea grass, passing by the Nereid's likeness. Putting a hand to his abdomen, he felt an uneasy rumbling. Ios saw this and handed Delos a burlap pouch which contained bread and cheese. Of course, thought Delos, this was what being hungry felt like. On Olympos, gods eat nectar and ambrosia, but not out of hunger, but more for enjoyment. Ios pushed the cart up to the path, removed some seaweed from the wheels, and walked forward.

Delos discovered quickly that Ios liked to talk, and he learned more about the old man in a few minutes than most people might learn in a few days. He didn't mind, though. The morning air smelled of salt and fish, and he became fascinated with the seagulls circling over the cart, hoping to spy a loose fish to steal. Shorter, windswept marble pillars bordered the sandy path, and he could see trees in the distance. Ios told tales of "the one that got away" and the time when he was pulled into the surf while fishing. Delos couldn't help but be amused, thinking this man was a combination of his father's features, his brother Dionysos' dry humor, and Hermes' quick wit. If mortals were like Ios, thought Delos, perhaps his penance would be tolerable. In the distance, the ground leveled off and a narrower column marked a crossroads. Three men on horseback approached from the east, each dressed in armor and brightly colored tunics, and a chlamys over their shoulder. Judging from their manner, Delos surmised they were military men, although one of the three dressed more like a high priest. Having had his own high priests, he was quick to identify the aspect. Ios slowed his gait once he saw the men trotting down the path, and Delos noticed this.

"Is something wrong? Are these men not from Trapæzos?"

"Nay, my friend," Ios said.

The tone of the old man's voice told Delos all he needed to know, so he removed the bow and quiver from the cart furtively. If Ios noticed, he said nothing. When they were within earshot, a man wearing a pale green tunic and what Delos concluded was a royal standard addressed the fisherman.

"Good morn, Ios," he started. "How was your catch this day?"

Ios remained silent.

"I asked you a question!" the man shouted, dismounting. He stepped closer to Ios who, despite the circumstances, remained quiet and calm. "I can see you did well today, old man. You may actually take some home to your family after all." He poked around the cart at the bags of fish. Pulling a knife from his side, he slit open one sack and dumped it in the cart, fish wriggling in the morning sun.

Still, Ios remained silent. This had happened before.

Delos held an arrow in one hand and the bow in the other, watching the man in the pale green tunic. No one seemed to care about him, for the moment. The second armored man dismounted, but his temperament was worse. With a deep grunt, he lifted the cart from one side and flipped it over.

"I don't fear you, Galateian," Ios announced, pulling a dagger from his wrist scabbard.

"Why do these men harass you?" asked Delos.

"Because Trapæzos is a fishing village and Galateia is in the center of the desert. The high priest of Poseidon in Galateia offended the sea god by raping a young girl in his temple. Poseidon then made Galateia's only thriving river, Meander, barren of all life. The terror campaign of the Galateians has put them in ill favor with other nations, so they must harass and pillage, like common thieves. Don't let their royal insignia fool you, my friend. I would enjoy seeing them attempt this crime in Phrygeia; *that* land has a large army and would repel these vermin."

"The old one is bold, Polos. Perhaps he would lose his impudence if I cut out his tongue?" the man in the green tunic commented, removing a sword from his waist scabbard.

"Perhaps, Creon. And I'll dismember his friend, leaving his entrails to rot in the sun," Polos grinned.

The third man remained on his mount, but kept his distance from the other two. Perhaps he would be a voice of reason for them, or maybe he would coax them into frenzy. Regardless, Delos's eyes never left him. This first day on Gaea would end in death; only the Fates would know if it were his death, or Ios, or these marauders. On the other hand, would it be salvation to die and not endure an unknown period as a human? Something intrigued the man on horseback. While Delos had been watching Polos and Creon, the man had been watching Delos, especially his armband. With subtle gestures, he nudged the horse forward, hoping to get a better look. When he translated the symbols, his face paled.

"Brethren! Cease this at once! The fair-haired one is..."

Fearing the priest would give away his identity, Delos raised the bow and sent an arrow clear through the man's throat. His hands clutching his neck, the man fell off his horse, crimson life oozing into the earth. Creon charged at Delos, but another arrow found its mark in his chest. Delos brought the bow up to his cheek, nocked with another arrow.

"You have now twice insulted the sea god, first in his own shrine, and now by assaulting an innocent man near the sea. Unless you wish to see the Netherworld, turn and go," Delos instructed Polos. Delos admired Ios' courage in this.

The Galateian dropped his weapon, started to turn, but swung around. The arrow made a hollow thud as it penetrated Polos' head, killing him instantly. A hidden dagger fell from his hand. Delos had not been on Gaea more than an hour and already he had killed three mortals. Surely, the *Moirae* had a sense of humor, or of the macabre.

Ios stared at his companion, finally managing to speak. "Thank you, friend. I felt sure I would see Hades this day."

Delos lifted the cart back to its wheels and salvaged some of the undamaged burlap bags. Wolves or wild dogs would eventually consume the dead men. No doubt, Hermes had taken their souls. Gaea would claim what remained. Ios and Delos didn't speak until they arrived at a pennant denoting the boundary of Trapæzos.

# PART TWO: DELOS

## 5—ALLIANCES

"Here is where my story began, so pay heed, goddess of Justice.

"As we approached the border, marked only by a weathered flag bearing a fish, I could see the village, a collection of two-dozen straw huts built around the agora, and what a marketplace it was. Villagers moved about, bartering for produce or fabric, taking in the latest gossip, and sampling meats and other dishes from farmers and fishermen. I had never really taken an interest in mortal life, so this intrigued me. Women and their daughters gathered around the crude, rocky well, filling their amphorae with what had to be the only fresh water for miles. Older women covered their heads with tattered shawls, while younger women displayed long hair. I passed men chopping log after log for firewood, while others returned from their hunt bearing their prized boar and deer. As the men still lived, they must have given thanks to my sister, Artemis, before taking their aim.

"Children and the younger men and women nodded or genuflected at the elder folk. Odd. I had only ever seen that in the presence of the gods. Perhaps mortals share some traits with us. With them, I should say. Ios mentioned that he was one of the few men who actually did his own fishing, much to the chagrin of the ruling council. He did not expect others to care for him, despite his advanced age, a trait I am began to admire. 'My rest will come with Hermes takes my soul to Hades,' he told me.

"Ios called out to Kabos, the blacksmith here, working in his small forge that opened out into the plaza from a tent. Eager apprentices surrounded him, trying to lift his hammer, but the tool came down haphazardly on the anvil. I was reminded of my own handiwork of Hephæstos, something I hoped to have removed sooner than later. As we came closer to a small hut, a young man met us, Ios' son Maelodon, who asked about his father's bedraggled appearance without even noticing me. I used to look at Zeus that way, long ago. The boy took the sacks into the hut, but Ios pressed on toward another hut. He said we had to apprise the Council of Elders of Trapæzos of what had happened with the Galateians.

"Wooden icons hung on the outside of the hut. I was not going to dismay the Council by explaining that wooden icons and superstitions did not protect them. The gods did. Some, anyway. Regardless, we were to meet with the five High Elders who oversaw the town, and their eyes fell on me as if I were curiosity. They were apparently not accustomed to strangers helping them. Ios entered the hut first, bowing low to those who sat in darkness within these frail walls. As I entered through the beaded curtain, the pungent incense overpowered me. I was used to it in temples to me—to Apollo—but not this much. It, like the wooden icons, had no protective power, but these simple people would probably not wish to hear that. Ios relayed what happened and introduced me to the four people, two men and two women, who sat cross-legged on the floor around a hearth.

"On behalf of the Council, and the people of Trapæzos, they welcomed me. Rather, Adara, a red-haired woman with a strong face, ushered those words. The others sat tightlipped. I asked what they planned to do about the Galateians, but I was silenced abruptly by an elderly man who muttered something about protocol. I didn't like the warmth on the back of my neck and my flushed face. Embarrassment didn't feel like something I would enjoy, and it crept up on me before I could react. I found myself looking down, much like I had done on Olympos. Ios vouched for me before escorting me toward a side of the hut so the Council could deliberate. I was, apparently, not meant to offer my opinion in such matters, impudence I would have to forgive if I expected to live as a mortal man. I explained that asking questions brought about knowledge, and that silencing one who sought knowledge was disrespectful to me. Hospitality should be a priority, but—alas—in this small village, well, never mind. Apollo would have smote them, but Delos? I needed to develop a thicker skin.

"The Council placed me in Ios' care during my stay, and I should be afforded every courtesy for having saved such a prestigious member of the community. That, at least, was a comfort to me. My welcome at his humble hut more than made up for my recent experience. Ios' wife, Eiraena, a woman of austere beauty, invited me to sit and offered me a drink of water sweetened with pomegranate. It almost reminded me of nectar. As she scurried about, I noted that their home's furnishings were not akin to the throne room on Olympos by any means, but Eiraena kept it tidy and pleasant. Fishing nets and burlap sacks did not replace silk and velvet, but they comforted me. I found myself enrapt by the aroma of fresh bread baking, and smiled a little at the cracked clay cup filled with wildflowers on the table.

"Ios' wife embraced me, followed by 'May Hesteia watch over you.' Indeed she would, and those words warmed my mortal heart more than any fire. Any apprehensions I had about mortals were melting away, much like the beeswax candle that flickered on the table. I would have to remember these people when I reclaim my godhood. Certainly, they would be worthy of a god's gifts. Someday.

"Evening meal—that is what Eiraena called it— consisted of bread, pungent goat's cheese, boiled eggs, and grilled fish, slightly charred. My first meal in the mortal realm met with me having three servings which pleased Eiraena. Ambrosia would have paled in comparison. I had eaten with mortals before, but not with any family, mostly with passersby when I would dally in towns looking to satisfy a different appetite. Throughout the meal, I could feel Maelodon's eyes on my manacle, and I knew questions would follow.

"He asked what brought me to Trapæzos. I simply replied, 'Traveling the world at my father's request to gain some insight.' I did not think that satisfied him, but it would have to. For now. I think he noticed that my hands were free from calluses, but I changed the subject. I said I would continue westward to see what the land had to offer, but Ios' expression suddenly changed. He asked if I would travel by Themiskyra, but I had not thought that far ahead. He referred to the Amazons of Themyskira as men-haters. I filled the awkward silence by eating a salt-laden egg.

"Barbaric women warriors, he called them, having forsaken all male gods. My limited experience with them could not confirm or deny that. I assuaged him by saying I would do my best to avoid any problems if I were to venture that far west. Ios just continued to eat. After the meal, Maelodon excused himself and Eiraena cleared the dishes. Before leaving the hut, Maelodon invited me to join him and some friends for a swim at Triton's Cove.

• • •

"A few months later, Ios told me that Adara, the Council member who had addressed me when I first arrived had taken ill, having stepped on a harpy's egg. As the healer of Trapæzos, Ios had rudimentary knowledge of roots and herbs, poultices and potions, so he had visited Adara to see what he could do. Zotikos, the woman's husband, despaired greatly, more than I had ever seen in a mortal. My life with these people had taught me so much, and I found that my underlying arrogance and defensiveness was wearing down. The news of Adara's illness even had me feeling sadness, more so because I knew how poisonous a harpy's eggshell could be.

"Ios tried herbal remedies and incense to allow her to breathe more easily, but I knew it would only be a matter of time. I had come to understand that my mortality would help me understand that of those around me, since I didn't have the means to heal Adara through any divine means. Prayer vigils to Apollo and Aesculapius would go unheeded, not because these people were not worthy, but one of their gods was absent, and the other was dead. My son, Aesculapius, tried to resurrect the dead, and Zeus smote him. Hades was appeased, and that was all that mattered, I guess. Zeus and I would have our reckoning someday for many of his misdeeds. Of that, I was certain.

"I hadn't realized it until this incident with Adara, but I had become contemptuous of the gods. Without any contact from my brethren, I had lost interest in being among them. That might change in the future, but I didn't care all that much. While Ios cared for his patient, Maelodon and I spent time with Zotikos, mostly preparing him for the inevitable. Eiraena kept everyone fed and at ease, as much as she could. Soon, it wouldn't matter, though.

34

"Only hours past sunrise on the fourth day of her illness, Adara's soul passed into Hades with Hermes. Even though I wasn't able to see him take her soul, I could still feel the fluttering of his sandals as he whisked her away to meet Charon. Trapæzos mourned the loss for many weeks. I, too, cried, not only for Adara, but for Zotikos and their children, as well as for my losses. I had never really come to terms with my life change, and I wept enough tears to flood the earth with no Deucalion or Pyrrha to cast stones. My world had been changed forever. Mortality hurt.

"I spent much of the funerary banquet in quiet meditation beneath an oak tree. I didn't understand the irony until later. Zeus' tree gave me solace. The soul I had had learned all it could from Ios and his village. I needed to move on.

• • •

"Months passed, and I finally found the courage to make plans to leave Trapæzos. Before I could do that, though, I wanted to see the Grove of Artemis, a place of mysticism and solace. I had been afraid to go. At first light, one morning, I quietly took an oaken bow I had made and my quiver, venturing beyond Triton's Cove. It wasn't hard to miss. A canopy of myrtle trees formed over my head, guiding me to a clearing where I saw a stump, presumably an altar of some kind. Or it used to be. I remembered how to shoot, and made the stump my target, landing a dozen shafts into the dead wood. Each dull thud felt as if it had pierced my own heart."

"As I retrieved my arrows, a stag bounded before me, seven feet high from ear to hoof, stooping to graze not far from the stump. A voice embraced the wind, and I heard, 'A noble animal if ever one existed,' and it was a voice I knew well. With a stag that handsome, I knew she wouldn't be far behind. I remember our conversation well:

*'I told Zeus my prized stag had wandered off. It was the only way I could come down to see you.'*

*'Even if he knew, he wouldn't do anything to you. You're his favorite.' I said.* We both smiled.

*'Why do you remain here, brother, among these people?'*

*'These people, Artemis? They're noble and righteous people, and I have great respect for them. You would do well to spend some time among mortals, among people— the term mortal seems so degrading now.'*

She said nothing.

*'Have you ever been mortal, sister?'*

*'No, I have not, but I have taken on their form.'*

*'Not the same thing, I'm afraid. We have to handle our dilemmas as they come, without the ability to transform our enemies into chimerae.'*

*'Truer words were never spoken. We? You truly are one of them. I hope you find what you seek. May I give…?'*

*'No, thank you. I will manage. But, your visit is gift enough.'*

She smiled. *'Very well. But, mind the sunbeams, brother,'* she said, her wry smile vanishing into the air.

"In her wake, where the sun kissed the grass, lay three silver arrowheads, the kind that allowed the arrow to reappear in the archer's quiver after it was shot. A worthy gift. Our conversation wasn't that compelling, but it was pleasing to me to see her. And, I might have even given her some insight into mortality. Maybe.

"Seeing my sister again gave me the reason to think about what I'd seen and done in the time since I first came to Gaea. Despite Zeus' desire to punish me, I had learned much, and when we met again, I would have to rethink what I would do with the knowledge I had before I left Olympos. That depended largely on him.

• • •

"My last meal with Ios' family a few days later bore down on my like the heavens, and Ios was not interested in talking very much. When Eiraena cleared the plates,

Maelodon and his friend Pandaeros entered with a wrapped gift for me. I had never received anything in this fashion before, and I have to admit being quite eager to see what it was. I had no words when I saw that it was a bow of polished white oak, carved with images of life in Trapæzos. Apparently, the butcher's son created this for me as a show of gratitude from the village. I wasn't sure what I had done to deserve it. I had learned all I felt I could from this place and these people… they had shown me sides of humanity I would never have experienced as a god. I could hope that I would be able to share this with my brethren someday. I needed to explore more so that when I returned to Olympos, I could know more of this mortal world. The *Moirae* didn't keep counsel with me, but I just knew that my life had more purpose than the one I had lived. It was time to find out more."

# 6—LESSON LEARNED

**"T**hat experience, dear Justice, reminds me of an event that happened much later, 1962 C.E. to be exact, before the Separation of the Souls, but was a first for me for two reasons—it was the time when I served as an observer on the United Nations Security Council and when I stole a car.

• • •

"Sitting in the Security Council chamber in mortal form once more, I read each of the faces around me, faces that spoke without words of the turmoil and tensions this world put upon them. I was there at the request of Antonin Rasmanoff, the president of the U.N. Security Council, a man who—thanks to the machinations of Morpheos, who manipulates dreams and the subconscious—thought he knew me from an implanted memory of us attending the same college and, later, from working in the private sector as a consultant. We had met the night before at his hotel, since I had called him when I arrived, where I asked about this impending doom I had heard about. He invited me to act as an observer in the Security Council, to offer counsel if I could. He acted on the memory that I, Paul Fairmont, worked for the Greco-European Alliance, the consortium of countries who had forged a coalition within the past few years; acting as a consultant would give me the chance to see how the world was dealing with this threat Antonin had mentioned.

"After the Separation of the Souls, where we gods had to deal with the separate Olympian world, *Ge Theôn*, a realm where gods interacted with mortals, and the outer mortal world, *Oikoumene Broteios*, where the gods existed in a fading memory, I had wanted to see what the world of Humankind was like. If my wife and my son needed to relocate there, I needed to know just what a chaotic mess it would be. My scrying pool allowed me to see sporadic glimpses of life as well as communicate with mortals. As I scoured the nations of the world for news and insights through the blessed waters, I kept hearing about a forthcoming crisis that would do great harm to Gaea: a handful of the world's nations possessed missiles bearing bio-toxins, poisons that could obliterate all life, reducing the earth to an inert ball of dirt. In the outer world, Gaea had only enough energy to keep her form, despite the atrocities that humanity had inflicted upon her. Zeus limited my visit to one lunar cycle, and I would be without my Olympian powers, too. Time was too short.

"Each U.N. representative spoke of the great need for control, control over the rogue nations who tightened the tension through intimidation. Every once in a while, Antonin looked at me, for just a second, to gauge my reaction, but my expression never changed. Acting as an observer was something I had done in Trapæzos, and I had mastered stoicism well. I was to blend in here, not express my thoughts until I knew everything I needed to know. Blankets of paranoia shrouded this vast room, and despite the controlled expressions of the council members, I could see their souls tremble.

"During a break, I pulled Antonin to the side of the chamber.

'What is happening here?'

"He began to repeat the conflict and its effect on the assembled.

'No, Antonin. I hear their words, but they're empty. This is a show, but for whom?'

"His eyes toward the floor, he sighed deeply.

'When we spoke last night, I could hear your desperation. You tried to control yourself, but beneath your words, you were crying out for help,' I said.

'Not many know this, Paul, and it cannot leave this room. This council is a merely a figurehead. The whole U.N. is. The General Assembly voted a few years ago to grant autonomy to the world's recognized nations, and this autonomy forbids U.N. interference unless a nation requests assistance or the U.N. applies to help.'

'Applies? How long does that take?'

'Let's just say that the last application was made a year ago, and it still hasn't been granted.'

'So, the nations keep you at bay, of your own doing. They prefer their own power." I started to understand the fear. "Doesn't this contradict your own charter? Shouldn't this council be the one who makes U.N. policy?'

"He nodded.

"Our break ended. Four more hours of this spectacle I endured before we adjourned for the day. I decided to do some research by informally interviewing some of the members. My questions had to be precise. I couldn't risk raising suspicions that I was somehow involved in the politics. No one revealed anything directly, but when I asked about the governments, each spoke in what seemed like veiled code wrapped in silence. I spent much more time reading their body language and emotions than actually listening to their words. Words shield truths, and truth is one area I know intimately. I remembered listening to the members of the Council of Elders in Trapæzos prattle on about superficial issues, all the while speaking in their own language, an internal one. This language didn't contain syntax and verbs, but rather it was suffused with innuendo and slivers of truth. I understood. Should a spy be among them, he might learn about the inner workings of the village, learn some sacred knowledge meant for Trapæzans only. So, they spoke in code.

"This council in New York City could learn quite a bit from its ancient progenitor. Instead of a code, an underlying comprehension, they spoke the language of fear and incapacity.

"After my meetings, I walked the city for a while, and I then saw the cause of their fear. It wasn't the nations who possessed the bio-toxins that could eviscerate the planet. These people feared themselves. Not having lived here, I could easily see the cameras disguised as signposts, the technology this world shouldn't even know yet, and remembered how I had to have my palm and retina scanned when I entered the building. Paranoia was a way of life. When I made contact through dreams before I left Olympos, I learned about the palm and eye scans, adding my own information to the U.N. computers. It didn't occur to me as to why until that moment in the city. None of this should be happening now.

"Rasmanoff arranged a car service to drive me back to the house I was staying in at East Hampton on the east end of Long Island. A week prior, I had arrived there because something about the seashore intrigued me. Standing on the wave-battered southern shore of Long Island, I had noticed that morning at sunrise how the cool wavelets crept up the sand and kissed my feet, dampening the slacks of my gray pinstripe suit, but I didn't care. On a shore like that, I had entered the mortal world a few millennia ago as a penance, but it wasn't a hoary fisherman who greeted me that morning, but rather a few dozen squawking gulls that

41

hovered over me like miniature harpies. Sunrise, one that painted the sky in broad strokes, scattered shards of orange and red over the ocean, truly a worthy tribute not only to me as the sun god, but to Poseidon. Places like this almost made me want to relinquish my godhood again, but those were thoughts for another day. Later that morning, I had met Sally, an elderly woman I saw at the farmer's market where I had stopped after walking back from the beach. She questioned my attire while judging which tomato to purchase, and we started talking. When she learned I had just arrived without a place to stay, she quickly told me I would stay with her, something about me reminding her of her son. Who was I to question that?

"The night I returned from the meeting, Sally prepared dinner for us, something she wouldn't let me do. Eiræna had taught me some simple dishes when I stayed with her and Ios, but Sally wanted me to be her guest. I wanted to talk to her about what I had learned to get some perspective, but I decided I shouldn't involve her. We spent the remainder of the evening walking the beach with her regaling me of stories from her past, of frolicking on this beach as a young woman before, during, and after her two marriages. She had grown up in that house, too. I stayed in the guesthouse, a more ramshackle clapboard dwelling adorned with seashells and marine art. Even though the smaller house had its own kitchen, Sally insisted I eat with her on the porch every morning. Her cancer debilitating her slowly, I saw a resemblance between her and Adara with each passing day, and like with Adara, I could do nothing to help without my healing power.

• • •

"Another day with the council members provided more insight into their mindset. Antonin pulled me aside this time during a short recess. The air seemed to vibrate with his pulse, and his tension reached out to me.

'Paul, as you can see, I don't know what else we can do. With Cuba, Russia, and the other rogue nations not willing to stand down with their missiles, we might need to spend more time worrying about how to react to biohazards than how to diffuse this.'

'You're not serious. Instead of being proactive, you're going to wait until it's too late. Once that chemical gets airborne, life dies, Antonin. All life. It might take a few weeks, maybe months, but the air and water will be contaminated. Within six months, I expect half the planet to be tainted. Less than a year? Everyone has a premature death sentence.'

'What do you expect us to do?' he said, raising his voice for the first time since we met. This wasn't a question as much as it was a legitimate cry for help.

'Here's a list of questions I need answered,' I said, slipping a piece of paper into his hand. 'Get me as much information as possible. I have a few ideas. Tell no one.'

"I had to bite my tongue throughout the rest of the façade of a meeting. These toothless people were willing to endorse their own death sentence, but I had to do something. I owed it to Gaea.

• • •

"As the limousine got closer to Sally's, I saw billowing smoke and flames lashing the air above the house. I jumped out of the car a few blocks away and ran the distance. Sally sat with a fireman on the porch of her house, a house I expected to be burned to the ground. Behind her house I saw the remains of the guesthouse, a fire truck shooting water over the charred remainder. Thankfully, no one was hurt. Once I knew she was fine, I walked over burnt wood and broken glass to retrieve my suitcase, a case designed to look like a 1960s suitcase but made from much sterner stuff. Inside contained a quantity of Hephæstian gold, my only means of currency in this world. Zeus only knew what I would have had to say to

43

explain why I possessed a satchel of gold coins. Thankfully, I was able to stash it on her back porch under a tarp before joining her as she spoke to police. According to her, around 5 p.m. when she was making dinner, she heard an explosion. The fire marshall seemed to think it was a gas leak, but I knew better. After the trucks and police left, I joined Sally for dinner, trying to bring as much normality back, but then I told her I wanted to see if I could find some of my belongings in the ruined house. Two hours later, I found materials that looked like wire and a piece of technology that Sally wouldn't have had lying around—the makings of a radio-controlled bomb. I called Antonin with what happened using a secure phone number, and he said he'd call me back in a little while.

"As I learned later that evening and had suspected, a thorough search of the council chamber turned up a listening device attached to the light fixture near where we had stood. Someone didn't want me to give Antonin and the council my ideas. Who knew what else they had learned? Who would care that much?

"The next morning, the car service never arrived. Not unexpected. The first time I went to meet Antonin, a friend of Sally's graciously drove me into the city, but this time, I couldn't risk involving anyone. I walked into town, giving myself that much time to think, but I had already made up my mind beforehand. Parked on a side street next to the butcher shop, I saw what I needed, a red 1962 Thunderbird. Thankfully, the residents of this town were more trusting than they should be as the driver's window was down. At 6:00 a.m., no one was awake yet, so I slipped inside and played with some of the wires until the car started. Observing the world through my scrying pool had taught me much. For as much as I hated to steal this car, I would find a way to repay the owner, but my priority was to get to the U.N. The meeting would start at 8:00, so

I would just make it before the security guards would seal the doors, a common practice when the council met.

"I had hoped the news of my death hadn't made it back to the city, but my palm and retinal scans didn't work. Whoever it was who had planned my demise had worked quickly. Guards watched me as I stepped aside, moving as quickly out of their line of vision as possible. Their guns would prove quite lethal to me if they believed I was a threat, and if I died before my powers returned, I'd be dead permanently. My last chance was to call the U.N. operator, but asking for Antonin would alert whoever it was that was looking for me. When Morpheos planted memories in his head, I asked for a failsafe, something I could use in the event of an emergency. I saw a woman walking toward the entry who I had seen before in the lobby and, pretending to have laryngitis, I asked her to call the operator for me and ask that a message be relayed to President Rasmanoff's secretary. She obliged me, and I offered to buy her coffee later to thank her. After I entered the lobby again, I feigned reading a newspaper until I saw Antonin and a few U.N. guards walk with deliberate steps toward the screening booth. The guard who had seen me unable to enter earlier intercepted them, but Antonin told him that I was needed in the Norwegian Room. When the guard balked, insisting I had failed the scans, the president of the U.N. Security stepped nose to nose with the guard.

'If this meeting fails to bring out the resolution this man can help broker because you detained him, I will hold you personally liable, strip you of your position, and put you in charge of sanitation. Do I make myself clear?'

"As we headed toward the chamber, Antonin confided that he didn't know if that would keep me safe, so whatever was to happen needed to happen soon.

"After calling the meeting to order, President Rasmanoff dispensed with the minutes from the prior meeting and informed the council that I would be addressing them briefly, under the U.N. ordinance allowing observers to address the Security Council with the president's consent. Muttering to themselves for a moment or two, the representatives weren't sure what I would say, as this wasn't the normal practice, but as soon as I stood, their voices stopped. Their hopeful anticipation impregnated the room.

'Ladies and gentlemen of the Security Council, Mr. Rasmanoff, I am Paul Fairmont, envoy from the Greco-European Alliance. Thank you for indulging me today. I have been observing you for the past week, listening to the conversations you have had regarding this recent threat you have named the 'Cuban Missile Crisis', but this is in fact a joint effort by Cuba, Russia, France, Australia, and Peru. The threat of bio-toxins has frozen the world in fear, and you are charged with addressing this global menace, but no resolution has emerged. None of those five countries has revealed why this need for destroying the earth, not that motivation would matter, but I think I can speak for all of us that this cannot be allowed to happen. When I look at all of you, I see your trepidation, your reluctance to change the status quo. This organization should be the bellwether, leading the nations of the world into solidarity.

'We live in a world where nations close their doors to others, keeping their people in check through technology. It's no wonder that Cuba, Russia, and the other three countries won't dismantle these weapons—they have no incentive to do it. By the time the U.N. gets approval to bring in peacekeeping groups, if at all, the earth could be lurching toward its doom. Once in the ecosystem, these toxins can never be removed. We must act today.

'I know how you can not only help the U.N. escape its figurehead status—a self-imposed one, from what I can tell—but also ensure that this kind of microcosmic oligarchy of terror cannot take root. Long ago, I visited a village where its own council of elders, itself comprised of people from all over their region, handled its business swiftly and purposely. I have never spoken of what I saw until now, but I feel this is necessary. When they saw conflict arise in their province, they sent a group of half a dozen to a dozen carefully chosen individuals, from warriors to healers, from diplomats to poets, to address the conflict as covertly as needed. Neighboring villages did not always give overt consent, but they knew within that someone else's perspective would prove vital. Sometimes, these cadres traveled across the land into neighboring provinces to learn more about other villages. The key, though, was having specialists, not simply those willing to help. This idea would work well now.

'Just as an example, Spain has some of the world's top biochemical engineers, Italy has a keen diplomatic corps, and Egypt and Israel have strong military strategists. Take from the best, form a task force that specializes in bio-toxic weapons, and go into these impediment nations to locate, dismantle, and destroy these weapons. I know some might think you seek to impose martial law, but you are not there to murder, rule, or enslave anyone—you simply want to eradicate global threats. You've empowered the world to create autonomy all around you. Now is the time to—'

"Armed men in dark green uniforms stormed into the room, obviously looking for *me*. They were too late, though. I had planted the seeds. While most of the representatives scattered under the tables or behind chairs, Rasmanoff and about ten others created a wall of people behind which I was escorted out of the chamber through a private entrance. Now paranoid myself that anyone around me could easily target me, I circled the block a few times, finding a small coffee shop where I sat, shielding my face behind a newspaper. A waiter approached me about thirty minutes later, asked to take my order, and dropped a piece of paper on the table.

*'Thank you. You started a conversation. We'll be in touch.'*

"Antonin signed it, 'In your debt.' That might come in handy someday.

• • •

"A few miles from East Hampton, I stopped at a gas station. As I was returning from the cashier, the attendant finished washing my windshield, commenting on what a "fast beauty" the car was and how, with 340 horsepower, I needed to take good care not to overdo it. He added that not everyone could drive a car like this one.

'You should see the horsepower I normally have,' I muttered, slipping two dollars in his hand as I got behind the wheel, knowing he wouldn't get the reference.

"As I had thought, no one even knew the car was missing when I returned it next to the butcher shop. A pawn shop in Manhattan was quite accommodating when I handed over half a dozen solid gold coins, so I left an envelope on the seat with about $1000 American and a thank you note before I walked back to Sally's. I still worried that someone might come after me, but I had been quite careful to watch for anything out of the ordinary. A week passed without incident, and I woke up early the following Saturday to a phone call. It was Antonin.

'I thought you should know first that those guards were mercenaries hired to kill you, but they never revealed who hired them. They await sentencing as we speak. Second, we passed the Task Force Division charter with an overwhelming majority. I don't know if you realize how persuasive your comments really were, Paul. Task Force: Alpha was deployed at 2 a.m. to Cuba. After that, it heads to Russia, Australia, France, and then Peru. I have full confidence we'll be successful. You should see them, these young men and women, so eager to get out there and help bring peace.'

'We both know I can't show my face at the U.N. for a while. It's better that I be forgotten. You have what you need now, anyway,' I said.

'And here I was going to ask you to be the liaison to the Task Force Division from the Greco-European Alliance, too.'

"I couldn't tell if he was kidding or not.

• • •

"I had less than two weeks left before the lunar cycle would end, so I spent it with Sally who finally started to let me cook some meals for her, and it turns out, I make great lasagna. I felt it wouldn't be long before she would succumb to her illness and leave this plane, and my grief over Adara's loss returned, incapacitating me. Who would have thought, after all that time had passed, that one woman's death would resonate with me so much? Sally and I took a few more walks on the beach over the next week until her legs couldn't carry her weight anymore. Most evenings, we sat on the porch, watching the sun set, and she sipped her coffee. Most days, I worked in the yard, catering to her flower beds, while she sat in a lawn chair and told me about her life. That was one thing I had never had with Adara—closure.

"The night before I left, Sally napped after dinner, and I watched the news on television. I nearly fell off the sofa when I heard the U.N. correspondent tell us that the bio-toxic threat that had hovered over the world had ended, peacefully, quietly. That morning, a representative from the Australian government revealed that it would be dismantling the weapons that could have poisoned the earth five times over. When asked by the news anchor what happened, the representative simply replied that it had reconsidered taking such heinous actions. Allegedly,

France and Peru would follow suit. The Task Force had miraculously prevailed. This time.

"At sunrise on the last day, I noticed Sally hadn't awakened yet. Her breathing was weak and her pulse thready. She had told me early on that she had wanted to die in her home, but she didn't deserve this. I would have to return to the Olympian realm soon, and my powers would return just beforehand. Her hand felt so fragile in mine, and her face had that innocence a child has before it's tainted by so much misery. I sat back in the chair next to her bed, her hand still in mine, and I stared at the ceiling. By late afternoon, I saw the moon's ethereal shape rising, and soon night would come, releasing me from my self-imposed mortality. Leaning over her face, I kissed her forehead, my lips moistened from tears touching her delicate skin. Just before I left, I gave her a parting gift: she would awaken in the morning fully cured, the one gift I couldn't give Adara.

"I finally had come full circle.

• • •

"My journey from Trapæzos brought me to more enlightenment, too, so I want to return to that part of my story."

# 7—TRUST

"An hour out of Trapæzos, the landscape shifted from grassy meadows bordered with sparse forests and ocean-tempered shorelines to dense woodlands where sunlight filtered through leafy canopies. I rode a clearly traveled path with a few days worth of food on a mare the Council of Elders gave me. Before I had decided to leave, I had asked Eiraena to fashion a sleeved cloak that would cover my arms so that my wristband would be hidden. The villagers never asked about it, so I was never concerned. Ios mentioned a few villages I would pass through in heading west, so I was able to replenish my food and water, as well as give the horse an ample rest.

"Some of the towns didn't have the welcoming eyes that I had seen in Trapæzos, and I saw much distrust and fear of foreigners. Moving westward would prove to be intriguing then, if I had to keep an eye on my belongings and my safety. When I stopped in Tripolis, I slept on my horse, keeping my bow and quiver always within reach. I had never been so elated to see a sunrise so I could depart.

51

Perhaps this was merely happenstance, but my gut knew better.

"In Ordu, buildings smoldered from being razed to the ground, and people wore shredded, soiled garments, keeping weapons in full view to ward off potential marauders. Despair and grief followed me, and I half expected to see Eris, discord's keeper, skulking about the debris. A woman in the distance, kneeling in the dirt, cried over the dead body of her infant son, an arrow having pierced its heart. The baby could not have been more than a week old. Who would dare slay an innocent child barely out of its mother's womb? Savages. Under Ares' influence, Humankind could do such heinous things.

"Between villages, the path became obscured by rockslides and fallen trees, so I left the path and delved into the forest, a dank mist covering my travels. It didn't take long for fear to rise, and the hairs on my arms tingled. I was just about to reach for my bow when half a dozen masked warriors emerged from the trees, each brandishing a weapon. The masks resembled animals: an eagle, a wolf, a cat. I was good with my bow, quite good in fact, but I just knew I wouldn't fare well facing animal-faced warriors so I dropped my bow arm. The eagle-headed warrior pushed up the mask, and I knew without question I was facing Amazons.

"I had trespassed on Amazon land, grunted one woman. But when I apologized, another woman cracked a spear on the back of my head. I was only to speak when spoken to, apparently. The one who struck me, Cydippe, was told, by the eagle-bearing warrior, to let me speak. I explained how I came to be on their land, and I must have been convincing as they offered me an escort, armed of course, into their city. They bound my hands and made me walk on the ground, taking my mare with them separately. After a short while, the mists parted, and I stood awed before a grand marble gate flanked by a wall almost fifty feet tall. Atop the wall stood battle-ready Amazons. Pushed through the gate, I found myself in the center of their agora, the only man, and as I walked, each woman, child, or crone spat on me. Another woman, Astraia, was to take me to the dungeon. I had walked into a prophecy, it would seem.

"Humiliating me through their main city, Astraia threw me into an iron cage when we arrived at the dungeon. I was not alone. Men, some who had been there for years it seemed, sat in similar cages, fecal matter rotting in the corners. Not even the Stymphalian birds reeked like this. Manacled or chained, each one had given up hope of ever been free. As an Olympian, would I have cared? I do as a man. Rope burns on my wrists drew my attention to my own manacle, a different kind of punishment, but one just the same. I hadn't given much thought to it, but knowing it would end at some point gave me a little solace.

• • •

"Through the tiniest window at the top of my cell, new morning light pushed its way through, a sunrise I would miss. I longed to see the wheel burst forth from the east each day—it made me smile to see a new day emerge. Astraia entered and wisps of dust followed her. She asked the guard how I was faring, and her response was simply, 'Alive.' She asked about this prophecy that I heard about when they captured me, assuming I had something to do with it: 'On the brightest night, a man with a metal arm will destroy the chosen of Artemis.' The captain of the guard had told Astraia, apparently, that she thought I was this man because of the manacle. They didn't trust me because I didn't fight back. I knew better than to attempt such a fruitless act. Their queen commanded that I was to be killed immediately if I had anything to do with this prophecy. My words would have fallen on death ears, and an Amazon fist would fall on me, so I kept my silence.

"I learned that, if I were innocent, one suggestion was that I would be brought to the breeding stables. I didn't imagine coupling with an Amazon would be a safe experience, much like watching a praying mantis mate. The queen didn't like that idea, though, from what I could hear. I would simply be blindfolded and led beyond the forest to Lycastus, a town not far from Themyskira. Astraia and my guard probably didn't think I was very smart, so they weren't speaking softly. From what I could gather, their queen, Danaë, wanted to fight against the oppression of men who sought to harm them, but not every man. It seemed that these two women didn't entirely agree.

"Taraeis, the captain of the guard, arrived, a taller woman armed for battle. Her sneer in my direction didn't bode well, or perhaps she was just that way. She informed the others that a second regiment should attend to the outer wall since their other queen, Otari, would soon return. Both monarchs in one place made her nervous. I was then left to the company of squalor and the stench of ripe urine.

• • •

"A dagger rattling on my cage woke me from the slumber I had attempted, and a burly woman with short-cropped hair threw me a piece of stale bread and an animal skin half-filled with water. As I had heard from Ios of some Amazons, she had one breast, but my lingering stare brought with it an explanation: a wild boar bit it off during a hunt. If not for her sister sealing the wound with her torch, she'd be dead. This tribe didn't mutilate its bodies by living up to rumors. I suffered through my meal as the bread tasted of mold and fecal matter, and the water... well, I didn't want to question its taste too much.

"Astraia returned later to retrieve me. The queen requested an audience with her newest prisoner. Daylight burned my eyes as we walked to the palace entrance, a sensation that had never happened before. Before I could be allowed to enter the palace, however, I was to bathe and be given clean clothes. Amazon guards watched as I did this, probably to unnerve me. I took my time, and made sure they saw me naked just enough to make them uncomfortable. Unlike the withered men in the dungeon, I was much sturdier and well proportioned. Of course, my smiling didn't help. My new meager tunic was just enough to cover my genitals, undoubtedly meant to humiliate me, but I had worn much less as a god. Often.

"Nonetheless, I donned a new cloak, which thankfully covered my manacle—no sense in questions this early in the day, and was escorted to their Chamber of Ministry where I saw a bevy of well-dressed Amazons. Danaë was easy to spot, her silver crown with a crescent moon on her brow, but also her stance, not as stiff as the others. She had a silver belt, etched with glyphs similar to my manacle, no doubt a gift of Artemis. The crescent moon emblems showed her fealty to my sister. The other Amazons each bore a cuirass emblazoned with a variety of animals. I recognized a few from my first meeting in the forest.

"A woman in a white robe touched my arm, taking hold of the manacle, her eyes closed. An oracle. She wouldn't recognize me in this mortal form, but all oracles knew me, or rather, Apollo. She told the queen she didn't think I was the man in the prophecy, but her mind could not render a clear picture. Taraeis didn't trust me, but I could tell she wore her anger and distrust like an outer skin, shielding her from some past pain. Danaë dismissed the others, something I didn't expect, and asked me to sit with her. She did something else I didn't expect—she apologized for how her warriors had treated me. 'Not all Amazons distrust men, Delos,' she told me. 'Only those who choose to remain ignorant.' To hear her speak so harshly of her own people, well, it took me off guard. Her instincts told her I was no threat, she told me, but until the prophecy had passed, she had no choice but to be careful.

"She offered me water, and it tasted in fact like water. After indulging me a few cups, she commented that she expected that I was not as she expected either. 'Men regard us as savages who drink the blood of men during rituals to Artemis which, if they understood our beliefs they would know, goes against the teachings of our goddess.' This I knew to be true. Artemis never asked for her followers to drink blood, and human sacrifice was anathema to the gods. Tantalus, a son of Zeus, thought to test the gods' omniscience by serving his own son Pelops to them, but when we—they—discovered this, they restored Pelops and punished Tantalus by making him stand in a pool of water waist high. Grapes dangling above him moved out of reach when he tried to eat; the water lowered when he tried to drink—his eternal punishment.

"I asked if men had any place in Amazon society, and Danaë replied they did, and offered me a little history lesson. Daughters of Ares and Harmonia, Amazons settled north of the Euxine Sea. The queen then, Lysippe, had a son, Tanais, whom Aphrodite favored, but the young man chose to remain chaste like Artemis. Out of revenge for spurning all the goddess' efforts to seduce him, she cursed him to know lust for no one else but his mother. Ashamed, he flung himself into the river and drowned. When Lysippe learned of the tragedy, she renamed the river Tanais. Her oracle advised her to take her tribe and leave the area, should her son's spirit return as evil. The tribe marched around the Euxine to the mouth of the river Thermodon whereupon it split into three groups, each forming a separate city. Lysippe's tribe formed Themiskyra, the center for all Amazon law. Many of the women from other tribes joined them here, bringing knowledge of architecture, farming, education, and different warfare techniques. To perpetuate the race, Lysippe's Amazons mated with the men of a neighboring village, Gargareia, during the Seeding Ritual. Amazons chose worthy breeding stock from the village, took them into the woods, mated, and left the men to return to their homes. Some killed any man who did not meet with their standards. If they gave birth to male children, most were killed by strangulation or smothering, but they returned a few to the men to rear. All females were brought here.

"A matriarchal society, women were the leaders, warriors, hunters, and mothers to the Amazon girls. Men provide them with children, nothing more, and made poor slaves because they wore out too easily. Amazons had ten times the strength of a man. What would take a man a day to complete, an Amazon would accomplish in a few hours.

"Themiskyra had two queens, I learned. Queen Otari handled defense, trained the warriors, and planned the expeditions. Danaë handled the domestic affairs. They shared the rule, always deferring to one another before making any major decisions. Artemis was their chief goddess, which would make my sister happy, but they did worship other goddesses. They did respect the male gods, but that was the extent of their fealty.

"I challenged her a bit. Amazons drank wine, but yet offered no thanks to Dionysus. They followed Apollo's prophecies, took advantage of Zeus' rainstorms, and Poseidon's grace to cross the sea. Even Ares, who sired them, received no allegiance. Like it or not, I proposed, the gods did indeed have a place in Amazon life. Danaë smiled. Then, she asked my feelings about women.

"As a youth, I considered women to be my equals, especially my sister. I learned at my mother's knee to respect women for their intelligence, wit, and strengths. Unfortunately, as I grew into adolescence and young adulthood, I forgot those lessons and regarded women, as my father did, as nothing more than amusement for my bed. I know now that was a mistake. During my stay in Trapæzos, I helped care for an elder of the village who died of poison. Her suffering was long and grueling, and

57

watching her die was the most difficult thing I had ever had to do. I watched the daily prayer vigil congregate around her hut for days, offering prayers to the gods for her health to return. I had no idea how important she was to the village, and I learned shortly after her death she had been one of the original citizens of the village, and had helped establish the laws and principles of Trapæzos. From then on, my respect for her and all women grew, replacing my older, more perverse ideas. So, in answer to her question, I felt women had as much of a place in the world as men do, and in some cases more so. I only wished more men understood how vital women were to all creation, and one of my intentions was, ultimately, to fall in love.

"As the words left my mouth, I almost didn't remember saying them, but it was true. I wanted to fall in love. Perhaps, despite that Zeus wanted me far from Olympos knowing what I know, I was sent to Gaea to learn how to fall in love. Would that be so terrible a lesson?

"I asked about my belongings and my horse, both of which had been locked away. The queen felt I wasn't a threat to her or her people, and asked me to swear an oath to Artemis that I would not do any harm to them. Of course, I complied. She would have me escorted to the city gates where I would be free to go, and in the off chance I did make a hostile gesture, the next one I would greet would be Hades. She called for Taraeis and Astraia to return my belongings and escort me back to the road. Astraia informed me my horse would be returned when I reached the road, not before.

"Just as we reached the gate, two men on horseback stormed through, riding toward the palace. Abandoning me, the guards returned to the palace. I should have left the city and continued on my journey, but an instinct, something I had learned we mortals had on occasion, kept me from going. Covering my head with the cloak, I took advantage of the tumult to find my way back to the palace, avoiding the keen Amazon eyes perched on the walls. I found my way behind the palace near the Chamber of Ministry and climbed a nearby oak tree so that I could remain hidden but have a clear view. Two dark-skinned men pointed their swords at Danaë and bound her to her throne. Animal hides covered them from head to toe, and both wore beaded headdresses and face paint. Wherever they were from, they had a strategic advantage, or somehow knew how to sneak up on an Amazon. She struggled against her bonds, but she could not break them, something which surprised me. The man furthest from me stepped forward a bit, and metal rings from wrist to elbow covered the arm he stretched out.

"The man with a metal arm, I thought. And with a full moon rising this night, the prophecy was about to come true. Other Amazons entered the room, but Danaë would die if they tried to help her. I could see the anger in the eyes of the assailants, and they would risk their lives for this. Amazons would as well. This would not bode well for either party. I had to do something to repay the kindness Danaë had shown me.

"Branches blocked my view, and the men kept moving around, so it was hard for me to take aim, but I had nocked an arrow in my bow. Voices raged within the room, and I couldn't make out what the men were saying, but I took advantage of the distraction to the men and released my finger. A dull thud, followed by seeing the man fall, assured me my aim had been true. A surge of energy passed through me, and I found myself leaping to the window ledge. Even though I warned the other man not to move or he would die where he stood, he reached for a throwing knife. A dagger to his side ended the assault. Danaë had escaped her bonds with a hidden dagger and used my distraction to her advantage. I lowered my bow and jumped into the room. Taraeis saluted me and said she would not soon forget my risking my life for their queen. Unlike other Amazons, the captain did not want to remain ignorant.

"The queen thanked me and then asked me for something. My name. What she didn't say was that she was in control of the situation the entire time, but I think I knew that. An Amazon, especially a queen, would not be easily brought to heel. She ordered the marauders' corpses burned in accordance with tradition, for even though they had been enemies of the state, they deserved to die well. I was invited to stay, this time in guest chambers in the palace.

"The next morning, over a meal, the queen saw fit to explain why these two men had come to Themyskira. Otari had led an attack on Sparta, took their general, Proxiteles, as her mate for the Seeding Ritual, and left him humiliated miles from his troops. He swore revenge should their paths cross again. On the return trip, Otari's ship met with Poseidon's fury and she was washed ashore on the northern coast of Afrika with half a dozen Amazons. Native tribesmen took advantage of the women, not knowing Otari was with child. News of her capture made it to the Akhaean mainland, Sparta in particular. Proxiteles took three years to arrange the means, but he eventually sought out Otari in Afrika. He learned from the local tribesmen that she had given birth to a boy and a girl, but had strangled the boy with his own umbilical cord, an act which caused the natives to kill the remaining Amazons. Proxiteles wanted the pleasure of Otari's death on his sword, but he could not kill her, so he left her with the natives and whatever justice they deemed appropriate. Danaë had managed to retrieve her sister from the natives, but the infant was kidnapped and hidden before she could be taken back to Themyskira. The price for the infant would be her mother's head. Since the Amazon queen would not comply, assassins were sent to take it by force. They didn't know Otari was afield on a mission, so they would take Danaë's instead.

"In the weeks that followed, my presence became less of a nuisance and some of the women tried to learn from my experiences in other places to gauge the understanding of men. I think they tolerated me more than trusted me, despite that I had saved their queen's life. I took the challenge of breaking down some of the boundaries between the Amazons and everyone else to heart, and I put the penance aside to concentrate on other issues. I usually kept to myself, but I could tell some of the women wanted to trust outsiders again, but they just didn't know how. The key was finding commonalities. One event in particular helped to break down some of the walls. I needed to share something with these women, and I knew just what to do.

"One dusky morning, I had brought my bow with me to get in some practice. Without divine ichor flowing through me, I actually had to practice a bit more to keep up my skills, something that took much getting used to, especially for an arrogant son of Zeus. An assemblage of Amazon archers in the distance had been training since dawn with straw targets, and I needed to prove myself. Peering at them from behind a tree, I did my best to keep myself hidden. Just after one warrior had collected her arrows, I sent three shafts screaming toward the heart of the straw figures. As they whistled past, each warrior turned to see who had fired the shots, a few brandishing their steel. Walking over to them, I could hear the gasps at how dead center my shots had been. I wasn't a god anymore, but my marksmanship hadn't faltered.

"Oritheia, one of the most vocal about a man being among them, now looked at me a little differently. Without saying anything, I retrieved my arrows. I started to walk back to the city when she challenged me. She pointed to a cedar tree about half a mile away, and jokingly said that if

I could hit it with one arrow, she would carry me back to the palace. Another Amazon said she would stand near to make sure I did indeed hit the target. I nocked three arrows at once and sent them off. A few minutes later, a flustered Amazon announced that not only did she see my arrows hit the same spot, but she also saw them disappear. I pulled three arrows from quiver, and they took a step back. They had seen arrowheads like this before and knew they could only have come from Artemis. No one questioned how I had come to have them, and I enjoyed being carried back to the palace.

"My celebrity status had gotten to the queen's ear, and she told me how she came to be queen of Themyskira which involved a visit from Artemis. She had defeated others in tournament—something my archery challenge had made her remember—and had taken her second to be Otari. I remembered from the prophecy that the man with the metal arm would come to destroy the chosen of Artemis, a fair honor indeed. Perhaps my sister had indirectly arranged for us to meet for some purpose. Our conversation changed to matters of state, but not of defense. An idea had come to the queen and she wanted to see how I felt about it. By now, neighboring lands would know of my residence with the Amazons, and Danaë asked if I might consider working as an ambassador of a sort, promoting trade with other cities in the region. Some would see it as a possible deception to take them off guard, opening themselves up to attack, but some would actually find my position to be worthy of their ear. I told her I would give it some serious consideration.

"Food surpasses all, it would seem, and with a declining harvest, my first task as Amazonian emissary was to approach Lycastos to the west. After two months of debate and capitulation later, I succeeded in arranging the accord. Themyskira would extend its protection over Lycastos in exchange for grain and other produce. An agrarian community, the Lycastans put aside their apprehension and were willing to make this work. I wished the Trapæzans had been so fortunate with their surrounding villages. That Galateian incident haunted me still. Heading up the cultural exchange, I helped broker an agreement where envoys from each city helped the other through the transition. Quite frankly, I was amazed at how willing both cultures were to do this.

"During this time of internal adjustment, I noticed, on two separate occasions, the arrival of an entourage to the palace at odd hours of the night, a time which precluded me from seeing the identities of the visiting faction. I could estimate five in the party, each one in full battle dress. Danaë had visits from all over the region now, so I didn't worry much about it. A few weeks later, though, five Amazons and I returned from Ordu when I saw a white mare in front of the palace, the standard not an Amazon's. I learned it was the Arkadeian queen, a childhood friend of Danaë's. Oritheia offered to introduce me as I might come across Arkadeians in my travels.

"The moment I entered the Chamber of Ministry, Danaë ushered me to meet Alkinoë, the Arkadeian queen. Ginger blonde hair formed a tight braid down the queen's back, in contrast to Danaë, whose braid was wound around the back of her head and held in place with a silver hair comb. They almost looked like sisters. Something familiar shone in Alkinoë's face, but I couldn't place it. I had seen her before. She commented that I was the man who had done what no other could do, and I gently kissed her extended hand. I was invited to dine with them after they finished their business, something I found I would enjoy more than most things. A smile I couldn't easily remove told me my sister Artemis's hand, or perhaps Aphrodite's, was stirring up something.

• • •

"Over dinner, I figured out where I knew Alkinoë, and the chill I felt sobered me a little. A thousand or so years ago, I, well, Apollo, pursued a mysterious woman, a simple farm girl, and we grew to love one another in one day. We made love by the sea that night, and our time together brought me in touch with a great and awesome power, as if I had loved the earth itself. Indeed, I had. A voice on the wind told me to go to Arkadeia, a pristine pastoral valley untouched by humankind. In the center of the verdant landscape, I fell to the ground and wept like I had never in my existence. This woman was an incarnation of Gaea, who had sought to experience life in a way she had never before. A honeyed voice told me to cast one thousand stones into the rippling river beside me, and from that act, Arkadeia the city-state rose.

"The gods aided me in bestowing great gifts on this most sacred of people, and they remained loyal to Apollo and Gaea, the sun and the Earth. Blessed with virtues and strength of character, these people created a vibrant culture, forging a monarchy. I watched as they prospered, sheltered in their valley. I felt a tie to this queen, somewhere between patriarch and something more. I shook off my reverie and rejoined the conversation. Alkinoë and Danaë explained how they had come to be friends, two victims of a bloody battle when their civilizations were young, before their royal stations. An alliance had been forged by the Arkadeian and Themyskiran monarchs, a first since their creation, but due to their divine origins, it seemed proper to create such an pact. Later, through ritual and tournament, both women had become Sisters of the Labrys, lifelong friends. Despite their distance, with Arkadeia being on the Peloponnesus and Themyskira on the Euxine banks, both remained staunch allies. Alkinoë's perfumed skin had me enrapt throughout the evening, and I did my best not to let my eyes linger. After the meal, the Arkadeian entourage took its leave, and I assumed it would be many months before our paths would cross again.

• • •

"One morning, a few months later, Taraeis woke me to let me know that an advance guard had sent word that Otari was returning. She knew nothing of the recent events, and the captain felt it would be better if I left the city until Danaë could broach that news at the proper time. Otari's hatred of men ran deeper than the Styx, and my presence in the palace, as opposed to the stables or dungeon, would raise her ire. Amazon guards would escort me to the gates and into Gargareia where I could arrange safe passage somewhere beyond the Thermodon. Before she left, I asked why the Arkadeians had left at night when they could have traveled further in daylight. Taraeis told me to ask the queen, and then she left me to dress and pack my things.

"Danaë and I shared a quick morning meal, and I asked her about the nighttime departure. Normal travel would take months, but the Royal House of Arkadeia possessed a crystal, the PortalBearer, forged in the First Fires, that could use the mind's eye to open a gateway. I commented that I didn't think the Amazons possessed such a trinket to get me out of the city faster, and the queen simply shook her head. I didn't have much time to leave, so I thanked her for her hospitality, saluted her, and left the chamber. I saw a familiar soldier bearing the Arkadeian standard in the hall, and I asked if the queen had come. He pointed to the royal library.

"Alkinoë had come for a scroll that the Amazons possessed. After explaining my predicament, I gently asked if I could accompany her back home, letting her know that I was aware of the PortalBearer. After a slight hesitation, she agreed to let me, but I needed to be ready immediately. Suddenly, I heard a commotion in the hall, and dozens of Amazon warriors in perfect alignment escorted Queen Otari into the palace and toward the Chamber of Ministry. Thinking quickly, Alkinoë gave me her cloak. I understood. Keeping my head covered, I managed to leave the palace undetected as an Arkadeian, retrieved my belongings, and met the queen and her entourage by the city gate. War cries emanated from the palace, and I knew that someone had told Otari of my presence. With strength I didn't know she had, Alkinoë hoisted me onto her horse singlehanded, and we galloped out of the city into the misty forest."

# 8—DISCORD

**"T**his reminds me of a time in the future about a year after the Task Force Division began its mission to address global issues and work toward spreading peace. Early 1963 I believe, before the Separation of the Souls, I poked my head into the outer mortal world once again while I prepared to move my family, but this time, I killed a man in Namibia.

• • •

"Traveling from Olympian time and space to that of the mortal realm actually takes quite a bit of energy, so when I arrived in Windhoek, Namibia, I had to head right for the Hôtel Parisienne. And, Hephæstian gold never ceased to amaze me. With the exchange rate, one coin gave me about 10,000 South African rands, plenty of money for my lunar cycle. Unlike my last sojourn, I really had no impetus for this visit other than to see how countries of the world fared. While enjoying my breakfast the next morning, reading the *Allgemeine Zeitung*, I noticed a small article about the U.N. and its newest peacekeeping agency. Of course, this was relegated to below the fold, but it still made me smile to see those seeds I had planted had borne sweet fruit.

"Later that morning, I wandered downtown to a farmer's market on Goethe Street, although most of the produce seemed underwhelming and shriveled in the sun. Nonetheless, I did what I do best and took in the surroundings. An intriguing dichotomy arose as I wandered up and down the booths: the line between the destitute and the prosperous was certainly not gray. Once I got to Independence Avenue one block away, I could see the larger homes of Bahnhof Street in the distance. One street closer to me was clothed in refuse and adorned with the homeless. A stroll down Bahnhof took me to Mandume, and then into a part of the city I should have avoided. Without my powers, I could easily find myself in unfortunate circumstances without a way to help myself. I may be skilled in combat, but that wouldn't help me if I were facing bullets flying past. I took a left down Meinert Street, and a young girl, no older than sixteen, ran past me, almost knocking me down. Even without ties to my godhood, I sensed something was wrong and tried to follow her, but she knew the streets better than I did, and I lost her a few blocks away. I deduced it was simply one more casualty of a society that didn't aid the helpless as much as it should.

"To be cautious, I let the Greco-European embassy in Windhoek know I was in town because, if I were to disappear, I would want someone to come looking for me. Plus, it afforded me some diplomatic immunity. My curiosity often got the better of me, and I didn't want to have to pass my few weeks as a mortal in a Namibian jail or worse, if such a thing existed.

"At the hotel, the concierge had told me about a symphony playing at the Alte Feste, and I met the Namibian cultural attaché in the lobby who directed me, after some idle chatter, to a quaint restaurant a few blocks

68

away. Windhoek was abuzz, and vendors lined the streets, selling everything from clothing to souvenirs and food. Not quite the agora in Athens, but it entertained me. I had stopped at one table to examine some bolts of fabric when, again, I saw the same girl from the night before huddled in the shadows eating something, perhaps some bread. This time, I got closer to her before she took off into the crowd, and when I chased her down some of the darker streets, I saw her duck into one alley off Meinert Street again. A dead end—tattered fabric hung on the brick walls, surrounded by fetid trash and perhaps a dead animal or two. At least now I was sure where she went, but how she disappeared was anyone's guess. She had my attention now.

"Some days had passed before I found myself in that part of the city again, and this time I noticed how people stared at me. It wasn't a question of skin color since other fair-skinned people lived or traveled to Namibia; this was about presence. Something about my mere presence here was off-putting. A stranger to them, they were to me as well, although I had become quite familiar with the few blocks I had run through in the past week. I sensed apprehension mostly, although some outright feared me, especially younger women and children. At the corner of Kaiserstrasse and Meinert Street, I found a café, if you could call it that, with three tables and a violinist and waited.

"I had almost finished reading the newspaper cover to cover when I saw her skulking about across the street, a parcel beneath her arm. Her sunken cheeks and eyes announced her malnourishment, but her clothing, a motley patchwork of faded fabric, hid that well and gave her places to hide things. Rummaging through street trash, she pocketed what she found and kept her eye on the passersby. I sipped my coffee without taking my eyes from her, glancing down at the paper if she turned toward me.

Once she disappeared down the alley again, I followed, and this time watched as she ducked under one of the cloth pieces hanging on the wall. Beneath the panel, a tunnel revealed itself, one carved from the brick wall and leading into an abyss. Only about fifteen feet long, I emerged slowly behind dilapidated wooden boxes in an outdoor courtyard surrounded by tall brick walls, but the evening sheltered the back end of this place so I couldn't tell just how big it was. Once my eyes adjusted, they widened. Huddling in the shadows, dozens of women and children sat, some wrapped in newspaper, others sleeping on dirty cloth. Making my way through the labyrinth of shadow, keeping myself from being discovered, I entered an open area where moonlight showered down, illuminating everyone, including me. Like a disturbed hive, the women and children immediately scurried around to hide behind wooden boxes and broken down farm equipment, trying to hide from me. Muffled sobbing came from everywhere. They weren't just scared; I terrified them.

"Taking a lesson from the Amazons on how to engage a hostile force when unarmed, I put my hands up, palms out, to show I meant them no harm. I tried English, but they didn't understand. I thought about speaking to them in another language that I knew, but then men's voices came from just beyond a door in the building, so I took my place behind the boxes. Cowering felt unnatural to me, but if the Amazons had taught me anything it was to assess a potential battle to understand the enemy. Four men slithered from the doorway, gruff voices speaking German and reeking of cheap rum and cigarettes. One man, pudgy in a trench coat, snatched one of the women by the arm; she whimpered as the man pulled her to her feet and stepped uncomfortably close to her. From what the darkness revealed to me, he was caressing her face with the back of his hand, but then he slapped her cheek, forcing out a pained cry. As he moved her toward the door,

I could see a trickle of blood at the corner of her mouth, her face moist with tears. I wanted to leap on them and tear them to shreds with my bare hands, but I'd be gunned down in seconds, judging by the pistols tucked into the men's trousers. Once they left, I heard the deadbolts lock. These women were prisoners, but why?

"Stepping back into the moonlight, I saw the girl I followed sitting with one of the women who appeared to be injured, her left eye bandaged. When the girl's eyes met mine, her scorn made the hair on my arms stand on end. I waved her over to me, but she wouldn't move. I moved a few steps forward, but she grabbed a broken broom handle and threatened me. Nothing I could do right then would make them trust me, but I knew I had to help them.

"Back at the hotel, I filled a rucksack with some blankets, towels, and loaves of bread I had bought at the market. Once the moon was high, I returned to the alley, emptying the contents for them before leaving. I had to start building some sort of trust before I could assess what was happening. Even with my diplomatic connections, I'd be putting these people at risk if I acted rashly. As soon as I knew enough, I could help them more.

"The following day, I brought more supplies, and the girl stared at me for a while from a palpable distance, probably trying to figure out why I was doing this. It was too soon to make contact, though.

"She actually acknowledged me the next time with a slight nod of the head, but she wouldn't approach me. I hoped she was realizing I wasn't an enemy. I would have to wait two days before returning.

"On my next visit, the girl who had waved a broom handle at me a few days earlier approached me, keeping about ten feet from me.

'Danke,' she uttered. This was the first time I saw her eyes, blue with gold flecks, shimmering in the moonlight. A minute level of trust was still trust, and I would take it.

'Gern geschehen,' I replied. And it truly was my pleasure to be able to help. I asked what this place was.

'Hölle,' she said. Hell indeed.

"She walked away, but I slowly followed, and she looked back every few seconds to see just how close I was. Some of the women and girls smiled at me, that noncommittal smile you give someone when you're not sure just who they are or whether they can be trusted. They still feared me, and that was probably for the best since I didn't want them to trust anyone who just came in and gave them supplies. I finally found out her name—Laina. Many of these women came from abroad, I learned, as wives or concubines of Namibian militia, the corrupt ones anyway. When the men tired of them, they brought them to this place. A few had arrived as younger girls and had grown up here. If they were lucky, they had food once a week, but they weren't always that lucky. Any animal foolish enough to get trapped here became a meal: rats, pigeons, dogs, cats. My provisions, meager as they were, had actually saved a few from starvation. Laina said that the men didn't much care what happened to the women as long as they could provide the required services. Her revelation surprised me, more that she would tell me something than the content itself. When we arrived back by the hidden entry, I heard the deadbolts unlatch. Laina pushed me behind a box and silenced me.

'Whatever happens, you can't interfere.'

"I didn't like the sound of that.

"Some of the same men entered, this time accompanied by an adolescent boy playing a small flute. His music darkened an already tenebrous place with its eerie playfulness. Two of the men found a young woman sitting by one much older and grabbed her by the arms. Instead of taking her from the courtyard to meet whatever fate those before her had experienced, the men turned her to face the wall, holding her, while another man unbuckled his belt. The sour smell of old rum and stale cigarettes permeated the air. The woman writhed and screamed, but a man holding her arm shoved a blood and urine-stained rag in her mouth. The man behind her lifted up her skirt. I couldn't watch the rest. Her muffled cries tore at my heart, but if I tried to do anything, surely people would be hurt, or killed. Just when I thought it couldn't get worse, it did. The other two men took turns with her. I had to keep reminding myself that if I made one move, one or more of these women would die.

"Alone again with the women about thirty minutes later, Laina found me. This happened every so often, she said, when one of the women spoke out against what they wanted her to do. I asked if it had ever happened to her. She turned away.

'No. To my mother and sister.'

"She also said the men wouldn't return that night. A shrill cry from the other end of the courtyard brought us to a darkened corner where a girl, probably no more than eleven or twelve, knelt next to a woman's body. Laina tried to console the girl, but her cries grew. I crouched down to see, and it was the woman I had just watched being defiled, a gaping wound in her abdomen and a bloody piece of metal lying on the ground. She took her own life, Laina told me, rather than bear the shame of that ever happening again. I was shown a corner of the courtyard where the dead go, each lying on the earth unprepared for the underworld. More than a dozen women and children were lined up, covered with the blankets I had provided. This was how they showed their respect for the dead.

"This would end. On Gaea's name, I swear it.

• • •

"I didn't have much time left before the lunar cycle would end, so I needed to act quickly. If Zeus hadn't restricted me, I could have taken care of this by now. My subsequent visits consisted of bringing broom handles, knives—anything I could find that would fit in my rucksack. I had started to gain the women's trust, reminding me of my place as a man among women who needed to defend themselves. Not as organized as the Amazons, these women had the inner strength to survive, but not always the outer courage to fight back. If Athene were with me, she could endow them with the strength of great warriors or even free them into her care, but I was alone here without any Olympian intervention. No deus ex machina. Ironic, eh?

"Instead of just bringing bread or meat to sustain their bodies, or blankets and clothes to shield them from the cold nights, I spoke to them about courage, self-worth, and fighting back. A resistant audience for certain, but I had to try. If even a dozen women stood up to these men, they might actually have a chance. Not all of them spoke German, but enough understood to share with others my sentiment. My hand gestures, an Amazonian language that a few taught me while I was in Themiskyra, helped convey what my words couldn't. Before I left that night, I asked Laina why the women didn't just escape through the opening in the wall, the same opening that allowed her or me to pass into the alley. Did they fear being killed?

'Fear of death doesn't hold them back. Shame does. Many of these women are far from home with no means to return, and with their self-worth torn from them along with their innocence, they have given up caring.'

'How did you get here?' I asked.

'My parents moved here for jobs, and I started school here a few years ago. When some of the militia came for my father to fight, they took my mother and me here. I don't know what happened to him, but I pray for him.'

"From what I could tell, Laina had the courage to leave—she had many times. I wanted to know what kept her coming back.

'Hope.'

"That was all I needed to know. I had two more nights before I would have to leave these women, and I wouldn't be able to return for quite some time. Even if they were all killed, I wanted them to die with some sense of pride.

• • •

"The next morning, I went to the Greco-European Embassy to speak with anyone who could help me arrange sanctuary for these women without revealing too much yet. Unfortunately, without specific details, they would be unable to help. Explaining in hypothetical situations started to make me look suspicious, so I stopped trying. Should any police force attempt to rush in there on some heroic mission, it might cause agitated fingers to pull triggers, and I didn't want the deaths of these women on my conscience. I did have one other recourse, however, and took advantage of the international phone lines of the embassy to call a friend in New York. Once a secured line was created, I divulged everything I knew and told him I would be leaving town in two days. He assured me that a task force would meet me in Windhoek.

"Every time I had gone back to the courtyard, I had taken a mental count of the women and children, and the number hadn't changed since my last visit: 37 women and twelve girls. Laina made sure each one had some sort of weapon tucked away in the folds of her clothing or hidden near her, and even the elderly women, despite Laina's protests, demanded to have something. She knew it was their right, regardless of the outcome. The next night would be my last night to see them, and at sundown I would return to Olympos, so I spent the night in the courtyard, telling them more stories of the ancient Amazon warriors who prevailed over their conquerors time and time again, learning how to fight back and assert themselves. To them, they were fantastical stories of magic and hope, but to me, they were real experiences of women I knew well. As the night passed, I even acted out great scenes of battle that had been told to me by Danaë and some of her sisters. These women of the courtyard, armed in newspaper and tattered cloth, sat taller, listening intently, even though most of them couldn't understand much of the story. As the moon passed across the sky, the pale silver illuminated everything, highlighting the shapes gathered around me. In quiet fires their souls burned for victory over their captors, and part of me knew that no matter what happened, they would all be triumphant in some way or another.

"In my mind, as I was teaching them ancient ways of women who prevailed over their adversaries, drumbeats echoed, and in their bodies, heartbeats echoed, each pulse like a blacksmith's hammer, forging steel.

• • •

"I slept most of the day away, having not returned to my hotel room until just before sunrise. My heart remained with the women and children since I knew I would be gone by nightfall. Saving them might not be entirely possible, but I owed it to them to keep hope. My plan was to return to the courtyard once more to spend my remaining hours with them. Late afternoon, after five p.m., I entered the alley for the last time, ready to take my count, but I heard noises beyond the fabric that made my pulse quicken. Bursting through the other side, I was grabbed by two men while two others tied my arms behind me. They had been waiting for me. I had been so pre-occupied with helping them that I never assumed the men would be watching; they hadn't done anything about the supplies I had brought. A quick scan of the area assured me that the weapons we had all hidden the night before remained safely tucked away beneath newspaper and refuse as nothing had been moved. While I writhed against my bonds, the adolescent boy played a tune, trying to disguise the noises of the courtyard with lilting musical notes.

Before I knew what was happening, I was gagged with a dusty shirt that was tied around my head, and then the horror began.

"With night falling, half a dozen men came through the doorway that usually remained bolted, seizing women and girls within arm's reach. Three of the men pushed their captives against the wall and forced themselves between unwilling legs, but only one was able to reach her knife she had kept beneath her headscarf, reaching between her legs, severing the man from his manhood. He leapt back, shrieking, releasing his grip on his victim so he could place both hands over the bloody wound. And the flute player played on. Seeing her sister's success, another of the women freed one of her hands and forced her thumb into her assailant's eye socket. Two more men had entered and had dragged young girls to the back of the courtyard by the hair. One of the men, trying to unbuckle his belt one-handed, felt a cold knife blade puncture his chest, plunged by the girl beneath him. He fell back, ripping the knife from his wound, but the serrated edge made a bigger gash. Like a growing inferno, a wave of confidence washed over these women, each one fueled by a deep rage that, only at that moment, they had the courage to free.

"A tall man with a pencil mustache aimed a pistol at an oncoming girl, armed with a metal shank, but like angry bees, the women swarmed him, his own cries muffled by flailing gunshots that flew aimlessly into the sky. And the flutist played on.

"Just as the moon rose, I felt my power rise within me. My ropes disintegrated, and my gag became dust. My eyes blazed, two suns driving out the madness. Decimated and disemboweled, men lay all about, oozing the last of their life into the earth. In the distance, beyond the walls, I heard sirens singing. Antonin had sent help. From across the dusty, blood-drenched square, I saw the one I wanted, the one among them who would not escape so easily, dying from a broom handle or a knife. He had no place to run, and so he played on. Standing before him, I saw his eyes meet mine, and then I saw the puddle of urine form beneath him.

'Like bold Marsyas from ages past, who brazenly challenged me to a music contest, you challenge me as well, thinking your tune will soothe and obscure the chaos around you. As was Marsyas' punishment for his hubris, so this is yours now. While you played, others suffered, stripped of their dignity, so I strip something from you.'

"With a thought, I flayed him, the man's skin slowly ripping from his body. He opened his mouth to scream, but I denied him his voice. For him, no sound he could create would cover his suffering.

• • •

"Before I was drawn back to my time and place, I saw Laina rallying the women, empowering them. Through both the alley and the doorway, a U.N. task force flooded in, taken aback by these women who stood tall and no longer felt shame. As she saw me fade away, Laina knew, while these people were there to help, she and her sisters were their own salvation.

"They were true Amazons.

"I have wandered from my original tale, with so many things to tell you, dear Justice, so let me continue."

# 9—BIRTHRIGHT

"Once we hit the dark Euxine Sea looming before us, she told me I might feel a little disoriented entering the portal. The gem's enchantment let the bearer rip a hole into time and space. Holding the amulet by the chain, Alkinoë let the morning sunlight activate the magic, and a small aperture opened up just before us hovering over the surf. Mirage-like, the image seemed unclear to me, but she knew where she was going, commanding the horse forward. Instinctively, I held on to the queen's waist, fearing I might fall off, but before I could get my bearings, we had landed on the other side of the portal with the others. I loosened my grip on Alkinoë as we trotted down the path as if nothing had happened. Traveling as a god was nothing like that, and I actually felt a sense of hesitation if would have to do it again anytime soon.

"Arkadeia's idyllic landscape looked nothing like Themyskira's forests or Trapæzos' windswept coastline. Cypress trees and mountains seemed to undergird the horizon, Mt. Menalon to the west, its cloud-cloaked peak standing in majesty over the valley. Far to the southeast, in the Parnonas range, towered the peak Megali Tourla, and to the north rose Mt. Kyllene, the birthplace of Hermes, with Mt. Taygetos in the south—the largest mountain in the Peloponnese. I suddenly felt a little saddle-weary, but had no intention of stopping. She pointed out a walled capital city, Tegea, nestled in the valley below. I asked her why, if the crystal could open a portal anywhere, why we didn't just go to the city. 'I like to ride,' was her response.

"The queen grew curious about me, so I had to become creative with my response lest I reveal too much about my penance. I let her know I was from the Pieræa province, near Thessaly, which wasn't untrue as that was where Olympos sat. All I would tell her was that I rode horseback until Platamonas, then a transport ship brought me into the Euxine where I ended up in Trapæzos. I so wanted to tell her the truth.

"The city gates towered over me, and I realized that Tegea was much larger than Themyskira. Much larger. Soldiers lined the walls, but one had to look for them to see them. The captain of the guard, Cleisthenes, greeted us. I had met him on one of the prior visits to the Amazons. Alkinoë instructed him I was a guest and should be afforded all the privileges of an Amazonian emissary, and then she instructed him to take the scroll to the oracle. After I dismounted, I wandered the agora of the city for a while, taking in everything about this city, the one I helped bring about. Apollo and I are the same. I can surely take credit for everything that I did before my penance without betraying my mortality. This is *my* city.

"I acquired a small chunk of cheese and some bread before exiting the agora and entering the main thoroughfare of Tegea. Towering above the city were the twin marble shrines: Gaea's and mine. I hadn't seen or been in one since my arrival as a man. As I arrived at my temple, I passed through the colonnade and removed my shoes, as was the custom. Entering the naos, the inner chamber, I noticed the fire-filled braziers and smelled the heady incense. How I missed that. The statue with my likeness towered above the supplicants, and I prayed, yes prayed, to whomever was listening that these people wouldn't see the resemblance.

"I think Zeus knew this would happen, and he wanted me to be disgusted by the burnt offering on the altar. These people were praying to a god who no longer resided on Olympos, but they didn't know that. I felt ashamed of the attention, but what could I do? By the altar I knelt, and I cried. This was almost too much. Too close to being a god again. Tears that rivaled the rivers Alpheus and Peneus when Herakles cleansed the Augean stables flowed out of me. I looked at my sodden hands, my mortal hands, finite and blood-filled. Everything about me felt awkward here: my face, my fingerprints, my hair, my heartbeat. I read, or tried to read, the inscription on my manacle. My mortal blood flowed away from my brain, and I felt lightheaded.

"Walking away from the shrine, I found great irony in that I was once *Apollo Alexikakos*, the Healer, but I felt struck down in my own temple. Was Zeus testing me? Had I failed? I left the agora and was shown to my quarters in the palace where I chose to sit in the all-consuming darkness.

• • •

"I remained in the room, darkened to keep my once-loved light away from my eyes. Whatever meager meals I ate provided no succor, fueling my dejection. Alkinoë only knew that I felt ill, most likely from my travels through the portal. I watched the agora day and night. Could I ever be like these people? Who was to say how long my penance would last... Months more? Years, perhaps. I, who once commanded the sun-chariot took more comfort under and an inky sky, with pinpoints of light from constellations and a pale moon to placate me. Many a night I awoke screaming, shaking, swathed in sweat, haunted by dreams.

Morpheos heard me not when I begged him to leave me alone. The aching needed to end.

"On a morning I remember vividly, I took my morning meal in my room and performed a rite of cleansing. Where I was to go, I needed to be pure. Perhaps I would find what I needed in my sister's shrine. My first stop was to a builder who sold me a pot of hot pitch and bristle brush. In an empty alley, I covered my manacle, enduring the heat. I made my way to Artemis' temple, made my offering, and knelt before the marble table. No other god did I trust as much as my sister. '*Goddess of life, huntress celestial, heed my call for guidance.*'

"I put myself into an abstraction, controlling my breathing until I no longer felt my physical self. In my mind, I was in an open, sun-drenched field, a single stag with white horns staring back at me. No words came, no questions, just pure thought. And, then it was over. The offering burnt to ash; I must have been in my stupor for well over an hour. Whatever my sister wanted me to know was somewhere in my subconscious and would appear when I needed to know. Albeit a short visit to the temple, I did feel a little better, but only the *Moirae* knew the outcome.

"Entering the palace, a lieutenant barely old enough to wear the beard on his face led me to the megaron, a great hall to rival any on Olympos, to see Alkinoë at her desk. Without pleasantries, she immediately brought my attention to a few unfurled scrolls. Up until a few months ago, she told me, her oracle could not scry in Apollo's temple. What she and the High Priest did know was that an unspeakable evil was approaching, waves flooding the farmland. The Amazonian oracle had learned the same information. For the first time, I felt her voice ripple with concern. This wasn't a natural disaster as Arkadeia was land-locked. I did have an idea about some malevolence approaching, but I could not even put it into words, not without Zeus knowing, and I could not be sure this was the same. That was a bargaining element I did not wish to use just yet.

"Alkinoë wanted me to use my diplomatic skills and seek out what neighboring lands knew of this cataclysm. Unfortunately, due to their ties with Themyskira, Arkadeia didn't have allies with everyone. Certain places like Korintheia, Argolis, Messineia looked at them with contempt. The more I discussed this with her, the more we both realized this could destroy more than just one country. It could ultimately threaten the strength of Olympos with the loss of so many people, people who offered their fealty to the gods.

"I met with Aegialeos from Akhæa as well as the monarchs from other adjacent territories with great success, but it would appear Clotho, Lachesis, and Atropos were bored and sought to play cat's cradle with their woven strings.

• • •

"One of my last places to go was Lakoneia, but on the morning I was to meet with the oracle to discuss the prophecy, a Spartan messenger brought word from Tyndareos, the king, denouncing the conference because of Arkadeia's ties with the Amazons. Proxiteles had soured his liege. When Lakoneian troops threatened to undo the work I had done, I had no choice but to meet the king.

"When I mentioned this to Alkinoë, she insisted she come along, and I was not going to challenge her. Using the PortalBearer, we arrived in Lakoneia just before nightfall in the palace hall, the only place the queen could think to go. Tyndareos' guards didn't quite know what to do when we appeared, but before we could all engage in some fruitless melee, the king's voice brought everyone to heel.

"A man of average height and build, with short gray hair and beard, Tyndareos looked pallid and squat next to the Arkadeian queen. He dryly commented that he would expect such an act from Demosthenes, but not from her. I then learned that Alkinoë had been married before, but her husband died on the battlefield. He then suggested that the assassination attempt we had planned had been thwarted and would hear nothing of the prophecy. Evidently, the fact that we had come unarmed didn't matter. I said that he was mistaken, and that we had to speak with his oracle, but he came nose to nose with me, saying that if I valued my life, I would hold my tongue. *Just one thunderbolt, Zeus. Fry this sorry excuse of a sovereign*, I thought.

"Alkinoë snarled and instructed him to summon his oracle, and not to threaten me again. He had the guard retrieve Giron, the oracle, and then asked about this prophecy. His condescension kindled my ire. Standing next to his king, the oracle looked like a rat. A rat next to a snake, how fitting. She repeated the words from memory:

"*When blood-red tides wash over, the fangs of war shall cleave the flesh of the dove, making a path for death. Only when the earth resides inside the heart of pure light can life begin anew.*

"Giron stiffened. He had heard those words before, commenting as such to his sovereign. Just as we thought he might see reason, he shouted to his guards to place Alkinoë in a holding cell and me in the palace dungeon. As the guards removed her, the queen shouted that no harm should come to me. Had she tried to escape, I might have been killed. She was immortal, but I wasn't. Dungeons seemed to be my fallback place of residence, too. My first night in the dungeon, I was introduced to the mastix. So much for no harm.

"Hours of lashings brought the guards no closer to an assassination plot, but it did rip my back apart. Pain I had never experienced almost caused me to pass out. I kept

Alkinoë in my mind, hoping to high Olympos that no harm would come to her as it had to me. Hades' fury wouldn't stand a chance against me if one drop of her blood flowed. Since the mastix wasn't getting the answers the guard wanted, he chose his studded gauntlet against my head. That, he found out, was an error in judgment as an unconscious man cannot speak. Before my consciousness left me, I peered into my jailer's vacuous eyes, hoping some shred of mercy would stay his hand. None came.

"Day three of my imprisonment meant I received food, if that's what one could call it. No word about Alkinoë. Guards were tight-lipped. I dreamt of her, her safety, her escaping and getting an army. Tyndareos needed to pay.

"Day seven. Her soft skin. Her compassionate eyes deeper than Tartaros. If I could get lost in her eyes, I would never want to be found. My back was numb from the mastix. I wondered what flesh remained to feel pain at all. Sleep was little comfort, but he wouldn't whip me when I slept.

"Two weeks. Merciful Gaea, please watch over Alkinoë. Her grace, her auburn hair, her mind... dear, sweet Artemis, I begged her to hear my plea and watch over her. My guard, Stolycos, and one other spoke of her, but softly, so I couldn't hear them. She had returned to Arkadeia. Casualties of war I understood well. I had become one. Praise Olympos she was home.

"Week three. Barely received water. No food. No more mastix. Tyndareos thought I would die anyway.

"*Blood-red tides. Fangs of war. Flesh of dove.* My mortality was oozing away from me. My flesh eaten by rats at night. *Earth in a pure heart.* I thought a month had passed, but I had lost all sense of time. *Hermes Psychopompos*, brother... I wanted him to claim me right then. Didn't want him to wait until I was dead. Alkinoë. I wanted her to mourn for me, burn a pyre for me.

• • •

85

"Ice cold water woke me from my near death, and Stolycos shouted for me to stand. Buckets of ice water were meant to bathe me. Clean clothes were meant to give me back some shred of dignity. Much of the pitch on my manacle had fallen off from the mastix striking it. I didn't care who knew anymore. I was barely coherent, muttering Alkinoë's name over and over and over. Chained, I was taken from the dungeon into the harsh daylight which I had not seen in more than six weeks. From under a stone I had come, and I was going to see the snake, venomous fangs at the ready. He was lucky I was so weak or I would have killed him with my bare hands.

"Standing before Tyndareos in the throne room, I felt small. Pitiable. Stripped bare of who I was. He offered me some bread and cheese. I didn't care if he had poisoned me at that point. Death would have been a better place to be. He stared at me. Another offer from the Spartan king— serve him for one month and stay alive. Hades was mocking my prayers for death.

"He would let me look at ancient texts regarding the prophecy—*if* I debased myself by serving him. Next to Tyndareos' slithering demeanor, Python was a garden snake. As long as Alkinoë was safe, I would do it... whatever he wanted me to do. He signaled to a guard who then left the chamber. Whatever shred of dignity I had wasn't worth keeping if she weren't free.

"Thirty days of my life I could give. For her.

"I told him that I was at his disposal. If a snake could smile, it would look just like the Spartan king, fangs and all.

I didn't know for quite some time that Alkinoë had already returned to Arkadeia, gathering forces to storm the Lakoneian territories. She was prepared to wage war for my return.

• • •

"Among my many duties was the laborious task of the king's hygiene, which involved his morning bath. Not a moment passed when I didn't think of drowning him in his own tub. The ignominy of bathing him—all of him—made me wince. Never had a god, or once-god, been so debased, and after the first day, when I went back to my chamber, I emptied my stomach into the nearest urn. But, I would have to do this every day, so I had to remember to clean the urn often.

"When Tyndareos didn't need me, I was cleaning out the stables, by hand if the shovel were missing. If I was lucky, he would let me bathe after such an activity, but that wasn't often. Sleep happened so sporadically that I had forgotten what it felt like to close my eyes for an extended period. I took my meals with the other servants; they showered me with pity through their eyes as we weren't allowed to communicate at all. When I did have to go in public, I had to wear a threadbare cloak to keep my face from view. I came to be known as the cursed one, or Tyndareos' pet. I had even heard a rumor that I was a demon from Tartaros given human form and only the king could control me. Only the guards and the king knew my true face. Perhaps the most mortifying was when Tyndareos instructed me to carry a hydria with me at all times, should he need to urinate. He never aimed well. And, I was to clean the hydria, and then myself—in that order.

"I had been instructed not to speak with anyone, except the king himself, so when Giron, the seer, skulked up to me one morning, I felt I was being tested. Having been charged with cleaning the megaron, I ignored his attempts at conversation, but he placed a hand on my shoulder followed by a plaintive, 'Please.' He swore his oath of oracular privilege to me, invoking Apollo's name, so I felt obligated at least to listen. Giron admitted that I was speaking truthfully about the prophecy, and that he

87

felt I was more than I appeared to be. I tried to deny that, but he then asked why I hid my wristband. He knew I wouldn't answer, so I had proven a point.

"Tyndareos, he felt, was but one of two of my masters, and the wristband marked another servitude, one I wished to keep hidden. He said he wished to help me leave Sparta. I wanted to know why, and he shared with me how he received the scar that ran down his face, the skirmish where he lost his right eye. He had been a beggar all over Akhæa, shunned for his prophetic gifts, until the day Tyndareos learned from soldiers who harassed the street urchins that one of Giron's prophecies would aid Sparta. From that day on, the half-blind man with second sight afforded himself a place in the royal palace serving the king. Giron would bring me the scrolls as an act of contrition for allying himself to such a despotic man. I refused.

"Honor must come first, I told him. My pledge to serve Tyndareos had to play out or my word would be meaningless. My humiliation at the hands of the king would have no purpose or meaning if I found a way around it for self-serving reasons. The *Moirae*, I told him, would see to it I was a free man when that was my destiny. The same was true for my penance to Zeus, although I didn't voice that thought. Giron pulled his hood over his head and left the megaron, and we never spoke again.

• • •

"Helios' chariot bathed the landscape with iridescence on the morning of my release from Tyndareos' subjugation, a gift to me, to one who had served his horses well. The king's voice shattered the moment, and I was called forth to bathe and dress him. I would have rather slept with a Gorgon.

"Adjusting his tunic, my mind elsewhere, I heard him comment that I didn't seem pleased. I muttered that the day wasn't over yet, simply because I knew he had me until sundown. My next task: feed the snake. Tyndareos never took his eyes off me while I stuck forks of food in his mouth, and he chewed slowly, smiling. I wanted to stab the fork through his forehead or slit his throat with the knife on the table or, better yet, disembowel him. Instead, I simply wiped his chin when he was finished eating. Justice would someday be served, even if it weren't by my hand.

"A servant entered, a youth whose eyes never left the floor, bringing another plate of food, and placed it in front of me. My eyes, however, bore into Tyndareos, wondering what further humiliation he had planned, but he merely gestured for me to eat. And eat I did. A form of gratitude for my service, he commented, since I had served him so well.

"Giron appeared from the shadows, as rats often do, and glided over to his king, whispering something. A guard was left to watch me as Tyndareos stormed from the chamber, Giron in tow. I continued to eat, the bread and cheese tasting better than ambrosia and nectar on Olympos at this point.

"Moments later, both returned, the king raging that had he listened to his oracle, none of this would be happening. Word of the prophecy had gotten out, and the people had begun to panic, crowding the Temple of Apollo for guidance. Hysteria festered as the hours passed, throngs of citizens filtering into the palace, and the guards struggled to keep them out. Like a growing tide, they moved themselves into the marble halls, inching their way toward the megaron.

"Soldiers escorted Tyndareos, Giron, and me from the fracas, the king shouting all the while. As we were escorted from the palace, I spoke up and asked about Alkinoë. Sparta's king suddenly stopped his tirade and just looked at me. It was at that moment I knew she wasn't in Sparta and probably hadn't been. Not having any leverage or advantage, I continued with the royal entourage, gritting my teeth. Shuffling toward a safer vantage point in the city, I glimpsed a soldier with a mastix attached to his hip, and my blood ran from my face: all that torture was for nothing more than Tyndareos' amusement. He needed no knowledge from me about an assassination attempt. Gods... he would pay.

"I hadn't noticed earlier, but someone in the crowd of soldiers had been eyeing me, being careful not to let anyone see. At our destination, a marble stronghold behind the palace, much of the phalanx encircled the building, but a handful remained with us. When I had a chance to move, I sidled over to the wall behind a column where I was then met with a soldier, but he didn't have the Spartan standard on his armor. Covering his cuirass was a leather flap with the Lakoneian emblem, but beneath it, I saw a familiar insignia, that of Arkadeia. Without words, he greeted me, his genuflection a vicarious greeting from the queen. He palmed an object and gently tossed it to me; it was the crystal and a note. At my earliest convenience, I was to meet this soldier by the palace entrance after sunset. I had to make one stop first.

• • •

"Standing at the gates of Sparta, carrying the dead soldier who had aided me and the scroll I found in the oracle's chambers, I followed the road until I reached a clearing, somewhere I knew that the moon would be brightest after sundown. Aeclys, the young man who risked his life to find me, died when an arrow from a Spartan soldier missed *me* as we raced through the agora. Before he died, I learned that Alkinoë didn't have the time to collect an army, so she hand-picked a few soldiers to sneak into the city and retrieve me. Two were discovered days into their mission, but Aeclys adapted to his surroundings well. I would bring him back with me to bury him in his homeland. To my recollection, no human had ever died trying to save me before. Now, three Arkadeian souls sat at the Stygian bank, awaiting Charon's craft, all because of me.

"Waiting for nightfall, I watched the sun chariot set. I had never truly taken the time to look at the panoply of colors when I drove the steeds below the horizon: misty orange, then crimson, then purple. Colors blended into each other, merging into darkness, giving way for Selene's moon chariot to rise in the heavens. When the pale disk reached its zenith, a shower of silver irradiated the land. It was time to go. The crystal spun on its thread, spinning one way and then the other, catching the rays of light. Finding the place I remembered the most in Arkadeia, I concentrated until it was as if I were there and then watched as the prism of light emanating from the crystal pried open a spatial rift. Before me, gardens of Arkadeia lay, but the image in my mind had not matched the image I saw. Carefully lifting Aeclys, I stepped through and fell to my knees, the air evacuating my body against my will. The sheer shock took a few moments to register, and then the portal closed behind me, leaving me in this place I had once loved to see. The city of Tegea lay in ruin.

"I lowered the dead soldier to the ground, said a silent prayer, placed an *obolos* under his tongue, and scanned the devastation. Once vital and lush, the gardens had withered from being trampled, either by human, horse, or other. Splashes of blood blotched the earth in places, and this once structured natural oasis was no more.

"The agora, once the thriving and active cultural center, had been razed, some of the buildings and carts still smoldering. Mangled corpses brought waves of nausea to me, but my own shock suppressed them. The remains of women and children, their lives cleaved from them by swords or battle-axes, made me dry heave from the stench. A frenzy of vultures fed on the raw, exposed flesh, each bird ripping its meal apart with no pity or remorse. Only one I knew of could bring this destruction. What I once thought was puddles of blood were swatches of red cloth, a war banner that had been decimated by the melee. *When blood-red tides wash ashore, the fangs of war shall cleave the flesh of the dove, making a path for death.*

"I vaulted over the deceased and the debris, screaming for Alkinoë, thinking she must be nearby, engaged in some protracted battle with the forces of evil and hatred. As I reached the palace, I took the steps two at a time, my heart ricocheting in my chest. Decapitated bodies of Arkadeian soldiers, blood spilling from any wound, sat piled along the terrace. The Royal Guard had done its best to defend the palace, leaving their bodies as a testament to their duty. Men and women that I had come to know well, gone.

"Severed limbs hung from the walls while blood dripped toward the floor. Blessed Aphrodite, the stench of decay and death lingered like a thick fog, making the marble halls a slaughterhouse. I realized... all of the bodies were headless. One final indignation to otherwise stalwart and loyal soldiers. From within the megaron, resonant, guttural growling ripped through my ears, and I picked up a discarded sword, a makhaira coated with blood, already knowing it would be useless. I found it odd that no soldiers stopped me, but my determination clouded my thoughts.

"Scant torchlight allowed me to see shadows in the other chamber, shadows only one creature I knew could make. Before I knew what hit me, I flew back against the wall, the sword flying from my grip. A war hound. Leaning over my head, sending its fetid breath washing over me, the beast should have torn me to pieces, but it hadn't. Hearing a familiar voice call it back, I knew more would be in store for me. The dog backed away, its feral eyes never leaving me, Polemos—a hound of Ares—oozed venom from its fangs onto the polished marble, etching trails of caustic saliva.

"Makhaira in hand once more, although futile, I followed the acrid canine breath to its source. I demanded to know about Alkinoë, but Ares glanced sideways, muttering that she'd been deposed. Hanging against the wall, her wrists bound with bloodied ropes and war-ravaged chains, Arkadeia's queen was the war god's trophy. Again my pulse surged, seeing the battle-scarred face. Pieces of armor had been ripped from her, no doubt by Polemos or his four-legged sibling seated next to him. I moved toward her, not caring about my own life, growling my disgust, and a hound lurched forward and snapped at me. Ares shouted *'Kakos!'*, and the creature lay back down, its eyes attached to my steps. I almost wished the war hound had devoured me.

"I wanted to take her down and bury her with honor, but Ares said she amused him. Lifting her chin to see her face, landscaped with bruises the color of Tartaros, I gasped. I had no choice. For the first time since Leto brought me into the world, I had to perform the greatest act of humility.

"I knelt before Ares in supplication.

"With any compassion he had, I implored him to let me give her a warrior's burial, according to tradition. Surely the god of war would indulge me this one request, with me on my knees. Whether it was because of this act or because I was worn down emotionally and physically exhausted from enslavement to Tyndareos, I finally wept.

"Silence blanketed us both, one god and his mortal brother. Tears I didn't know I had, from the depths of my own personal underworld, rose forth, flooding my face and the chamber floor, diluting the half-dried puddles of Alkinoë's blood.

"I looked up to see Ares lift the war helmet from his head, revealing his face irreparably scarred from unending hostilities fueled by his own bile, and our eyes met. He told me she fought valiantly. Fifty of his finest warriors

93

fell to her blade within the first moments of battle. Dozens more were no match for her skill. He called it a glorious triumph, although a short-lived one.

"Lost in the moment, reliving each sword struck and spear thrown, war's master was enrapt by an orgiastic expression of power. He felt strengthened, aroused as well, while I was drained of my will and desire to live. Humanity had beaten me. Then, it happened.

'*Take her*,' Ares told me. A moment of compassion.

"I took her lifeless body to the only place I knew to go, the Temple of Gaea, to perform the rites of the dead. I wouldn't glorify Hades with this woman's soul. He'd see her soon enough. Her lifeless body on the cold stone altar, I dressed her wounds with scraps of cloth I found outside and mopped her skin clean of blood and dirt. I couldn't bear seeing her like this, but I suppressed my tears this time. I had a ritual to perform, and I wouldn't mar her memory with hesitation. I kissed her forehead and told her I loved her.

"I loved her.

"Kneeling before the white table, I heard a voice enter my mind, like fog creeping over the ocean. I knew this voice. Anger at this sacrilege, she felt. Salvation would come, she told me. My human mind struggled to hold the words, but my pain grounded me enough to understand what I needed to do. Such was the will of the Earth Mother, Gaea, the *Matêr Pantôn*. Idle she could no longer be.

• • •

"She told me where to look in the naos of her shrine. Behind the altar lay a secret chamber, one known only to her high priests, and now to me. I slid a marble partition in the wall aside, revealing a panel carved with an eagle holding the sun and earth between the tips of its wings: the insignia of the chosen of Apollo and Gaea. Placing my palms on the raised surface, I pulled the wings apart,

94

sliding open a small closet. On two marble pegs hung a sword forged by the Earth Mother in the First Fires—the *Kiphos Gaias*—the Sword of Gaea. Brushed golden Earthsteel made up the hilt, the cross guard tapered down toward the pommel. In the center of the guard sat a blue jewel, triangular, embedded in a recess. The narrow, tapered silver blade had an edge sharp enough to split a centaur hair, and the fuller ran two-thirds down the blade, etched with similar glyphs from my wristband. Protruding from the pommel was a ring. As I removed the sword from its sheath, a humming echoed throughout the temple, the blade singing to me. Again, Gaea's voice instructed me. Once I expunged the evil of Ares, I would perform a rite of purification, restoring the glory to Arkadeia. She assured me that the sword would strengthen me to fight the coming battle with Ares, as well as protect me from harm, but I had to allow the sword to perform the task.

"I was no match for Ares. This I knew. I was ready to sacrifice myself for the Arkadeian people and their queen. Alkinoë's body would be safe now, so I returned to the megaron where, as I suspected, Ares still sat, gloating. Polemos and Kakos were gone, no doubt gone back to the Areopagus, Ares' hill.

"I would reclaim this land in Gaea's name, I told my brother, whose laughter spurred me on. This close to the sword, I could feel the electricity it exuded. Three steps closer I walked, and I unsheathed the blade, one that Ares had never seen, and it intrigued him, but he remained unmoved. One way or another, I announced, this would end here.

"With an unseen gesture, he brought his dark warriors from the shadows, two dozen armored wraiths, their eye sockets vacant of anything but vile torment and blind savagery. My brother wouldn't even face me in battle. So be it. Possessed by a rage I never knew I could muster, I jumped into the phalanx, the Sword of Gaea an extension of my arm. With every strike they managed to make on me, I came back with a parry or thrust, even when my own blood ran down my arms or from slices to my leg. Let the sword do the work, Gaea had told me, since I was forcing my own emotions onto the task. Clouded by vengeance, I wasn't able to take down Ares' warriors because I was doing it all wrong—I was on the offensive. A change in strategy that went against everything I felt surfaced.

As each sword strike came, I became defensive, never striking a blow against another. Slowly, I gave myself over to the sword, allowing it to control my movements, and with fluidity I slowly saw the tenor of the battle shift. Without my anger and with only my desire to block, I put all my trust into Gaea, knowing that she would never let me come to harm. Black blades came crashing down, but each kissed the Earthsteel in my hands. My movements were a dance, a rhythmic ebb and flow that eventually drew all the power from these soldiers of death, until—finally—my movements stopped altogether. One by one, the extensions of Ares' will retreated back to the shadows until I once again stood before my brother.

"That was enough to goad him into picking up his own sword, three times the size of mine. I stood my ground. When the blades struck each other, sparks flew, and I didn't fly into the wall, as I had expected, although I did falter a little. He toyed with me, as Polemos or Kakos would with his prey, and his war blade whistled around as he brought it down toward my head. Each time I felt my sword would break or bend, but it remained whole and strong, and this augmented my courage. And, I learned, that the sword strengthened me through Gaea's regenerative will. Ares didn't know that.

"He struck wildly, crashing his sword onto mine over and over again, trying to get me to falter, but I was empowered. While he possessed greater skill, I was a quick learner, and I remembered my sparring with Athene

96

ages ago. Ares insisted on demeaning me, trying to wear down my ego so that I would slip up, but I simply smiled at his remarks. He didn't like that one bit. A war chant came from his lips, a special song he sang in an ancient tongue, his mantra on the battlefield. As long as he continued to sing it, he focused even more on victory. For some reason, Gaea's words from the temple came back to me repeatedly, but I didn't understand yet what to do.

"In yet another attempt to throw me off, Ares summoned his war hounds once again to enter the fracas, each one materializing before me in a cloud of squalid mist. Polemos lashed at me with a taloned paw, just missing my head before I backed out of the way, but Kakos, a more cantankerous canine, swept his barbed tail, tripping me, just before he leapt across the chamber. Marble cracked where metallic talons struck, and before he could spring again, I swung my blade around and struck. Unlike god-forged metal of Ares' sword, flesh—even of a war hound—cleaved much more easily, and Kakos limped toward his master missing one paw. Faster than Hermes it seemed, Polemos tackled me, snapping his jaws at my sword arm. The war god thought a two-pronged assault would help, and his sword met mine while I lay on my back. Even with Gaea's protection, I felt Ares' raw power reverberate through me.

"To even the playing field, I boldly rolled under Polemos' heaving torso before he could react and thrust upward until my blade was buried in his abdomen and protruding the other side. With both hounds wounded and whimpering, Ares' distraction became my advantage.

"Emboldened by the Earth, and giving myself over to her completely, I became one with the *Kiphos Gaias*. With a stalemate quickly approaching, I had to strategize a little differently, but I became lost in thought, and Ares took advantage of that. A well-swung blow knocked me to the floor, loosening my grip on the sacred sword. A tinkling sound caught my ear, and I saw the crystal on the marble beneath me. Ares hadn't noticed or didn't care, so I snatched it up, and then a deeply hidden memory shook loose in my mind. Shoving the crystal into the open ring at the end of the hilt, I saw the metal grasp it, fusing itself to the glassy object. At that moment, the *Kiphos Gaias* became *Thyroros*, the PortalBearer.

"Ares tired of this clash, especially since he wasn't winning, leaped across the chamber, swinging his sword down as he descended. As our swords met, the vibrations went through me, cracking the floor, but leaving me intact. Twice more he simply tried to pummel me, but the living blade in my hands wouldn't accept defeat. He was giving over his control to his bloodlust now, and it was at that moment when Gaea showed me an image in my mind. I knew what to do.

"Shifting my body weight, I moved out of the way before Ares could strike, giving me only moments to use the flickering torchlight to initiate the crystal's magic. With a sweeping motion, I opened a portal, the sword parting space and time simultaneously. His mind addled with power, Ares sprang forward, his arms over his head, both hands wrapped around the hilt of his sword. Before he could move out of the way, his forward momentum carried him into the dimensional chasm, which then closed behind him. It was done.

"I whispered, *'For you, Alkinoë'*, before I lost consciousness.

• • •

"I awoke hours later, as if from a horrendous dream, but the smell of death, reinforced by corpses and hound's blood brought me back to a harsh reality. I returned to Alkinoë. Leaning over her body, now still, I managed a few words: *'Ares is vanquished.'*

"What would I do now? Where would I go? How many other lands in the Peloponnese had met with the same fate? With the sword sheathed, I felt mortal again. Ares' defeat didn't assuage my guilt or pain, so what was the point of all this madness and destruction? And where were the other gods? Had Ares destroyed them, too? Through a temple window, I saw a crescent moon floating in the heavens—Artemis was there, but what could she do? I couldn't keep my eyes open anymore, so I gave myself over to Morpheos to heal.

"At sunrise two days later, while still in my reverie, Gaea spoke to me about the Ritual Cleansing. After I was fully awake, I no longer ached, all my scars and wounds had vanished, and my mind felt clear for the first time in many months. The rite would take time and preparation, and I felt like I was in a place mentally where I could do it, unburdened by so many things.

"A slit in the stone in the niche where I had first received it accepted the blade, a key of a sort. The wall parted, and I entered a small room with an open ceiling and a unique altar: a large piece of oak, hewn from one trunk and carved with ancient glyphs similar to the ones on my wristband, sat on a marble plinth. Following Gaea's instructions, I set the scabbard on the table, unsheathed the sword, and placed it into a narrow opening in the table. The jeweled hilt aligned with the opening above. I had done everything Gaea asked me to do. All that I had left was meditation.

"Kneeling, I brought my mind to a place where I could fully receive the Earth Mother's power and whispered a sacred chant, the words flowing out of my mouth in a language older than the gods, as quickly as she spoke them to me:

*'Khaos, womb of creation, I call upon you.*
*Gaea, mother of all, I implore you.*
*Olympeia, spirit of the sacred mount.*
*I beseech you, fount of life, purge this land of death.*
*I supplicate myself to you.*

*Remove blood's stain from Gaea's flesh.'*

"I repeated this without end during the entire ritual.

"As I felt myself merge with my Earth Mother, she embraced my soul in a way words cannot describe. A presence rose from beneath me, providing a link from aether into reality. Through the floor, into my body, through my chest, my arms, fingers, and even into my mind, I felt her.

"The sun reached its zenith, its golden beams cascading into the chamber and falling upon not only the PortalBearer crystal, but also the Eye of Gaea, embedded in the hilt's center. Tremors vibrated throughout the temple, almost as if an entity were awakening from a long slumber. Acting in tandem, both crystals took in the sunlight, sending forth a blue bolt of energy that passed through me, as if I were a human prism, filtering the light even further. My body rose until I was completely enveloped in this azure energy, and from my body departed an eagle made of pure light, and this bird of power flew from the shrine, bathing everything in its essence. I could see through its eyes.

"Unleashed, the eagle radiated a cleansing light, vanquishing blood and death, purifying the landscape by removing all the dead. As she and my former godself had done when first creating this civilization, the eagle took stones—Gaea's bones—and created a new Arkadeia, giving each stone life in human form, like Deucalion and Pyrrha had done after the Great Flood. Hades controlled the underworld, and he would not allow any souls of the slain to return, but he promised them eternity in Elysium. This Arkadeia would be Olympos' glory once more, willing to serve Gaea and Apollo. With its task completed, the great bird flew off into the sky, rejoining the sun.

"I, too, felt replenished, and I returned to Alkinoë, sword at my side, to wish her one final farewell. Her cold hand in mine felt unnatural, and I wished I could join her

100

wherever she was, for it would be better than being without her.

*'I will miss you, my sweet Alkinoë. I love you,'* I whispered, gently touching her hand with my lips.

"I was about to curse Zeus, for having me experience all I had, only to come to this one moment, when I thought I felt her hand move. Surely, Hades would not be that cruel. I squeezed her hand, sharing myself with her, and then I felt it. Her pulse. Her cheeks had more color than earlier, and I thought I saw her chest rise and fall slightly. Gaea had healed her for me. She must not have been entirely dead. Alkinoë's eyes fluttered open, and she turned toward me. A faint smile, and then her weak voice uttered, *'I love you, too.'*

"Scooping her into my arms, I held her, praising Gaea. I swore by all that was holy, on the River Styx itself, to love her and only her forever. I knew the severity of such an oath, and I intended to keep it. She kissed me, and her touch did as much to heal my soul as Gaea had my form, perhaps more. I helped her to stand so we could assess this new Arkadeia together when I heard a faint crack.

"I looked down at the sign of my penance, and it had cracked completely through.

*'Blessed Gaea...'*

"Alkinoë didn't know what this meant. Without thinking, I told her my penance had ended. She didn't understand, but we would have much time for explanations. I tried to pull apart the metal, to make sure it was indeed broken, but I couldn't. Then, I heard a voice offering me help.

"It was Zeus.

"He thought it would be fitting that the one who had bound me into his penance should be the one to remove me from it.

"Alkinoë, poor sweet Alkinoë, had no idea before whom she stood. I held her hand, kissed her forehead, and

101

placed my wrist on the altar. Once Zeus summoned a thunderbolt, I think she understood better. Invoking Khaos, Gaea, and Olympos itself, Zeus ended my penance and touched the manacle with the thunderbolt, melting it into a puddle. My godhood flowed back into me, a rushing torrent of energy unmatched by any flood. No longer did I need to call myself after my birthplace.

"Before the queen of Arkadeia stood Phoebos Apollo, the Shining One. As I was before, I would be again.

• • •

"The *Moirae* began my tapestry of divinity once more, with new thread and purpose, but I had seen other things through Gaea's eyes; I now had other plans. I had learned of the existence of one more *Protogenos*, one unspoken, untouched by thought, and one duly deserving of the gods' reverence.

"Olympeia, Gaea's sister, and Spirit of the Sacred Mountain upon which Titans once stood, and where gods dwelled now, would have to be known. A new era would begin for the gods, and I would aid in its arrival.

And yet, I wondered why Zeus would free me, since he knew I had knowledge that could cause him great harm."

# 10—HOPE

"The past and the future stand tethered to each other, and sometimes those events bring memories to rise. The end of my mortality back then ignites the memory from my last visit to the *Oikoumene Broteios*.

"Every time I traveled from Olympos to the inhabited mortal world, I became increasingly more aware of just how flawed humanity was. Don't misunderstand: immortals have their share of failings, too. I don't have to tell you, Justice, since you've been around as long as I have, perhaps longer. But, before I sent my family across from *Ge Theôn*, something I needed to do because of the Separation of the Souls, I needed to see for myself more than just New York City or Windhoek. Gaea's vast surface held much to see, and I had to see just how much this world had changed from what I knew it should have been. Why my vision had not been as clouded as the other gods remained a mystery; perhaps it's my tie to truth. Immortality blinded the gods. Of all Olympians, I think I've changed the most, and there has to be a reason. When the Fates allow, I will know.

"Before I sent my wife and child into an unknown—you'll find out later just how agonizing it was. Too hard to go into at the moment.

"One lunar cycle would have to be enough to show me just how radically the mortal world had evolved from the moment Nyx shattered the Sacred Scales, because I knew things were just not right.

• • •

"Hephæstian gold would help me travel once more, but Morpheos' aid I didn't need; my traveling would be purely scouting. Culture in June 1970 hadn't changed much since I was there just seven years earlier, but now the eyes of unobstructed truth would see all. I had no humanitarian mission this time. I was, for all intentions, a tourist.

"San Francisco's hilly landscape was my first stop, and I just wandered around the city, finding a hotel in Nob Hill as my home base, as it were. Like New York City, every street corner showed cameras, some cleverly hidden in architectural elements, while others were mounted to the corners of buildings. Paranoia had borne a sour fruit here, and the people had gotten used to the taste; it tasted of distrust. Banks had armed guards outside, automatic weapons gripped tightly. I understood that, but even the McDonald's wasn't without its protection. Such insanity.

"Clarity of thought helped me to see visions, visions of what should have been. How in Gaea's name I could see that, I had no idea, but there they were—clear pictures of a different San Francisco. Then, they faded just as quickly. Even without my immortal ichor flowing through me, my eyes could peel back the veneer of falsehood that adhered itself to everything. I needed some perspective.

"The Champs-Élysées in Paris. Main Street in Billings, Montana. Jenkins Corners in Abilene, Texas. All of these places shared one thing in common—an underlying mistrust and fear simmering beneath the surface of their humanity. And, here I am, a toothless god in a land who had all but forgotten my kind.

"I needed something to anchor me.

"A woman pushing a stroller down S. Claiborne Avenue, New Orleans—she couldn't have been more than 25—was slyly plucked from the street in daylight while I watched by two men in navy shirts, detained for two hours in a dilapidated brick building, and put back on the street, looking no worse for wear. Well, maybe her cheeks were red and her accelerated pulse was palpable. Cautiously, I asked her what happened, but she didn't want to talk to me, pushing the stroller through a crowd and disappeared. A young black man in dusty jeans and a flannel shirt sitting on a stoop saw me and invited me to join him. "She was grilled," he said. "Grilled to see what she knew." When I pressed him further, he said, "I don't know nothin' else," and scurried off like I'd scared him. I saw similar happenings in Barcelona, Moscow, and even Sydney. But, time was running out for me to find the place I wanted.

"Spiteful primordial beings. Had Nyx had even a second of forethought of what might happen, well… hindsight would always be wiser than the current situation.

• • •

"The last city I saw before I had to return to my realm looked no different from any other city, nor did it have fewer cameras, retinal scanners, armed guards, or metal detectors. Surveillance helicopters flew overheard every fifteen minutes or so, but no one even paid attention anymore. Downtown saw throngs of businessmen, merchants, housewives, children, and myriad other personalities all weaving amongst one another in this intricate tapestry of urban life.

"A hot pretzel with mustard from a food vendor went down very well with a cup of coffee while I sat on the silky green grass of the park in town. While this city wasn't as tall as others or even as vast, it possessed a charm that I couldn't ignore. Nonetheless, the familiar yoke of chaos weighed heavily on me. Families took their children out on this day to play in the sun or eat a packed meal on a blanket, simple joys that helped take my mind off the obvious issues. This park, its grassy lawns surrounding a small pond on which boats shaped like swans moved as gracefully as their feathered counterparts, became an oasis for me. While scanning the advertisements for housing in the local paper, I came across a listing for a brownstone apartment for a reasonable price, and its location seemed appropriate for a woman and her child to live there, for a time anyway. I wasn't entirely convinced, though, as I hadn't become any more enamored of this city than any other I had seen. My heart felt leaden when I thought about leaving my family here, in this world without the gods and with Humankind of questionable character.

"Just as I thought I had finally talked myself out of this city, I looked up and saw a young boy, around three, playing on his own, but not out of view of his parents, not an entirely unfamiliar site here. He must have imagined himself as an eagle or hawk, as he ran around in circles, arms outstretched, a blue towel tied around his neck like a cape. It made me laugh. Soon, two older boys about ten years old walked over to this would-be bird and began to taunt him. At first, the little one didn't see the others, as he was so caught up in his own joyful reverie, but they became hard to miss when they stood in his way, calling him names. More chaos the world didn't need.

"The boy stopped and looked at his adversaries with a layer of tears in his eyes to where his cheeks sparkled in the sunlight. As his eyes welled, one tear fell down his face. He blinked a few times quickly, not quite knowing what to do. His parents were not looking at that moment, so I prepared to stand, but before I could, though, a girl came over, maybe eight years old, and stepped nose to nose with the other two, telling them to leave the boy alone. The boys started to yell, but the girl pushed the boys away, not thinking of the risk to herself. The parents heard the commotion, instructing the girl to bring her brother back to them. She didn't move until the other boys begrudgingly walked off and then untied the blue towel from her brother's neck, using it to wipe his tears. Taking his hand, she returned to her parents. I overheard the father praising his little girl for her act of bravery.

"And there it was—hope for humanity: one child against two, protecting an innocent. Later that day, I eagerly signed the contract on the brownstone at 1236 Commonwealth Avenue in Boston.

"The end of my penance meant I could finally resume my rightful place among the gods, as Apollo, but it brought with it other challenges, some manageable and some nearly insurmountable. But, you, dear Justice, need to know what happened after I reclaimed my godhood once again."

# PART THREE: APOLLO

## 11—BLOODLINES

"Six months passed after Arkadeia's rebirth and changes needed to happen. I could no longer be an aloof, whimsical immortal, acting as I wished without consequence. If my penance had shown me nothing else, it was that, whatever we did—god or mortal alike—consequences followed. These new Arkadeians were as determined as their predecessors, rebuilding a city they never knew through memories that lingered in the ruins. It would take time for them to adjust to life, but they had time to do so. My first task, then, was to protect the people I had helped bring back, so I built stronger ramparts around the city of Tegea made of god-hewn stone. Hephæstos, having seen what I had endured, put aside our squabbles and helped me reinforce the city. He and I might never see things the same way, but we both agreed that Ares' befouling of such a sacred city, among others in Akhæa, would not go unaided. I swore a Stygian oath that Arkadeia, under my protection, would never be vulnerable again. This time, Gaea joined me in this venture, so sun and earth would protect its people.

"Alkinoë, adjusting to my identity and the miraculous resurrection of her city, agreed to marry me, and we did so in the Temple of Hera. Not since the marriage of Peleus and Thetis had gods and mortals seen such a celebration. Much to my surprise, my smithy brother offered us two thrones, forged in Earthsteel, as a wedding present. I remembered the day, in his forge, when he attached the manacle to my wrist. I had wanted to throttle the life from him then, but now, I understood what it meant to be in the shadow of the gods, as he had been relegated to the sooty forge beneath Olympos. Appreciated for his craft he might be, but not for his heart. Even Aphrodite chose Ares as her lover even after taking Hephæstos as her husband. I had a new found respect for the blacksmith.

"After the nuptials, my bride and I rekindled trade compacts with the neighboring lands, those that had survived the prophecy. I learned that other cities benefited from the benevolence of Olympian power, but alas, they didn't have Gaea's magnificence to heal. Whereas before my penance I wouldn't have cared, now I felt intense remorse. Too much loss. But, growth would begin again.

"Tegea became an even stronger metropolis than before, and an influx of visitors helped to stimulate the economy. One morning, while the queen and I were between trade settlements, a man entered the megaron with a twine-tied parchment that announced the bearer, Orestes, was bringing an offering from Antiope, queen of Athens, to replace our lost captain of the Royal Guard. An act of munificence we had not expected, we both agreed to this. Accord began with acceptance.

"According to *xenia*, we must show hospitality to all guests, and Orestes received a meal and a chance to rest before returning to Athens. Antiope would know we accepted this most generous offer.

• • •

"Midday, two leather armored men entered the city through the main gate. One, a dark-haired man of athletic stature, bearing a bronze hawk-emblazoned cuirass and shouldering a makhaira, moved with purpose and pride. A seasoned Athenian warrior, he enjoyed the genuflecting of the citizens his station afforded him as he passed through the agora. Well-worn leather sandals left a deep imprint in the dirt road and a raptor's eyes surveilled all, as if whatever his eyes could see, and that which they could not, was under his protection. His companion, a few inches shorter but equally as brawny, wore burnished gold armor and his well-used sword hung from a waist-borne scabbard. Like my own mark of servitude, he bore a steel manacle, his allegiance to Athene for all to see. Unlike mine, however, he wore his willingly.

"They found the palace quite easily as it was the second tallest building in the city and found Queen Alkinoë in the Hall of Defense, where matters of military importance came to fruition, pacing gently in front of a marble table where lay PortalBearer. After her first husband's death, Alkinoë became queen regnant of Arkadeia, as both she and Demosthenes ruled equally. After she and I married, she bestowed that same honor upon me, both of us ruling equally. She ruled, with my counsel, and I supported her. If we didn't agree, we met in private to discuss the matter. Arkadeia would always see two monarchs in accord.

"Sagacious in battle strategy, Alkinoë could assess any soldier's worth within moments of meeting him or her. She had already assigned him to the barracks to be near the soldiers as well as assigned him a cultural envoy. Heavy footsteps and a commotion in the outer corridor signaled her of his arrival. Her keen assessment began the moment he walked in the chamber, and he carried himself with almost too much pride. He gave her an Athenian salute, yet custom dictated that one greet a sovereign with that country's gesture. I suspected this might not bode well.

"He was Lykaon, from Attika province, city of Athens. Audaciously, he asked whether *xenia* had been afforded to the messenger sent to announce him. Alkinoë didn't reply. The man with him was Eristokles, a travel escort, who departed the moment his presence was no longer required. More oddities.

"The queen gestured for Lykaon to sit, but he respectfully replied that he preferred to stand. A look from her could silence a rowdy phalanx, but now it simply dismissed her entourage. I sat amused across the room. Once she was within a few feet of him, she firmly reminded him that he was no longer in Athens. No one sat in her presence if she was standing, and no one stood before her if she sat. If he couldn't cleave himself from his Athenian alliance, then he could not serve her.

"He sat. And then apologized for the effrontery.

"After learning some basic information from him, she stood, unsheathed *Thyroros*, and instructed him to kneel. Sunbeams from the window above shone through the jewel in the center of the sword, the Eye of Gaea, and bathed him in cerulean light. It was through her hand, and Gaea's presence, that Lykaon of Athens swore his fealty to the Royal House of Arkadeia, to perform faithfully the duties of his office, the Lokagos, Captain of the Royal Guard.

"Blue radiance yielded to sunlight once more, and Lykaon found himself arrayed in armor of golden Earthsteel, bearing the eagle, sun, and earth standard of Arkadeia on his cuirass. Indeed all his raiment had changed, including the sword he carried, now bearing a different royal insignia.

'*Athena skepe meta sou*,' she added. 'May Athene protect you.' Indeed she would.

"As if on cue, Alepos, Lykaon's second-in-command, entered. A seasoned warrior in his own right, he did not aspire to climb the ranks to become Lokagos; he was content being ypolokagos, or first lieutenant. Alepos escorted his superior officer to his new quarters in the barracks. The captain would hold an inspection of his troops at dawn on the proving grounds. Lykaon found his accommodations less austere than those in Athens, but all he wanted to do was sleep. When he awoke later, two maidens had drawn a bath for him and were ready to bathe him. Quietly noting his discomfort, they left, only to be replaced with a young man, bearing a washcloth.

• • •

"At sunrise, Lykaon put the army through rigorous drills, testing their limits and their skills. Despite his loyalty, he doubted Arkadeian soldiers possessed the requisite abilities to perform successfully, but much to his surprise, they were reasonably well trained. Alkinoë went to check on his progress and proceeded to humble him at the archery concourse. He needed to know that she was neither a commoner nor was she in need of protection. Later, he was reminded that Arkadeians, as children of Apollo and Gaea, shared in many of those divine qualities, and using a bow was second nature to her. The people, she informed him, were not first generation citizens, so he would have more success with them.

"She didn't need to observe Lykaon often, but once in a while, she would ride out to the proving grounds. Her new captain was demonstrating some hand-to-hand combat maneuvers, using Diogenes, a lesser trained warrior, as his sparring partner. Despite the hard-edged deportment he showed to Alkinoë and me, the Lokagos demonstrated compassion and understanding, a trait my wife wasn't sure he owned. Diogenes had some skill with a quarterstaff, but Lykaon had more. The Arkadeian soldier learned a lesson or two in humility when he thought he could take on the former Athenian warrior. Lykaon told them that they were soldiers by position, warriors by training. Moving from the former to the latter took time and devotion to the craft.

• • •

"I once found Lykaon at the blacksmith's forge, overseeing the artisan sharpen the blades used in that day's exercises. Not one sword could leave if it didn't pass his test: splitting a human hair lengthwise. That told me he cared not only for the men and women he trained, but also for their weapons. Well-worn they should be, he told me, but their edge should be honed often. He felt the same about the army. I didn't need to say nothing to him, but my hand on his shoulder would be all the approval he required.

• • •

"Even though I had come to know my wife well since we first met, I constantly admired her as I learned more and more about her past, a past I wouldn't have noted prior to my time as a mortal man.

"Athene had trained her, and Alkinoë learned how to temper her fighting ability with wisdom and mercy. Battle, an art practiced and honed, possessed a rhythm like finely orchestrated music. As an adolescent, all she yearned for was to be in the king's army, fighting alongside Arkadeia's finest soldiers. She trained much during those years, sparring with anyone who would, and she excelled, but out of skill grew arrogance. Back then, she worried more about hubris against the gods more than against her peers. It only took once, though, one time to be bested which squelched that self-satisfaction. During one of the tournaments held every year in my honor, a Tegean visitor reputed as a trainer of warriors would become a pivotal individual. Achilles, son of Peleus and Thetis, took lessons from him, as did the apiarist and herdsman Aristeios, and his son, the hunter Actaeon. My son, Aesculapios, also apprenticed with this noble warrior, taking from him the healing arts. When Alkinoë met Chiron, however, she learned that there was a fine line between prowess and humility, and a warrior needed to know it.

"As an adolescent girl, maturity burgeoned within. Restraint was also new. She acted like a thunderbolt gone astray. At thirteen, she volunteered to go up against a warrior schooled by the centaur. Some claimed she was outmaneuvered. Repeatedly. Conceit and desire just to win flawed her; she knew the motions and maneuvers, but she had forgotten Athene's wisdom—her stratagems—behind them. Once the tournament ended, she spoke to no one. This story was hard for her to tell me. Despite the praise from her peers as they passed her, she saw only the dirt road, wishing its dust could cover her shame. Waiting for her, just outside her quarters, Chiron's face invited her. His smile put her at ease, and she listened to him. He brought no weapons, no armor, no shield upon which to base his words. He simply spoke about what it meant to be a warrior, awakening in Alkinoë the grey-eyed goddess' advice and wisdom, some of which he himself had taught Zeus' daughter. Being a warrior was not more important than being. She had to know the outcome before she engaged in combat, verbal or physical. An open-ended battle would surely end in defeat, he told her. Visualize what you expect, and then bring it to be. Being the victor was the goal, and the how would come. It was rumored that even Zeus took counsel with him, but Zeus denied it.

"Chiron visited her twice more before he left Arkadeia, and he charged her with challenging herself, leaving the raw warrior behind. She would remain immature until she embraced his vision. Veteran warriors mesmerized her, but from each she took a movement, a flick of the wrist, a flexing of muscle, until she learned to master those techniques, taking ownership of her own ability. The "dance of the warrior" she wished to perform with grace and deportment took years of training, instruction not only in the art of battle, but in also the weaving of psychological webs to reinforce her core. Chiron had also instilled within her a love of learning, so mathematics, history, and philosophy had just as much merit as how to hold a sword or quarterstaff properly. Alkinoë spent much of her youth sparring with her brothers and friends between tournaments, hoping to participate in the Tegean Games, a festival for the masses, but a tournament designed for the elite. She never boasted of her abilities, but rather let others do that for her while she smiled in ways that shielded her with humility. Destiny would decree that she would hold power and authority, and when she turned twenty, that augury happened.

"She had been married for only a few years when her first husband, Demosthenes, suggested she enter the Tegean Games with him. He enjoyed flexing his muscles, battling against his peers to raise his standard. He had invited Alkinoë to join him partly to have her share in the exhilaration, and partly to impress her.

"The combatants came from all over. Five thousand participants diminished into a few hundred after the elimination trials that were almost as rigorous as the actual events themselves. Primarily for entertainment value, the games demonstrated talent, prowess, and augmented the reputation of not only the combatant, but also his or her city of origin. Cities with many contestants usually received royal scouts who would look for the finest men and women to recruit for the Arkadeian army. Both Demosthenes and Alkinoë had made it to the finals after a few more qualifying events, but by the quarterstaff event, only Alkinoë had proceeded; Demosthenes had lost his footing during the wrestling match and had been pinned. Alkinoë would fight against nine others. Almost as soon as the starting horn's blast faded, she took three contestants out of the running. Two hours of heated clashing later, and circumstances disqualified four more warriors: either by an adversary disarming him or by falling to the ground.

"A wiry Spartan warrior had challenged Alkinoë one on one, but the melee had only lasted twenty minutes when the Spartan's pride outweighed his honor, and he tasted dirt. Alkinoë's last two opponents, spry like grasshoppers, kept her vigilant and made her work for every minute she had been able to stay in the arena. The dull thud of the staves clashing came in such rapid succession it sounded like a war of woodpeckers. Worn down, but recalling Pallas' words and Chiron's support, she pushed toward victory. The last challenger had been a Mycenæan man, mostly muscle. When she finally knocked the staff from his hand, the spectators erupted into an ovation that lasted ten minutes.

"Once the excitement settled, the Captain of the Royal Guard had presented Alkinoë—scratched, battered, and bruised—with the golden laurel crown. From the stands, a shrill cry echoed, however, and a woman screamed that the king, Aleos—grandson of Arcas, founder of Arkadeia—who had been sitting in the Sovereign's Box, had collapsed. Having no apparent heirs, the king spent his days in the Temple of Gaea, communing with the goddess behind closed doors, ordering that he not be disturbed. On the day of his passing, soldiers found what remained of his clothing on the floor of the shrine, his body taken by the Divine Mother, and his soul escorted by *Hermes Psychopompos* inside Hades' gates. On the altar was written in the king's hand an order that decreed the rule and sovereignty of Arkadeia should pass to his son, one revealed to him through conferring with Gaea, a man whose genealogy had been hidden from all, including the man himself, because his mother was divine, a *Protogenos*, in fact. She had never procreated with a mortal, so her son would be a demigod. As the augury had

116

stated, Alkinoë would come to rule Arkadeia, not due to her warrior ability, but rather because she was married to the man whose mother was the Earth itself.

"Demosthenes would only accept this revelation on the condition that his wife shared equally the rule; he did not want her to be queen consort, a position that held no real power. Like the Olympian *triandria*—Zeus, Hades, and Poseidon—the new king and queen drew lots to decide which aspect of governing each would take: Demosthenes would manage the military and defense, and Alkinoë would handle diplomacy. Henceforth, this would be part of the law of succession. This way, should one of them die, the other had full right of rule.

• • •

"It became custom that either Alkinoë or I would accompany our captain to the forge. Lykaon continued to inspect each hammered xiphos to where both sides of the steel could split a block of marble; each single-edged, curved makhaira could cleave skin from bone, and each kopis could sever a limb so cleanly, it would take a few moments for blood to flow—as close to perfection as they could be. Originally wooden back when the army started, each aspis, or round shield, was of an Earthsteel alloy and embossed with a standard of Arkadeia: an eagle with outstretched wings grasping a symbol for Gaea with a sun between the wings. He would make sure that the Royal Guard was both armed and trained enough to defeat a Hekatonkheire.

"One morning, while she watched the fires birth their tempered offspring, Alkinoë needed to leave the forge due to nausea.

• • •

"Alkinoë heaved her insides into a krater for a few weeks, and I stayed at her bedside unless something dire needed my attention. Lykaon would inform me if such an occurrence happened, though, so I could focus my

117

attention on my wife. Watching her in eruptive agony, I felt my own innards churn, and I could do nothing to help her. Ironic that a god of healing had no charm or magical words or gesture to wave this away. Her default position, when she wasn't vomiting, was to gather the bed sheets around her and pull her legs to her chest, as close as possible.

"A priestess advised me that this routine would happen for a few more weeks, but she needed to speak with me outside of the chamber. Delicately, she asked if I had felt anything about this pregnancy, something perhaps the god of prophecy would know. I hadn't. She reminded me that this child was the offspring of a god and one whose parentage was the same god and a *Protogenos*. He or she would grow into great power, the likes of which had never been seen, since *Protogenoi* did not typically mate with gods. With this much power, surely he or she would rise to challenge Zeus himself. I hadn't considered any of that part aside from serving on Olympos. My son or daughter would need to be groomed not only for taking the throne of Arkadeia, but also a seat on Mount Olympos.

"If Zeus saw this possibility, what would he do? Would I have time to speak with him before the birth? New questions, but no answers. I would have to speak with Zeus soon, about this and my discovery of Gaea's concealed sister. After the birth, I would go to *Zeus Hypatos*, the Most High, who would open the Hall of Tribunals to all immortals, even *Protogenoi*. Once I told them of her existence—of Olympeia—everything would change. Everything.

• • •

"Months passed. Alkinoë spent ten hours in labor, and she would have rather battled the fire-breathing Khimæra, Ladon, and even the hundred-handed Hekatonkheires simultaneously. I preferred the cacophonous death rattle of Python at Delphi to the wailing in my bedchamber. Both of us would be disappointed. I had usually moved on to another woman long before a child came of our union, so now I had to endure both the pain Alkinoë was in as well as the anxiety of what my father might do.

"I decided to join her at her bedside. Even with this clamor, I felt the hair on my nape stand on end. *He* had arrived. I didn't want to confront Zeus here. Not at this moment. My attention needed to be on Alkinoë. I gradually moved to the back of the chamber where burgundy curtains puddled on the floor in the corner. Stealth didn't become Zeus, but apparently lurking in the shadows was one of his new practices. As a god of truth, I abhorred this hiding. He muttered something about seeing hope for Olympos in the child, but I let him know that, while the *Moirae* may have spun the thread, by Styx, I would let no one make him or her a puppet of the gods' folly. Zeus stood in silence, his calmness a harbinger of dread, and I didn't need to be prophetic to know that.

"After he removed my earth-bound punishment, I ultimately forgave him, keeping my other knowledge to myself. Gaea's priests burst forth with auguries about my child's fate, the child who would forever connect Olympos and Arkadeia. Visions of 'spilled blood of the queen,' 'stony hindrance,' and 'web of light,' recurred, but not even the most wise could unravel the mysteries. Alkinoë heard none of this, at my request, and the birth would be as normal as possible, despite the lineage. Groomed properly, my child could threaten whatever tenuous balance still existed between gods and Man, and I trembled at the thought. Screams pulled my attention back to my queen, a woman held down by her handmaids.

"Two hours later, the world welcomed my son. Cleansed of afterbirth, he was placed in his mother's arms. Zeus asked to see the boy, his grandson. My wife gestured for us both to approach. Zeus inched toward the bed, overtaken by the arrival. Warmth radiated from his face, the hint of a smile peeking from beneath his white beard, and Alkinoë relaxed her maternal embrace, ready to present the boy to his grandfather. As Zeus was within inches of the bed, his smile seemed to flatten, and tremors took hold of the palace, cracking marble walls and knocking servants to the floor. The earthenware bowl containing the bloody water and cloth shattered on the floor. I jumped toward my wife, but the sky god thrust his hand behind him, encasing me in serpentine tendrils of lightning. Building in severity, the earthquake was thought to be Zeus' doing, a distraction so he could abduct the baby, but the lord of Olympos hadn't moved. In fact, he couldn't move. Growing up his legs was a layer of rock, binding him to the floor.

"Gaea knew... Gaea knew Zeus' intent.

"Since the Earth Mother anteceded Zeus, her power superseded his and, knowing the prophecies, she would not let him trifle with her great-great grandson, especially not one brought about by an Arkadeian and *Apollo Epikourios*, the Healer. Unfortunately, this same descendant progression prevented me from breaking free of Zeus's power, despite my efforts.

"Storm clouds, beckoned by their master, churned above the palace, assailing Tegea with raindrops like arrows from mist-laden bows. No amount of energy Zeus expended removed the rocky encasement. Divine ichor leeched from his hand as he worked in vain to break free. Gaea had him in her chthonic grasp, and she would not let go. Alkinoë, too, had an iron grip on her son, whose shrill wailing added one more layer to the cacophony of crackling thunderbolts, pelting rain, and the bellowing sky god. Pain beyond that which I had ever felt made me cry out, the final indignity the Arkadeian queen would endure. Guided by warrior instinct alone, she reached beneath the mattress and pulled forth an Earthsteel scabbard, drawing the Sword of Gaea, PortalBearer. Her infant clutched to

120

her chest, she pointed the weapon inches from Zeus' neck, his torso now fully cocooned in stone.

"She demanded that Zeus release her husband or we would see if the sword could kill a god.

"To threaten a god was a heinous crime, and Zeus summoned a thunderbolt to strike her, but the sword dampened the impact, dispersing the energy. Gaea would not only curtail Zeus, but she would also protect her daughter, and Kronos' youngest son could do nothing. Another electric discharge struck Alkinoë, and again the power fizzled out. She took two steps forward, lining the blade to his neck, willing to sever his head if necessary, consequences be damned.

"She *ordered* him to release me.

"Ichor-stained stone covered most of his body, including his left arm and most of his chest. Filaments of living light sparked from his eyes, eyes that had lost their sanity. I thought that, deep within his mania, he knew she could kill him, and he probably wondered in that moment whether she would risk the Erinyes' torment. Or, would they come at all, since Gaea rarely interceded in the affairs of gods or Man, but would defend her daughter because of this child. Zeus, who had strategized with Poseidon and Hades on how to take down Kronos and had taken the flint sickle given to him by his mother, the one forged by the very goddess who held him in her inexorable grip, and beaten his father in the Titanomachia, knew he would lose so much if this human ended his life. As I fell to the floor, free of the lightning, I knew my father would find another moment when he would spirit away his grandson and teach him the ways of an Olympian king. I would have to prepare.

"Zeus threatened that this was not over. Alkinoë, however, commanded that he vow a Stygian oath that he would never try this again, or she would slit his throat.

Nothing could have severed her grip on either the sword or our son.

"Stentorian laughter gave her his reply. I informed him that she would do it, and take great pleasure at watching his ichor drain away. I also warned him that if he ever touched my son again, I would bring the wrath of all of Olympos upon him.

"How dare I threaten him with the wrath of Olympos, he shouted. He said he *was* Olympos.

"Convulsing worse than before, the ground beneath the impotent Zeus split open, swallowing the sky god. The fissure repaired itself, showing no sign of any damage. Alkinoë uttered that Gaea could have him, but I knew this was not Gaea. Another voice I had heard in my head. And it wasn't Hades. Gaea's sister, Olympeia, after his act of hubris declaring *he* was the sacred mountain, imprisoned him in Gaea's *adyton* where the scales used to reside, deep within Olympos.

"For the moment, my son was safe.

• • •

"Ten days later, after the *aphridromia*, the ceremony where I ritually asserted my paternity of the child, the sweet sounds of salpinx horns sang throughout the city just after sunrise in honor of the Dekate, a feast where the child was named before friends and family. In this case, we had invited the general populace to share in this glorious celebration. So as not to overshadow the peoples' affection and distract the attention from the child, the gods who attended took on mortal guises, proud to attend such an auspicious occasion. Bearing *opteria*—gifts for the child— citizens thronged into Gaea's temple, its doorway lined with olive wreaths, anxious to find a good spot to see the naming of their Crown Prince. As there was no statue devoted to Gaea, the naos contained a marble table set for offerings; but this day, it would be where the heir apparent's cradle would lie. Lining both sides of the chamber were the Royal Guard, present as a symbolic gesture of protection since no one would dare attack a temple, especially not that of *Gaea Kourotrophos*, Nurse of the Young. The Arkadeian army, on high alert, had readied itself to stand against any marauders, even the gods themselves. I had already held council with Hera and the others, however, and she would not only reign in her husband's stead, but she also assured me that Zeus' divine punishment would not inspire vengeance against the Arkadeian people. She asked, though, that I return to Olympos soon to illuminate the rest of the pantheon on the existence of Olympeia.

"We named him Phoebos Demetrios, Shining Son of the Earth.

After the ceremony, Lykaon approached, hoping that the *Moirae* be kind to my son as they weave the tapestry of his life. He also hoped Gaea and the gods would watch over him, this new heir to both Arkadeia and Olympos.

"May they indeed."

# 12—OLYMPEIA

**"A**kheron's waters lapped at the shore, moved by no apparent wind, as I waited for Charon's arrival. Arrayed as an Olympian not an Arkadeian, I descended into Hades' realm as *Apollo Apotropaeus*, he who averts evil, to speak to Zeus. Black poplars and willows of Persephone's grove, through which I traveled to reach the river from Oceanos, brought out the melancholy I had felt at various times of my existence; such was its power.

"One polished *obolos* persuaded Charon to ferry me to the path that led to Cerberos and the gates that opened upon the fields of asphodel, a food of the dead. An appeal to the Unseen One, Hades, allowed me to pass through the gates unhindered by Ekhidna's three-headed canine offspring. Through the Valley of Mourning I traveled until I reached the cave within which lay the way to Gaea's *adyton*, a place so hallowed that none except Nyx had ever seen it, let alone entered it, except after the loss of the *Hieros Zugos*. No path truly existed, but Olympeia told me the way, for it was only me, of all the gods, she trusted. The god of reason, I understood the underlying principles that guided the *Protogenoi*. A healer, I connected with both her and Gaea, as those who replenish. A god of music, I grasped the cosmic harmonies constructed of space and time, existence and oblivion. That my mother was Leto, a goddess of motherhood in her own right, didn't hurt either.

"Meandering through the darkness, a living entity in this realm, guided by an internal compass, I trusted Olympeia implicitly, else she wouldn't guide me. For what seemed like days, I walked in complete blackness, a great irony for one who commanded the fiery steeds who drew the chariot of the sun. I had come to learn that I enjoyed the darkness, though, as a place of reflection. At times, the path seemed to descend, although I had to wonder how much further into the underworld I could go. Other times, I felt a change in landscape beneath my sandals, as if someone were leading me up an incline where I hoped I might exit some cave opening and see the world of Man once again. I missed illumination, dancing shadows cast by fire that bounced seductively, whimsically. To conjure light, to cause even my one finger to glow and see my way would imply mistrust, and I wanted this bond to remain. Not since being in the company of Leto did I feel so reassured, so at ease. If the gods or Humankind had known her, they would call her *Olympeia Polyphorbos*, the All-Nourishing. Soon, they would.

"In the distance, as I perceived it, something glowed, a small ember far from me. As the space between that light and me shortened, I also saw something moving, something elucidated by presence and absence of shadow. It seemed as if an hour passed before I could get closer to it, and I made out a face, its silver beard a beacon in the living obscurity. The rest of the figure was captured within the cave wall, his entire body embedded like a raw gem. This far beneath the sky, he could not call forth the gift bestowed upon him by Argês, Brontês, and Steropês,

125

children of Ouranos and Gaea; here, he lay impotent with no Cyclopean gifts to channel. Lightning cannot live in nebulous absence of light, but attached to the wall next to Zeus was a lone torch, its fire different somehow here beneath Hades' realm.

"As a cerebral voice she spoke with me, in a language she allowed me to comprehend, one that predated the gods. I knew why she brought me here.

"I broke the silence by informing my father that I had a story to tell him.

"When Khaos came forth, Gaea Matêr Pantôn, the All-Mother, emerged next, but clinging to her amorphous form was an unseen entity. When Gaea became the Earth Mother, her sister—Olympeia—became one with her, bonded for all eternity, taking refuge in the form of a mountain that would bear her name. The Titans received the mountain Olympos as their home, and Gaea kept her sister's identity hidden. Initially empowered not only by youth, but also by the prophecy that foretold Kronos' demise, the Titans gained power through Olympeia who had sworn to sustain whomever Gaea bequeathed the mountain. After Zeus deposed his father and imprisoned the Titans, Gaea dispatched Typhon to destroy him and his siblings, but he imprisoned the dragon beneath Mt. Aetna, forcing Gaea to cede Olympos, and her sister's power, to him, Poseidon, Hades, Hera, Demeter, and Hesteia. Consequently, we all amassed power because of an ancient contract.

"Zeus' triumphs were due in large part to Olympeia and her replenishing power, unknown to all until now. She asked for nothing, not even gratitude, since we were never meant to know of her existence. His hubris had brought this imprisonment upon him. Regardless of his sovereignty over the gods themselves, he was not Olympos. She was.

"Deafening darkness overcame me once the words stopped. Olympeia spoke to me once more. I noted that his silence highlighted not only his wrongdoing against Demetrios, but also against Olympeia. She had put my father's fate in my hands. Zeus replied that he would not beg for mercy, but I commented that I had no intention of being merciful. My task was to deliver justice for the crime he was to commit against my son, and I would take a lesson from him: he would remain here for as long as I was human. That gave him one year to atone. Hera would rule in his absence, and I promised her I would disclose what I knew. As a god of truth, I couldn't deceive to cause harm. Mount Olympos might be a different place upon his return.

• • •

"A few days in Tegea to see my wife and child helped refocus me. So much of the cosmos would change, and it would affect all races of Humankind as well as the gods, which ultimately meant me as well. I was already changed, and the *Moirae* were weaving intricate fabric already. Tegea would be the first city in Arkadeia, in the world, to erect a shrine to Olympeia, paying homage to the one whose energies helped birth the known world, despite all prior misconceptions. I couldn't even fathom how this knowledge would change how Humankind worshipped the gods, if they would lose followers or gain them. How would the nations of the world learn about this revelation? I could use the oracles in my temples, but I would have to handle this delicately. Rewriting history would have devastating consequences, but not telling Humankind would be a greater disservice.

"I appeared on Olympos in the Hall of Tribunals with Hera holding council with Hades and Poseidon, both of whom would need something of this importance to leave their respective realms. Hesteia sat on the edge of the hearth, a ring of stone surrounding the fire pit, pushing the embers around with her hands until the flames burned at the intensity she desired.

127

"Hera called out to me, addressing me as Phoebos. All was ready, she said, and she was anxious to hear what I had to say, as well as about Zeus. I told her my decision. Poseidon and Hades hadn't expected my callousness. The queen of Olympos trusted me to bring about whatever justice was necessary, and Olympeia trusted me with the decision. My uncle from the oceans commented that he hoped his solitude would provide him with as much as wisdom as mine did for me. Summoned by Hera, the remaining *Tettareskaidekatheon*—Fourteen Olympians— filled their thrones promptly, each god or goddess curious to hear what I had to say, and it was not the time to equivocate.

"All we had ever known was false, and I was duty-bound to eradicate this falsehood, as god of truth. Khaos brought forth *Protogenoi* who designed the cosmos, the awareness into which Fate thrust us, and a piece of this awareness had remained veiled from us, for reasons passing comprehension. The cleansing ritual to remove the stain of Ares' maleficence from Arkadeia not long ago lifted a veil of dark ignorance from me. In order to purify the land, not only would Gaea's aid be required, but also her sister's, the *Protogenos*, Olympeia. Unlike the other primordial ones who may move freely about the cosmos, Olympeia was bound to this mountain, giving her name to it. She imparted part of herself within us, as she did with the Titans before, nurturing us especially when mortal worship vacillated. In fact, she was obliged to nurture any to whom Gaea bestowed Mount Olympos. As I told Zeus, we couldn't unlearn this, but rather we must embrace it, grow with it.

"Once the mortal world heard about this revelation, I had to hope they would revere our mountain's spirit, offering her their love. Some would not believe; others would believe to the exclusion of the gods themselves, and we had to accept that. One couldn't ignore or change a force of nature. Without the Scales, balance didn't exist unless we strove to keep it, and the consequences to the cosmos would be dire indeed. I asked the gods: do we venture forth into the unknown future, the yet unwoven Fate which lies before us, or do we cling to archaic ideologies and paradigms?

"After some silence, an unlikely voice decimated the taut stillness. Hesteia, staring into the fire, asked what choice we truly had. This was reality, was it not? What good would it do to debate and argue about something that, as I had put it, we couldn't unlearn? She called for a vote to be done with it. Poseidon, stupefied not only by a sense of purpose from his sister who seldom spoke, but also by her willingness to take a stand, concurred, as did Hades, Demeter, and Hera. Pallas Athene wished to discuss it further, bringing to light the very real possibility that Humankind would forget the Pantheon of Olympos, weakening the gods. I reiterated that change did not have to be bad; it could provide clarity and direction, something Olympos could use more of. Hera extended her arms, summoning forth a torch to hover before each immortal. All in favor would ignite his or her torch; any opposed would not.

"Thirteen gods voted, and thirteen torches burst into flame. The *Moirae*'s loom would soon yield a polychromatic cloth, intertwining threads from Ananke, also known as Adrastæia—the Inevitable One.

• • •

"Seated next to the scrying pool in the Hall of Prophecy, a place few gods ever saw on Olympos, I conferred with Olympeia after the vote; I would become her voice for the gods. A solitary ball of fire hovered over the water, beams of light reflecting off the sacred glasslike waters, creating a magical, mesmerizing kaleidoscope. An image formed.

"I told her that, yes, I had seen what was coming, too, and we could do nothing about it."

# 13—COMING TO TERMS

"On Demetrios' tenth birthday, he would meet his mentor in politics, philosophy, logic, academics, and even warfare. We brought up our son as an equal to the other children in Tegea, despite being in the line of succession. Tutored privately since he could speak, Demetrios played as any boy would with his friends, mostly children of soldiers and others who served the monarchy. Any Arkadeian child could play in the prince's private courtyard with him, since we didn't feel he was in any danger.

"One early morning, escorted to the Hall of Tribunals by one of his attendants, the young prince ran up the steps to the throne, leaping into my lap. Fortunately, I had only been reading some communiqués from other dignitaries in the Peloponnese and not meeting them in person. I reminded him that he was getting a little too heavy to jump on me, pointing to his own throne between his mother's and mine. He promptly replied that he could learn better how to be king if he could see what I was doing. It was that phrase "to be king" that brought back the memory of when Zeus' imprisonment ended, and I remembered nine years earlier when I sojourned back through the innards of Gaea to the *adyton*.

• • •

"I didn't delight in seeing Zeus, but the day came—one year later—when I said I would return to release him from his stony prison. Much had happened since my last visit, and Olympos had reveled in having recognized Olympeia into their hearts. Communicating through oracular channels, and through dreams by way of Morpheos, I chose my words carefully, with guidance from Athene, wisdom's mistress, and most received this revelation well. High priests and priestesses, selected from Gaea's attendants, traveled to those cities that were reluctant to believe. Divinely gifted priests conferred with council after council of skeptics, interpreting the cryptic messages I sent to those who were less able to comprehend their oracles. Time would be the vehicle for understanding, and faith would come.

"Zeus' mind bubbled with a mixture of rage and humility, frustration and empathy, and the sole torch illuminated his face, showing little change since my last visit, but how much change could there be since gods don't age as mortals do?

"His voice, softer and controlled, uttered how he felt her flourish around him, sustain him. That was her purpose, I said. Like a rushing stream, or a raging river, her essence moved through him, he continued, knowing I understood. He realized that she spoke through me on Olympos and the world of Man. Something about the timbre of his voice, I mused. Zeus' breath could alter the course of rivers, grind down mountains. But now? The underpinning of the king of gods still existed, but did he understand the absolute comprehension of she who fed both Titans and gods? Could I still trust him, he who would have taken my son for the glory of Olympos? That was why I had returned, to know.

"Trying to gain his attention, he mumbled something about a contemptible existence. I tried again. Hubris, he said, and how the gods dared... I didn't care about his mental state. I needed to know whether he would try to take my son again. He who could decimate a nation with but a raised eyebrow now stared, glassy-eyed, at me. I thought my father might have become unwoven, and sound leeched out of Zeus' mouth, but I couldn't hear him.

"Demetrios was *my* heir, he said, vowing not to interfere—on one condition. Between Olympos and Arkadeia he must choose upon reaching adulthood. Should he elect to remain my prince, Zeus would not pursue it further. If he elected to join Zeus on Olympos, I would stand by that decision.

"At his eighteenth year—not one day sooner—I told my father.

"He swore a Stygian oath, one that would render him voiceless for nine years should he break it. I trusted that his omniscience faltered in the cavernous bowels of the underworld, overshadowed by Gaea and her sister's presence. He couldn't know what Demetrios would choose. If it was Olympeia's will, I told her, she could return Zeus to Olympos. I was satisfied.

Onerous awkwardness accompanied my father's reestablishment to the throne—his disgrace had brought him low—but the pantheon accepted his return because he was their true sovereign. Kronos' youngest son would forever have to bear his shame and simultaneously command respect, a delicate task. As I had told him, Olympos would be different, and the gods' future lay in the hands of the Arkadeian prince. Zeus would never violate a sacred vow, no matter what his deepest desires might be. Waiting until Demetrios' coming of age would be a trifle, since time passed differently for immortals, and he had promised to accept whatever decision Demetrios would make, but not even Olympos' monarch could defy the spirit of the mountain itself.

• • •

"By the time he was eighteen, having already garnered some military experience in minor skirmishes alongside the Arkadeian army—assigned to the Blue Guard—as well as having been tutored in the humanities by Chiron, Demetrios had begrudgingly matured, although he remained a spirited young man. Despite his mentor's best efforts, my son had succumbed to the adolescent distractions: raiding the royal wine stores to revel in the Temple of Dionysos with some of his peers in the Blue Guard, avoiding his tutoring to go swimming in the River Alpheos, and racing chariots through the streets of Tegea. Being the prince didn't preclude him from discipline, however. He spent three days in the stables, not only bathing all the horses, but also removing all of the excrement from the stalls—with his hands. My son's behavior reminded me of my own mischief as a younger god, some of which had brought my penance upon me, although the knowledge I possessed about Zeus was a large part of that, too. I wanted to instill within Demetrios the possibility that he, too, could feel disgrace before greater consequences would come for further indiscretions. Neither Alkinoë nor I would tolerate such insolence from our son, the young man who represented Arkadeia's future. Chiron worked closely with us to find ways to teach the young man how best to act when being groomed to rule. Unlike his peers, he didn't have the luxury to be puerile.

"I showed Demetrios about diplomacy, hoping he would remember these lessons, and I encouraged him to ask questions of envoys or even comment in discussions. He had his mother's patience and my ability to reason. The longer he spent with Chiron, the more Demetrios shed his juvenility, embracing his role as the crown prince one task at a time. While he revered all the gods, he had chosen his custodial relationship to be with Gaea, spending hours in silent meditation each day. Before sunrise, he could be found kneeling before her altar, uttering his prayers and entreaties for wisdom. Although disputed by some of the priests, Demetrios claimed to have communicated with the Earth Mother directly, in a divine reverie, receiving insight and knowledge about matters beyond the concerns of Humankind. Named for the Earth itself, he shared a sacred kinship with Gaea, and rumors flew that he took the *Asulos Pistis*—the Sacred Pledge—where a suppliant offers himself or herself to a *Protogenos*, in this case, Mother Earth. During his ruminations, he would learn chthonic concepts, those ideas that were literally rooted in his faith and in the realities of the regions beneath the Earth's surface. He learned the true nature of her existence, as well as that of Olympeia, but she forbade him to speak about it. Like me, Demetrios developed a profound respect for she who imbued the sacred mountain with its inexhaustible power. Zeus feared this deep-seated respect because he knew that Demetrios' destiny was inexplicably tied to Olympos, and he wanted to be tied to his grandson.

• • •

"The day had arrived, and Hermes escorted my son to visit Zeus.

"He couldn't be Olympos' heir, he told his grandfather. Arkadeia's crown prince needed to remain in Arkadeia. Awkward silence followed, and the king of the gods didn't respond. Demetrios started to repeat his answer, but he was cut off. Zeus had indeed heard him. It was not his choice to make, Demetrios said. It was the will of Gaea, and we needed to obey it. Zeus knew better than to speak out against the Earth Mother, but crashing, percussive thunder outside made clear the monarch's feelings.

135

"He had learned his lessons well about diplomacy, my son had. Zeus had wanted my son to rule Olympos at some point, but that had never been done before. Olympian monarchs-to-be deposed their predecessors; prophecy dictated that. Monarchs did not select their replacements. But, that was not the issue.

"Rhea's youngest announced that, as *Zeus Agetor,* he who commanded the gods would choose his heir if he deemed it so.

"Demetrios said no. And his reason was quite legitimate—he was *hemitheos*. All it took was one word for Zeus to slump back into his throne, thunder hissing into silence at that one word—demigod.

"That was why Demetrios couldn't rule Mount Olympos. Through Gaea, he had learned that when she gave the Titans this mountain, and later the gods, the only stipulation she made was that the sovereign must be *teleios*—complete. A demigod would not be able to fulfill the prophecy, the divinely sanctioned patricide that Zeus feared so much. Demetrios said he would sit with his grandfather on occasion or even hold counsel with Pallas Athene, but only a true son of Zeus had rights to the throne, and I knew that I didn't want it.

"At once relieved and perplexed, Kronos' son thrust out his lower lip beneath his beard, nodding ever so slightly. This child had the courage to defy him. His omniscience grew cloudy about my son, and the haze concerned him. In most cases, a well placed thunderbolt or edict usually put an end to his concerns, but in this case, he would simply keep an eye on Demetrios, the heir apparent of Arkadeia. My son had done well.

"Demetrios returned to Arkadeia, to Tegea, but Zeus had a favor to ask, one that I didn't learn about until later from my son.

# 14—WHAT MUST BE

"I, Demetrios, knew better than to bring certain issues to my parents' attention, especially those from my grandfather. The last time I played 'Hermes the messenger', my father went raging to Olympos and left the priests beside themselves with worry that Zeus would smite all of the Peloponnese. Ironically, my father had done the same thing, telling me things that my mother shouldn't know but invariably ended up getting to her. For as much as Apollo railed against his father's tactics, he used them, too, and I often thought I would rather face the wrath of Hera over my mother's. The queen of Arkadeia couldn't bring down bolts of lightning or send a plague of locusts, but her ire could make the captains of the Blue and Red Guards wet themselves. I'd seen it.

"Zeus' errand would be carried out in secret, if only to avoid the chastisement I knew I would receive, and I had no aspirations on hand-shoveling horse dung. What convinced me were Zeus' words, 'Balance, there must always be balance,' and I believed my grandsire. Whether that would come back to haunt me was anyone's guess.

"Arrayed in my royal armor boasting the Arkadeian standard, *Thyroros* hanging from my belt, I rode my mount through the city gates, galloping into the Arkadeian countryside, my heartbeat keeping time with the hooves. I had not openly deceived my parents when I told them I would be on a military maneuver, but I neglected to tell them I would be taking the sword. I could see months, if not years, of dung in my future—or worse—should I fail to complete this errand.

At the crossroads leading to Akhæa and Elis, I dismounted just in time to see the messenger arrive. I knew that I wouldn't make the distance to meet Hermes on foot, but I also knew that the horse could never go where I was going; not even my father's immortal fiery horses could make this journey. A smack on the horse's rump sent it back toward Tegea while the winged herald took me to the cave entrance through which I could complete his task. From within the earth's innards, a fetid stench of decaying meat escaped, but this is where I needed to be, and Hermes could go no further, to this part of the underworld, unless through Zeus' decree.

"Invoking Gaea's protection over me, Hermes flitted back to Olympos, an airy place perfumed with nectar. You would think one who escorted souls to the shores of Styx could endure the stench of Hades.

"So close to the open air, the first few feet of the cave were free of the viscous residue left by forlorn souls. But once I reached steps carved into the floor, descending into the living darkness, the torchlight illuminated what remained of those souls that had made it near to the exit, only to be reduced to otherworldly ooze. Without Hades' consent, those who made it past Cerberos, the king of the underworld cursed, never able to experience the warm blanket of my father's light. The stairs curved a little to the right, and my torch extinguished, but I knew this would happen. Now, only my faith in Gaea and Olympeia would guide me through the labyrinthine depths.

"When my father had described this descent to me after his meeting with Zeus, I had no frame of reference, but it did seem like days had passed, or maybe hours, and my skin crawled. Whether it was literally crawling with something otherworldly or simply a sensation, I didn't care, and the passing air tickled the hair on my arms and nape. I mouthed prayers to keep myself focused, not knowing how much warning I would have before I encountered anything. Chiron, over the years, had told me stories of daimones and other offspring of Ekhidna, especially ways in which one would dispatch them, but I really didn't think my mentor knew I would eventually face any of these chthonic creatures, did he? Flapping wings in the distance—but who could tell how far away anything was—had my eyes darting around the darkness and my right hand resting on the sword's hilt. What intrigued me was that I could barely hear my own footsteps, but it sometimes felt as if the ground beneath me was not so much ground but the spine of some Hadean denizen. Perhaps a trick, I mused. In my mind, I asked why I could bring no light with me, and—in unison—both Gaea and her sister replied that no light from above could pierce the dark from below. Some things I had to take on faith. This wasn't the time to rebel.

"From time to time, they would whisper to me that they were there, with me. I wasn't sure if that was less to reassure me of their protection and more to reassure me of their mere presence. My father had never mentioned having to battle with anything on his journey to see Zeus, but maybe he had kept that knowledge from me so as not to frighten me. Surely, either Gaea or Olympeia would give warning. After all, Gaea *was* the Earth, from the surface where the fields and oceans stretched for miles to the obscurity beneath them. Sometimes I felt like everything I did was a test of my mettle, from fighting with the armed forces to slinging horse dung to meeting with diplomats. And now, would I be able to do as Zeus asked? Imbued with only my birthright and the sword that it represented, I would go down to and return from places few heroes had never been before: Herakles, Orpheus, Theseus, and Odysseus, among others. Each paid a price, I knew. What would mine be?

"At what seemed like an open space, a landing of sorts, which I could only sense, the walls' faint iridescence gave credence to shadow and movement. Freeing my sword, I smelled its approach before I felt the slimy surface brush against me. Swinging wildly, hoping to make contact, I tried to listen to the swishing and whooshing to find my target. Not far from me, a light grew in which stood a figure, almost human.

"I heard my name in a disembodied voice say it was here for me. I could almost place it, but whether it was male or female, I couldn't discern. Light, a living mass it seemed, expanded around this figure focusing the image for me. I was then sure it was a male voice, vaguely familiar, telling me not to fight him, and that Zeus had sent him to help me on my quest. The moment I recognized the voice, the visuals tightened for my eyes.

"It was Lykaon, the captain of the guard. I asked why Zeus sent him and whether my parents knew he was with me. Once I addressed this figure, I suddenly felt that Lykaon was indeed with me more so. The captain stepped closer, and I could even smell him, the leather of his armor, the pungent odor of his horse. I started to relax, extending my hand for a traditional greeting, a mutual wrist hold, a sign of respect among the military, but Lykaon shook my hand, then pulled me into a firm embrace.

"I asked if he was all right as I could feel him trembling. I told him he had nothing to fear as the Sisters

140

were guiding me. The hug lasted a little longer than usual, and Lykaon whispered into my ear, *'Demetrios, I need you to hold me. My lover has returned to Athens. I need you.'*

"I could feel the captain's warm breath on my neck, and I tried to push away, but something kept me from moving. Although I knew this wasn't right, I also knew I had been infatuated with Lykaon since I was a boy. With my duties to the kingdom, I had never had time for a companion, although I had stolen moments with a boyhood friend and peer in the Blue Guard. For Lykaon to make such an advance, so intense a gesture, was unthinkable since it would mean his immediate termination and return to Athens, disgraced. No one approached me without my explicit permission. This wasn't right. The more I tried to think this through, the more passionate Lykaon became, tightening his hold, and it wasn't altogether unpleasant. Unexpectedly, I remembered Zeus, and how my grandfather almost abducted me the day I was born. Against my will. This was against my...

"I shouted, *'No!'*, drawing my sword, the dark blue jewels glinting in the ambient light. I brought up my knee, extricating myself from Lykaon's hold. He was *not* Lykaon. The man repeated how lost he was without his companion, and that only I could help him. In another place and time, this wouldn't have bothered me, but I didn't know who this was, despite his appearance.

"He moved forward again, his arms reaching for an embrace, but I gripped my sword with both hands, shuffling around the darkness. Just when I thought I had my eye on the figure, it moved, mist-like, until it was behind me. One arm wrapped itself around me waist, the other across my chest, gripping my arm gently. I could again feel the warm breath on the back of my neck and ear, the pungent leather, the bristly facial hair as it scraped against me.

"This apparition told me I couldn't deny him, that it was what I wanted, and that he was finally here... for me. The honeyed yet masculine voice enticed me, dazed me, and I didn't notice the face morphing, at first, becoming serpent-like, its shiny fangs sliding down my neck. Immobilized, I was ready to give in, but I had a flash of the day I was born, snippets of images where I saw Zeus moving closer to me, ready to snatch me—against my will—before Gaea rooted the sky god to the floor. Against my will. Against...

"A shrill cry came from the body of Lykaon with a serpent's head, its fangs a hair's breadth away from piercing my neck, the double-edged *Thyroros* jutting through its head. Releasing its snakelike hold on me, the body crumpled into the dark. I cleaned my sword on my cloak and sheathed it.

"All I could muster was, *'Damned empusai. Lead on, Gaea.'*

"This endless meandering had purpose, and the adrenaline had me walking a bit taller down the tenebrous path; my hand didn't rest as much on the pommel, as I had started to adjust to this absence of light, of life. I thought about when my eyes would get used to the dark in my bedchamber while I stared up at the ceiling, and I could recognize how the shadows told me where the columns were or where the tapestries hung against the wall, but just barely. Here, no shades of gray helped me, but I sensed boundaries and depth, I just didn't know how. Experience, as Chiron told me, would teach me things that formal learning would not; deception would not ensnare me again. In fact, I would rather slash first and ask questions afterward in this place.

"Balance, Zeus told me. Fire emblazoned that word in my mind, so that would be how I could justify what Zeus sent me to do. Olympeia revealed more secrets to me as I walked, things I would need to know. Without any

142

warning, the path became almost vertical, and I slid down into what I thought was Tartaros, at times tumbling headfirst. One hand instinctively attached itself to the sword. I wouldn't lose that. After what felt like a few hours, although was probably more like a few minutes, I stopped in a cave where I could actually see. As I assessed the area, I noted that a ceiling was somewhere above, obscured by shadow, and the light seemed to glow from the walls, but it wasn't natural light. Air moved over me in waves, wafting me with a rank stench of carrion and blood, and I tried not to surrender to nausea. What sounded like growling or grunting echoed as much as it could in this soundless place, and I drew my sword, still stained with empusai blood. Like stones grating together, a rumbling voice broke the silence, at first hard to hear. I could make out three tall cave openings, bars of godly metal either keeping something out or keeping me in. The rumble came again, but closer, and the stone pulsated, signaling footsteps coming toward the bars. More of that stench washed over me, this time from all three caves, and I couldn't stop the urge to vomit this time.

Gaea could shrug and rip the Earth in two, and her children could all but do the same. *Megalê Thea*, the Great Goddess as she was known by some cults, begat many offspring, but Ouranos asked that Mount Olympos go to his favored Titans, while he imprisoned the rest of her children in Tartaros and other parts of the underworld. In an irony of which the Muses still sing, Zeus set free the orb-eyed Cyclopes and the Hekatonkheires from their prison to aid him in vanquishing the Titans, who were subsequently imprisoned in those maddening depths. Kronos' youngest succeeded largely because of two gifts: a flint scythe used by his father to castrate Ouranos, and thunder and lightning, created in the First Fires by the Sons of the Anvil, the Cyclopes: Brontês, Steropês, and Argês. The Hundred-Handed Ones, however useful in

143

Zeus' plan to knock the Titans from Olympos' heights by throwing giant boulders, aroused the sky god's paranoia, and he put them back in Tartaros in three caves, enclosed by Earthsteel bars.

"I stood before the central cave, stepping on rocks to get closer, but I lost my footing and fell into the pile, soon realizing they were not rocks at all. Amid the mound, I saw serpents' skeletons, lion's heads, boar tusks, and metallic scales—the well-scavenged remains of Campe. So, Zeus had left her remains in front of those she was to be guarding. Intriguing, Grandfather. I now knew those who reeked of death and were coming to dine on royal flesh.

"A voice like grinding bone beneath rock made my blood run cold, and I stumbled back from the bars, kicking Campe's bones out of my way. I couldn't see anything but shadowy movement, and the dozens of darkened spots on the bars I believed were hands on the first cave, hands that I hoped could not reach through. When I felt safe enough, I replied that I was a son of Apollo, heir to the Arkadeian throne. Giving one's lineage gave credibility, my father told me, especially when confronted by formidable adversaries—in this case, three chthonic megalithic sons of Gaea.

"A multitude of hands gripped all three sets of bars, and fifty voices, in unison, from the middle cave spoke more clearly than the first of the three brethren, although still sounding like gravel. I recognized him as Briareos the Strong. I agreed that I had wandered far from Apollo's light, but I was on a mission for Zeus. A cacophony of 150 voices erupted from all three caves, with each captive shaking his bars, but I stood my ground, aware of *Thyroros* at all times. I didn't know if one sword could even protect me from 300 hands. From the cave furthest to the right, a deeper voice rose above the others.

144

"To Gyges of the Earth, I responded that Zeus' decisions were not always met with unilateral support. I, for one, didn't always agree with how Zeus handled family, and he was wrong to lock them away again—

"I couldn't explain why, but I suddenly felt a wave of fear, not mine: theirs. More grating voices tripped over one another, and the harmonious dissonance was gone. She accompanied me on my journey, I told Cottos, imploring him not to fear. They didn't mean Gaea, their mother. Olympeia grounded me, I added. She sustained, not diminished, those she favored.

"Their agitation at Zeus' name, and perhaps my affiliation with the king of gods, wouldn't bode well for me, but perhaps something else would. I had thought Gaea would have told them that her sister had imprisoned Zeus in the *adyton*, but she hadn't. Intriguing.

"Grumbles and more bar rattling ensued. She hadn't wished to fuel their enmity for Zeus. Their present enthusiasm at knowing who accompanied me, however, conveyed joy, not anger. Mighty as these three gods of storms were, I found them to be amiable. As my father had once told me: allies came from places one least expected: a fishing village or even Amazons.

"Why had Gaea not freed her children, I thought, or stood up to Zeus, since she must have been outraged when he imprisoned those who had helped him defeat Kronos and the Titans. Her response to me was not what he would have expected.

"The prophecy that enabled Zeus to remove Kronos from power required her withdrawal from the divine sphere. Even a *Protogenos* had to abide by a prophetic edict. But, yet, she had intervened on my behalf the day I was born. Musing over Gaea's words, I considered the plight of the Hekatonkheires, prisoners within their own mother's body, like children grudgingly returned to the womb. I would do Zeus' task, but I had my limits as to what I would endure from my grandfather, and perhaps this is why Zeus wanted me on Olympos.

"I couldn't bear to see them a victim of Zeus' suspicion, so I released them into their mother's care. Gaea would tend to their needs once more. Grunts and more bar shaking followed. They asked why I did this, and I simply replied, *'Balance.'*

"The first Earthsteel weapon, *Thyroros* sliced through the bars with ease and enabled the Hundred-Handed Ones to emerge from their cave-like cells. Not obscured by shadow any longer, I saw why they had those names, and fear pulsed through me in waves. Briareos spoke, his raspy intonations sounding much more like human speech, like me. I had honored them, he said, and they pledged their fealty to me.

"One of the massive black arms extended toward me, and I touched the elephantine hand to seal the bond. Elated as I was, I couldn't help but be unsettled by their frightening appearance, each towering over me like three mountains. Cottos stepped forward, his gargantuan feet as big as triremes, carrying an obsidian box that he handed to me. They had been keepers of an ancient amulet forged in the First Fires, for their father, Ouranos. I looked inside to see a disk of silver Earthsteel with twelve jewels encrusting an outer ring. Inside this ring, corresponding to the jewels, were twelve glyphs representing the Zodiac. At the center sat a red jewel, said to be the *Ophthalmos Ouranou*, the Eye of Ouranos. Only Gaea's forlorn mate knew what power this jewel possessed, and with his essence rejoined with Khaos, it was unlikely that anyone would ever discover it.

'*Krios, Tavros, Didimoi, Karkinos,*' I whispered, speaking the names of the Zodiac as my eyes fell on the respective gemstone. '*Leon, Parthenos, Zugos, Skorpios, Toksotis, Aigokeros, Udrokoeus, Ikhthyes.*'

"Cottos cautioned me that names had power in this realm. Saying them too loudly or too many times would invoke them. I didn't know that. I thanked the Hekatonkheire for his wisdom and the amulet, but asked that they keep it a little longer until I returned from my quest. I returned to the dark path, but now, the darkness didn't concern me as much. Journeying along the stretch of this impervious Tartarean blackness gave me time to consider my place in this cosmic amusement for the *Moirae*. Born of Olympian and *Protogenos* ancestry, allied with the life force of the sacred mountain, and now a bonded ally with three storm gods, I could appreciate Zeus' omniscient concerns better as well as the irony that I never asked for any of this. Moving up the divine ladder was never an aspiration of mine. Ruling my people with compassion and wisdom was more of what I had in mind.

"The air temperature around me dropped dramatically to where my teeth chattered and my eyes went numb, and then came the despair and sorrow and grief in waves. Olympeia counseled me to remain on the path, to follow where she guided me, since I would soon be in a place so sacrosanct that even to look, or try to look, at what would be around me would bring on a madness from which there was no return. I pulled my helmet over my head, my eyes toward the ground, or at least where I thought the ground should be.

"Arkadeia's beleaguering winters, with ice storms and blizzards to blanket the region until Persephone surfaced from her Hadean sovereignty, were temperate compared to the bitterness carried through the obscurity through which I traveled. My faith in both the Earth Mother and her sister kept me from faltering, keeping me from succumbing to the rawness. From the heart of Tartaros, where I headed, blew this breath of anguish, this killer of hope. Panic grew from within my gut, spreading like a cancer, moving through my chest and arms as I neared this sepulchral place, this place I could never see but had to pass through with only my devotion to be my beacon. A few steps later, without Gaea or Olympeia telling me, I knew I was there, and the talons of terror snatched me, tearing apart my resolve, one piece at a time. I had arrived where none save Zeus himself had ever seen, and even the god of gods had felt the same emotions I felt; no one was immune from such soul-shredding agony.

"Here was where Kronos was buried.

"Beyond this cavernous maw lay the prison that held the Titans, less austere perhaps than the final resting place of the Titan king, but no light could ever shine here, not one iota of illumination for that would be all that was necessary to shatter the stony cells in which Zeus sealed the other eleven children of Gaea and Ouranos. I raised my head, since Gaea wanted me to see this place, but nothing stood before me except emptiness and the occasional silhouette of a glyph marking each tomb. Of all the stories told to glorify the Titanomachia, I had never learned how fragile the barrier between this sepulcher and the outer world was. Despite being the son of an Olympian, the pangs of guilt rife within me, coupled with shame, brought me to tears. The Golden Age of Kronos and his siblings would have destroyed Gaea—I knew that—but my ever-present empathy about their fate, Zeus having encasing them in living stone, begat regret. The longer I spent in this place, the more I realized I could never accede to my grandfather.

"Leaving the catacombs behind, the ice in my veins melted, warming my extremities. Even my eyes no longer felt numb. No empusai or lamiae would ever venture close to this place, so I felt safe for a while, but at some point I would probably have to engage some subterranean denizen eager to drain my blood or gnaw on my bones and sinew. Thoughts of daimones gorging on my flesh made me hungry.

148

"The sound of rushing water in the distance splintered the silence, and I was eager to see something other than death and misery, not realizing that little else existed here. Around a darkened bend, percussive water against rock crashed louder in my ears, raging with the force of a storm. Waves of heat collided into me, enough for me to remove my helmet, and the play of light and shadow in grayscale made my heart race. I reached a stone bridge, heard the tumbling waters, but smelled decay. Looking over the edge, gripping the jagged rock which pulsed with life, I gaped at the river of black fire which slithered through Tartaros—Phlegethon. Known for its fires that burn but do not devour, the river flowed among four others that twisted through the underworld: the wailing *Potamos Kokytos* from which the lamentations of the dead could be heard; the *Potamos Akheron*, river of pain in which the dead would relinquish their agony, but if a living person were to fall into its waters, he would feel the anguish that had leached into it from every soul; the *Potamos Lethe*, whose waters brought forgetfulness of their earthly life to the souls entering Hades' realm; and the *Potamos Styx*, river of hatred. Like Akheron, the Stygæan waters received the hatred from those souls who entered it, and it smelled the most foul of all the *Potamoi*.

"Shuffling along the bouldered bridge, about as wide as I was tall, my eyes bounced from one side to the other, intrigued by the undulating fire which looked more like flickering black water, hoping to keep my balance. Walls of heat rose with concussive force, sucking the breath from me as I managed to focus one step at a time. Midway across, I saw something drop above my head, something alive, and I freed my sword. In my peripheral vision, I saw something approach and jumped up, bringing my knees in close. Was it a snake or some kind of tail? As soon as I regained solid footing, I took a defensive stance, squinting to see what amorphous creature had settled before me.

149

Another swipe from the opposite side, and I jumped back a few steps. Whatever it was hissed loudly with each strike, and golden eyes shimmered in the near-dark.

"A creature wailed that none would pass, one called Keuthonymos. I had wandered through this gods-forsaken realm, putting my faith in the Earth and Olympos, and I would pass if I so wished it.

"Meeting the challenge, the ophidian creature vaulted toward me, razor-sharp claws outstretched, but the sword forged by the Earth Mother blocked the attack. Always aware of where I was in relation to the river, I pushed past my desire to rest, and forced all my hand-to-hand combat experience to the surface. A swish of the monster's tail took my legs out from under me, making me vulnerable, but I had had enough of this melee: the only way to cross the bridge was to destroy it. A strong shove with my foot loosened the fanged one, giving me a few seconds to roll out of the way and pray to Athene that I be able to cleave the bridge in two. Earthsteel clanged against rock with blind fury on my first try, but I knew the edge could split the stone. The second time, with my mind clearly focused on the task, I sliced through as if it were soft flesh, cracking a gap between both sides. My opponent and I fell toward the flaming river.

"With an upward thrust, I stabbed the underside of the stone, concentrating on it holding me up. Will power kept me attached while Keuthonymos plummeted into the blazing river, toward the swampy pool where all five *Potamoi* met near Hades' shrine. The climb back to the top of the severed bridge took longer, and my sweaty fingers couldn't grip the stone as strongly. Lying on my back, my lungs heaving, I thanked Athene for training me well. After a quick jump across the gap, I parted from Phlegethon, hoping I would never have to see that river again, but I feared I might have to traverse the bridge on my return trip.

"I spoke out loud, suggesting that my guardians could aid my quest at any point, if they so chose, but Gaea and Olympeia said nothing in reply.

"As my trek continued, I knew I'd face more obstacles—since those who travel the underworld did so at the whim of Tartaros—although I didn't think Keuthonymos was much of a challenge. Time passed differently here, and I was afraid when I returned to Arkadeia, I would find a land devoid of a monarchy, but I had made a promise to Zeus. I wasn't sure how much more I could take, even with my heightened stamina and training, since even a demigod would need to rest. Despite my parentage, I never called myself a *hemitheos* as it smacked of arrogance, and I had enough problems without having to add more kindling to the fire of my ego. I had never tapped into the divine power within primarily because I wanted to be able to handle myself as a man, and someday as a king, without the benefit of Olympian energy. It was a well that, once I had drunk from it, I would thirst only for that and nothing else.

"Gaea knew I required rest, as the comfort of sleep would heal my wounds, internal and external, for a time. Soon, she would take care of me, I felt.

"Again, the darkness yielded to an unnatural light, and I heard a soothing voice slither into my ears.

*'Come, my child, come,'* said the voice, honey to my ears. *'Find me in the dark. Find me in thy heart.'*

"A niche in the cave, carved by teeth and illuminated by a flaming brazier of wrought Earthsteel, opened before me, and when my eyes adjusted, both wonder and fear ensnared me. My eyes followed the end of a serpent's tail, coiled around a dilapidated pillar of stone, to where scales merged into the flesh of a female torso, laden with breasts. Her arms, open to accept me, ended in talon-like hands, but her face in the soft glow of the flames reminded me of my mother. In my mind, I knew who she was, but I didn't

151

fear her, even though many heroes had encountered her offspring in their own tests of valor. Herakles had bested her son, the Lernæan Hydra, with torches to his severed heads, and had wrestled with Cerberos, the *Kuna tou Aidou,* or Hound of Hades. Bellerophon had choked her son, the Khimæra, with molten lead dripping from a spearhead. Her daughter, the Sphinx, outdone when Oedipus solved her riddle, cast herself off a cliff. But, Gaea's daughter by Tartaros would not be brought down; in fact, she would bring forth new progeny to go up against heroes of every generation, monsters more inconceivable than those who had come before. Ekhidna would prevail.

"Collapsing into her serpentine embrace, I suckled at one of her nipples, taking nourishment from her milk, the same milk that had fed her grotesque brood for eons. I had respect for her and those she birthed, however, as a daughter of Gaea, and humbled myself in her coils. As she fed me, the tip of her tail cautiously moved toward the sword, slinking from the tip of the sheath toward the pommel. Her scales brushed against the hilt, curling around it, caressing it, but then releasing it. She had no designs on the blade itself; her mother forged it, and she wished to touch its grandeur. I had no fear.

"Hypnos and his son, Morpheos, came from the darkness, touching my brow and brought me some of the peace I needed to continue my journey because the next task would be the hardest. Fulfillment of Zeus' request was inevitable.

• • •

"When I opened my eyes, I was alone. Dreams had flowed through my mind, but I couldn't remember what they were; I did, however, have a clarity I had not had earlier, and this made me more at ease in my confusion. Cold stone replaced a warm serpentine embrace, the polished scales of her tail having held me tightly against her bosom. A more rudimentary kinship with her other offspring I felt, wondering if I, too, had become chthonic and more earth-bound. This rejuvenation I experienced, as if being reborn, gave me the strength to continue; in fact, I felt stronger after this encounter than I had before I left Arkadeia. Did the mother of all monsters know I would need bolstering before this last part of my journey, or was she just doing what maternal creatures do when put before children in need of nurturing? Wet-nursing this *hemitheos* did more than any training from Pallas Athene or advice from any oracle: it emboldened me, and my ego could use some reinforcing if I were going to accomplish this forthcoming task.

"Leaving the rocky recess, I took up the path once more, realizing that Tartaros was not an evil place, and those within it harbored no malice toward me; they were simply doing what they were born to do, as was I. I wondered if wisdom I had gained had literally illuminated his path, because I now could see more, and the path meandered through Gaea's bones in ways my mind could barely conceive. My perception of this place would forever alter how I interacted with those in the upper world, and I would want to compare what I had learned with what my mentor, Chiron, had experienced, since the noble centaur had seen things beyond that of any mortal.

"When hours, or days, had passed—who could tell, Olympeia cautioned me that I would need to draw from all my worldly understanding to perform that which Zeus asked of me. Even though I felt stronger and more capable, both *Protogenoi* advised me not to give in to overconfidence; I should trust in her and Gaea, no matter what. I repeated my *Asulos Pistis*, devoting my life to the one whose power birthed Titans, the gods, and fostered the mountain upon which they ruled.

Narrowing to where my shoulders touched both sides of the passage, the path descended gradually, as did the temperature of the underworld, and I knew I was near my destination. My visual acuity diminished, but my other senses could feel a source of power ahead of me: my skin tingled from the proximity, and I instinctively gripped my sword.

Devoid of seeing it with my eyes, as the fickle dark enshrouded me once again, I sensed the path widen. Squinting, I perceived what I thought was a pinpoint of light, but my mind could be playing tricks. I used my outstretched arms, fingers splayed, to guide me, knowing that gnarling gurgle in my gut to be the birth of fear. Every few steps, I waved my arms, expecting to hit stone or worse, and my heartbeat radiated throughout my limbs, my face, and my eyes. Able to catch the pinpoint flickering, growing into a larger light source, I shuffled my feet forward, my breath deepening. A voice rose to my ears, jarring me.

'...*knew he would send someone to fetch me,*' the voice labored to say. '...*would not let me rot... forever.*'

"Unable to speak, I inched forward, my eyes adjusting to the torch hovering not far from me. Gaea reassured me she would be by my side. The closer I got, I could hear the entity's breath, difficult and raspy, and I wondered if I were ready for a fight, should it come to that. Once I could discern who this was, I understood why Zeus had sent me down into Gaea's *adyton*. Balance had to resume, and if Zeus couldn't have Apollo's son, he would have a suitable alternative.

"Ares.

"Unlike Zeus, whose punishment consisted of encasement in stone, thick Earthsteel chains shackled the war god's arms to the wall while more chains attached his legs to the ground. An added layer of debasement had him naked, his skin bloodied from underworld daimones who wished to taste an Olympian's ichor. When he raised his head to see who had come to this place, his hollow eyes

154

had lost their pugilistic luster. I saw nothing but destruction and death in them, and I remembered the story of how this son of Zeus had defiled my home and had tried to kill my mother.

"He asked who I was, but this time, I only spat my name. He didn't deserve my title.

"Wisdom dictated that I not reveal too much just yet or my emotions would cloud my judgment. I told my uncle that Zeus wanted him back on Olympos where he could keep an eye on him. Balance had to be restored. Ares suggested that, once free, he would try to kill me. I simply told him, brandishing my sword, that Zeus wanted his son returned, but he didn't specify alive. And, those chains bound his godhood until Zeus removed them with my father's sanction.

"He asked who told me that, thinking that might make me doubt. I told him Gaea, but that made him laugh. Arrogance.

"It would take some time to return him to Olympos, Ares told me, and that, before we had left this realm, my carcass would feed his hounds after Eurynomos, the corpse-eater of the underworld, had had his fill.

"I laughed. Arrangements had been made to ensure his safe delivery to Zeus. Appearing out of the obscurity, two daimones dragged behind them a bronze *pithos* inscribed with glyphs of pre-Olympian origins. For a god who had traversed blood-soaked battlefields alongside Deimos and Phobos and had been party to more wanton annihilation than any other deity, Ares' face paled at the sight of the stone jar, recalling the time when the giants Otos and Ephialtes had imprisoned him for over a year until Hermes freed him. The war god hung his head, and his body went limp.

"Shame. The one weapon against which he had no defense, and I had not done a thing.

"Four quick sword strokes separated the chains from the wall and floor, and Ares crumpled to the base of the cavern. I told him to get in. No signs of life came from him, and I moved in closer to see, prodding the fallen god with my foot. Ares reached out, grabbed my leg, and shoved me into the wall. Even though he had no more strength than an average man while the chains remained attached, he had adrenaline to fuel him, and he rammed his forearm into my throat. Athene had trained me with weapons from Olympos' armory, at the behest of Chiron, so I knew how to engage a combatant hand-to-hand, even a god, but I had never thought I would engage *Ares Brotoloigos*—Ares the Murderous. He beat me with the chains until I bled from everywhere, and kept striking me, but Zeus had charged me to do this one task, and do it I would, so I fought back—hard. Rolling around in Tartaros was not what either one of us had expected to be doing, and neither of us had his bearings or a strategy. This was simply two combatants thrashing one another senseless, and it aroused much in Ares. Even with all his battlefield experience, he had no weapon, no armor, and no protection. As we struggled to restrain each other, I finally freed his sword arm.

"I ordered him to release me or return to Olympos a eunuch, pressing the cold blade against Ares' inner thigh. If this edge could sever Earthsteel chains, surely it would do the same to his manhood. How formidable was an emasculated war god?

"Again, possible shame—or threat of such—had won out over brawn, and Ares reluctantly climbed into the container at sword point, pulling the chains in before I secured the lid. An advantage of an ensorcelled pithos is that it sealed instantly.

Holding the jeweled pommel up to the torch, Gaea flared the flames with enough light to shine through the gem, activating its magic. In a circular motion, I cut a hole into the realm of Olympos, in the Hall of Tribunals, and kicked the jar through the portal before following, leaving Tartaros behind. I managed a silent thanks to the Earth Mother before collapsing at the base of Zeus' throne."

# 15–SANCTUARY

"One didn't ignore a summons from Zeus, so when I arrived on Olympos, seeing my son Demetrios lying lifeless on a marble table in front of Zeus' throne, grief pierced my heart. The back of my hand stroked my son's blood-caked cheek, and I noticed the tattered armor and *Thyroros* still in his tight grip.

*'Blessed Gaea...'*

"My mind raged, flashing into ways I would punish all of Olympos if my son were indeed dead, but my heart simply wanted to know one thing: why?

"Stepping down from the dais, Zeus came to my side, informing me that he was proud of Demetrios, but I shouldn't worry: he was weakened, not dead.

"I demanded to know why he had sent my son to Tartaros, but—in truth—I knew why. I wanted more. Zeus, again, simply said that balance was the key. Demetrios had refused his offer since he was *hemitheos*, so a suitable replacement was needed.

"Turning to see the pithos, I discharged a shaft of sunlight to shatter it, ultimately releasing my brother. Zeus reminded me that, without my sanction, Ares couldn't assume his rightful place on Olympos. My brother was needed, apparently. So be it, but I wasn't finished with him.

"He took a Stygian oath that he would never set foot in Arkadeia again, for any reason. I looked back at my father, who swore to uphold Ares' words as well. In this, Zeus knew all too well what I had endured when the warmonger decimated my people. Ares knew that if he trifled with his father, a thunderbolt would ensure Olympos needed a new war god.

"The chains clinked open, and I carried my vanquished brother, dropping him by the sky god's feet, stating that he was Zeus' responsibility. I was taking my son and going home."

• • •

Somewhere beneath Olympos:

*"Sisters Three, from threads untwined,*
*Sisters Three, from skeins unfurled,*
*The price of lost balance must be paid,*
*Order and Chaos, two paths to tread,*
*Istos Anankes! Istos Aphuktos!*
*Loom of Destiny! Inevitable Loom!*
*One has become two, two paths to tread.*
*Klotho unfurls threads in pairs,*
*Lakhesis measures twice for one self,*
*Atropos cuts two ends to life!*
*Which Fate holds fast? Which Life holds true?*

• • •

"Fever dreams plagued me for days after the *Moirae* sang, and I always awoke holding my head, the pain worse each night. Flashes of the *Omphalos* at Delphi, the center of the cosmos, shattering repeatedly in my mind were not the real concern: prophetic dreams were birthed in shrouds of mystery, left for the priests and oracles to decipher. I, though, needed no intermediary—I *was* the quintessential oracle. Why I would dream of the stone that represented the navel of the cosmos crumbling was beyond my understanding, but the pain had more to do with my confusion more than my actual ability to comprehend the symbolism.

"I had also walked through Tegea and had seen the perplexity on the faces; something was adrift. People seemed conflicted, almost lost in their own mind. Having previously dismissed it as fatigue or even illness, both common in a large city, my dreams started to contextualize their cerebral absence from the world around them.

"Alkinoë had decided to sleep outside Demetrios' chamber since he returned to Tegea, even though he had fully recuperated from his odyssey to Tartaros. News of the prince's success spread through Arkadeia like fire on a river of oil, and his reputation grew just as vehemently. Besting the god of war, even a weakened one, gave his mentor great pride, too. Chiron's satisfaction had little to do with his triumphs with Demetrios, but rather had more to do with Demetrios' triumphs over his own impediments, namely his immaturity. With Olympian balance restored, and Zeus sated for the moment, Chiron hoped his charge could take hold of his destiny to lead his people by setting better examples, at some point in the future claiming the throne when I relinquished it. Unlikely to perish as an immortal god, I would someday transfer my authority to Demetrios. Presently, my torment kept me from my duties, so Alkinoë presided over the business of running the monarchy, with our son learning from her extensive experience.

"Many prophetic dreams originated from Ananke, the *Protogenos* of Necessity, but I knew these dreams came from the *Moirae*, more as a cry for assistance, though, than a true prophecy. Beneath Olympos lay numerous caverns, meandering deep beneath the earth's surface, some perilous to traverse, others simply dark and mysterious. Hermitlike, the *Moirae* performed their sole three-fold task in a cavern just outside the gates of Hades. Just inside, in an antechamber of sorts, three paths extended into darkness, only one leading to their *istos*, their loom. The other two led to unmentionable places from which no one, god or mortal, could return without Hades' consent, something he was loath to give even on good days. Interestingly enough, the destinations changed sporadically, so unless one knew precisely which path to take, and when, he could never enter the looming chamber. A circular fire pit, embers glowing like the red eyes of daimones, sat in the middle of this entrance, and it was here that I stood. They would sense my arrival, something I had rarely done, and materialize in smoky puffs from the coals.

*'We greet thee, Apollo the Oblique, son of Zeus,'* they said, their voices a unity. My prophecies had a tendency to be vague, apparently.

"And I greeted them, Weavers of Fate, daughters of Ananke. They knew why I had come.

"Even in the presence of a god, the *Moirae* never brought anything from the loom chamber. It was an inviolable law written by Khaos. Klotho, Lakhesis, and Atropos faded in and out, reappearing in different places along the circle of stones surrounding the fire.

"They sang of two looms, two skeins, of Fate divided. They coalesced into one another on occasion, making their harmony that much more profound. The scales... Order and Chaos... They sang of two. Of two worlds.

"I didn't understand yet what they meant. Of two worlds? But, the Fates rarely answered a question directly.

"Prepare them, they instructed me. Two threads for one self could not be. Prepare them. Prepare them, I repeated, hoping the meaning would come forth, but it didn't.

"Then, a shiver of recognition rippled through me, and I left the Fates. Zeus was holding counsel with grey-eyed Athene, her owl perched on her shoulder, when I burst into the Hall of Tribunals.

"I needed them both. Immediately.

"Zeus must have seen my pallid, grave expression and escorted my sister to meet me.

"We were in peril, I told them. What I had learned from the *Moirae* would change the cosmos and the nature of all things.

"At Athene's behest, I clarified my meaning. We had never given much thought or discussion to the implications of the *Hieros Zugos* being destroyed, since we had observed no noticeable effects. We always assumed that when we did see something, it would be blatant, like the sinking of Atlantis when a piece of the Scales crashed into the ocean or Ares' decimation of Arkadeia. Since those events, we had seen nothing else that dire. Yes, mortals had waged wars and committed atrocities, but not to the same level. Over the past few months, I had seen my people, the Arkadeians, walking around in a cloud of confusion. At first, people would lose track of themselves in conversations or daily tasks. Common among humans, yes, but not when a majority would seem to drift into a reverie, only to return to their conversation or task glassy-eyed, fear lurking beneath their lack of control. Following this came the fever dreams…

"I assured them this wasn't normal human behavior, but something about the way Zeus asked urged me to know more. Had he seen something? Perhaps. Veiled in mortal guises, he and Hera had gone to Crete, paying a visit to the *Diktaeon Andron*, the cave where he was wet-nursed by Amaltheia, and mingling with the local villagers, testing their *xenia*."

"They noticed the same thing I had just described: an absent-mindedness among the people where they were

162

cognizant of themselves one moment, but lost in another. I believed I knew why. The *Hieros Zugos* kept the balance of Order and Chaos flawlessly, leveling off that which would tilt the pans in ways not even the gods could conceive. Waves of energy rippled through all that existed, in a sense, tethering the cosmos to the Scales. When disarray would increase, it would trigger the Scales to send out pulses of power to generate a corresponding stability. This was how it kept equilibrium. The moment Nyx shattered them, those waves undulated not only forward, but also backward, back to the moment Khaos came into being. Everything from that moment on started a new course for the cosmos, a new reality. Almost every moment, almost every event—no matter how small—was somehow different from how it happened originally, or would happen. An example would be the Titanomachia: it happened in both realities, but the means by which the gods assumed control was infinitesimally different after the Scales' destruction. Even the gods' own behavior was not as it was, but we didn't know how the cataclysm had altered it.

"Here is why the *Moirae* called to me, I told Zeus. Somehow, the Istos Anankes had become two distinct looms, spinning two threads for each individual, mortal or immortal. One thread marked out the life they lived now, and the other marked out the life they lived before, or should have lived.

"Ascending the steps to his throne, Zeus turned to face us. That was why they were bewildered, he commented. In their minds, they were living two lives. Two threads for one self could not be.

"That was precisely what the *Moirae* had told me. We gods would be affected soon, as well, if we didn't act. Athene, perhaps for the first time in her existence, asked what to do.

163

"What did one do with two realities, I asked her. How did wisdom reign here?

"In short, she began, two realities should dictate two worlds. But, simplicity had never been a watchword for the cosmos. Making that happen would go back to our own beginnings, when Khaos spawned the *Protogenoi*, but she had given up her essence to fuel that which we enjoyed as our existence.

"I saw truth in what she said, and departed hastily, an idea brewing. I needed to consult one other in this matter.

• • •

"No one saw me enter the shrine or the *adyton*, the one in Gaea's temple in the center of Tegea. In this designated place, the mortal equivalent to that which existed within the Earth itself, I communed undisturbed with the Great Mother, asking her guidance. She, too, was disturbed by this revelation, and as we spoke, yet another voice emerged, a voice seldom heard. She would do what Gaea had done for her ever since her birth: take on a custodial task. She felt her destiny would be fulfilled in this singular moment.

"I asked what it was that she wished to do.

"Her plan reminded me of my earlier conversation with Athene, something which I had not considered. My mind then jumped to how this reality schism began—Zeus neglecting to consult a *Protogenos*, among other things. Olympeia's idea could not erase what had already transpired, but it could at least offer a solution to the immediate dilemma with the Fates. Now, a *Protogenos* would act for the benefit of humanity and godhood, something Nyx hadn't considered when she reacted to Zeus. We could reach some sort of balance, and it was just as Athene had said it would be—simplicity.

"Olympeia's influence covered the Olympos of the gods, or *Olympos Theôn*: not the Earth-bound mountain— *Olympos Anthropon*—that was Gaea's. *Olympos Theôn*

164

was the one consigned to us immortal gods who existed outside of time. Mortals understood it as a place which hovered atop the real mountain, but that was not truly how it existed. It was a separate plane not constrained by mortal concepts, like gravity. Humans aged and died; gods did not. Preternatural power through Olympeia pervaded *Olympos Theôn*, giving it life, and the gods were able to manifest themselves among humans and influence the world.

"Gaea would create a second earthly realm, one where the duplicate souls would go, and life would continue there with little influence or interference of the gods. *Oikoumene Broteios*, the inhabited mortal world, would be governed by Ananke, with the second loom—an unexpected outcome of the Scales' destruction—weaving the threads of life for these mortals. The *Ge Theôn*, the earthly realm governed by the gods, would be where I would reside in Arkadeia.

"Whatever residual energy remained from the Olympian gods in the *Oikoumene Broteios* would dissipate and remain hidden, and these mortals would live with only a fading memory of what once was. As generations would pass, they would abandon the gods entirely, finding faith elsewhere. In this way, the conflict of two fates for one self would be abated. By Zeus' decree, this schism would take hold during the Separation of the Souls and, for the first time since Khaos existed at the beginning of the cosmos, all godly powers would be in unanimous agreement. Order out of chaos, indeed. Done correctly, mortals would not know that they were splitting into two selves, each with a distinct fate. Such concentrated godly power in the *Ge Theôn* would bring about immortality and eternal youth for those who lived in that realm. As long as the gods remained strong, these two worlds would never encounter one another again.

165

"Well, that was how it should have worked. There *was* that prophecy that still hadn't come to pass... yet."

# PART FOUR: OF MANKIND

## 16—CALL TO ADVENTURE

**EBC 2 (Chad, Africa)** "For WPR News, this is Adelaide Montgomery. The United Nations issued Task Force: Delta to N'Djamena, the capital of the Republic of Chad early this morning to quell an uprising of the Chadian army against its own government, namely President Marzey and Prime Minister Ungindo. After snipers managed to kill the prime minister, Delta operatives swarmed in the direction of the gunfire, arresting two suspects believed to have fired the M16 assault rifles into the palace. After securing the area, Delta chief operative Neil O'Reilly announced that his group had the situation under control."

• • •

2008 C.E. An abandoned tenement in San Francisco, in the *Oikoumene Broteios*.

Caked with dust and cockroach excrement, cobwebs mocking the tapestries from Fate's loom and strewn over old furniture, water-stained paintings, and forsaken baby toys, a basement room sat empty—inhabited by darkness for far too long—keeping company with rodents and spiders, Ekhidna's clutch in miniature. Mildew, the pungent perfume of neglect and desertion, saturated the air. Opaque with dust and spider webs, a window near the ceiling consented to allow pale moonlight in, a desiccated shell of a spider hanging from a thread in the glow, an austere reminder of Arachne's fate. Against the far wall, a wooden staircase ran, a few of the treads having completely disintegrated.

Light cascaded down the stairs like a rushing cataract when the upper door opened to the alley, twelve cloaked individuals descending into this diminutive Tartaros, barely disturbing the dust. The first one carried two torches, and the second one cradled a scroll wrapped in leather. December winds brought a Borean chill, diluting the heady scent of decay, and from beneath the hoods, frosty, serpentine breaths escaped. Wraith-like, the figures hovered across the soiled cement floor to a large wooden table, warped from age and moisture, and draped with a black cloth. Like the Siren song heard by Odysseus, the frigid air whistled as it squeezed through cracks in the window casing.

One individual placed the thick animal skin on the table, and the scroll unfurled on its own. From the folds of the cloaks, each individual removed a black candle and placed it on the table. The book bearer's voice, as deep as the underworld, took control of the silence.

"All is aligned. We begin."

Joining hands, the leader touched the scroll and then pointed to the center of the table. Each candle ignited, invading the darkness, and then the recitation began.

"Gods of the Five Rivers, we call upon thee—*Potamoi Akheron*, *Phlegethon*, *Styx*, *Kokytos*, and *Lethe*, hear our plea. Attend us, thou who embody pain, fire, woe, wailing, and forgetfulness! Gods of the Underworld, show us that you are among us."

Wind whistled outside, a clarion call inviting chaos, and a cold, piercing gust splintered the windows, but the consecrated flames barely shivered.

168

"According to the ancient text, we have assembled twelve in the service of *Potamoi Haidou*, Rivers of the Underworld—to right that which has wronged all of creation," continued the speaker, his voice raised over the whistling bluster. "We swear our fealty to you. We are yours to command."

Moonlight filled the room and, beneath the cowls of the cloaks, the eyes of the assembled smoldered like fire. As they allowed the immortal spirits of the Five Rivers to fill them, the leader began his chant in ancient Greek. According to the ritual, he and the others repeated it eleven times, their voices unifying.

"By our kinship with Tartaros, Erebos, and Thanatos, this coven invokes thee—take Hades' own and open the Underworld between the *Ge Theôn* and the *Oikoumene Broteios*! Let the children of Ekhidna find the paths from the world of Olympos to the world of Man!"

As the incantation grew louder, darkness festered like algae in bloom until all they could see was an eerie glow from the book. The all-consuming obscurity even absorbed the candles and torchlight, and the earth seized. San Franciscans would think it was one of their many earthquakes, unaware of its occult source. Seconds later, the quaking stopped, and the ebony entity dissipated. The coven leader released his hands and the scroll closed. Distant thunder echoed, but that was not part of the ritual. The other eleven suddenly convulsed, sputtering forth blood and bile, and then falling to the floor, dead. The remaining supplicant seethed at the apparent assassination of his cohorts. Without the complete circle, the spell lost some of its potency. Eleven deceased bodies shriveled, turned to dust, and vanished within the earthen floor. The cloaked one smirked.

"You may have taken my coven, *Zeus Kolastes*, but the invocation is true. I will rebuild to ensure that the creatures of the darkness shall walk in this world, wreaking devastation on the mortal world. You had the chance to make this right, but you did not, and now the dwellers of Hades shall torment Gaea."

A louder crack of thunder preceded a desperate burst of energy stretching from a distant shrouded mountaintop in another plane, surging through the cloaked man who shook uncontrollably and heaved blood through his nose and mouth. Falling to the floor a quivering mass of bodily fluids and skin, Gaea claimed the body, leaving the black cloth behind. Millennia ago, *Hermes Psychopompos* would have escorted the soul to the underworld, but the necromancer had none—the price he paid. Despite Zeus' revenge, however, the deed was complete, and the *Protogenoi* would need to have mercy on all Humankind.

Zeus all but exhausted whatever power he had left on this task, and how it was left to mortals to take up where he left off.

# 17—THE SANDMAN COMETH

**Radio Moscow** "For WPR News, this is Aleksandra Sokolov in Moscow. Technicians at the nuclear power plant in Novodvinsk in Arkhangelskaya oblast had to call in Task Force: Iota to help contain a uranium leak on Monday. Although not accustomed to accepting help from outside agencies, the Russian government acquiesced to the United Nations when the latter, threatening sanctions, insisted on sending in nuclear technicians. Scientists at Moscow University say the leak may have contaminated parts of the Dvina River, a source of drinking water for the region. Task Force technicians will release the test results on the water by the end of the week."

• • •

Enshrouded by liquid white robes, a figure hovered—unmoving, yet ubiquitous—above the jagged peaks of the Olympos of Humankind, a place essentially devoid of godly energy, but a parallel to a mountain in another realm. Empowered by those who dream, mortal and immortal alike knew him by many names, but most knew him as Morpheos, the god of the dreamscape. He wafted down toward the mortal realm at the urging of the Moira in search of those exceptional enough to receive the most

171

hallowed of dreams, those of prophecy. Rarely given to mortals, these enigmatic dreams required the help of a true Oracle to discern their meaning, and in this new age, Oracles were hard to find. The dreamscape had changed over the millennia since the gods had ruled, and Morpheos knew his time as an immortal might be ending. Driven by instinct alone, he traveled to the mortal realm of Earth. Descending closer, he split himself into multiple rays of light—dreamweavers—that headed out in various directions. One such dreamweaver sailed the ether toward the city of Boston, Massachusetts, to the apartment of a sleeping woman, Aleta Halston. As a warm breeze, he entered her bedroom through a window cracked open and undulated around her like a boa constrictor, tightening his coils of reverie around her sleeping body. Sprinkling dream sand over her eyelids, he departed hastily, letting the dreams grow inside her mind.

Impassioned thunder echoed throughout Aleta as her thoughts coalesced like binding mist. Upon a stony crag poking into the unlit sky she stood, and a cloak of pure white feathers enveloped her, rising and falling in the wind, as the scent of rain overwhelmed her and tickled her nostrils. Black thunderclouds gathered; the resounding thunder screamed past her from the horizon and tendrils of stark lightning danced above her, igniting the heavens. With the tumult of the storm growing to full force, she felt the rain pelting her ebony skin, yet caressing her. Drops of water trickled down her body beneath the feathers, and she turned her face skyward as the water cascaded down. The storm's essence, its very power, filled her, and then she heard a voice whose echoing words were both familiar yet enigmatic, *"Silver Sister of the Sky, your fate awaits you where prophecy is truth."* A strident crash of thunder and a dazzling flash of lightning awakened her from her guided vision, and when she was fully conscious, she gasped as she saw a small, white feather on her pillow.

• • •

As the morning sun painted the sky a pastel hue, the streets of Boston flowed with life, the veins and arteries of a living creature. Highways and back roads pulsed with automobiles, taxis, buses, and trucks, stopping and starting like the beating of a heart. Downtown, a young man sat at a sidewalk coffee shop, the Beanery, just off Commonwealth Avenue, a few blocks down from the gold-domed State House. Sitting at a wrought iron table outside the café, he ordered a double cappuccino, a bagel, and a copy of the *Globe*. Blaring car horns, vociferous taxi drivers, footfalls of rushing people—all the city's sounds—washed over him like so much background noise. A daily routine, he caught up on the world's events, paying close attention to the articles concerning wildlife or animals. A non-conformist at heart, right down to the clothes he wore, he preferred the casual to the formal. Leaning back in the iron chair, one foot on the seat next to him, he sipped the frothy coffee that had arrived somewhere between page one and page six. In his gray T-shirt, gray khakis with the elastic cuff, and his favorite hiking boots, in addition to his close-cropped blond hair, one might think he was a Marine, but Brandon Jeffries didn't have a warrior's heart, at least not for physical combat. An assistant zoologist at Northeastern University, he collected data on animal species throughout the world, examined population demographics and habitats, as well as tracked animals in the wild. He defended the endangered animals that had no protectors; he fought his battles in the academic milieu, teaching others about helping to preserve wildlife and maintain the delicate ecosystems of the planet. His clothing and appearance were not just a personal choice; they made his job easier by keeping to the simpler things.

Flipping through the comics, he stopped at the horoscopes for the first time in months. He sometimes liked to read them all and then take only the parts he liked as his own personal horoscope. As he finished the last one, a line of text made him linger a moment longer: "*Keeper of the Twelve, your fate awaits you where prophecy is truth.*" Next to the words was printed a small feather.

• • •

As the morning sun rose, brushstrokes on the wind painted the heavens a soft orange and blue. Off Washington Street in the suburb of Brookline sat a Victorian 'fixer-upper', a gingerbread house. In the sitting room, Sarah Bishop worked diligently at the potter's wheel to put the last touches on a unique clay vase. Since she lived alone, her living room was her studio, skirted with bookshelves laden with pots, bowls, and figurines—some fired, some not. She pulled her short red hair out of her face with a rubber band, but a few stray wisps dangled down, framing her cheeks. Clay-encrusted hands, gifted tools, shaped the murky mud and gave it new life, worthy of a gallery according to some. Like her mother before her, she created something from nothing. Her sponge, filled with the precise amount of water deftly created texture and contour in the workable mud. Scrutinizing eyes watched the shape evolve into something alive and inspiring. Every so often, her foot pumped the pedal for the wheel to spin faster and then she let it slow naturally. She could have used an electric wheel, but she preferred working in the same manner as her mother and grandmother. Once she achieved the desired shape, she stopped the wheel and drew a taut wire underneath the clay to sever it from the platform, like birthing a child. A timer rang, and she carefully placed the curvaceous piece on the shelf while placing an air-dried piece in a heated kiln. The pot she removed from the kiln she placed on a cooling rack while she went to the sink to wash her hands. Upon her return, she spun the pot on the stand to examine for cracks or blemishes, and saw a line of words imprinted in the side of the clay, *"Daughter of the lost kingdom, your fate awaits you where prophecy is truth."* Her fingers brushed the words to make sure they were not some illusion. As she examined the clay further for any more anomalous etchings, the imprint of a small feather at the bottom, no bigger than her thumbnail, caught her eye.

• • •

Danelos scanned the labels of a few boxes of newly arrived artifacts before pulling a large box off the shelf. Wiping it down with a cloth, he brought it to the desk where he examined all the incoming relics. Gently removing the cover, he carefully withdrew a fragment of marble, a remnant of ages past. Picking up the soft-bristle brush, he gingerly dislodged dirt to reveal more of the ancient treasure. He yawned and stretched, his arms flexing behind his head. Some archaeologists had porters and helpers who were brought along on digs to move large pieces or stubborn rocks, but he chose to do the labor himself, claiming it helped keep him focused and in shape, his 6'2" frame intimidating the freshmen who took his introductory classes. To know him, though, one would see a straightforward, easygoing individual. He would rather wear jeans, a T-shirt, and his favorite black leather biker boots than the stuffy suit and tie of his colleagues. The laborious task of cleaning, marking, cataloguing, and storing the artifacts ate into his schedule, but he loved pulling back the layers of the past through his work. After he finished with the segment of the column, he removed another object from the box, a weathered stone with etchings unfamiliar to him. Since his job was to catalogue only those items he could identify, he simply placed it in a smaller box, labeled it 'unknown', and placed it to the side of the desk. Time permitting, he would examine this artifact before he went home. Stretching again, he pulled an elastic band from the drawer and tied back his hair into a neat ponytail. After completing his master's degrees in

175

both Greco-Roman archaeology and World History, he didn't have any weekends to himself, especially since the university had not assigned him a new assistant. Danelos set the last item in the box on the desk and peeled away the shreds of newspaper to reveal an ancient kylix—a shallow, long-stemmed drinking cup. Judging the piece to be from the Early Iron Age, he was astonished to see that nothing marred the surface of the black paint. Around the cup's rim was a white feather, symbolism he had never seen on a piece this old. The artistry was distinctive, the paint on this kylix sharing no remote similarities to others he had examined. Trying to find any timeworn imperfections with his magnifying glass, he cleared away some dirt from what looked like letters in some form of ancient Greek. As the dust fell away, the words became legible and his expression hardened: *"Heir of the Mountain, your fate awaits you where prophecy is truth."*

Two months passed, and the strange events that had transpired for these four mortals coalesced with other lost memories. Prophecy, however, wouldn't remain dismissed for long.

• • •

Early one Sunday morning, as Aleta stepped out into the hallway of her apartment building to retrieve the newspaper, she saw a postcard attached to the front page advertising a gala event at the Museum of Natural History the coming weekend. The museum would serve wine and hors d'oeuvres, and patrons could tour some of the museum's newest exhibits. Setting the paper on her kitchen table, she threw the card in the trash. Who had time to go to the museum, she thought. A short while later, after she emerged from a shower, she went to get a bottled water from the refrigerator, and sitting on the kitchen table once again was the postcard. Bewildered, but still not interested, she tore the card into pieces and tossed it in the trash. After she finished getting dressed an hour later,

Aleta went to pour a cup of coffee. As she took a sip, she glanced back at the table and almost dropped the cup. The card was sitting on the table again, in one piece. It was at that moment she tried to remember the last time she had been to the museum.

Brandon, while running down by the Charles River, spotted a billboard advertising the same museum event, but it wasn't a postcard that kept reappearing. Rather, a sign seemed to be on every building he saw, no matter where he turned. When he stooped to tie his shoe, he saw a newspaper by the curb and it, too, had the information about the event. Shrugging it off as coincidence, assuming the museum was doing a mass media explosion, he finished his workout, seeing the same information six more times. As soon as got home, he looked up the museum online and found the event. With exhibits on pre-Columbian animal remains making the rounds to Boston, this was something he didn't think he could ignore.

Working feverishly to clean her house before she started her work, Sarah took a few minutes to check her email since she wouldn't be able to do that later with her hands caked with clay. Deleting messages that she had already read or were spam, she accidentally double-clicked on one from the Museum of Natural History, noticing the event that would be the next weekend. Even with her interest in pottery and sculpture, she wouldn't have the time to invest to go the new exhibits, so she deleted the email. Seconds later, a new message appeared from the museum, but she deleted it, thinking she had some sort of email virus. After three more emails came, she turned off the computer, but—like it or not—she now had the event in the back of her mind, and she loved the inspiration she received from ancient pottery.

• • •

Not since the arrival of the Elgin Marbles two years earlier had the museum gone to such lengths to make the

177

evening truly a spectacle. With a black and silver theme, the lobby sparkled with crystals and silver ornaments, hanging from the ceiling to mimic stars, and a gaggle of docents flitted about, greeting guests, ensuring they received all the help they required. High-end restaurants from all over Boston catered the event, each supplying a bevy of servers to carry trays of food, delicacies from all over the world. An open bar, situated by the entrance, served the finest wines from dozens of countries. On the landing where two expansive staircases met, musicians from the Boston Symphony played, each in black formal attire. Even though the musicians themselves blended into the surroundings, their music transcended the cacophony of voices, creating a blanket of sound to heighten the mood. Black lacquer boxes situated throughout the lobby allowed people to donate to the museum at their whim, and each box had its own tuxedo-clad guard, a consequence of the chaos that had woven itself through the city over the years. With surveillance cameras jutting from every corner, the guards were superfluous, but the City Council insisted on having armed protection in case of any trouble, which is ironic: Boston had been one of the most fortified cities in the U.S. since the United Nations Task Forces went into effect in 1962.

When the museum opened its doors to the public in 1975, the UNTF assigned operatives to keep the artifacts free from criminal activity so the museum wouldn't have to spend money on security since the allocations for exhibits came from other government agencies, specifically the National Archaeology Council. As of 1998, the Museum of Natural History affiliated itself with the Museum of Science, also in Boston, making it the largest historical conglomerate on the Eastern seaboard. Research fellowships allowed graduate students with many Boston colleges and universities the opportunity to do funded research without having to find sponsors. Danelos

Fairmont, a 2002 doctoral graduate of the Classical Archaeology program at Boston University, became one of the first research fellows to receive a teaching position under the new federal guidelines that allowed for students not yet finished with their degrees. At 28, he became one of the youngest faculty members to receive grants to go on half a dozen digs in places like Egypt, Syria, Greece, and Siberia. His appearance at the gala event meant he could share his latest discoveries with those in his field, but also with those who might be willing to support the museum. Even though he would need to get background checks on potential donors (something the UNTF required), he could make initial contact and set up these donors with basic information about the exhibits, just enough to promote interest. This night, he would be hosting something altogether different, little did he know.

From early in life, Danelos never conformed to the status quo, something that confounded his mother until she learned that it just didn't work for him. Since he did well in school, no one cared that he skirted the boundary of the typical; even at the museum, he wore his own version of professional attire. As this was a formal event, he wore black; if anyone had a problem with his black leather pants, black button-up shirt, and biker boots, they'd have to ask him to leave. Tuxedoes made him look plastic, he thought, and he could rarely find one that would fit him right. Years of working on digs, moving stone artifacts and digging ditches, in addition to his fitness interests, had crafted a solid frame, one that didn't work so well with confining clothing, like bowties and jackets. The inexperienced should follow convention, he would say, and those who know what they're doing should break it. He felt his work should be the basis for judgment, not his clothes. As long as he presented himself well, he never caught any opposition from his department chair or the trustees who occasionally popped into his office.

Danelos snatched a dirty martini off a passing silver tray, swallowed it, and placed the glass back on the tray before the waiter was too far away. For as much as he loved his job, he knew this would be a long night and one that he might enjoy more if he weren't completely sober. Before he could grab another glass, he saw a striking woman enter in a silver sleeveless evening gown, her close-cropped dark hair flanked by dangling silver earrings. She seemed a little overwhelmed by the crowd, but stuck to the side of the lobby, sipping a glass of Pinot Noir. When she and Danelos made momentary eye contact, he nodded and smiled. Some colleagues addressed him, so he turned to speak with them, wishing the waiter would return with more martinis. It never ceased to amaze him how superficial people could be when they needed something, especially money or prestige. These colleagues had asked Danelos to speak at a symposium about the dichotomy of modern technology and ancient archaeology, but he had to refuse respectfully. He told them it was because he had made a prior arrangement, but he knew they wouldn't pay him, and that was something he promised himself once he received his doctorate: no paycheck, no product.

About an hour into the evening, and three martinis later, he had already made his obligatory rounds to those whom he needed to see and found momentary solace leaning against a marble pillar, hoping to avoid contact from some of the more insipid guests who wanted nothing more than to talk.

"Hiding?" a voice from behind asked him.

A woman with shoulder-length red hair and a black sequin dress stood behind him, delicately holding a glass of Shiraz.

"Am I that obvious?" he asked, trying to think if he'd met her before.

She smiled. "Not many men here providing structural support for the building. This sort of thing not your style?"

"Nah, it's fine. I work with the museum, actually, so I become a target for those who support research or exhibits."

"Ah. Everyone wants his name on a wing or a project?"

"Something like that."

"Sarah Bishop," she said, extending her free hand.

He shook it gently. "Danelos Fairmont."

"So, what are you working on, if you don't mind me asking?"

"I recently helped excavate some artifacts from temple ruins in northern Greece. We managed to bring back some whole pieces, too. The exhibit's down the hall, if you want to see. We tried to reconstruct what the environment would have been like thousands of years ago, too. I think we did pretty well, if I do say so."

"Well, I've mingled with a few folks here, and I'm about ready to move onto something else, so lead the way."

Intrigued that she'd expressed interest, Danelos led her through the crowd toward a banner that read, "Thessalian Dig: Temple of the Moira." Just before the entrance stood the same dark-haired woman he had seen earlier, the one with the silver gown, chatting with a young man.

"Let me know when you want to see the research we've done, Brandon. It's mostly genetics, but I think you'd find it helpful with what you're doing," she said, sipping her drink.

"Thanks, Aleta. I appreciate it. Who would have thought I'd run across another animal advocate tonight? You know, it's funny you mentioned almost becoming a veterinarian. I'd thought about veterinary medicine, but a zoological grant came along in grad school and had my name all over it."

As they passed, Sarah, who'd had a few glasses of wine, leaned over and said, "Hey, come on! He's going to give us a private tour of his exhibit."

This part of the museum wouldn't be open to the public for another hour or so, after the cocktail hour ended, but Danelos felt like showing off a bit, and Sarah had no desire to mill about the museum lobby. After they passed through the replica of a temple entrance, the grandeur and expertise of museum facsimile construction took over Sarah. Much of what she saw was plaster and paint, the original pieces marked as such, but she found it hard to tell the difference. That was the idea, she supposed. Ancient pieces of pottery and other clay objects intrigued her, but the whole room had her rapt attention, to the point that she forgot that others were in the room. While she had been examining each wall niche, both Brandon and Aleta appeared, obviously attracted by Sarah's impassioned, partially intoxicated suggestion. This first room, darkened with only spotlights on the smaller pieces, had the smaller finds, each one painstakingly marked and catalogued by Danelos, who stood in the corner, arms behind his back, waiting to see if they had any questions. Not wanting others to enter, but willing to entertain those who had, he closed the door to the exhibition, locking it from the inside. At first, he thought Brandon and Aleta seemed less than amused, but as they walked further into the room, he could tell they felt compelled to lean in to read the information cards.

Another doorway led into the inner chamber where Danelos' prized find sat, a scrying pool from the temple, almost intact, minus a few marble blocks. Each piece interlocked together so well that he could actually fill it with water, just as it would have been in ancient days. About six feet across, the pool sat in the middle of the chamber with gas-powered torches on the wall to cast light in nuanced ways.

"I'm Danelos Fairmont, and I work for the museum in the Antiquities department as well as teach classes in Classical History and Archaeology at BU and Harvard. About a year ago, I was in northern Greece, and I came upon a site that had gone unexamined by anyone in my field, so I procured the financing to do a preliminary dig. Once those who funded me saw the potential for more coming from the site, I received full funding to excavate. The shrine was in ruins, but my team and I were able to unearth this scrying pool from the Temple of the Moira, or Ananke, the goddess of inevitability, or Fate, as some of you might call her. A scrying pool had many purposes when they were in use," Danelos continued. "Some priests of the gods used them to divine the future or see the past, but others used them as a means of communication with their chosen deity. In the case of the Moira, legends say she would commune with the most worthy, but rarely. Some sources say that if you get an audience with Fate, your life's thread shortens, but no one knows by how much."

"Do you actually believe in things like the Moira?" Sarah asked, her fingers grazing the cool stone.

"I suppose I do," Danelos replied, "but I don't worship the gods. My mother was strangely atheistic, but I grew up with Greek myths from her. Go figure. I think that's what intrigued me about the ancient world."

Mesmerized by the dim light and the circular room, Brandon, Aleta, and Sarah shuffled around the pool, occasionally brushing against the stone. When all three did so at once, a few ripples danced across the surface but went unnoticed.

"Do you really think the Moira exists, or existed?" Aleta asked, adjusting her earrings in her reflection.

"Hard to say. If she did, the ancient world has long since vanished with only pocket groups, mostly in the Mediterranean, who still worship the gods, although some are scattered throughout the world. It's said that the ancient gods grew in power through their worshippers. If she still does exist, though, I'm guessing she's lying low."

They all laughed a little, but suddenly became quiet, as if they realized they were in a holy place, even though this was a reproduction. A few more times, all three touched the stone ring simultaneously, generating more ripples. Danelos stepped closer to explain more about the symbolism etched on the side of the pool and placed his hands on the stones.

Silently at first, the waters swirled around, a gentle mist rising from the surface. A whisper crept into the chamber, a silken voice,

"*Four not born of godly word, two of vessel, two of sword...*"

Aleta noticed the water moving and jumped back.

"Nice effects, Dan. What is that, ancient Greek?"

Again the voices spoke, this time a little louder, "*Four not born of godly word, two of vessel, two of sword...*"

"Yeah, that was Greek, but there are no special effects in this exhibit," he replied, his eyes darting about.

Spinning faster like a captured maelstrom, the pool generated more mist, and the gaslights flared. This time the words came loudly, this time in English, "Four not born of godly word, two of vessel, two of sword..."

"What the hell is happening?" erupted Aleta. "Okay, Dan, you've done a great job with this exhibit, but I think it's time to shut off the special effects."

"It's not me, Aleta," he repeated. "Okay, everyone, let's just go. Maybe a technician installed something he shouldn't have from another exhibit."

Moving toward the exit, the four stopped when they realized the door was no longer there. Sarah turned around.

"Guys, look at the pool."

From the spinning waters, a figure rose, cloaked in swirling white mist. In her hands, she held a skein of ivory thread.

"The fount of prophecy flows like quicksilver, mortals. Your touch has brought me here."

"Okay, your technicians get extra points for this, Danelos," Brandon uttered.

A pair of flashing eyes turned toward him. "Only those most worthy, bound by divine prophecy, can summon me. I have seen your likenesses in the loom."

Danelos was about to speak, but the figure anticipated his question.

"I am Ananke. And you are of the prophecy, mortal, as are you all. You must go where prophecy is truth."

Slowly backing toward where the door used to be, Sarah shrieked when the two pillars that flanked the exit fell across her path and shattered.

"What do you want with us?" Brandon shouted, taking steps forward. He realized this was no longer a special effect, but he wasn't sure exactly what it was, either.

"What do I want with *you*?" Ananke asked. "You summoned *me*."

"Okay, Ananke, or whoever you are," Danelos said. "What do you mean our touch brought you here?" For the moment, he was giving credence to the apparition.

Into the mist, Ananke vanished, but coalesced outside the pool as an elderly woman, cloaked in shimmering fabric. Barefoot and bearing a spindle, she walked over to Danelos.

"You four share a destiny, a destiny woven together as threads in a cloth. Overlapping at times, each thread comes back upon itself in a way I have never seen. You have no conception of how much an enigma you are, Heir of the Mountain."

He knew that phrase.

"Why did you call me that?"

"That is not for me to say. Each of you will need to find the truth. Your touch called me here because, together, prophecy binds you all into a fate woven before you were born. You are mortal, but your ancestry connects you to the gods."

Their shared confusion silenced them.

"I know you do not believe. Not yet. I can only tell you things that will not affect the outcome of the prophecy."

Aleta raised an eyebrow. "How do I know this isn't some Pinot Noir-induced stupor, and I'm not sitting right now in the middle of the lobby?"

A wrinkled smile spread across Ananke's face. "You do not, child. Faith is something you must come to on your own. I cannot force you to accept this, any more than I can expect you to accept the fate that will befall you... all of you."

"Is anyone else bothered by this?" Brandon asked.

"A little," answered Aleta. "I just want to understand why we're still in this room with this woman who thinks she's Fate personified."

Ananke approached Aleta, who towered over the cloaked woman by a good two inches thanks to her black Ferragamos.

"Touch the spindle."

Aleta moved her hand slightly, staring into eyes that spoke of stars and planets, life and death, and she felt strangely at peace. She let her fingers graze the thread, never taking her eyes off Ananke. At the moment of contact, memories inundated her mind, pictures of the mountains where she grew up as a child, flashes of the animals she had rescued and brought to her mother, a veterinarian. A father's death, a sister's illness in remission, a mother's disgrace... all passing through her in a way that she could feel every emotion she had ever felt, every moment of joy or pain, doubt or shame, greed and generosity. And feathers. Ananke lowered the skein of thread.

"I cannot show you the future, but I can show you the past. Now do you believe?"

Aleta walked into a shadowy part of the chamber, hiding her tears.

Fate approached Brandon and Sarah; each had a similar reaction. Danelos walked toward Ananke, but she put out a hand to stop him.

"No, mortal. Not even the past. You are not meant for such knowledge. Not yet."

Sarah's eyes met Aleta's as she touched her arm. Different life experiences, but the same reaction to reliving them. Although only a few feet separated him from the two, Brandon understood. Some people say that seeing your life flash before your eyes changes you; apparently, it does. Danelos watched the others, not realizing he had taken a few steps back. He watched them process the information they must have seen, and a twinge of jealousy made his stomach flip. Why was he not allowed to know? What images from his past was he not supposed to see? Ananke removed three small strands of thread from the skein, braided them together, and held them out to him.

"If you wish to see what they saw, take this. Then, you will understand."

His first instinct was to take the threads, see their memories, and feel a sense of understanding along with them. Just before he held out his hand, he pulled it back.

"They're their memories, not mine. They will have no meaning to me, and I'll feel as if I've intruded on their lives. No thanks."

Ananke replaced the threads in the skein. "Wise decision. When you are ready to know about your past, Heir of the Mountain, you will know," she whispered.

Joining Danelos, Aleta's eyes met his.

"Trust me. Some things are best left in the past."

187

Taking her place in the scrying pool, Ananke told them, "*Believe. Trust. And, remember, your fate awaits you where prophecy is truth.*"

As the waters and mists ceased swirling, all that remained in the pool were a few ripples, and then they, too, stopped. Like a polished mirror, the water showed no evidence of movement at all, as if it were truly glass. Awkward glances thickened the tension.

"Did you hear what she said?" Brandon asked, fumbling in his pocket.

"Yeah, why?" Danelos replied.

Brandon removed a small piece of paper from his wallet. "I'd say this would sound weird, but under the circumstances, I don't think so. I was reading the horoscopes last weekend when I found this."

Danelos read the clipping and passed it to Sarah and Aleta. "Well, adding to the bizarre, I catalogued an ancient bowl a week ago that had that very phrase etched into it, in Greek."

"Guys," started Sarah, "a clay pot I fired had the very same phrase on it along with a feather."

"A feather? I'll ante up here, too. Last weekend, I had a strange dream, but in it, I heard the same phrase. And, when I woke up, somehow a feather was on my pillow," Aleta said, hands on her hips. "Wow. My therapist doesn't even know this."

Not really knowing what to say, Danelos stammered that they should probably get back to the reception, and the four parted ways until the end of the evening. Denial shrouds even those whose minds are willing to receive most things. Shattering reality to rebuild a new truth comes at a price—loss of ignorance. They didn't know what to say to each other let alone anyone else about what had happened, so they nodded at each other occasionally in the lobby. A few hours later, just as Aleta was about to step into a cab to head home, she saw Brandon talking with Sarah.

"Aleta! Wait up!" shouted Sarah.

Aleta let the cab leave. Not sure what to say, she asked them if they wanted to grab some coffee somewhere. It seemed like the thing to do. If Fate wanted them to be together, then at least they should get to know one another, she thought. Why she suddenly felt the need to do that was anyone's guess.

"The Beanery on Comm. Ave.," Brandon said. "Excellent coffee. Better frozen yogurt. You know you want some." His goofy grin made them laugh.

As another Yellow cab approached, Sarah whistled loudly. The other two looked at each other and then at her.

"Hey, I grew up in the city. You have to make your presence known," she winked, getting into the cab. "Come on. Fro-yo awaits."

En route, Brandon realized he had taken one of Danelos's business cards from the exhibit, so he sent a text message,

"Beanery on Comm @ 11 p.m. Ur buyin. - Brandon"

• • •

"That had to be some of the best yogurt I've ever had."

"I would think so, Aleta. You had two."

"Girl, I'll just do some more Pilates, that's all," Aleta replied, scraping the bowl with her spoon. "What's on your mind, Dan?"

He smiled, caught off guard a little, and his eyes said it all.

"Ah, I was hoping it was something else. But, oh well. So, what now?" she asked, leaning back in the booth.

"You guys tell me. My gut tells me that it was for real. Don't ask me why." Danelos answered, folding his hands behind his head.

189

"Well, you're the expert. What does 'where prophecy is truth' mean?" Brandon asked, knocking back his second double espresso.

Danelos, spying the surveillance camera in the corner, leaned forward on the table, "The only place I can think of, and mind you, there may be others, is the one place where prophecy was known to have unimaginable power—Delphi."

"As in the Oracle of…?" Sarah asked.

"Oh, honey, I love Greece, but when I go, I go to Santorini or Mykonos."

"Aleta, I don't think Dan's talking about going for a vacation," Brandon chortled.

"So, Ananke wants us to go to Greece? On whose dime?"

"Heh. Exactly, Aleta," Sarah said. "Okay, folks, I have to get up early to do some more clay work. We've exchanged numbers, right? Let's talk about this another time."

Noticing that it was well past midnight, they parted ways, but Danelos stayed up for a while on his balcony, the starry night a comfort to him. That experience in the museum felt too real, too familiar. He'd been to Delphi before, during graduate school, and he had seen some of the ancient scrolls archaeologists had found in the antechambers, the prophecies that priests had carefully written down—misquoting a prophecy could spell disaster. Normally, the sibyl would only speak the prophecies, leaving no tangible record, but she couldn't stop someone else from writing them down. Dan would enjoy the opportunity to see how this scenario would play out, but he didn't think the others would, and Ananke said prophecy linked them. As a child, he remembered learning about such things from his mother, since she said he had Greek ancestry, but after a while, she stopped.

While he stared at the heavens, a shadow passed over his head, and he thought it might be a bird or maybe a bat, but the stench that followed reminded him more of a garbage scow, one hauling decomposing flesh. That was the sign for him to go inside and try to sleep.

# 18—PROPHECY AND TRUTH

**EBC 4 (London, England)** "From WPR News, this is Jack Redding in London. Sources close to Israeli Prime Minister Avraham told reporters at yesterday's press conference that both he and Egypt/Palestinian Prime Minister Al-Fasan would use whatever force necessary to keep their people safe from outsiders and the civil wars breaking out all over the Middle East. Despite the United Nations' insistence on fortifying the borders of Israel and Palestine with Task Force: Rho operatives, both countries—who signed the Middle East Accords in 1948 just after Israel's inception—wish to use their own military. The UN will respect their wishes, but will be ready to move Rho operatives into the field if necessary."

• • •

Later in the week, a padded envelope arrived at Sarah's house with no return address and the words "Urgent/Time Sensitive" stamped in red across the front. She had just finished washing her hands after firing some pots and didn't think to look down the street to see who delivered the package, but the loud knocking on the door had jarred her from her potter's wheel. On the kitchen table, she poured the contents: a round trip plane ticket, her passport, and an envelope filled with Euros, five hundred to be exact. The note attached read: "Oracle of Delphi. Noon. Saturday, June 21. Sarah Bishop, your fate awaits you where prophecy is truth." Three days from today, she thought. Whoever this is isn't wasting time and also had her passport updated since her trip to Australia as a child. That freaked her out more than anything did, but combined with the events at the museum, she thought it made sense in a strange way. Rereading the note with the hope that she would figure something out, Sarah snatched up her cell phone on the first ring.

"Oh, hey Aleta. Aha. Yup. Brandon called you? Yeah, me, too. Hmm. What about Dan? Oh, he called Brandon? I guess I'll see you at 6:00 tomorrow morning at Logan, then."

• • •

Stepping out into the early morning just beyond the doors of the Athens International Airport, Brandon, Sarah, and Aleta collapsed onto a bench while Danelos finalized the rental car. They couldn't help but notice no shortage of surveillance cameras attached to light poles, the front of the building, and even some of the potted trees lining the drop off area. America wasn't the only country to watch its citizens, apparently.

"Does anyone know what time it is here? I am so lost," asked Sarah, fumbling with her watch.

Brandon mumbled, "It's 4:15 a.m. It's seven hours later than the States." He had his head leaning back against the bench, his eyes closed.

"Perfect. I'm such a morning person," snorted Aleta. "This had better be good. That's all I'm saying."

A few minutes later, the rumbling of a 2002 Jeep Wrangler got them standing. Brandon put their bags in the back and then hopped in the front seat; apparently, the women wanted to sit in the back, probably to sleep.

"So," Brandon started, "How far is Delphi from here?"

Danelos checked the GPS. "About 120 miles, which is close to two hours... less than that when I drive." He grinned. "But before we do anything else, do we want to get settled into a hotel room at all, take a nap?"

"I just want to do this before I lose my mind," Aleta replied. "Maybe we'll even find out who gave us the plane tickets and spending money, right? I'm only into this because of the coincidence. Because, it's either real, or I'm in a coma somewhere."

"You're just a ray of sunshine," Brandon joked. "C'mon, it's an adventure. Let's just see what happens. My vote is, drive on. Let's just get to Delphi."

After an hour or so, Aleta had to admit to herself that the landscape was beautiful, and being in Greece was, after all, on her 'to do' list. Maybe they'd have time to do some sightseeing before they went home. This time together at least gave them the opportunity to learn more about each other, and they realized they actually did have some things in common: both Brandon and Aleta were animal lovers, and Sarah and Danelos loved sushi. Everyone loved frozen yogurt. Whatever was happening, Fate couldn't have picked a more diverse group of people. Each person's personality added something to the group dynamic, making the group that much more interwoven, like the cloth from the loom. Only, they didn't know that yet.

Sarah giggled a lot when Aleta spoke mostly because Aleta had this casual sense of humor that always took people off guard. One minute she could be serious, and the next, she'd come out with a bit of sarcasm, a quip, or even an expression which would put everyone into hysterics. Born in the S. Bronx, she grew up—of all places—in Colorado just outside of Boulder. City girl met country, and the country was never the same. Aleta's mother, a veterinarian, had to start a new life, and Colorado was as good a place as any to do it. Being a black girl in a predominantly white town, back in the 70's, Aleta Halston,

194

an only child, developed strength of character from her single mother, two singular women who worked so well together. Sarah, on the other hand, grew up in Boston; not exactly a street kid, but more street savvy. Mom and grandma were potters, products of the 60's with their carefree style and tie-dyed shirts. Raised a Wiccan, Sarah found peace in knowing that all of the elements worked in conjunction with another: earth, air, fire, water, and spirit. At home in the woods or on a mountain path, she could survive with little or nothing. Her father took her to the shore as often as he could, explaining the extraordinary power of the earth and its forces. She couldn't have asked for more supportive parents; it crushed her when they divorced. They're best friends now, but marriage wasn't for them. A few months after the divorce was final, her father moved in with his new boyfriend. That was fifteen years ago. Now, Sarah's in a Jeep driving toward one of the holiest sites in the world with people just shy of being complete strangers. Brandon was right—it's an adventure.

Tapping his hand on his knee to some Greek rock music and taking in the countryside, Brandon smiled to himself as he thought about what had happened in the past week. Normally comfortable by himself, he found he truly liked being with these people, and he thought Aleta was just too funny. He wasn't sure if Sarah liked him or maybe that was more of his ego, but he felt a connection he couldn't explain. He felt at ease, as if he had known them his whole life. From the first moment in the museum, his usual defense mechanism of pulling back didn't surface, something he'd have fun explaining to his therapist. Adopted as an infant, he grew up an only child of some privilege, although his adopted father, Maxwell, liked his son to work for whatever he wanted. Not the worst father, he was an absentee one, though, because business kept him away from his wife, Angela, and their son. If international business did nothing else, it drove wedges between people, teaching Brandon how to be more reticent over the years, but it also made him more self-sufficient. Whenever Max came back from trips, he always brought Brandon stuffed animals. By the time the boy was ten, he virtually had a zoo, but while some children were content making their toys talk and play games, Brandon wanted to know why zebras had stripes or why armadillos rolled into a ball to protect themselves. This passion for learning became something his mother could foster since she stayed at home, being able to read to her son or show Brandon web sites that explained animal behaviors. Taking very little from his parents financially, he did let them pay for his education since he knew he would take care of them at some point. Now, his education was paying off, and his zoological interests made him a contender on the national level with research and grants. He might even find something on this trip that would augment his career. It would certainly augment something, but his career might not be it. He did find, though, that he liked Greek rock music.

"Hey. I've been thinking about something. Ever since I can remember knowing how to read, I've read fantasy novels and comic books, back when I used to hide under my blanket and read with a flashlight. In those stories, there always seemed to be that one character who just refused to be a part of the journey, you know? That guy or girl who wouldn't believe or just felt that this new path was just too crazy. We've all seemed to be on board for this adventure from the beginning. Why? I mean, I've been wavering back and forth about this for a while now, and I know why I'm in. How about you guys?"

"This all sounds so much like the stories I heard from my mother when I was a kid, so I'm just intrigued by it all," Danelos said. "It just feels right to me."

Sarah brushed a few stray hairs back. "Seeing those memories in the museum. That's what did it for me. How could I deny that that happened? As a Wiccan, I feel spiritually tied to the world, so the idea that something greater than me exists isn't so far fetched. I don't know exactly. I feel like I'm in the right place."

"You know, as a scientist, I fully immerse myself in facts and hypotheses, data and mathematics. But, after what happened to me, I can't help but think something wants more from me, call it a higher power or maybe a god or gods. I've given this so much thought, and I almost didn't come on this trip. But, I said to myself, 'Aleta, if you don't do this, you will never know the answers to all those questions. You'll never find meaning to this.' And, I need empirical data to back up what I know. What better way than to just take a few risks. Maybe we're all being manipulated. Hell, maybe I'm still at home sleeping."

Brandon lingered on her words a moment longer. "At first, this all seemed so easy, so arranged. But, maybe it's supposed to be that way. We still have time to back out, I guess, if we want to. I don't see the karmic police coming to take us into existential custody, y'know?"

The last twenty minutes of the drive passed quickly, and soon there were signs pointing the way. Sunrise dusted the landscape with a yellow tinge, bringing to life the hills. Danelos headed down a pebble road down to where visitors were to park to take tours of the ancient shrine. As soon as the Jeep stopped, Aleta woke up, her eyes darting back and forth. Realizing they were finally there, she nudged Sarah, who woke up slowly. They gathered what they were taking and headed down to the visitor's office where they expected to see at least a few more people. The tour guide's booth was empty, and no one could be seen anywhere. Since no signs dissuaded them from proceeding, Danelos just kept walking down the path that led to the site. He hadn't been here in quite some time, but some of the landmarks were familiar. This area had lush vegetation and trees covering somewhat rocky terrain, but

197

time had changed some of it; tourism had done the rest. It was a short walk to the main site, and they didn't seem to be in any hurry to get there. A cloudless sky hung over them, embracing them. Ouranos was long gone, but his gift to Humankind remained.

The earth started to tremble, shaking loose rocks and stone fragments all round them. Clouds of dust rose up, and small cracks appeared in the ground. To stay together, they grabbed onto each other, but Sarah lost her footing and fell. Covering her head with her arms, she prayed that the tremors would stop. Dust coated her mouth and her nostrils, and she couldn't see the others. As mysteriously as the shaking started, it stopped. Quickly assessing the area, she saw Brandon crouching down a few feet from her, and Danelos and Aleta were kneeling on the ground about ten feet away, but everyone seemed to be all right.

"Everybody good?" Brandon shouted, coughing from the dust. He went over to see how Sarah was doing.

"Yea, just peachy," Aleta answered, wiping her hands on her pants. Danelos seemed okay, but he had not stood up or moved.

"Dan, you okay?" Brandon put his hand on Danelos's shoulder.

"Yeah. Give me a second." He leaned over, his hands on the ground, staring at the earth.

He reached up; Brandon grabbed his wrist and slowly helped him to stand, and then supported his elbow.

"I'm fine. Thanks, Brandon."

"What happened?" Sarah asked, lightly touching his arm.

"I'm not sure. I think I just breathed in some of the dust. I just can't believe there was an earthquake. Hasn't been one in central Greece in a long time."

A few minutes later, he seemed fine, so he continued walking down the path. Once they were within view of the shrine, Danelos stopped short. A fissure, about ten feet long and six inches wide in the middle crossed their path, no doubt from the earthquake, a yellow serpentine mist rising into the air. As if in pain, Danelos dropped to his knees, his face right in the middle of the mist and screamed, his voice echoing throughout the countryside. This time the others didn't move. Danelos's screaming died down, and he lifted his face skyward while outstretching his arms. He started muttering incoherent phrases and making grand gestures with his hands. Images flooded his mind, cascading together and merging, then diverging away. First, he saw a starry sky, pierced by a sword of gleaming gold, and then images of the sun and the earth colliding, exploding into tiny pieces. The next image was a collage of the sky again, but with twelve bright stars, surrounding an eagle. The last image showed a military-type insignia surrounded by a whirlwind of fire and water. The images stop abruptly, causing Danelos to lurch backward. Swimming back through a sea of awareness, he sat up, and within moments, he was fine, as if nothing had happened. Brandon and the others were looking at him, and he could see their fear. Brushing himself off, he stood.

Brandon asked, "What the hell was that?" as he put a hand on Danelos's shoulder. "You okay now?"

"All I remember was breathing in some of those vapors and then my mind just opened up. All these images and symbols just raged through me. I can't even begin to explain them, but they were bizarre."

"Do you want to go back? Do you need to lie down?" asked Sarah.

"No, really, I'm fine."

"Danelos, we don't know what those vapors were or if they were poisonous. Maybe we should get you to a doctor. This can wait."

"Aleta, really, I'm fine. My head's clearing. If you guys want to continue, I'm game," he replied.

Brandon shrugged and said, "If the man is game, then so am I." He started to walk down the path.

"Girl, this is too strange, but I'll be damned if I know what's going on," Aleta remarked to Sarah, both trying to keep up with Danelos.

"Here's an interesting archaeological fact for you," started Danelos, "Some say that the stone at Delphi, the *Omphalos*, is the same one which the Titan Kronos regurgitated when Zeus gave him a potion designed to make him throw up the children he had eaten whole. In ancient times, people considered the stone the center of the world and the priests would anoint it with oil daily. In modern times, Delphi holds no real significance except to those archaeologists or historians, like me, who the legend captivates. This shrine is also sacred to Gaea and some believe that those who worship the earth are doubly blessed with prophetic visions from the sibyl of Apollo."

"Sibyl?"

"Sorry, Sarah," he smiled. "A sibyl was a priestess who sat on a tripod stool over a crack in the earth from which these hallucinogenic vapors rose. She would inhale the vapors, chew on a laurel leaf, and some believed she would see prophetic visions from Apollo. Then, an oracle would decipher the visions and give them to whoever sought the prophecy."

"Forgive me for pointing out the obvious, but didn't you see visions after breathing some vapors from that crack back there?" asked Aleta.

Danelos chuckled. "Yea, I did. But I'm not a sibyl, or an oracle. That was just a freak happening."

Aleta smirked.

The site was within view, and Danelos again stopped, but this time he only paused a moment and then moved on. His eyes were playing tricks on him, though. He stopped again, staring straight ahead.

"*Pros Theôn...*" he uttered.

"Excuse me?" Aleta asked.

"'By the gods', but that was ancient Greek, and I don't know that much of it, except what I read off archaeological finds. I saw something up ahead, and my mouth just uttered those words. Maybe I heard the phrase somewhere," he said, trailing off. He thought the vapors might be making him hallucinate, but he remained quiet about it.

"If I didn't know any better, I'd expect to hear Rod Serling about now," replied Aleta, waving her arms.

Danelos fixed his gaze again on the path before them, and his amazement came out in English this time. "Do you all see that?" he asked, pointing toward the site of Delphi.

"All I see are some trees and ruins. Why, what do you see?"

"Brandon, would you believe me if I told you I don't see ruins. I see Delphi."

"I think those vapors are still affecting him," Aleta muttered to Sarah.

Danelos quickened and stopped before a dirt path adorned with shattered marble and stone. "This is not possible," he uttered, "How would you explain this?"

"Explain what, Dan? All we see are crumbled columns. Exactly what do you see?" asked Brandon, worried that Danelos's encounter with the vapors was more than he claimed.

"A bull. A bronze bull. Over there, can't you see it?"

"They're coming take you away, ha ha," sang Aleta.

"I'm not crazy! I see it standing before me like I see you," Danelos retorted. "Come here, Sarah, take a look at this." He reached his hand back and found Sarah's hand. "Don't you see the bull?"

Sarah blinked a few times, and then smiled like someone under the influence of a drug. Aleta and Brandon approached them warily.

"What do you see, Sarah? Ruins, right?"

201

"I…I don't know… Wait. Aleta, I do see something… like an image coming into focus. Yes. Yes, I do see a bull!" she shrieked, "Holy… I can see it. Come here, guys," she said, gripping Brandon's arm.

Brandon squinted a moment, and then his whole face changed. "Uh, I see it too," he replied, "This is… this is amazing. Are we high or something? Maybe we all breathed in those vapors."

Aleta walked closer to Danelos, but kept her distance.

"Is this a joke?" she asked, but replacing her normal humor was an underlying quivering.

He held out his hand without taking his eyes of the sight before him. With trepidation, she placed her hand in his. Her brown eyes widened, at first with shock, and then with pleasant amazement.

"This is Delphi as it was in my ancestors' time," muttered Danelos, who walked down the clearly marked path of the Sacred Way. Still connected, they passed the Korkyran bull, which glistened in the sunlight, and they gawked at two semi-circular monuments on either side of the path—one honoring the Seven Epigonoi, the seven offspring of those who fought at Thebes, and the other the Monument of the Kings. Further on the left sat the Sikonian Thesauros, a treasure house, in all its glory of Doric style. High up to the right sat the pinnacle of the path—the Temple of Apollo—but they would reach it soon enough. As they proceeded, their eyes stayed affixed on the shimmering marble and stone. If they were indeed hallucinating, then it was a most pleasant one. As the path turned to the right, they saw the *Omphalos*, the navel of the world that the priests anointed with holy oil. Just past the navel sat the Thesauros of the Athenians and then the Bouleuterion, where the members of the Delphic Parliament had had their meetings. At the center of the holy ground of Gaea rested the Sibylline Rock where the first soothsayer supposedly had given the first oracles to Gaea. A bit further was the sacred fountain that Python guarded before Apollo slew it. A smaller rock, the Stone of Leto, sat beyond the sibyl's rock. Some said that Leto sat here with her son Apollo and urged him to slay Python. The Naxian Sphinx, that guarded the path, sat high atop its column. The bright beams of the sun shined through the columns of the shrine of Apollo casting shadows that seemed to dance on the ground below. Danelos, almost in tears, led his friends up the path, pointing out the Stoa of the Athenians, a covered walkway adorned with columns on the outside and a wall on the inside.

No one said a word, except Danelos, since they all began to see this anachronistic mirage. If it weren't for their walking, they would look almost statue-like themselves, since they uttered no sounds. Up on the right sat the Serpent Column, something that made them all gasp. The column showed three marble snakes intertwined all the way to the top, where a golden cauldron sat. Strangely enough, flames flickered in the cauldron—the first appearance of anything remotely living also being there with them. Danelos was more aware of his stampeding heartbeat. The others gripped one another tighter as they had to look up to see the top of the pediment stretched across the entrance of the temple. With each calculated step, they made their way to the sacred shrine of Apollo. The four separated, but their perception remained. Danelos unknowingly bowed his head upon entering. The floor, a shimmering marble, was vacant except for a large throne that sat at the far end and a hestia, or hearth, situated in the center. Six feet across and unmarred by ash or flame, it glowed slightly, as if embers still burned within it. Their steps echoed ominously as they examined the majestic ceiling and columns, which by all rights should have been dust. Like gentle fingers, a warm breeze caressed them and carried the perfume of laurel and fir. Danelos walked over to the hestia and noticed the wood was almost used up. Walking a few steps around, he saw a few pieces of laurel wood, picked them up, and tossed them on the dying embers. A column of flame erupted from the pit, almost touching the ceiling, and a wave of heat knocked Danelos to the floor, dazed.

"You know," Sarah started, trying to help Danelos to sit up, "this would all be so much easier if we knew what the hell we were doing here."

"I hear that," replied Aleta, "this defies a whole list of scientific laws, never mind logic. I don't suppose one of those visions you had could help explain this?"

Danelos was about to speak, but he smelled that familiar odor of the mist he had encountered earlier. On the other side of the temple, wisps of smoke curled up toward the ceiling, but someone was there. He didn't know how, but he could sense it. Seated on a golden tripod over a crack in the marble floor was a cloaked figure whose head was down. Muttering escaped from the covered head in words and phrases, but certainly not in English, or in any form of Greek Danelos had heard. As he moved closer to the figure, seemingly a woman, he realized that the smoke didn't bother him as it had earlier. Perhaps he was used to it. Next to the tripod sat a painted pot with a laurel tree growing from it, and a hand wrapped in cloth pulled a leaf from the tree and put it under the hood. While this woman chewed the leaf, the muttering grew louder while her exhaled breath scattered the mist.

"That *is* ancient Greek," Danelos thought. "But, what is she saying?"

The others followed behind him, since he seemed to know what he was doing. As soon as Danelos was within arm's reach, the woman lifted her head, still muttering. The more she said, the more he understood. Sarah reached up to his arm,

"What's she saying?" she whispered.

204

Not taking his eyes off the woman, he now deduced she had to be the Delphic Oracle. At some point, he realized she was repeating herself, so he turned toward the others and gestured for something to write with, but he didn't speak; he mumbled words to himself just the Oracle was. Sarah handed him a cell phone, and he tapped out a text message of what he heard as quickly as he could before he became more confused. Smoke rose, giving the air around them a greenish haze, but only Danelos and the Oracle seemed affected by it. Afraid to move, Aleta just made eye contact with Brandon and Sarah, but their expression was the same—what was happening?

Twenty minutes passed, and Danelos finally turned toward his companions.

"Okay, I think I have it."

"Have what?" Aleta asked.

"A prophecy. Our prophecy. The one Ananke told us about."

Sarah's confusion spread to the others. "So... what did she say?"

"I'll translate the best I can, but we've heard some of this before," Danelos replied.

*"Four not born of godly word*
*Two of vessel, two of sword,*
*Keep vigil over Gaea's kin*
*From Keto's progeny within.*
*Lead day's darkness to finds its path*
*Let spirit restore balance without wrath.*
*Four for Gaea, four must be,*
*For being lacks uncertainty."*

"Well, that clears things up, doesn't it," Aleta smirked.

"I'm just repeating what she said. It doesn't really help, does it?"

Making their way back toward the Jeep, the Oracle uttered more that the others would never hear,

*"Now with words released, the augury takes hold,*

205

*That which was kept at bay may now unfold,*
 *Portals work both ways, doors to one, doors to all,*
*Powers of the past who heed the call,*
*Fate's loomed path leads to dark unknown,*
*For seeds of the future have yet to be sown.*
*Four must prepare, four fight the past*
*Or nothing more in this world will last."*

Mist rose up and swirled around them, blinding them from each other, and when it dissipated, they found themselves at the base of the ruins of Delphi, a Delphi long since eroded through time and the elements. In the air, a Delphic whisper escaped the temple— "*Hoi theoi humas fulasoien.*" 'May the gods protect you'. Silence enveloped the ride back to the hotel, although they had much to discuss, and the plane ride back was the same. Too much to understand, too quickly. Mortal minds needed time to adjust to otherworldly events, although many of these ideas cross over into dreams and fantasies. Unfortunately, time was one thing that never truly stopped, and it did not bind prophecies. Like it or not, the events of the ancient past would affect the present, and these four would have to be ready. They had no choice.

# 19—CONTROLLING DESTINY

**KALW (San Francisco)** "For WPR News, this is Michael Harris in San Francisco. Firefighters had to work through the night putting out a raging fire at Mitchell Matthews High School when lightning struck the science wing late last night during a massive thunderstorm. The fire spread throughout the building due to a fuel leak in the heating system, and Governor Adams had to call in Task Force: Alpha to assist. Task Force agents helped get the fire under control within an hour, minimizing the damage to the rest of the building. Witnesses claim the storm formed quickly, almost unnaturally, and disappeared almost as quickly."

• • •

Three months later.

Drawn from its scabbard, the sacred blade screamed, golden Earthsteel glistening in the Atlantic moonlight. The two-headed creature was scarcely noticeable in the darkness and Danelos' hands, one above the other, gripped the hilt until he felt the etched metal dig into his palms, his heart beating in his head that seemed to pulse into the sword, bringing it to life. As the furry form maneuvered over the grassy field, its guttural growl portended an inevitable confrontation, but Danelos' instincts were blind to the signal. Such was the nature of the beast to generate confusion right before it struck. In the gauzy darkness, that dangerous time of twilight when human eyes scarcely perceive, a serpentine hiss hovered around them. From deep within the obscurity struck a snakehead with fangs that Danelos quickly deflected with his sword. Before he could find his bearings, again the head lurched forward. It didn't want to attack him directly; if it had, it would have aimed at a more vulnerable place. These lunges were tactical—this creature wanted to know exactly where it could strike with its jaws, two sets, and fangs oozing caustic venom that would dissolve steel. For some reason, this monster showed up in Bar Harbor, Maine of all places, but where the portals existed, these monsters tended to appear. Danelos had managed to lure it into an uninhabited area, but he didn't know how long that would last. If it had the capacity to strategize, it could lure him somewhere more populated, endangering innocent lives. He'd have to vanquish this thing and do it with minimal loss.

A whistling sound approached, and a boulder, no doubt thrown by the serpent-like tail, hurtled toward Danelos. He jumped out of its path, swinging the blade down, slicing the rock in two just as it reached him, both stony halves plummeting to the ground like a marionette with its strings severed.

"So, this is how you want to play," muttered Danelos.

Another smaller rock came careening at him, and it, too, met the same fate. Following that, a cement chunk sailed toward him, but he dispatched it as well.

"Bring it," Danelos announced, flipping the blade around.

With that, five other rocks, unearthed by the massive paws, flew at him at once, all but one falling to the ground in pieces having been kissed by Earthsteel. The last boulder hit him square in the chest, knocking the wind from him and sending him back fifteen feet while the animal moved closer. Regaining his composure, but thrown off a bit by the proximity to his adversary, Danelos leaped to his feet, sheathed his sword, and darted into a park surrounded by trees, careful to look for bystanders. This time, when the boulder came toward him, no sword in hand, he instinctively threw up his left arm to shield his face and the stone shattered into dust.

"That'll work, too," he said to himself. The manacle had created an invisible shield.

As the dust cleared, all he could see was a massive oak trunk, bitten off toward the base, cast toward him. He knew this wouldn't be pretty. Again, the sword came free from its sheath, just in time to come crashing down on the trunk, slicing it in half lengthwise. A second oak knocked Danelos to the ground. Teeth gritted, he threw the tree back. A third collided with it, splintering both. Intuitively, he gave himself enough room to maneuver. As the last tree whistled closer, he jumped into the air, knowing he wouldn't get a good angle to use the sword, and he hoped the manacle would do what it had done before. The impact pulverized the tree as it struck his invisible shield, something he would have to ask Hephæstos about at some point, but knocked him down.

The four-legged assailant finally stepped into the moonlight, and Danelos recognized it as Orthros, a sibling to Cerberos. One of Hades' hounds. Excellent, he thought. Fiery eyes flared in the darkness. At such close range, the confusion Orthros generated took Danelos off guard, and this time when the serpent tail lunged, it headed for the throat. A swift move of his left arm placed his manacle in the way, and the fangs bounced off Earthsteel with a clang. Recoiling, the snakehead bit Danelos' wrist, immobilizing it long enough to stagger him. Both feral dog heads reached out to snatch a bite, but they snapped shut just shy of his torso. Even though the manacle was unbreakable, he felt the pressure applied by snake jaws as well as a burning sensation from where drops of venom dripped down his arm. If he was going to free himself, it had to be soon before he couldn't concentrate.

This time, when a mouth attacked him, he kicked it back, enabling his sword arm to come down on the snout, breaking the grip on his wrist. Orthros didn't like having his muzzle smacked, and a louder growl signaled a change in strategy. Danelos stepped back a bit to survey the scene just in time to see the dog leaping for him. Taking a firm grasp of his sword, he jumped forward stabbing upward into the chest. Momentum kept Orthros' body moving as the sword ripped through his abdomen. Crashing to the ground, its innards hanging free, the underworld canine attempted to get to its feet, but he couldn't get enough strength to push his body up. Sidestepping clear of the frothing mouths, Danelos stood behind them as swung down hard, severing them from their necks, silencing Orthros.

"Back to Hades, mutt," he uttered as he watched the creature melt into gelatinous ooze and get absorbed back into the earth.

He sat on a bench a few feet away from the dead grassy patch where the hellish hound once lay.

His sword back in its shoulder sheath, both became invisible. His chest still ached from when the rock hit him, but he would heal. He wondered how the others were faring, no doubt engaged in similar skirmishes. While he regained his breath, Danelos' mind wandered back to when he had come to be fighting underworld dwellers.

• • •

After he returned from Greece with Brandon, Sarah, and Aleta, fitful dreams plagued Danelos. Every night, he writhed in sweat-drenched sheets, only to wake in the morning both physically and mentally exhausted. Jumbled visions of a mirror reflecting a crown, monstrous creatures, and scattered memories of a place he had never

seen flew through his mind; he also saw skeins of wool
unfurling into piles of string that melted into pools of
darkness. He had tried sleeping aids and even a doctor's
visit for his nightmares, but nothing helped. He knew it
had some connection to the visit to Delphi, but he couldn't
make sense of it. He hadn't even looked at the prophecy
more than once or twice since he came home. This
problem would soon rectify itself, but not until he
experienced one more night of those lurid dreams, tossing
about, his sheets winding themselves around him and
terrifying images forced upon him. Not even Morpheos
would venture into this territory.

This time, he muttered foreign words, gradually
building to a louder mix of nonsensical sounds. As the
scenes played in his mind, they flashed faster and faster,
until he finally screamed loud enough to shake himself
from his sleep. He sat up, lightheaded, his heart pounding.
His bearings lost, he stopped thrashing to look around,
realizing he had flipped himself around, his head at the end
of the bed. Untangling himself from the web of linen, he
sat on the edge of the bed, hands gripping the edges of the
mattress, as if the mattress was the key to his sanity. In the
haze, he sensed something was different, but he was so
tired from lack of sleep that he simply arranged the sheet
again and fell back against the pillow, hoping to be rid of
the dreams just once. He prayed that he could just have
one night of peace.

A short time later, piercing the window, the sun's rays
burst through like arrows, bathing the room in warm gold.
Danelos gradually awoke, but kept his eyes closed since
opening them would mean he had to face the reality of
actually being awake. The right side of his face warmed,
and something told him that was not right, since his
window was on the left side of the room, but he just
thought he had spun himself around on the bed again. The
breeze through the window didn't smell of car exhaust and

the pretzel vendor at the corner of Commonwealth Avenue and St. Paul Street who always started selling at 6:00 a.m. It smelled of lilac and rose, mixed with a purity he did not recognize. A sense of dread forced itself upon him and he sat up, eyes darting throughout the room, a room that was not his. Sheets of a fabric he had never felt before, softer than silk and of a white that no amount of bleach would produce in his washing machine, covered him. As his eyes scrutinized the room, he saw walls of white stone, perhaps marble, with fluted columns in each corner stretching to the ceiling about twenty feet up. Draping the window was a sheer fabric that puddled on the floor, obscure enough to diffuse the light. No glass prevented the morning breeze from coursing through the window, bringing with it the rose perfume. He peeked under the sheet and realized that, wherever he was, he was naked. His last memory before going to sleep was reading, and he must have dozed off, but he could not find the book in the bed. As each minute passed, he doubted whether he was dreaming more and more.

Wrapping the sheet around him, having seen no trace of his clothes, he opened the strange door and peered down a hall of marble walls divided on each side by more columns. He had not gone ten steps when he heard someone speaking, presumably to him, in a language reminiscent of Greek.

"Halt! Who are you?"

At hearing the man's voice, Danelos started to turn around and threw his hands in the air, dropping the sheet. Now he not only stood in a place he did not know, but he was naked in front of someone he did not know, but who looked like a Greek soldier, wearing armor reminiscent of an ancient time. When Danelos did not reply, the man drew his sword and took on a defensive posture.

"I ask you once more. Who are you?"

When Danelos turned fully around, the soldier lowered and re-sheathed his sword, genuflecting with his face to the floor. He recognized the language as an early form of Greek, but not one he knew well. Maybe this was the dream related to the Delphi prophecy?

"My apologies, Your Highness. You do not normally leave your chamber undressed."

The man remained on one knee, his eyes down, and Danelos did not know what to say. Your Highness? Who did this man think he was? Thinking quickly, he wondered if the Greek he spoke would be enough for this man to understand. He thought it best to speak in short sentences.

"It's all right. No harm done. You may go."

"As you wish," the soldier replied, his eyes averted as he rose, and departed, almost running.

Danelos could not believe it worked. Surely the Greek he spoke was not the same dialect the soldier knew. Perhaps the man did not question someone obviously of a higher station. Nevertheless, he needed to find out what was happening to him. Ripping a hole in the sheet to put his head through, he snatched a piece of curtain cording from against the wall and fashioned a makeshift tunic, hoping it would be enough to keep him out of further trouble. After his visit from Ananke and the Delphic Oracle, he didn't know what to expect. A few hallways later, he stumbled across a chamber guarded by two lieutenants, spears in hand. His ears were ringing, and he realized that was his heart beating. Getting as close as he could to the door without being noticed, he tried to listen to the voices he heard within. The same dialect of Greek, he thought, but not as recognizable, probably because they were speaking more softly or just more quickly. Danelos knew his only chance of finding out where he was would be to enter that room, but he was not only unarmed, but also unprepared for what to say as his excuse. Hoping the

Greek he knew would do the job, he was ready to address the soldiers, but they saw him first.

"Good day, Your Highness. The captain of the guard is expecting you."

Oh good, he thought. Even more madness to endure. How could he pull off being this person? But, who was he being confused with?

"Forgive me, Prince Demetrios, but what are you wearing? Is that a bed sheet tied with a curtain cord?" asked the lieutenant, trying to keep from smiling.

"You question me?" barked Danelos, starting to become accustomed to this role he now had to play. He now knew he was mistaken for royalty. That might help later on.

Having realized he had overstepped his bounds, the soldier resumed his stance by the door, moving his gaze from the man he assumed was his prince.

"Of course not, Your Highness."

"As you were."

Glaring at the sentry, Danelos walked through the door and felt like he wanted to vomit, disbelieving he had been able to somehow convince that soldier he was this Demetrios. With walls draped in jewel tone fabrics of deep red, purple, and blue, adorned with gold and silver ornaments, and a polished marble floor, the room staggered his mind. His eyes followed a purple carpet to a dais on which sat two ornately carved thrones, both white marble and Earthsteel. A wine-colored mantle lay on one throne while one of spun silver sat on the other. Behind these enormous chairs, on the wall, was a golden disk surrounded by a circle, a stylized sun, its gold and silver rays of different lengths. Bewildered, Danelos didn't hear someone walk up behind him.

"I was beginning to wonder if you would rise before the sun set."

214

Turning around quickly, he realized almost instantly that this man before him was no one to mess with, a bronze xiphos hanging at his side. Standing about his height, the soldier wore leather armor, pteruges, and greaves. He held his helmet, with white plume, against his side. For some reason, Danelos couldn't help but feel this man looked familiar.

"Are you well, Demetrios? You seem a bit pale. And strangely attired."

"Yes. Yes, I'm fine. I was having some disturbing dreams which kept me up most of the night."

"Perhaps we can get a sleeping draught for you from the chemist? Olympos knows how much dreams can drain a man's faculties."

"No, that won't be necessary." He was beginning to feel more comfortable, but he didn't know the name of the soldier. Was he the captain of the guard?

"I came to see you about the troop exercises, since we agreed to meet again after you had taken some time to look at my plans. What do you think?"

Now he was stuck. What could he say that would appease this man, the man who had the power to dismember him? Surely, the soldier would realize that he was not the prince at some point. A voice from behind him saved him from answering, but it also added a new level of intrigue.

"Yes, what *do* you think? Apparently, my captain has mistaken you for me," the man said.

The soldier drew his sword, taking a defensive stance to protect his prince.

"Who are you? Identify yourself!" he announced, ready to strike.

Danelos held his hands up. "I—I'm Danelos Fairmont. I don't know why I'm here. I woke up in a different place, with no memory of how I got here. Is that sword really necessary?"

"Lykaon, stand down. I sense he is not here to hurt me." Demetrios was shielding the truth, but he wasn't sure himself what the entire truth was.

The captain of the guard reluctantly resheathed his weapon but stayed between Danelos and his prince.

"Leave us, Captain. I can take it from here."

Demetrios gestured for Danelos to sit. "Tell me, Danelos Fairmont, how exactly did you find your way here?"

"I told you. I was asleep, or trying to sleep anyway. When I woke up, I was apparently in your room. Where exactly is here, anyway?"

Demetrios leaned against the marble table leaving a short distance between him and his guest. Leave your adversary an out, he thought. If he felt trapped, he might react rashly.

"I am Demetrios, prince of Arkadeia, son of Apollo and Alkinoë. Dreams have great power, and it would seem they moved you here from where you are from. Just where would that be?"

"Boston. Boston, Massachusetts. I'd venture to guess that you don't know where that is."

Another man's voice broke in near the entrance to the chamber. "He wouldn't know it, but I would."

"Father," said Demetrios, bowing. "This is…"

"Danelos. Yes, I know who he is. Welcome to Arkadeia. I suppose the time has come, hasn't it. The Fates do like to weave, do they not?"

The Fates, Danelos thought. More than one?

"You know this man?" Demetrios asked.

"In a manner of speaking, but that's a matter for later. Demetrios, let me speak with Danelos alone."

Bowing again, the prince took his leave.

"So, I understand you've been to Delphi. Mind-numbing place, isn't it? That whole leaf chewing idea wasn't mine. Have you made any sense of the prophecy?"

"Wait. You know about that? And, no, we haven't."

Apollo smiled. "You will… in time. Yes, I know about that. That temple is mine, after all."

Apollo watched as the revelation finally hit Danelos.

"Apollo?"

"Yes. After you met with Ananke, we felt your presence stronger in the *Oikoumene Broteios*. That prompted your visit to Delphi, and your dreams that brought you here."

"Oikou…"

"It means 'the inhabited mortal world'. I have much to tell you, but not much time to do it, I'm afraid."

Apollo knew if he told Danelos too much, he would overwhelm him, even though that wouldn't last long, but sometimes too much knowledge at once could be debilitating. He managed to explain about Nyx, the Scales, and the two looms. Then, he explained the *Ge Theôn* and *Oikoumene Broteios*, but leaving out that the latter realm contained a copy of everyone in the former. Explaining that would be too much information for Danelos, and he might hesitate. Afterward, after the task was complete, he would explain everything.

"Let's assume what you say is true, and you are who you say you are. Prove it, then. I'm a man of science and data. Show me some empirical data."

"How would you propose I do that?" Apollo asked.

"I don't know. I'd ask you to prove to me that you're Apollo, but according to legend, if a god revealed his true form, a mortal would die from seeing such raw power."

"Quite true. Poor Semele learned that the hard way. Dionysus still has issues with Zeus about it. I do have a way I can show you without endangering your life."

Apollo poured some wine into two goblets while he was speaking and casually handed one to Danelos, both drinking a little. Hospitality—*xenia*—was paramount.

217

They left the palace on foot, taking a garden path alongside the building about two hundred yards just south toward the stables. Two sentries opened the thirty-foot, ornately carved wooden doors for them, closing them after Apollo and his guest entered.

"There must be dozens of horses here," remarked Danelos, as he looked as far as he could down the row of stalls lining both sides of the building. A pungent aroma of animal and manure lingered.

"Hundreds," said Apollo, continuing down the corridor.

After they passed through the main stable, they exited the back of the building and continued toward a marble structure of similar build. The doors, intricately carved gold, bearing a half of a sun emblem on each side, parted for Apollo as he went within a few feet of them. Danelos noticed no smell of horse or manure here, but did hear neighing in the back stall. Shadows cast on the walls, from what seemed to be flickering fire, caught his attention. As they reached the stall entrance, Danelos felt beads of sweat down his back as the heat grew more intense. A constant, heavy heartbeat pounded in his chest, but he couldn't tell if it were nervousness or his body reacting to the scorching heat.

"Perhaps this will be the proof you require," commented Apollo, pointing at two fiery stallions, seven feet from hoof to the top of their heads. "These are Lampos and Actaeon, two of the steeds who drive the chariot of the sun."

Helios had long since retired from this task, so he gave his own mounts to Apollo so that he could use them to drive the sun across the heavens. Æthion, 'he who is fiery red', Asterope, 'he of the starry eyes', Bronte, 'he who is thunder', and Phlegon, 'he who is the burning' drove the chariot most often. Other horses resided in the Olympian stables, since having too many fiery steeds in Arkadeia would put the people in danger should the horses get loose. Danelos, mesmerized by the flickering of their manes, started to believe Apollo, but what he did next would confirm his beliefs.

"Would you like to touch them?" Apollo asked. "Normally, any mortal merely walking through the door of this stable would be incinerated, hence why no guards stand by the doors, but I added something to the wine, a bit of ambrosia, so that you might have this opportunity, but only for a few moments."

Danelos locked eyes with Apollo. The food of the gods, he thought.

"Yes. Come now. Step forward slowly. Start with Lampos as he is less temperamental."

Danelos approached the horses who, sensing a stranger, neighed wildly for a moment, but soon calmed when they realized their master was allowing this mortal man to come near them. Unsure, Danelos reached up and gently touched Lampos' neck, barely grazing the hair, then becoming more confident, he stroked the iridescent mane a little more firmly. The sensation felt like running one's hand through frayed cotton threads, but warmer. Much warmer. Lampos marked his approval by stamping his front hooves in succession a few times and nodding his head. It seemed as if the horse knew him. Actaeon stepped forward and poked his nose under Danelos' other arm, lifting it over his neck, so that both horses had the experience of being touched by a mortal man for the first time.

"We should go. The ambrosia will wear off soon, and we have much to discuss. Plus, you are completely drenched in your own sweat," Apollo said. "All right, boys, you have had your fun. Now, my friend and I must take our leave of you, but I will return later."

Convinced of Apollo's claim, Danelos walked away reluctantly, wishing he could spend just a few more moments with those amazing creatures. Once they left the stables, the cooler air dried his body and brought his temperature back to normal levels. No words could possibly express what he was thinking at that moment or what he could ever tell anyone of this experience. Part of him knew that he would never be able to share this, and he was actually glad of that. The walk back to the palace seemed to take less time, probably because Danelos was lost in thought the entire way, not paying as much attention to the countryside as he had upon his arrival. To avoid unnecessary attention, Apollo silently transformed Danelos' makeshift garb into something more fitting, the latter not being the wiser. Arriving at the palace, two sergeants flanking the doors saluted and bowed to their king and the man who they perceived as their prince. Carved in each door was half a sun so that, closed, showed a royal seal: a sun with gilded rays streaming forth surrounding a raised spherical shape.

"Danelos, come sit. I have more to tell you. It will seem superfluous later, but now, I need to explain. Gaea and I created the Arkadeian people a millennia ago, and they exhibit attributes from both of us—they are healers, lovers of music, and archers. They hold reason and truth above all else, and they draw forth strength from the earth itself, making them physically more capable than an average mortal. Only a few other races, namely the Amazons of Themiskyra or the Myrmidones of Thessaly, equal them in sheer force. In addition, they are not bound by mortality. In this *Ge Theôn*, they don't grow old as quickly, nor do they die naturally, but they can be killed. As children of a *Protogenos* and an Olympian god, they have been given privileges that other races do not enjoy, namely they have been trained by my sister, Athene, in battle skill and strategy, and many of them have fought wars against demons from Tartaros alongside heroes like Odysseus and Achilles. They worship the entire pantheon of gods, but Gaea and I are their patron gods. The only reason I am not on Olympos now is because I wish to groom Demetrios to reign over Arkadeia."

"What about Demetrios' mother, Alkinoë? Is she here?"

Apollo's face darkened. He couldn't tell him the truth. Not yet. As a god of truth, it physically hurt him to keep this knowledge from Danelos. He wouldn't lie, though.

"She no longer resides in Arkadeia."

Danelos knew better than to press the issue.

"So, Apollo, what else do you want me to know? I feel like I have learned so much already, but I'd like to know when I eventually go back home. I will go back, yes?"

"Yes, you will most certainly go back. But, I will tell you more later. Come, let me show you around the city."

A perfunctory outing, Apollo knew deep down this was all so unnecessary, but it had to be done. All throughout the city, Danelos asked questions, but some of this city seemed so familiar to him. He chalked it up to his visits to Greece in some of the villages that still had agoras, or markets. It dawned on him that Apollo had no problem passing him off as his son, the prince, but he felt uncomfortable being that recognized. Touring the temples, Apollo pointed him toward the Temple of Gaea, the highest place in Tegea, and the Shrine of the Fates at the furthest part of town, separated from all the other temples. Danelos didn't understand why Apollo kept referring to the Fates in the plural; he only knew of Ananke from all the stories he had heard and the myths he had read as a child.

Before returning to the palace, they walked by the proving grounds where Arkadeian soldiers trained ten hours a day, mastering such skills as swordplay, archery, and hand to hand combat. Demetrios had engaged a friend in some sparring, using quarterstaffs, and he moved so fluidly that Danelos couldn't help but stare and smile.

221

Apollo caught his companion's expression and realized time was a crucial adversary here. After the prince defeated his sparring partner, he saw his father and Danelos.

"Care to engage me?" Demetrios asked, wiping the sweat from his brow as he walked over.

Danelos took up a staff, more because he didn't want to insult the prince than actually knowing how to use it. Demetrios took it easy on his new partner at first, measuring out his skill. He could tell Danelos had done some martial arts training, but he wasn't a finely tuned Arkadeian warrior. Three swift moves and Danelos was on his back, the prince's foot on his chest.

"It's time, isn't it, brother?" a female voice said from behind Apollo, who never took his eyes off the two men.

"Yes. As soon as they have finished, you may take him. He has to know what to do."

"Of course. Wisdom and fate deem it so."

Three more matches finished, and Danelos, covered in dirt and sweat, returned to Apollo and his companion. Something about the woman made Danelos avert his eyes.

"Well played, Danelos. My son would make a warrior of you yet."

"I think that pleasure belongs to me," smiled the woman, her grey eyes glimmering in the daylight.

Garbed in silver armor, a snake-frilled metallic cloak around her neck, clasped with a snake-haired woman's face, she stood as tall as Apollo, but she seemed taller. Not far, perched on an oak branch, an owl sat surveying the landscape.

"Danelos, my sister has taken an interest in training you. She senses you have potential."

Nodding mechanically, understanding who she was, he took Athene's hand, and the two melted into the breeze. Demetrios, engaged with a new partner, grinned as he knew what that training entailed. Apollo's austere expression became softer once he realized what would happen. *The Fates must be served*, he thought. *Only then will prophecy become truth.*

• • •

A fortnight passed in Arkadeia, and the day had come when threads of destiny woven so long ago would see their fruition. Apollo and Demetrios visited with dignitaries from Euboea, hoping to draw up a trade agreement; after Herakles dispatched Pyraekhmes, the king of Euboea, the son of Zeus helped the king's son, Nestor, establish a stronger monarchy for the island. Nestor decreed no horses could live on the island, however, since Pyraekhmes' own steeds had ripped him apart. Loyalties came at a price, though, and Apollo decided it would be better to find a price amenable to Nestor in order to engage in commerce. In his peripheral vision, Apollo noticed an owl perched in a high window, but he didn't hear it arrive.

Oaken doors carved with intricate designs burst open and an armor-clad man entered, a silver helmet with a white plume shielding his identity. Apollo thought the man looked familiar, but he seemed almost bigger. Lykaon went to draw his sword, but the man removed his helmet, revealing a familiar, yet altogether different, face. One doesn't train with Athene without taking some innocence from her pupil.

"Danelos!" exclaimed Demetrios, embracing his look-alike. "Welcome back to Tegea."

"It's good to see you, too, Your Highness," Danelos replied, surprised by this show of emotion from someone of such high station.

"It would seem your training went well. I almost did not recognize you."

Danelos would not have recognized himself if he had seen himself in a mirror. Not only was he a better fighter and strategist, but he also had put on some muscle. He had worked out back in Boston, but what he had just experieneced made his gym days look like child's play. A royal feast welcomed Danelos back, and the whole city rejoiced. Apollo wanted the spectacle and the mirth since he knew what would come. Returning from such a divine encounter was a glorious event, worthy of wine and song. Into the late hours they celebrated, Danelos sharing his experience with the soldiers, who now looked upon him with reverence and camaraderie.

A few hours before sunrise, Danelos, who in his drunken stupor had managed to remove the silver armor but had fallen asleep in his leather armor, was awakened by a noise in the throne room, prompting him to grab his sword. Only a few torches lit the hall, since the revelers had left to go back to their homes, so he had the advantage of stealth on his side to see who or what had caused the disturbance. His training had awakened something in him that he had never experienced before, a sense of awareness. No one guarded the throne room. Odd, he thought, since it contained sensitive materials and valuable objects. When he had arrived in Arkadeia, soldiers stood guard at the entrance, unless that they only did so when Apollo or Demetrios were inside. Who would dare skulk around the royal palace? Perhaps Apollo or his son had risen early. In the dimness of the throne room, he saw shadows lurking about, so he stayed close to the wall, hiding behind pillars every few feet. No light might have been an advantage for him in some ways, but it also provided a challenge.

He sensed someone approaching and drew his sword, lunging in the darkness, anxious to use his newly honed skills. With one lucky move, he felt his sword pierce something soft, and then heard a moan as the assailant fell to the floor. By feeling over the body, he learned that this man was masked, so he assumed the others would be as well. His sword guided him throughout the chamber, hoping to catch someone by surprise, but a sharp pain shot

224

through his head as someone hit him with a sword pommel or staff. His blade clanged against the marble floor, certain to scatter the other assailants. Getting his silent wish, a hand-to-hand melee started when two aggressors jumped him. Once he had his bearings, he removed his dagger, sticking it deep into one man's neck, but the man pulled back, taking the dagger with him. He elbowed another man in the face, hearing the nose break, and kicked back, breaking the man's knee. Moonlight started trickling into the windows high above the throne room, casting barely enough light to see by, leaving an owl-shaped shadow on the opposite wall. Danelos found himself in the middle of the room, unprotected by pillars, and swordless. Turning quickly, he pushed his fist into the obscurity, connecting with another body who would no longer have a need for his sword. Armed once more, Danelos heard footsteps in the hall, hoping it was Lykaon or Demetrios with reinforcements, but only saw another figure cloaked in shadow. Without thinking, he spun around, thrusting his sword into the dark. The owl hooted loudly, flapping its wings and flying around the top of the room. In that moment, he knew he had made a grave error and his blood ran cold. All the braziers lit by themselves, bright light exploding into the throne room. He saw three men he did not recognize lying in pools of their own blood, but when he turned toward the door, the figure he saw was not a masked intruder.

"Demetrios! Are you all right? Did I hurt you?" he shouted, running over.

The prince, blood trickling from the side of his mouth, looked up at Danelos.

"Fear not," he coughed, "You did what you were trained to do."

With those words, Prince Demetrios closed his eyes.

225

"No... no... no!" shouted Danelos, trying to stop the flow of blood from Demetrios' chest. How could his training have failed him? How did he not know?

Lykaon burst into the room, and stopped cold when he saw Danelos, covered in blood, leaning over the body. Before the captain could do anything, but sword in hand, a blur and a breeze whirred by, hovering over the body. His winged sandals fluttering faster than the eye could see, the god Hermes motioned his caduceus toward the body of the fallen Arkadeian prince.

"Stop," said Apollo. "That soul is not for you to take, my brother."

Hermes, in his role as *Hermes Psychopompos*, guide of souls, took the spirits of the deceased to the shores of Styx where they awaited transport to the underworld.

"Only Hades or Zeus may stay my hand, Phoebos," replied the messenger god.

A dark cloud seeped through the marble floor, an obsidian smoke, and in its wake stood one of the two gods of which Hermes spoke.

"Heed your brother, Hermes. Prophecy requires the soul of Demetrios."

"As you wish, Lord Hades," said the winged one, bowing in deference to his uncle and fluttering to his brother's side.

Apollo changed his appearance to seem more like a son of Zeus and helped Danelos to his feet.

"Such is the will of the *Moirae*," Apollo began, looking into Danelos' eyes. "He will not be lost to us. Those Sisters who weave the tapestry of life have other plans for my son."

*Again with the plural*, Danelos thought. He couldn't speak. Apollo cleansed him with a gesture, removing all traces of the blood, and put a hand on each of the young man's shoulders.

"You fulfilled part of a greater destiny, Danelos. Now I can tell you everything."

No longer needed, Hades returned to the underworld, but Hermes remained, flitting about like a hummingbird. Apollo took Danelos and sat with him on the steps of the dais.

"I need you to listen carefully. If you remember, I told you about the *Ge Theôn*, the realm of the gods, and the *Oikoumene Broteios*, the inhabited world of mortals. One of the side effects of the Scales being destroyed was that a new loom emerged, weaving entirely new fates for those who lived on Gaea. Since a person cannot live two separate fates, Gaea used great energy to create another earthly plane within which this world could reside. The three *Moirae* spin and tend the original loom here, while Ananke tends the new loom in your world. That's why you question the plurality of the word Fate when you see or hear it. You only know of the one Fate, or Moira—Ananke.

"Where you are now is guided by *Olympos Theôn*, the Olympos of the gods. The world in which you live contains *Olympos Anthropon*, the Olympos of Man. In that realm, the mountain has no godly power, since the gods remained here. Very little of the Olympian magic exists in your world, Danelos. But, unlike the second earthly place Gaea created, there exists only one Hades, Tartaros, Erebos, and so on. Those realms are linked to you're your world and mine."

"I'm beginning to understand," said Danelos. "But, just what does this have to do with me? With my friends? What about Demetrios?"

"I'm getting to that. When the gods learned that humankind was housing two fated souls within one body, the solution was to bring the newer one to the outer world during the Separation of the Souls. Life would continue on as it needed to, except that that world would be devoid of greater Olympian power, since the gods chose to reside here. As a god of prophecy, I understood far more of the future than my fellow gods, so when I had to send the second self of my son, Demetrios, into your world, I had to change things. Alkinoë and I went into that world to accompany Demetrios, to make certain he would find a place in the new existence, but in doing so, my wife had to give up her immortality. When we arrived, it was 1970, and we established human identities to fit in, making a life for ourselves for a while before we decided to deal with Demetrios' other self. I knew of the prophecy that you and your friends learned about, so I had to find a way to work around it."

"Why? Why would our prophecy have anything to do with you, Alkinoë, and Demetrios? What identities did you take?"

"Keep listenining, Danelos. I took Demetrios' soul and implanted it within Alkinoë's womb so she would give birth to a mortal child, since she was now mortal. Shortly after he was born, I had to return here to help groom Demetrios for his eventual kingship of Arkadeia, and because my own Olympian power was waning in the other world."

Danelos' intuition was taking hold. "Apollo. What mortal name did you take? What was your son's name?"

Apollo didn't really have to say anything, since his eyes did it for him.

"Fairmont. You took the name Fairmont, didn't you?"

"And named my son Danelos. Yes, you are Demetrios's other self, born into a mortal body. You are, in fact, my son."

"Now I understand the first line of the prophecy. *Four not born of godly word...* Since I was born a mortal, the prophecy would include me. So, why did I have to kill Demetrios? Isn't he also me?"

"In a way, yes. He is you. An earlier you."

"So, what happens now?"

Hermes, who had been hovering the background, flew over.

"Danelos, my brother wants you to reclaim Demetrios'... your soul. When you do, you will have reclaimed your entire existence. That is why I could not escort Demetrios' soul to the underworld."

"Wouldn't that make me immortal? Doesn't that negate the prophecy? And, if Demetrios was immortal, how was I able to kill him?"

"Think about it," Apollo said.

It took a little while, but Danelos finally realized everything.

"Clever. The prophecy said 'not born of godly word'. I wasn't born immortal, but by claiming Demetrios' soul, I can become one now without having any effect on the prophecy. I still don't understand how I was able to kill Demetrios."

"Arkadeians are immortal, not invulnerable to harm. As my descendents, they would heal from any wound or any disease not immediately fatal," Apollo replied.

Silence dropped like a heavy cloth over them while Danelos processed all that he had learned. He walked over to Demetrios' lifeless body and crouched down.

"How does it work? How do I claim his... my soul?"

Hermes flew over. Touching Demetrios' body with his caduceus, he removed the intangible essence of the Arkadeian prince, and by touching Danelos, Hermes transferred that essence.

"That's it?"

"What were you expecting?" Apollo said. "A flood of memories or emotions? In time, as you adjust to being whole again, you will remember your entire existence. And, since I know you are thinking it, you are Danelos Fairmont, son of Paul and Allison Fairmont. It would be easier to think that you just changed your name, since that is the only part of you that is different from the man you were here."

Apollo approached Danelos with a different look in his eye. Now he could acknowledge his son for who he was. Now the god of truth could embrace the entire truth.

"It goes without saying you'll need time to adjust. You know where to find me now, and I will show you how to return here should you need to do so. But first, I want to show you something," Apollo said. "Take my hand."

As he did, they both appeared in Apollo's shrine in Tegea where a pool of water sprawled before them. It reminded Danelos of the scrying pool around which he and his friends had seen the vision from Ananke.

"Watch closely."

Apollo reached over and touched the water's surface. As the ripples subsided, Danelos saw a familiar place.

"Boston," he whispered. For a moment, he thought he was going home.

"Take a good look at your city. What do you see?"

Danelos watched a busy Commonwealth Avenue, people bustling about and cars in motion. He was ready to reply that he saw nothing out of the ordinary, but slowly his awareness became sharper, assessing the situation as a trained warrior would. Above the clamor of the day to day living, he saw carefully placed cameras attached to the corners of buildings and atop telephone poles. He had always known they were there, but he did not know how many or why. The overall tenor of the city seemed on edge and something was out of alignment, but he did not know what. He sensed an underlying tension emitted by everyone, even though they did not outwardly appear as such.

"You see it, don't you? You sense something isn't quite right."

All Danelos could do was nod, staring into the pool.

"The Scales that Nyx destroyed were not simply ornamental; they were forged in the First Fires, in the heart of Khaos herself. Before all life came this one holy object. Order must balance with Chaos, Danelos. Remember that. Just as scales measure weight, these measure proportion. When one side is tipped, the other side must shift to make a balance. If a great evil is loosed upon the world, eventually a greater good will emerge to create equilibrium. *Isorropia*, Danelos. Without evil, however, good cannot exist, for a scale needs two sides, so when goodness becomes a much greater force, a malevolent evil comes forth again create symmetry.

"The Boston you see is one of many possible cities it could have been. Ever since the destruction of the *Hieros Zugos*, nothing can balance. In your world exist factions of great goodness, or those who would seek to impose order on the chaotic society that has emerged, but—simultaneously—a strong evil is growing with nothing to keep it in check. From that wickedness, prophecy foretells of Gaea being rendered inert because of the greater chaos. What lives in the underworld here can travel to the underworld in your realm. Ekhidna's offspring will keep leaching into a world that cannot fight them because they don't have the means. Eventually, those creatures will destroy that world. If the *Oikoumene Broteios* is destroyed, the *Ge Theôn* would feel the repercussions. Eventually, creation would collapse in on itself. *Isorropia*. Restore the balance, and civilization survives.

"In your world, governments control everything, but put forth a guise of benevolence and concern. Those cameras you see were placed there for your protection, you were told. Concealed agents of various governmental agencies roam cities like Boston, imposing silent martial law. They track everywhere you go, everything you buy, your choice of music, literature... Those cameras and that technology record all of your life. I know this because I

231

have watched mortals and, somehow, they have managed to thrive in a sea of deception and cultural disease. Such is the nature of humanity, flourishing against all odds, a true testament to this Iron Age. I am afraid, however, that your survival will be sorely tested. Danelos, I speak the truth. The *Moirae* weave a delicate tapestry with threads that intertwine. I don't know why you of all people were chosen for this, but I do know that the Fates aren't capricious. You see with new eyes, Danelos. Use that new vision to comprehend what I tell you. Ultimately, you choose."

Danelos uttered, "Two roads diverged in a wood, and I—I took the one less traveled by, and that has made all the difference. I always did like Frost."

With that, he and Apollo vanished.

• • •

"Now what."

Soot covered the entrance to the *Kalkeion Hephaestou*, the forge of Hephæstos, the heat coming forth like hot dragon's breath, although not as hot as the stables of Apollo. Flickering torches lined the walls of the cave and Apollo would not accompany his son into the depths. Echoes of hammer hitting anvil reverberated off the stone, piercing Danelos' ears and filling him with dread as he moved closer to the source. Opening into a cavern, caked with dust and filth, the path became more pronounced with stepping stones crafted from the finest marble.

"May Gaea smile upon you, mortal, since the *Moirae* have not," chuckled Hephæstos, his voice like metal against metal. "Step forward."

Danelos' feet moved slowly as his eyes took in the surroundings. Sparks flew from the forge, showering him with stinging balls of light. He was not aware of the forge god until he stood before the great anvil, some ten feet wide. In his left hand, Hephæstos gripped tongs that held an object in place, and in his right hand, he wielded a hammer worn with use and time, but as powerful as ever. As soon as the hammering stopped, Hephæstos cooled the object in a wooden bucket of water, wisps of steam hissing and snaking into the air, evaporating almost as quickly as they formed. Snatching a buffing cloth from his belt, the god polished the object until it gleamed like a celestial body. Danelos, both dumbfounded and delighted by this experience, broke from his reverie when instructed to stick out his left arm. All at once, Hephæstos firmly held the arm with one hand while placing the manacle on Danelos' wrist with the other. Despite how hot he thought it would be, Danelos was surprised at how cool the band was against his skin.

"Squeeze the band around your wrist," grunted the blacksmith. "The seam will seal itself."

"What is this for?"

"This marks your service to Olympos…and your fate," grumbled Hephæstos. "The next time you see Apollo, ask him about his visit to my forge." He laughed haughtily. "Fettered to the gods. Heh," he muttered.

Intricate markings on the metal dazzled Danelos, but also intrigued him as they were in a language he could barely understand. Ever since he had become an archaeologist, he had become familiar with metals of all sorts, hoping to identify the substance of weapons he would find at digs all over the world. This metallic substance felt light, like aluminum, but Hephæstos informed him that nothing could damage Earthsteel; other gods used the same metal for their weapons. Only two forges could work with such a metal, commented the soot-laden blacksmith, and he wiped down his hammer with a stained cloth before placing it lovingly on its hook on the wall. Danelos didn't think to ask about the other forge. Nodding in uncertain gratitude, he left the cavern, continually glancing down at his wrist. Hermes waited for him, hovering just inches above the dusty earth. Without a

233

word, the messenger god touched his young charge with the winged caduceus, transporting both back to the throne room of the Arkadeian palace. Apollo and Lykaon had patiently waited for Danelos' return.

"You will adjust to that band, my son," said Apollo, unconsciously rubbing his left wrist, remembering the penance he had served not too long ago. "We have other matters to which we must attend."

The sun god walked behind the thrones, knowing Danelos would follow him, and stopped before the wall. Lykaon caught up to them both, anxious to see how events would unfold.

"We must attend to one last task before I can send you back to the *Oikoumene Broteios*," Apollo began. "If you remember, you were the first in command of the Arkadeian army, bestowed upon you on your eighteenth birthday by your mother. Beyond this wall lies your personal armory with weapons you received as gifts from god and mortal alike. One item in particular I want you to have, but you must retrieve it. By lifting this segment of wall, you will gain entrance to the armory where what is now rightfully yours awaits you."

"Lift the wall? I can't do that. I don't even feel stronger than I did before," Danelos replied, shaking his head.

"Put your hands under the bottom of the wall and lift it," Apollo repeated.

Squatting down, Danelos pushed his hands, palm side up, into the thin crack between the wall and the floor. If only to humor Apollo, he pushed up, but nothing happened. A steady look from the sun god persuaded him to try again, this time putting all his energy into it. Sweat trickled down his temples, but, again, nothing happened. He reached back into his memories to a time when he knew how strong he was. Danelos pushed up hard, grunting as he braced his legs. Before he knew what happened, the wall went straight up into the ceiling, cracking the marble doorframe, sending chips of stone flying in all directions. Noticing the damage, he smiled shyly.

"Sorry about that."

Apollo responded, "That is one way to do it."

As the powder cleared, Danelos spotted what lay hidden behind the throne room—his armory. Spears hewn from oak trees and capped with sharp Earthsteel heads stood like a regiment of soldiers along the wall, and shields polished to perfection hung above them. Various suits of armor, leather and metal, stood on rough mannequins, their individual components meticulously laid out, ready for use. Half a dozen bows, also oak, that had seen battle many times before, hung on the wall, their quivers stocked with arrows and suspended alongside them. Each armament was in multiple, all except one. Hanging on two marble pegs directly in front of him was the sword, haughtily suspended in its leather scabbard. Bolted to the marble just above the blade, a metal plate read: *Thyroros*. PortalBearer. A living blade and part of Gaea, the sword radiated palpable power through Danelos. On the scabbard, even the chape, or tip, had ornately etched designs, much like the bulk of the sheath itself. He wrapped his right hand around the hilt, and every battle ever fought with the blade, every monster ever slain with it, every emotion he had ever felt while holding it, he felt in one eternal second. With one smooth motion, the sword came free of the scabbard, a high-pitched ringing sound reverberating off the marble walls.

"Praise Gaea," Danelos said. He remembered the sword.

"Indeed. She forged that blade herself before Hephæstos was born. It stayed in the *adyton* of Gaea deep within Erebos until I needed it to cleanse Arkadeia—"

"And defeat Ares. I remember."

235

Danelos surprised himself with that revelation, more like stating aloud that he remembered his past.

"In the center of the guard, she put a stone she called *Ophthalmos Gaias*—The Eye of Gaea. A stone of cerulean that would link the sword with her power so as long as she, the earth, existed, the sword would be indestructible. She imbued another cerulean stone with *ápeiri̱ órama*—boundless vision—and set it in the pommel of the hilt."

"Boundless vision?"

"You don't remember yet. When light passes through this gemstone, it ignites the power to open a portal into any place the bearer can see in his mind's eye. Simply knowing the place's name could open a portal there. Gaea forged it before all other weapons, so any weapon forged since cannot damage this sword. Furthermore, it is bound to you until your life ends or you pass it on to someone else worthy, and no one else may use the sword against you or use the power it wields to open any portals unless you deem it so, of your free will. This ability enables you to send your adversary to another place, even another time."

Danelos nodded. It was coming back to him a little at a time. To test his memory, he swiped the sword at a column, and it passed right through as if it were water.

"I didn't even feel the metal strike the marble," uttered Danelos, adrenaline coursing through his body.

"Come. Let us return to the throne room. Your time here is coming to an end."

Sliding the sword into its scabbard, Danelos followed Apollo from the armory and into the throne room. A mental gesture on the sun god's part made the severed column complete once more and closed the door, sealing the armory. Danelos had mixed feelings about going back home, although he did want to go; after all, he did have a life in Boston, but this experience had changed his altered perception of reality to the point that he would have to make some changes. Now that he had seen and understood aspects of his real life from an entirely different perspective, he did not know how he could live the lie he had been living. He had known about the surveillance cameras on some level, and he had wondered about other oddities the likes to which he had only given a passing thought, if that, but did not think they would impact his life. Knowing about the scales, however, forced him to think outside the box and accept possible realities. So much of what had transpired was surreal, but in some ways, it was not. It felt right, but he could not understand those feelings, at least not now. Lykaon's farewell to Danelos consisted of a firm handshake, an austere expression, and a "May the gods be with you" before he excused himself to run troop drills. No one had to say anything, but Danelos knew that Lykaon thought of him as a brother, as he did of Lykaon, and the latter had made his peace about the loss of Demetrios, also knowing that Danelos *was* he.

"So much of what you need to know will come to you," began Apollo. "Trust your memory. Remember one other thing: your strength comes from Gaea. Should you separate from her touch, you will lose that strength until you again touch her. Before you leave, do you have any questions? I know I have given you much to ponder and little time to question."

"Actually," Danelos said, "I do. I can't very well carry a sword around in the regular course of my day. Any suggestions? Also, this armband is not exactly discreet."

"As far as the sword, keep it with you at all times. Some will seek you out because of it, and you will need its protection. Only when you remove it from the scabbard will both be visible to you. Once replaced in its sheath, both will become invisible and intangible to others. When you are here, it will always be visible."

"And the armband?" Danelos asked, holding up his wrist.

Apollo smiled. "You will think of something. It is time to go. Repair the Scales, Danelos. You and your friends must succeed. You must."

A beam of sunlight shot through a window high in the throne room. Danelos unsheathed the sword and held the pommel to the light. A surge of electricity passed through the blade and Danelos looked one last time at Apollo.

"May Gaea watch over you, my son."

Taking a firm grip on the hilt, Danelos struck at the air a few times, opening a portal. Reality fell away from where he had cut, leaving an opening just big enough to pass through. Familiar smells from his apartment made his heart race. He made one last glance to Apollo who nodded his farewell before passing through the rift that sealed once he was on the other side.

Now Apollo would have to tell his people what had happened to their prince, and then he would have the task of ruling his homeland once more, alone.

• • •

Danelos, home in his apartment, walked over to the window and looked out at his city. The sun was rising. How apt, he thought. The aroma of hot pretzels filled his nostrils and he inhaled deeply. He was home, but he did miss the lilac and rose. He put the sword on his coffee table; he would deal with it later.

The hot water of his shower reminded him what it felt like to be clean, not that he really minded bathing in a pool in the palace, having servants to wait on his every need, having oils rubbed all over. However, standing all alone in a shower with a loofah and a bar of soap had its merit, too.

As he toweled his hair dry, he went to check his answering machine. Certainly, after all this time, his tape would be full. He'd have to find a new job, too. No messages. Odd. Just when he started to think something was wrong with the machine, he glanced at the digital date: October 10, 2009. That can't be right, he thought. On the kitchen table, he found his phone. Not only was it still fully charged, but also the date read October 10, 2009. He figured the third time would be the charm and turned on the television to Channel 9 News. That confirmed it. Scrolling across the bottom of the screen was the same date. He had been in Arkadeia for almost two months, or so he had thought, anyway. Only a few hours had passed in actuality, but that would be the hardest part to understand. All of the memories he had acquired in Arkadeia, for all those weeks of training and the experience with Demetrios, Apollo, and Lykaon—it all had happened in a span of hours.

Danelos looked at the sword on the coffee table right next to his Runner's magazine and mp3 player. He thought about his mother—how does he start *that* conversation? So much to think about, but not much time to do it. How would he tell all of this to Sarah, Aleta, and Brandon? How do you tell your friends you're an immortal demigod?

Reflecting on what Apollo said, he thought that Frost said it best: "And I took the road less traveled by, and that has made all the difference."

# 20—ELEMENTAL

**TNN (Tokyo)** "From WPR News, this is Hideyuki Sato. An outbreak of Ebola virus in Brunei has decimated a village just outside the capital city of Bandar Seri Begawan, allegedly due to a gorilla carcass local hunters brought into their village. Scientists with Task Force: Psi, specializing with medical emergencies, have quarantined contagious individuals in HazMat makeshift shelters until they can treat them with an experimental drug called Noctinase that has had success in monkeys. Newly elected Brunei president Ullala and the UN Task Force have worked together before when Task Force: Omega stepped in last year to deal with human rights violations during the old regime of President Durogo."

• • •

Standing in front of the manicured hedge and between two piles of marble remnants, Sarah tried her best to prevent the creature from reaching the passersby who had strolled into the park for an evening jaunt. The statues of Hermes and Artemis, nearest the people, shattered as the serpent's tail slammed into them, and Sarah used her power to control the elements to throw walls of earth up between the Lernæan hydra and the innocent people who

240

had no idea they might be food for a giant reptile. After hearing about the disturbance on the news, Danelos opened a portal to Paris near the Louvre, the first place he could think of in Paris that he had been to before, and it wasn't far from there to L'Parc Olympique, a park built where the Jardin de Tuileries used to be. Riots in 1992 caused by rogue Greek militants protesting an exhibit of artifacts at the Louvre used explosives to destroy the park, saying they were taking away a French landmark as the French had taken away the artifacts from the Greeks. Surrounded by the Rue de Rivoli to the north, the Avenue du Général Lemonnier to the east, the Voie Georges Pompidou and the River Seine to the south, and the Place de la Concorde to the west, the park contained one large fountain depicting Gaea cradling the Earth surrounded by a marble walk measuring fifty feet in all directions away from the fountain. Encircling this walk were fourteen stone pillars between which sat statues of the fourteen Olympian gods. Even though the *Oikoumene Broteios* did not exist in ancient times, when the gods sent the 'second selves' to this realm, these people carried with them knowledge of history and the ancient gods with them, building monuments to commemorate what they remembered as their past, even though the gods did not exist in this "inhabited mortal world." Walkways from the fountain toward the surrounding streets allowed access to the fountain from all sides, and the corners of the park contained small forests of oak, maple, and other deciduous trees where Parisians and tourists enjoyed many an evening stroll or even a morning run.

Sarah's knowledge of these chthonic monsters wasn't extensive, but she knew that only by decapitating a hydra and then cauterizing the severed necks could one destroy the monster. Since she only possessed her ring that allowed her to control the elements and nothing suitable for decapitation, she would have to improvise somehow.

241

The government could repair the park, she thought, but they couldn't replace people, so her primary objective was to keep the people away while she figured out a plan.

Caustic venom spewed forth at intervals from the heads, bathing the plants, animals, and marble statuary, the portentous sizzling sound it made on contact a warning that the poison would corrode anything coming too close. One of many underworld monsters she had seen over the past weeks, the hydra slithered across the garden, drawn to the sounds and smells of cafés lining the streets. Sarah mentally gestured at the water in the nearby fountain to collect into a spinning ball of liquid and careen toward the monstrosity heading toward Ares' statue. The shock of the blast sent the serpent tumbling, but not before its tail lashed out at a plinth beneath another statue, turning it to dust, causing the remaining statue to fall in Sarah's direction. Knowing she did not possess the strength to catch the marble icon, she created a raised soft earthen platform with a thought, catching the statue safely before another treasure could be lost. The French government had bought actual statues from the Greek Antiquities Board to use in the garden with the hopes of beautifying the area as well as honoring the long-standing accord eventually reached between both countries. Before she could think, Sarah sensed something behind her and, using her power, called up a strong wind to push back one of the hydra's heads. She had seen firsthand what the venom could do to marble and small animals; human flesh would respond in kind. Just before a serpent's head could snatch a couple entering from the south path, an earthen pillar created by Sarah's thoughts pushed its neck aside, making the monster lose its balance that gave her the chance to push it back even further with a solid rocklike projectile. This was getting her nowhere, and eventually either she wouldn't be able to save those in danger or the hydra would eat her. As it was nighttime, the hydra had the advantage of sticking close to the ground until it would rear its seven heads into a striking position.

Fighting an underworld creature that stood fifty feet at its tallest taxed her abilities, but she realized that she only her imagination limited what she could do. Able to reshape earth, fire, air, and water into whatever form she wanted, she had to find something that would incapacitate the hydra long enough to behead all seven heads. With enough people around beyond the park's boundaries unaware of the danger, Sarah had to use ingenuity, not her greatest strength, and she knew it. Using a considerable amount of mental energy, she pushed her mind deep into the earth, picturing a wall of soil rising up around the hydra. If she could maintain that long enough, containing the hydra in a makeshift pen, it might give her an extra few minutes to think of a plan. Crouching down, she touched with ground with both hands, and focused on the image in her mind. The sound of the earth ripping apart accompanied a ring of stone and rock that rose to thirty feet around the hissing spawn of Ekhidna—the highest she could muster without losing touch with the element. She hoped it would be enough. Her eyes darted around, looking for anything sharp enough to do the task. The fountain wasn't far away, but water wouldn't do anything to a water-beast. Wind couldn't decapitate anything, so that was out. The only fire she could sense was coming from the gaslight lamps on top of the columns that enclosed the fountain walk. She had the earth... so, no water or air, and fire was a possibility. As she repeated the list of the elements in her mind, she couldn't believe it could be that simple. It worked before. Could it work now?

The hydra was about to break through the wall, so she had to act quickly. She discerned through her connection with the earth that deep beneath the park—beneath most of Paris—was clay. Why hadn't she thought of it before? Changing her thoughts a bit, she caused the clay to rise up

243

and take the place of the dirt. Gradually, the wall of clay rose until it formed a dome with the hydra's seven heads poking through the top. Using one hand to guide her power with the clay, Sarah reached across to where the gaslights burned and summoned the fire. Flaring up enough to shatter the glass globes, the blazing flames followed her command, swirling around the clay dome, quickening until it had engulfed the structure. Once she had control of fire, she could feed it with air, so even if the gas were exhausted, it wouldn't matter. Sweat poured down her cheeks being in such close proximity to the conflagration, but she had to continue until she carried out her plan. Using the swirling oven, she created a kiln that baked the clay into a hard crust. As soon as she sensed this had happened, she extinguished the fire. Exhausted, she just wanted to collapse, but she had a few more things to do. Shrieking and hissing frenetically, the hydra squirmed within the dome until it cracked open, leaving massive shards of clay on the ground around it. Using the wind, Sarah positioned some of the fragments just right, and then called forth a gale force gust to push the hydra from behind. Not having a firm place to slither, it fell forward, impelled by air currents, landing in the pile of clay shards.

Her plan had succeeded. When the hydra fell, it severed its own heads on the considerable clay pieces, some as sharp as a battle-axe. Beckoning the fire from other gaslights, she bombarded the detached necks until the flames had sealed each one, silencing the monster for good. Like all underworld creatures, the hydra liquefied into primordial ooze that seeped back into the earth. For the moment, the people of Paris were safe. She would have to contact the local authorities about the damage to the park and hope they would understand what happened. For the moment, however, she sat on the edge of the fountain, looking up at the figure of Gaea, the Earth Mother, thanking her, and remembering how she became a mover of earth herself.

• • •

Three months earlier.

After setting the newly formed pot into the kiln, Sarah cleaned off her wheel and wiped down the machine. Having belonged to her grandmother, this potter's wheel held more memories than anything else she owned. Many an early Sunday morning Sarah would spend at her grandmother's side, watching the wheel spin and her grandmother's deft hands caress the malleable substance, covering everything with a rich brownish red. She threw her first pot at ten, made her first sculpture at twelve, and won her first award at sixteen at her high school's arts and crafts show. For as much as blood coursed through her veins, so did clay, in a manner of speaking. When her grandfather died, Sarah's grandmother took up molding and shaping clay as a means to pass the time and keep her mind off her loss, but as the years passed—and they passed rapidly—the elder woman became renowned for her ability to shape earth into objects of beauty.

The pot would need hours in the kiln and then time to cool down, so she knew she had the chance to take a hot bath and scour the red mud from her arms and hands. Just after eight o'clock, she drew the bath, tying back her red hair and winding it into a loose knot held together with a tortoise shell plastic clip. First, her toes sank into the steaming water and then her legs, followed slowly by her torso, until submerged to her neck. A soft, audible moan escaped her lips as she sank into the tub, knowing she had all the time she needed to relax. Working the wheel well required skill and a strong leg, especially since her wheel was foot-powered. Grandma did not believe in electric wheels; she said it took all the skill out of working the clay as well as diminishing the final product. Sarah, although no purist like her grandmother, used the older wheel when

245

she wanted to work off some tension or to channel her mentor. Her electric wheel, despite being variable, did not comfort her the same way. When she had to churn out pot after pot for customers, she would use the electric wheel. For special clients, like the one for this order, she broke out the older model.

Muscles began to relax and she stroked the once-dried clay from her arms while gently massaging them. She always took her baths almost scalding so the water would remain hot for a while before she had to get out. A folded towel on the edge of the tub served as a makeshift pillow as she closed her eyes. Sweat, laden with clay dust, trickled down the sides of her face, making reddish swirls as they melded into the tub water. Fatigue from the day's work overtook her and she slowly drifted to sleep.

Muffled noises woke her abruptly and she sat up, expecting water to overflow onto the floor, but instead, she sat on a woven mat, barely covered with a rough, horsehair blanket in a darkened space certainly not her bathroom. Her eyes darted nervously throughout the obscurity as her heart raced. The air smelled musty, almost fetid. Light flooded the room as the door flung open. Sarah screamed.

"Calm down," replied a soft male voice. "You are safe."

"Who are you, and where am I?" Sarah demanded. "Where are my clothes?"

"My wife found you in the river. We tried to rouse you, but you would not awaken, so we brought you to rest here in our home."

"Where am I? Who are you?" she asked again, as if she had heard nothing the man said to her.

"Kyros. I am High Elder of Parthos, once a prefecture of Atlantis."

"This can't be. I must be dreaming," she said, pushing herself against the wall.

A man of about sixty, Kyros poured some water flavored with pomegranate juice into a clay cup and handed it to Sarah, but she would not take it. He took a sip from the cup to prove to her it was all right and offered it again. This time, reluctantly, she took it from him, but she did not drink it.

"I don't understand. I was taking a bath, and I must have fallen asleep. Am I dreaming?"

"You were bathing in the river? We found no clothes by you."

"No, I was bathing in my bathtub. In my house. In Brighton. Please tell me I'm dreaming."

As her eyes began to adjust to the light around her, Sarah noticed that Kyros had a virtuous face covered with a braided white beard. His dark gray cloak, tied around his waist with frayed cording, showed signs of age and wear.

"I do not know this Brighton you speak of. Is it far from here?"

Her bewildered expression made him ask if she knew where she was. She had never heard of Parthos, but she kept reiterating that she must be dreaming. He smiled the way someone does when he does not know what to say.

"I will return later. My wife left some clothes for you on the chair. When you are ready, please come out and join us if you feel up to it."

Once he left, Sarah drank from her cup. Enough light came through the window even though a piece of cloth hung over it, and she found the clothes. The skirt and tunic, both of a soft Tyrian purple fabric, fit her reasonably well. Part of her still thought this was part of a very real dream and an even smaller part thought that someone or something had transported her to this Parthos, wherever it was. Her experiences with Ananke and at Delphi started to wear down her resistance to being in such a foreign place. She was not averse to alternative ideas or even the prospect of an alternative reality, but she just never

247

thought she would be part of one. Everything about the hut felt real to her – the floor, the still air, and even the pomegranate water – but she did not want to believe it.

As she pushed the door open, her eyes immediately squinted from the bright daylight, and it took her a few moments for her eyes to adjust. All around her she saw people dressed in a similar fashion to her, doing daily chores, washing clothes, cooking meals, and even gathering at the well, sharing the day's news and gossip. It felt as if someone had placed her on a movie set, but these people actually seemed to live this way. A few steps from the hut, she felt someone tap her on the shoulder and turned to see a woman, about her height, her wavy white hair cascading down her shoulders.

"I see you are feeling better," commented the woman, smiling. "And the clothing fits you well. Come join us."

The elder woman led her toward a group of other women the same age, each looking a little like her grandmother in some way.

"What is your name, young woman," an aged, crackling voice spoke.

"Sarah."

"You are certainly not from around here, are you?"

"Can you tell me where I am? I mean, where exactly is Parthos?" Sarah asked, not meaning to ignore the question.

Another woman, her silver hair braided down her back, replied, "Well, the original Parthos was a prefecture of Atlantis, but we have named this place, here on the Akhæan mainland, as our new home. How did you come to be in the river?"

Sarah's face stiffened. What would she tell them? Before she had a chance to offer any response, Kyros approached, greeting the others.

"Sarah, the Priestess has summoned you. Excuse us, ladies."

Kyros took Sarah's hand gently and escorted her to the other side of the village where a small thatched hut sat, a plume of smoke snaking its way from the tip of the roof. Aromatic lilac perfumed the air, almost like incense, and became much more apparent as she stood before the door.

"What does this priestess want with me?" She felt goose bumps rise on her arm.

"I was simply asked to bring you here, but you are in no danger. Poseidon protects the shrine."

Before she could question that, Sarah heard a soft voice call her from within the hut and pushed the door open. Darkness enshrouded her as she walked inside with only a smoldering fire in the center of the room to shed any light, casting dancing shadows on the walls.

"Come sit by the fire," the voice beckoned.

Hesitantly, she sat on one side of the glowing embers as the figure on the other side raised her arms in homage of the sea god.

"Fear not. Poseidon knows of your arrival and has asked me to speak with you. I do sense reluctance from you, and I know you think you are in a dream, but you have been brought here for a fated purpose."

"I don't understand," Sarah replied. "Who are you, and why do you think Poseidon wants anything to do with me?"

"I gave up my true identity a long time ago when I was selected as High Priestess to Lord Poseidon, but you may call me Hermæa. In your world, Poseidon and the other gods exist mainly in myth and legend. Here, Olympos rules supremely, and the gods are as real as you or I. Let me tell you a story. Not long ago..." began the old woman, her soft voice ensnaring Sarah, taking her mind off the present dilemma.

She wove together the history of an island kingdom set off the coast of Akhæa and ruled by a benevolent sovereign, a man whose destiny would set in motion a string of events that would forever change all history. Poseidon, the Earthshaker, brother of Zeus, fell in love with the goddess Cosumia, a daughter of Aether, the *Protogenos* of the Upper Air, the place where Olympos resided. To protect her, he built an island city surrounded by concentric islands where she would live out her life peacefully and rear his children, five sons who would share the sovereignty of the place named Oceaneia. As each son grew into manhood, he assumed a different royal station and took a wife from the mainland, settling in the palace made by Poseidon. In harmony they lived, and each king bore many children who, over time, helped to populate the idyllic city. As decades passed, the populace grew into tribes, and the governing body evolved to where tribal magistrates presided over parts of the island as well as the rings of islands. Families lived in concord and various parts of the monarchy traded with one another, each specializing in a certain interests: fishing, building, and scholarship, among others. Warfare was the only area not fostered, since everything the people needed they could get from one another, and they did not trade with the outside world of Akhæa, something forbidden by Oceaneian law. Curiosity of outworlders grew, however, and young men would surreptitiously travel in small boats to the mainland and spy on mainland activities, bringing back knowledge to their respective tribes. Once these ideas permeated the tribal society structure, dissention grew among those who had seen other ways and those who chose to live strictly by Oceaneian law, causing civil war. Knowledge of weaponry grew, primarily from observing the outworlders, and soon many tribal numbers dwindled. Poseidon grew angry and chose two sons from each of the five original kings—Atlas, Gadeiros, Ampheres, Euaimon, Mneseos, Autokhthon, Elasippos, Mestor, Azaes, and Diaprepres—putting them to tournament. Each would have to fight his brother or cousin to the death with the victor winning the right to rule over the entirety of Oceaneia unchallenged by anyone, and only this man would choose his heir. In this way, the first true monarchy of this island would be born.

Each man, armored and trained by Athene, entered the coliseum with a single objective: victory. For many days these men fought one another, each vying to outdo the other in battle and, after a week, only five men stood—Gadeiros, Mneseos, Mestor, Azaes, and Atlas. All of Olympos watched from above, each god and goddess secretly desiring one of the men to win. On the eighth day, Mneseos and Azaes killed each other in a sword melee. Another, Mestor, beheaded by Gadeiros, brought the number down to two. Remaining in the fight by the twelfth day were Gadeiros and Atlas, warriors equally matched, so much so that the combat lasted thirty days with neither one resting for more than a few hours before rekindling the fray. The following morning, Atlas approached Gadeiros in his camp, presenting the idea of a joint monarchy, with one sovereign for head of state and one for military leader. Initially, Gadeiros was reluctant, since this might show weakness as one man would not emerge as victor. After two days conferring with Atlas, they both realized that this would be the best option for Oceaneia and decided to tell the people. All that remained was to seek Poseidon's blessing.

In his temple, the sea god expressed disinclination, but did not give a final directive. He told them that they would know his answer when he was ready to give it. Although uneasy about their patron deity's response, the two men proceeded to the coliseum where they presented their plan to the masses. Of course, this did not please either side, but as they heard both Atlas and Gadeiros speak about the plans they had for Oceaneia, as well as how synchronized the men were in their presentation, an almost flawless joining of two strong leaders, they were willing to hear out

251

the rest of the proposal. After all, even if the two made the decision, the citizens would have to live with it, and no one wanted civil war. At one point, a man shouted a question from the stands about trade, and Atlas answered him directly and completely. Seeing this, other people asked equally important questions, and Gadeiros helped Atlas respond. A myriad of questions showered the two, but they continued to give concise and obviously well thought out answers.

After two hours, Atlas put the idea of approval to the people, but first they would have to appeal to Poseidon for his blessing. The High Priest of Poseidon gathered the people in prayer, their voices melding into a harmony of faith. Echoes of thunder from the distance moved closer, clouds roiling in the sky, growing darker, and tendrils of lightning sprayed over the skies – surely a sign from the gods. In the swirling clouds, a face formed, a bearded face with piercing eyes of azure. No one knew whether this portentous moment would bring about favor or disfavor, but the appearance of an eagle from high above, soaring to the ground with something in its talons made the crowd gasp. Circling above the balcony, the majestic bird hovered above Atlas and Gadeiros and opened its talons, letting two gold crowns fall into waiting hands. As quickly as it appeared, the bird vanished into the clouds, taking with it the storm. Hesitating but a moment, both men slowly placed a crown on the other's head, the definitive sign that they had formed a monarchy, and the gods blessed it.

From the crowd, a man's voice rose above the murmuring, declaring he had come to give his response to this decision, and he would not be outdone by his brother's show of approval. The throng parted, allowing the man to step unimpeded across the ground toward the balcony. He raised his trident, appearing from nowhere, toward the two newly crowned sovereigns, giving his consent for this

252

union to take place by summoning two smaller tridents, intricately carved by the forge god himself, and placed them in the monarchs' hands. Before he departed, he informed them that, as long as they revere him as their patron god, he would reward them. With no further words, he turned and walked back through the coliseum through a sea of kneeling worshippers, heads hung in respect, and vanished into mist at the gates.

With all eyes back on Atlas and Gadeiros, and a heavy silence still suspended over the crowd, a voice shouted,

"All hail King Atlas and King Gadeiros, sovereigns of Oceaneia!"

With those words, the people erupted in shouts of exuberant joy, thankful to have two such noble men leading their country. Then, something unexpected happened which would change everything. Gadeiros stepped forward, extending his hand over the crowd to silence them and again, a quick hush came, as the crowd was eager to hear what he had to say.

"When Poseidon established the tournament to decide the monarchy, we all knew this would either make us stronger, or break our spirit. Each of my brethren hungered for the chance to mold and shape this land and its people into the pride of Gaea and Olympos. We have celebrated victories and mourned losses to our fair country, knowing that each man gave his very life to uphold the standards of our homeland. When only Atlas and I remained, I knew I could do what I needed to do to ensure victory. I would overcome my friend and ally in combat, ensuring that Oceaneia would have the ruler for which it yearned. What I did not see, however, was what this was doing to you, the citizens. However, Atlas did, and he approached me with a solution that would bind our people once again. Without his brave act, defying the gods themselves, we would surely fight a heinous civil war, with many more lives lost. I wish to honor my cousin this day by proposing we rename our home 'Atlantis' – the island of Atlas – since without him, I do not feel we would be here before you now."

After Gadeiros ceased speaking, a short silence filled the air, but the uproarious shouts of the people shattered it, declaring their approval. For many years, both Atlas and Gadeiros ruled wisely, building a great nation revered by mainland monarchs and the gods as well.

Sarah had listened to the story carefully, hoping it somehow would help her get home, but Hermæa sensed the young woman's concern.

"There is but one more chapter to this tale, young one, and this will tell you what you need to know."

Sarah found it interesting that Hermæa said 'need to know' and not 'want to know'. Necessity implies she has to do something with this information, but her desire was to return home.

"Many years passed, and Gadeiros died in battle and Atlas met his fate on an expedition on the mainland. Gadeiros had no children, but Atlas had a son, Euenor, who took the throne and reigned well, keeping peace with Atlantis and the mainland. When Zeus took victory over Kronos and the Titans after the Great War, he sought counsel with many immortals, gods, some Titans who had remained neutral, and *Protogenoi*. All but one did Zeus summon—Nyx. Insulted by this effrontery, she destroyed a sacred set of Scales that held the balance of Order and Chaos. Euenor, having heard a portentous prophecy from his high priest, Agisthos, had already initiated an evacuation to the mainland, but he would remain with his homeland. All other members of the royal family, as well as thousands of Atlantæans, left their home and sailed for safety, but the wave came down hard on the island, sinking it beneath the waters. Not even Poseidon could aid his people, as he was still stunned by Nyx's actions for he knew the consequences. Many of the Atlantæans made it to safety, but hundreds did not. Those who would have drowned Poseidon transformed into fish so that their lives would be spared, warning them not to swim too close to the island since they could be caught and mistaken for food. Some survivors, including members of the royal family, ended up here, in this village, named for our home, Parthos. The world in which we live, the *Ge Theôn*, and the world where you are from, the *Oikoumene Broteios*, do not exist as they should. Morpheus has brought you here at the request of the *Moirae* to fulfill a prophecy, but I sense you know that already."

"Yes. The Delphic Oracle told us about it, but my friend Danelos hasn't deciphered it yet."

"He will. Delphic prophecies take time to unravel. You..."

Through the door burst a young man, heaving and sweaty. "My apologies, Priestess, but you must come quickly. Acastus has news!"

Despite the urgency, Hermæa slowly stood, took her time pulling her cloak over her head, and took Sarah's hand, leading her into the center of town where Parthosians were gathering around the well. Some had come from plowing the fields, others had come from the river, and all were clamoring about, like angry bees buzzing around the hive. Kyros met Hermæa and Sarah on the way, using his tall scepter to help him walk. Sarah noticed the head of the scepter was a trident, lending credibility to the story she had just heard. Hermæa had not told her how long ago this had happened, so she did not know who was a member of the royal family. The story also confirmed that she must really be in Parthos since she could not have dreamed any of this herself. The crowd parted as Kyros and Hermæa came closer, enabling them to speak directly with Acastus, a former member of the Atlantæan militia and one of Parthos' finest warriors. His weathered armor, bearing the crest of the trident on his cuirass, made him stand out from the others. Acastus had fought in prior wars between Atlantis and cities on the mainland, as well as having helped to protect the village of Parthos. Of the survivors, he was the only one with any military training. Removing his helmet, sweat poured down his forehead, matting his brown hair to his head.

"In my daily surveillance of the border, I saw troop movements to the north. I have no doubt that he has returned."

"Are you certain it is he, Acastus?" asked Kyros.

"As certain as Apollo's chariot that crosses the sky, I have seen him and his legions just beyond the ridge," he replied, pointing.

"The last time he came, we were almost destroyed! What can we do this time? We don't have the means to fight them," interrupted one of the men.

"We cannot retreat! We have nowhere else to go," added another.

Sarah whispered to Hermæa, "Who is this person?"

"The Warlord Phlegos," spat the High Priestess. "His reputation for killing was known even when Atlantis was at its peak. Ares sired him with a she-wolf, so the legend claims, and his ferocity is unmatched."

"What could he possibly want with Parthos? You don't seem to be a military power. What does he want?"

"As an outworlder, you would never have known the horror he unleashed—be thankful to whatever gods you worship. Phlegos and his warrior vermin infest Parthos once every year, so the news that he is near is no surprise, but it still puts the fear of Tartaros in all of us. He, it, whatever, claims we hold a sacred treasure, something beyond all the wealth on the mainland, and he seeks to find it. The last time he and his minions descended upon us, he took five of our citizens and a priest of Poseidon. Now our brethren endure in Elysium, one hopes. When Phlegos touches you, you feel your skin burning, but the flesh does not combust… nay, his fire eats the spirit away until nothing remains but a lifeless corpse. Some have said that nothing remains to enter the underworld."

Kyros, after hours of discussion in the village, convinced most of the people to return to their families so that he, the other elders, and Acastus could develop some sort of plan, but he did not sound entirely encouraged. Hermæa took Sarah to another part of Parthos where she could become more acclimated to the surroundings. Resigned to her situation, Sarah kept hope that she, or someone, would figure out a way to return home, although the likelihood seemed to diminish with every passing hour. While she wandered through the streets, she saw some people cowering in the shadows, and others stared at her, fearful she might be a danger to them. Fear is a powerful motivator, and with the knowledge that Phlegos' arrival was imminent, the citizens of Parthos were not willing to try to get to know Sarah.

In another open area, two aged women sat at pottery wheels, much more unsophisticated than even Sarah's grandmother's wheel, but nimble hands fashioned water jugs, deftly keeping the water at just the right amount to prevent the clay from collapsing or drying out. Staring at them, Sarah examined some of the finished pieces that had cooled from the kiln. She marveled at their skill in fashioned works of art and function since she had not seen another person throw clay since her grandmother died. When she did it, it felt as if she was channeling her grandmother, but to watch someone else do it seemed awkward, a bit disconnected. At the same time, some of the women sat in the same way that her grandmother had, or used the same sweeping motion with the wet cloth. As she picked up a small bowl, one of the women asked her if she would like to try making something. Smiling, Sarah gladly took a seat on the stool and humored one of the women who wanted to show her the basics. They didn't know Sarah had been a potter for years. After all that had happened, it felt good to do something she could control. Thinking her a quick study, the women admired her work and their ability to teach someone so quickly.

While she got lost in her work, an outlet for the frustration she had been feeling, a small crowd had gathered. By the end of the day, she had made two friends of the women and had gained some admirers as well as a little more acceptance. Kyros spied her and made his way in her direction. The meeting, having lasted much longer than anyone had expected, had yielded few results if any. Accompanying the elder was a young man, around Sarah's age, in a blue tunic and leather sandals. His left forearm bore a leather bracer and over his shoulder he carried a quiver and his bow. Unlike his father, the young man was clean-shaven, and his ash blond hair cut very short. She glanced up for just a moment when she heard Kyros' voice, but she did not stop the wheel until she had finished what she was doing.

"Sarah," began Kyros, "I see you have found something to occupy your time. This is my son, Tithonos. He was out hunting when you arrived and just returned."

Not one for too many words, Tithonos nodded and smiled in her direction; at least she thought it was a smile.

"When you are finished, I would be honored if you join us for our evening meal. As far as I can recall, you have not had anything since you arrived here. You must be quite hungry by now," Kyros said.

"Actually, I'm finished now," Sarah replied, wiping her hands on a piece of torn fabric. "I'll just set these pieces out to dry and then I'll be ready."

Tithonos said nothing on the walk back, but he did listen intently to Sarah as she talked about how wonderful she felt working with clay again. For the first time since her arrival, she expressed herself more openly and this pleased Kyros, despite the looming problem about to destroy the peace. As they entered Kyros' home, strong aromas of roasted meat filled Sarah's nostrils, along with the earthy smell of fresh bread. The meal allowed them to talk more openly than they had been able to since Sarah's arrival, since she had finally accepted her present situation. From time to time, Tithonos would ask her about Boston, her family and friends, and her duty; she understood that to mean her job. Kyros and his family were surprised to learn that she actually earned a living making pottery, but she explained that, in Boston, she actually has people who commission works from her, so she can ask whatever price she wishes. Talk of her family made her homesick, and that knotted feeling in her gut, the one she had when she arrived, started to return. Taking her cue from that, Kyros' wife, Pelageia, asked Sarah more about Boston. The more she described it, the more Tithonos said it sounded like the capital city of Atlantis with regard to its immense size and large buildings. Sarah asked if any pictures existed of the islands, but no one knew what that meant. As she described it further, Kyros went into another room and brought back a scroll of weathered parchment that revealed a drawing of the island taken from the top of the palace. From that, Sarah could see the concentric islands that surrounded the main city and how the monarchs had divided the kingdom. With a tearful eye, Kyros pointed out parts of the island that he remembered fondly, especially where he had met Pelagæa. He had barely reached adulthood when he had to leave the islands, but he remembered his home and family, both taken from him, except Tithonos and Pelagæa. Both he and his wife told Sarah story after story of their life in Atlantis, about how peaceful it was and how breathtakingly beautiful.

After the meal, Kyros excused himself since he had agreed to meet with the village elders about Phlegos. Sarah had wondered that, with the threat of danger so close, how he and his family could sit so calmly and enjoy a meal.

She would have thought he would have been doing what he could to forestall the problem, a problem that very well could destroy all they had built in Parthos. Boldly, she asked Kyros if she could accompany him to this meeting, but his reluctance was evident before he could reply. She insisted, primarily since this affected her, too, and she wanted to hear firsthand what the villagers were going to do. Tithonos, sensing his father did not wish her to go, tried to persuade her to join him and a few of his friends. Sarah, however, would not allow this to sway her, so she stood her ground, arms folded, until Kyros finally acquiesced, much to the chagrin of Tithonos.

"You must respect the council, Sarah. They will not tolerate any outbursts," Kyros said, gathering his cloak and walking stick. "Guests to Parthos do not normally sit in on council meetings, but considering the circumstances, I will allow it."

The meeting took place in a storm-wrought hut, its thatched roof letting moonlight shine in, casting shadows on the dirt floor. Kyros took the chair at the head of the table; Hermæa sat to his right, Acastus to his left with Sarah next to him, and the remaining elders formed a circle. Sprinkling a pungent powder over the smoldering coals, the High Priestess offered a prayer to Poseidon before turning over the proceedings to Kyros.

"We all have had time to deliberate as to how we can take on the problem of Phlegos. Acastus tells me that within two days time the warlord will have entered the grove of Artemis just outside the village. Suggestions?"

"What about leaving? Certainly if we took to the ocean, Lord Poseidon would aid us."

"In this matter, Theron, I fear that Poseidon has left this task to us and that he would not aid us," replied Hermæa, solemnly.

Xanthippe, a woman slightly older than Sarah, said, "I agree. Poseidon has always wished that we be his favored people... from a distance."

Her faith had been tested more times than she could remember.

"If we were to leave, and presumably we had the time, where would we go? I would not bring the wrath of Phlegos on any of our neighbors, especially after it took so long for us to arrange the treaties," Kyros responded.

"Then we fight!" Acastus said firmly, punctuated by his fist on the table. "We stand and fight, to the last!"

Sarah's heartbeat jumped when he spoke. She was not sure if she was afraid of him or impressed with his intensity. In any event, she saw he was not afraid to die for a cause.

"With what, Acastus? We have no weapons, only spears and a few bows. All the metal we had, we lost in the last raid that warmonger brought upon us. We were lucky then they did not slaughter us! No, we cannot fight," responded the blacksmith, Genadios.

"So, we allow ourselves to be killed? For what? Some treasure that that maniacal son of a she-wolf thinks we have? We have to do something," said Acastus.

Sarah wanted to say something, anything that would help. With no prior knowledge of Phlegos or his attacks, she had no innate sense of what to do. Without thinking, she asked the first thing that came to mind, her voice stopping everyone else from arguing.

"Does he have a weakness?"

Kyros shot her a look that scolded her for getting involved, but she just sat taller in her chair. Like it or not, she was now involved since she could not go home. All the others simply looked at one another.

"Does Phlegos have a weakness?" she asked again. "If he has one, maybe he can be slowed down if not stopped."

Acastus replied, "Not that I am aware of." His tone seemed as if he was shirking her question. After all, she was not a Parthosian. Of course they had investigated a weakness... or had they?

"Sarah, he has attacked our village repeatedly for many years. If he had had a weakness, we would have known," said Kyros, dismissively.

She pounded her fist on the table. "In case you've forgotten, I am here against my will, with no knowledge of how I got here. I have had to get used to the fact that, somehow, someone took me from my home and transplanted me in another world. Do you realize how hard that is to process? Maybe it's not that uncommon when you have gods, but I don't recall seeing people sudden fly around the space-time continuum. So, maybe this problem affects me, too, now. And another thing, don't dismiss me. I asked a simple question."

After she finished, she sat back, crossing her arms. Acastus seemed almost proud that she had done that. It seemed to break the tension.

"The Military Council in Atlantis made no mention of any weakness he had," said Acastus, "but that does not mean he does not have one. I am not even sure where we could find that information."

While the others just looked at one another, dumbfounded for the moment, Sarah's face lit up.

"Kyros, remember that drawing you showed me of Atlantis? That scroll? Are there other scrolls?"

"I have never seen any others. Do any of you know of other scrolls from Atlantis?"

Amid the shaking of heads, suddenly Hermæa remembered something.

"The altar in the shrine. Beneath it are two chests, one gilded, the other silver. In all the years we have been here, they have never been opened."

"Acastus, you and Genadios head to the shrine and see what you can find. If need be, bring the chests here," commanded Kyros.

Half an hour later, both chests arrived in the council chamber and their lids removed. The silver one contained holy relics that existed in the great Temple of Poseidon in Atlantis, but the gold chest contained at least fifty scrolls, sealed with the royal wax, and one piece of parchment with nothing written on it. At first, no one was willing to break the wax seals, but the monarchy had not existed for many years, a realization that made it easier for Kyros to break the first one. Most of the ones they examined were battle plans, ancient peace accords, and documents of state; frustration ceased further examination, leaving everyone defeated. The imminent danger presented by Phlegos and his marauders crept back into the pit of their stomachs, eroding whatever hope they might have created in their mind.

"I will do what is necessary," Hermæa said, "and return as soon as I can." She left, returning to the shrine.

"What will she do?" asked Sarah.

"Consult with Poseidon, a speculative measure at best since the Lord of the Seas does not often respond to a mortal summons. Rather, he tells her what she needs to tell us," replied Kyros.

"Is she in any danger?"

"Communing with the gods is never free from the potential of harm. I respect the gods, but they can be fickle and tempestuous when they wish to be. They wouldn't disagree with that," replied Xanthippe.

In the shrine of Poseidon, the High Priestess pulled her prayer robe over her head, and then lit two iron braziers, worn from years of use, with flaming bunches of sea grass. Softly speaking a mantra of sorts, she put herself into a trance, hoping to gain the favor of her patron deity. The shrine, only lit by the brazier flame, filled with grassy smoke, casting a haze throughout, and it was into this miasma her heart's desire was fulfilled. In the shadows, the silhouette of a man emerged, never showing his face, but Hermæa knew it was he. She spoke with him of their dilemma, asking him for guidance, but always cautious of her tone, as she did not want to offend him. His reply was brief, but told her what she needed to know, and then the door flew open, a great wind sweeping through, cleansing the place of worship of the holy incense, and extinguishing the brazier flames. She returned to the others, taking the blank parchment back to the shrine and leaving it on the altar.

Once again vacant, the sacrarium of Poseidon filled with perfumed smoke once more, for no other reason than he liked the fragrance of smoldering sea grass. Returning to corporeal form, he stood but a moment before another figure entered, materializing from the air. All knew her standard anywhere, especially on Olympos, where the fearsome aegis sat proudly on her chest, a way to frighten those who would be foolish enough to wage war against the goddess of battle arts.

"Why have you asked me here, Poseidon?" asked Athene, her grey eyes flashing.

The sea god's stoic countenance informed her that he was still a little bitter about their last encounter.

"I have need of a… favor."

"Why so despondent, dear uncle? You cannot still be sore about losing Athens to me, can you?

His silence hovered around him. She was right. The time had come to let that pass.

"No, not really. I need to call upon your prowess in stealth, actually. The warlord Phlegos will soon attack Parthos, but if the villagers knew his weakness, they could stop him. I do not possess the ability to circumvent Ares' watchful eye," he replied, "but you do. Find out for me? I

264

do not wish to arouse the wrath of Ares. He can be so bothersome."

"Resorting to flattery? Sometimes you can be so transparent. What makes you think I can find what you seek, assuming I were to help you? Surely, my brother would find out and warn his scion, thus ending the battle before it even starts."

"Ares cannot hear what is not spoken," Poseidon replied, glancing down at the blank parchment. "An ancient enchantment, so ancient—in fact—that any Olympian would not even bother with it, prevents even Zeus himself from reading what is on it. I am not asking you to spell it out for them. That would arouse Ares' suspicion. However, if you give them something to figure out on their own, then neither you nor I have actually told them anything."

She smirked. "Clever. Out of mutual contempt for my bellicose brother, I will do as you ask." In a cloud of mist, she vanished, returning just a few moments later.

Touching the parchment, she scorched the knowledge to it, and then dematerialized, vanishing to Olympos, but not before she performed one more task, a gift. The maker of earthquakes vanished, too, but not before he sent a gust of wind through the shrine, blowing the door open, a sign to Hermæa that the gods had left the temple. She grabbed the parchment, not even noticing Athene's other offering, returning to Kyros and the others. She thought her heart would pound its way through her chest before she reached them, anxious to see what aid her patron had given then, never knowing whether it would help or not.

"Poseidon conferred with Pallas Athene, mistress of battle arts, who put on this parchment information we can use to defeat Phlegos," said Hermæa. Carefully breaking the seal, she unraveled the golden paper.

Burned onto the surface were four symbols:

Hermæa's heart sank. Humanity knew the gods for their riddles, but this puzzle seemed untimely considering the circumstances. Only her staunch faith kept her from expressing her displeasure. All eyes stared intently at the four symbols, hoping they would have an epiphany, only no one spoke. Acastus, his features unyielding, traced the symbols with his finger, thinking that might somehow impart knowledge.

"Does Poseidon know that time is not a commodity we have?" he asked, sighing.

"Hush, Acastus," barked Hermæa. "Surely bringing his wrath upon us will not help. Be grateful for what we do have."

"You are correct, Priestess. I merely state my frustration with the situation, not with our Lord Poseidon," he replied, more to ease her than what he truly believed.

Sarah, helpless on so many levels, not the least of which was her unfamiliarity with these people, left the group to walk through the town. With each passing hour since her arrival in Parthos, her frustration had grown, but at the same time, she had resigned herself to the knowledge that this was her reality, too, and maybe she should do her best to decipher this divine puzzle. Tithonos followed her from the tent, his pace slowing to hers as he approached.

"I cannot begin to imagine what you feel, Sarah. Being an outsider is something I have never felt, having grown up in this community, but I will certainly listen and do what I can to make you feel less detached."

She barely smiled, still facing ahead. "Thank you, Tithonos. That means a lot to me right now, although it doesn't get rid of my anxiety. For some reason, I am here, and I have no idea how I got here or why I'm here. I am beginning to accept that I could be here forever, but the thought of never seeing my home or my family again, makes me angry. I don't think I've allowed myself to feel anything since so much has happened so quickly. What if I can't go home, Tithonos? What happens to me then?"

She could not keep the tears from coming anymore. Tithonos could not reply, for he did not know what to say, but he put his arm around her shoulder. This was the first physical contact she had really had with anyone and it felt reassuring that she was alive and not in some deathlike dream world, or wherever should could imagine herself. Where the dirt path merged that led to the ocean with the sand, both stared into the distance at an unforgiving horizon, a boundary to a world she did not know, nor wished to know, at that moment. A calm sea, like a polished mirror, sat before them, which only made her uneasy, thinking about the cliché of the 'calm before the storm'. Temperate breezes pushed against her from the vast ocean, combining the salty air with the smell of sea grass. Her mind thought for a moment that this was Poseidon's way of reassuring her all would be well, but this tested her faith, even more than when she had lost her parents. Time, as Acastus had mentioned, was certainly not abundant, and she hoped that someone would find a way to stop the attack. If she had to die, she did not want it to be with total strangers, in a time where no one would remember her, even though her fondness was beginning to grow for these people. Tithonos, sensing her disquiet, put his hand on her shoulder.

"Would you like some time to yourself?"

She shook her head. "No, I don't think so. Would you mind if we sat for a few minutes?"

They found a half buried log on the side of the path, worn from the elements, and watched silently as the clouds traveled across the pale blue sky. Tithonos wanted desperately to speak with her, but the words would not come. Whistling through the sea grass, the wind washed

267

over them, caressing them, perhaps in its own way trying to assuage the frustration. Sarah and he sat there for over an hour, at which point, she gently kissed him on the cheek before heading back to the village. He lingered for a moment, sitting up a little straighter and blushing before following her back.

When they rejoined the others, Sarah read on their faces that they had made no progress with the symbols. Consternation shadowed them, testing their patience and resolve.

"By the gods, why is this so difficult? They are just four symbols!" erupted Xanthippe, who had been pacing in the council chamber.

Kyros looked as if he were about to speak, but she cut him off. "If you say one more word about patience, old man, so help me, I will beat you with your own walking stick."

"We do not need to worry about Phlegos, it seems," interjected Theron, "for we will kill each other before he arrives."

"Enough! If you are not going to be productive, then you might as well go home!" shouted Acastus, pounding his hand on the table. "We do not need this right now."

Sarah moved closer to the parchment, carefully eyeing the symbols, hoping she would think of something insightful, but she drew a blank. Suddenly, though, she asked a question, not realizing she had asked it aloud.

"Why four symbols?"

"What? What do you mean? What kind of question—" Xanthippe snapped back.

"Let her speak," Kyros interrupted, trying not to let his impatience with Xanthippe show too much. "Go on, Sarah."

"We see four symbols here. Well, what comes in fours?"

"Four directions? North, south, east, and west," answered Theron.

"Four seasons," Acastus added.

A lengthy discussion emerged from their findings, no one coming any closer to what significance these meanings would have on their situation. The directions sounded plausible at first, but Phlegos was coming from the north, that much they knew, and this was summer, so why allude to other times of year. Sarah pulled Kyros aside and asked about other scrolls in the chests. Perhaps from whatever records they had kept from Atlantis, they could decipher this enigma. Gently touching her arm, Kyros had a passing notion that the gods might have sent Sarah as a voice of reason, if Xanthippe's harshness did not intimidate Sarah into silence first. He moved the remaining scrolls to the table, dividing them among the assembled, instructing them to examine each one scrupulously, leaving no detail ignored. Unfortunately, the Ancients wrote the scrolls in an Atlantæan dialect that Sarah could not read, so she sat next to Tithonos for moral support. These gods must be fickle, Sarah conjectured, since somehow she was able to understand and communicate with the Parthosians, but she could not read the text. Whatever forces were at work knew exactly what they were doing, a game to entertain idle gods. As the moon slowly crossed the heavens, illuminating the earth in silver, torches burned brightly in the council chamber, their flames dancing, casting sprightly shadows. Hours passed unnoticed until dawn, when Tithonos opened his last scroll. Crinkling parchment and murmurs had been the only sounds in the hut until now.

She could make no sense of the text, but something about the shapes embedded in the wax seal alarmed her. Unsure of what she had found, she pulled the three pieces of the red wax along the table with her index finger, putting them together. Tithonos glanced over to see what she was doing and his eyes widened. With new enthusiasm, he unfurled the light brown goatskin and, using his finger, slowly reading the words, but he found he could not. This wasn't the Atlantæan text he knew. Embedded in the manuscript were the four symbols, written separately, but the language was foreign to him. To be certain about the shapes, he studied the parchment with Athene's markings, his eyes dancing between both pieces of paper.

"Father, I think we have found something."

A first glance at the wording made Kyros' pulse race. He had not seen this dialect in many, many years, since he was a child. He leaned in, narrowing his eyes, hoping to catch a word or phrase. Hermæa moved next to him.

"Olympian script. By Poseidon's trident…this is the language of the gods, the one they speak among themselves. How would we have acquired such an object? This came from Olympos itself."

"How do you know this, Hermæa?" asked Acastus.

"As an apprentice to the High Priestess in Atlantis, I learned a few phrases, only the ones necessary to invoke our patron deity. Why would the monarchy have a need for this?"

"Well, what does it say?" asked Xanthippe.

From what she could tell, it described an ancient magic, earlier than Olympos, called the *Tetrastoikeia*— The Four Elements—earth, fire, air, and water. She also made out the name Hephæstos, the blacksmith of the gods, but she could not understand what he had to do with such ancient magic. According to legend, when Khaos first brought forth Gaea, the earth, she imbued her daughter with this primordial enchantment, giving her reign over the elements. Later in the reading, Hermæa pieced together that Gaea then bequeathed three of the dominions to other deities: two *Protogenoi*—Ær, god of air and Hydros, god of water—as well as an Olympian, Hephæstos, god of fire.

Gaea strengthened the *Tetrastoikeia* by connecting primordial energy to newer godly power, leaving herself as the binding agent. As long as she existed, the enchantment would exist, and an *Eklektos*, a chosen one, could use its power, but only through a key. The parchment did not say in what form the key existed, but only the heir of Atlantis would know what it was. Through this conduit, the rightful heir would guard the *Tetrastoikeia* until he or she would provide an heir, and so forth, until the end of Creation. Neither good nor evil, this preternatural power would perform for its heir, and only its heir. What could be determined was that, when combined, the four elements wielded power over anything divine since the *Tetrastoikeia* existed before Olympos, before the Titans, and before the gods. After she finished reading what she could, Hermæa looked even more despondent. She had not learned what she had hoped.

"How anticlimactic," muttered Xanthippe.

"Now what do we do? Was there anything we could use to help us defeat Phlegos? Do we even know what this key is?"

"No, Acastus," replied Kyros, sighing. "What we do know is that earth, fire, air, and water can somehow hurt the warlord, but we do not know how."

"Let us try to use logic. Unless he can fly, which we have not seen, he has to walk on the earth, so obviously that does not affect him adversely, and his helmet does not cover his mouth, so air has no effect. That leaves fire and water."

"I am not convinced, Theron. Ares spawned this creature of death, so anything is possible. If anything, I say we try fire," replied Xanthippe.

For a woman of such advanced age, her spirited nature came through clearly. About five feet tall, she did not present the most imposing image, but her gruff demeanor overcompensated for her lack of stature. Hermæa saw the sun rising and left to attend to morning prayers in the shrine. Moments later, she ran back into the hut, out of breath.

"Come quickly! You must come to the shrine!" she said, turning around and leaving once again.

One by one, they entered the holy structure to see Hermæa standing behind the altar, dumbfounded. The day before, Acastus had left a few whittled staffs, a handful of worn swords brought from Atlantis, and three bows with quivers, all empty. Part of the morning ritual constituted asking Poseidon to bless every venture, including going off to battle, so the soldier had brought the items with the hopes that the priestess would channel Poseidon's good will onto them. Now, as they stood, someone had replaced the original weapons with a dozen freshly forged swords, well-strung bows with stocked quivers, half a dozen quarterstaffs, and bronze shields. Without question, they had enough weapons for just about everyone able to fight.

"Praise Athene," cried Kyros. "As High Elder of Parthos, I charge you, Acastus, with the task of teaching as many men as there are swords how to wield such a weapon well enough to defend this village. Tithonos, gather the hunters and distribute the new bows. Xanthippe, whatever people Acastus does not take for the swords, you hand them a staff. The gods surely bless this venture, and we will fight to the end if necessary." Seeing this gift planted within him a sense of hope and the possibility of at least standing their ground.

Once Acastus had the men and some women assembled, he began the basics of how to hold a sword, how to use its weight in battle, and avoid being hit. He sent two of men, Lycurgos and Sophronios, as scouts to seek out how far away Phlegos and his men were from the village. Every moment counted now, and he made certain his focus did not waver. All of this preparation could be for naught if Phlegos and his army descended upon

Parthos too soon, but the villagers had to hope that the weapons were a sign the gods were on their side, or at least wanted them to have an advantage. Those with swords seemed to take to them quicker than most soldiers would, no doubt some sort of enchantment from Athene to help their skill. Surely the goddess was taking a risk aiding a mortal village, as she knew all too well the wrath of the war god. Acastus left them sparring with one another to check on other parts of the village where the hunters had started refining their aim. Meat, more of a luxury than a staple, was not easy to find, so the hunters who relied on their traps or bows did not have the same archery prowess as a trained soldier. Makeshift targets on the side of wagons allowed for more than enough practice. Some would see a promising, yet reluctant, warrior in Tithonos, who chose the way of the poet more than that of the fighter. Acastus had offered to train him as his replacement, but the young man turned him down, saying he was next in line as village elder and needed to keep his mind sharper than his sword. Leaving the young man behind, Acastus observed women gathering provisions for the village—jugs of water from the well, bushels of apples from the local orchard, and preserving that days' catch from the sea by wrapping it in salted cloth. Even the elder women performed with fervor, knowing all too well the wrath of the malevolence about to invade their home once again. His mind kept going back to the four elements, and the *Tetrastoikeia*, but he could not make sense of such mystical nonsense. Military maneuvers and troop deployment were his strength, not wondering if water sprinkled on his foe would make him melt. It took him a few hours to survey the entire village, bolstering confidence where he could and reassuring the less secure that everything would be all right, even though he knew he could not promise that. Morale, he thought, was paramount. If the people thought they could survive, then

273

they would try their hardest to keep the peaceful life they had fostered in this place. Hearing his name shouted across the village, he focused on one of the scouts running toward him.

"Acastus!" he started, catching his breath, "By my estimate, Phlegos will be at the edge of the grove of Artemis by dawn, which means only a few hours after that, they will be in the village," said Lycurgos.

"Where is Sophronios? Did I not tell you to stay together?"

"He ran ahead to see what else he could find out. I do not imagine he could have wandered too far, he knows we are more vulnerable during daylight."

"I cannot wonder about him now. Did you see any scouts from the warlord's party?"

"Nay, Acastus. I would think they would send a few, just to test us, but I saw nothing."

"That either means they will send them later, or they are able to hide themselves well in the daylight. Nevertheless, stay on guard by the border of the grove, preferably in the trees. Take a bow with you. If you see advancement, send an arrow toward the sea. Once we see that signal, we will prepare to engage them, and may the gods have mercy on our souls." He gently stroked his beard, with his other hand resting on the pommel of his sword.

Once Lycurgos returned to his post, Acastus continued his rounds. Now, they waited.

• • •

Sunrise would normally bring about a hustle of activity in daily chores. As the chariot of the sun god climbed higher above the horizon, Acastus gathered his makeshift soldiers together for one last inspection, offering advice from his vast experience helping to defend Atlantis. The men and women, gathered by the well in the center of

274

town, stood eager to receive whatever their leader could give them.

"Remember what I told you—only engage them if necessary. Strike hard. Your only job is to show these marauders we will not go down without fighting. This will be the last stand. For years, Phlegos has attacked us, knowing we would offer no resistance, but now we stand our ground. You know the risks, and I hope you have made peace with your families should this be your last day. We fight for our freedom! Should this be our final stand, we pray to Hades that we find comfort in Elysium."

Acastus, garbed in his bronze armor, emblazoned with a trident, the symbol of Poseidon, stood tall. Women and children moved to the farthest part of the village, closest to the sea, praying to whichever gods would listen that they should meet their fate quickly. Sarah, who had chosen to remain to Tithonos and the hunters, examined her bow nervously. Kyros' son, aware of Sarah's apprehension, searched for the words to say to ease her mind, but he knew that nothing would pacify her. She was not like any of the women in Parthos, and perhaps that is why he felt the way he did. She radiated strength, despite her pale complexion and distant look. He started to think that maybe he had grown fond of her in a way he had never felt toward another woman, but now would not be the time to tell her. Her red hair, pulled back from her face, shone in the morning sun's rays, making her seem goddess-like to him, unreachable. Regardless, he would do what he could to protect her. In that, he found strength to endure the day's unknown events. For the first time, he had something to believe in and that gave him courage.

Suddenly, an arrow soared overhead, heading for the sea, the signal Acastus had waited for all morning. Freeing his sword from its scabbard, letting the steel breathe, he stood ready. Unknown to Lycurgos, however, Phlegos' men, a scouting party of ten, covered the distance between the grove and the village seemingly with the speed of Hermes, striding confidently out of the woods, swords drawn, into Parthos. Within moments, they would be in the center of town and would engage Acastus and his improvised soldiers.

Covered head to toe in night-stained armor, bearing the wolf's head on each cuirass, Phlegos and his men didn't stop their advancement upon seeing the Parthosians, but paraded up to them, swords gripped tightly. One took a swing at Acastus, who parried the attack, but not without losing his balance, staggering back. The intruders hit with the force of ten men, swinging blindly at their adversaries, simple farmers and hunters. Even though outmatched, the villagers followed their leader's advice, avoiding direct contact unless required, and then striking to wound. Athene's enchanted weapons held their integrity against Phlegos' men, but the latter wore Ares' armor, forged by Hephæstos, and they did more damage. Villagers fell, unable to withstand the brute strength of the attackers, but most Parthosians managed to stand their ground. Only years of fear and anger could be channeled into strength, encouraged even more when volleys of arrows came whistling overhead, crashing into Phlegos' men, taking out dozens. Apparently, only Phlegos was invulnerable to attack from mortals, his men were not. A second spray of arrows, an unexpected assault, reinforced the idea that these villagers would not go down easily. One of Phlegos' men, pulling an arrow from his thigh, ordered his men to fall back to camp. Swords held high, the remaining Parthosians pursued them, but Acastus issued his own order to stand down. They had done what they could, confronting their enemies head on, but not without loss for both sides. Two of the attackers had been struck through the neck with arrows, and they died by choking on their own blood. Seven village men, bearing deep wounds and a few severed limbs, would be the first of Parthos to enter

Hades' realm in this conflict. Considering the skill and ferocity of the warlord's soldiers, they fared better than Acastus had expected. Once Lycurgos sent another arrow, a symbol that the aggressors had left the grove, the task of removing the dark-clad corpses began. Before they could get close enough to move the bodies, they shrank back in horror as the flesh immediately became dust, leaving the body armor behind. Some secrets they literally took to the grave.

Bodies of the fallen, in white funereal shrouds and a coin on each tongue, were cast upon a blazing pyre, sending their souls into the underworld. Families mourned as much as they could before they realized this attack had been a test to see what sort of reception Phlegos' army would receive. Now that they knew the Parthosians had weapons and would fight back, surely the next wave would be even more devastating. Acastus took an account of who remained so he could redistribute the weapons. As much as any Parthosian, he felt the loss of his comrades, but the bigger picture stood before him like a stone monolith. Assuming he would survive this, he would mourn properly, or hope that shades of the dead could mourn in the underworld if that was to be his fate.

According to regular reports from Lycurgos, who grew quickly into stealth, the amassed army was not moving yet, so perhaps the Parthosians, too, had some time to collect themselves and develop another strategy. Sarah had not given up on the idea of the *Tetrastoikeia*, but her lack of familiarity with this time or place made her inner quest almost impossible. The Council of Elders convened almost immediately after the hostilities ceased, sitting with Hermæa who could still not make any headway with the scroll describing the four elements. Hours of discussion produced nothing, but Kyros, Theron, and Xanthippe chose to stay behind and work on the enigma while Hermæa gathered the women and children in the shrine for

277

prayer. Without an oracle who would commune with the gods, they would all have to rely on Lycurgos, a thought that made some uneasy since he could fall asleep on his post or misinterpret the actions of the warlord's factions. No one had seen nor heard from Sophronios since he left, and the general thought was that he had perished on his quest, so his loss was added to the prayers in the shrine so that his soul would reach Elysium.

The following morning, just after sunrise, Lycurgos raced into the village.

"They are advancing! Acastus!"

No sooner had the words left his mouth when an arrowhead burst through Lycurgos' chest, dropping him immediately. Grabbing their weapons, the Parthosians charged for the path out of the woods, the only way to enter the village by land. Like a callous gale force wind, Phlegos' army charged, screaming battle cries into the throng, swinging wildly and hoping their sheer multitude would decimate their victims. Sarah and Hermæa helped lead the women and children to safety by the sea, hiding in a sea cave by the water's edge. Not large enough to protect the entire village, the cave would at least keep some safe while the battle waged. Once she could account for everyone, Sarah carefully raced back to the village, grabbing her bow and quiver along the way. War cries and screams deafened her as she found her way to the edges of the melee, seeing huts either burned from fire arrows or crushed beneath warhorse hooves. She kept to the sidelines, terrified for her life, but also fearing the loss of so many innocent people. The carnage that spread before her made her rage within, but her helplessness kept her from engaging any of the attackers. As she made her way around a corner, debris from dozens of clay pots and figurines littered the path. Crushed beneath the weight of a collapsed hut, the kiln lay cracked open, its embers smoking from contact with straw from the roof. So many pieces of pottery had been obliterated, the handiwork of these skilled craftswomen, the death of a culture. In the rubble, she recognized the pot she had made days earlier, now in pieces, and picked up some of the shards before she heard shouts behind her. Vaguely she could hear anguished cries that Phlegos himself was coming, which would assuredly mean the destruction of Parthos and everyone in it, including her. Above all the din, a pained cry came from the fray; it was Tithonos. Without thinking about herself, she ran out into the fighting, seeing his still body amid the others, a spear jutting from his heart. Dread overcame her, and she ran to his side, imploring him to get up, but after a few tries, she realized he was dead. The earth rumbled as more horses came from the forest, and she ran into the woods on the other side of the village, hiding behind a tree. All of this was too much for her, and she wept unceasingly, for Tithonos, Parthos, and for herself, knowing she would die. As she wiped the tears from her face, she still held the shard of pottery, its bare edges crumbling from the sweat in her hand. As if clouds of mystery evaporated, she had an epiphany. It made sense to her now, and she wondered why she had not thought of it earlier. Pulling an arrow from her quiver, she removed the arrowhead. The thin, leather thong tying her hair worked well to attach the piece of pottery to the arrow. She tugged on it just enough to make sure it would not come loose, praying that her conclusion was correct. One last deep breath and she returned to the village, bodies from both sides on the ground, some dead, others wounded. Fifty feet before her stood the scourge that had brought this destruction upon them. Off to the left, Tithonos' body lay, his lifeless face staring at her, fueling her rage. Fire rose from the depths of her soul, burning away her fear, and she slowly raised her bow. Stretching the string tighter, the arrow slowly slid across the shelf of the handle, until her right hand was next to her ear.

"Phlegos!" she screamed, her voice cracking, tears trickling down her cheeks.

At first, he stood unmoved, ordering his soldiers, but when Sarah screamed again, the words 'heartless murderer' caught his attention. He walked closer to her, intrigued, crunching bodies of the deceased. The warlord reached down, resting his gauntlet on the hilt of his sword.

"I want to see the face of the man who destroyed this village before I destroy *him*."

He laughed. "You amuse me, girl. Why should I not kill you right now?"

"Pray to Ares that he might save your soul because I don't care where it goes after you're gone."

She had never felt such rage, such passion, for anything before, not even her family or friends. Every hair on her body tingled while her muscles pulled the string taut. Fear kept her fingers from releasing the arrow.

"Ares protects me, little girl. Do you think you can hurt me with that? Now, put down the bow and surrender. It would be for the best. You would make an excellent concubine."

His eyes flared, revealing his divine heritage and his hubris. She wanted to wipe that sanctimonious look off his face, and she knew he was trying to get to her. Too late. The carnage had already pushed her way beyond the edge. Blood spatter and chunks of flesh on his black armor made her nauseated, but she would not relent, not now. Sarah noticed he nodded his head to the right just a little, a signal for one of his men to raise his bow. She knew that he would kill her as soon as she released the arrow, but she knew of no other way to end this. With so many Parthosians dead, she had to hold her ground. Distant shouts aroused Phlegos' suspicions, but he did not move.

"Demos, go see what that is," he ordered the archer.

"Yes, Lord Phlegos. What about the girl?"

"I will handle her."

They way he stressed 'handle' made Sarah shiver, not with fear, but with resolute anger. She would be no one's concubine.

"You know you cannot defeat me," he began, taking slow steps toward her, "so why not end this folly now. After all, I am the son of Ares. Not even the gods dare stand against him, or me."

Every few words, he moved closer, keeping his eyes on her, but his hand never left the hilt of the sword. He removed the sword, revealing the bloodstained blade. Her heart pounded in her chest, but she could not drop her bow. He moved closer. With every step, he crushed a body beneath his foot, bones cracking under the weight.

Twenty feet separated them now.

She wondered why none of his soldiers had tried to kill her yet, but realized that he was playing with her, and his men knew that. He did not think she could defeat him, so he was playing a game—why just kill her when he could humiliate her first.

Fifteen feet.

"Sarah! What are you doing?" shouted Kyros. "You will get yourself killed!"

She moved her head slightly in the direction of the voice, and Phlegos took the opportunity to lunge forward, his sword above his head. All she could hear was the plink of the bowstring as she let it go, releasing all the tension.

Ten feet.

Phlegos advanced, ignoring the arrow, until he felt it breach his armor, tearing into his chest, stopping him cold. He looked down in horror, his blood spilling onto the ground, but pushed a few more steps. His body burst into flames, consuming him entirely, rendering him into dust at her feet. The sulphur stench permeated the air as the dust blew away in the wind. Reacting to the fall of their leader, Phlegos' men drew their bows to kill Sarah, but a familiar voice erupted from the woods behind her.

"Drop your weapons!" shouted Sophronios.

Immediately, out of the woods, appeared a hundred warriors, bows drawn. Their armor, polished silver, with an eagle prominently emblazoned on each cuirass, flashed in the sun.

"I say again, drop your weapons."

Amid battle cries, the warlord's soldiers advanced, only to be stopped by a barrage of steel-tipped arrows. As each shaft hit, it produced a hollow thud, piercing flesh and ripping through bone. One by one, the dark army fell, and any remaining retreated back the way they had come.

Sophronios ran up to Sarah, whose hand bled from tightly gripping her bow.

"He is gone," he said gently. "He is gone. Let go of the bow. Everything is all right now."

She turned toward him and collapsed, the shock too much for her. Holding her gently, he lifted her up and carried her to the nearest hut, kicked the door open, and placed her on a bed. He found some water and a piece of cloth and gently cleaned her bleeding hands. He whispered a 'thank you' before he left the hut, waving over two soldiers.

"Let no one enter. She needs to rest."

Taking either side of the door, they staffed their post as if she were royalty.

• • •

Slowly Sarah's eyes fluttered open, adjusting to her surroundings, but too tired to move. She could make out the face of Kyros, his wife, and Hermæa, all smiling at her.

"Thank the gods," muttered Hermæa.

"Are you all right?" asked Kyros. "You have been asleep for three days."

"Three days?" Sarah replied softly. "How did I get here?"

"Sophronios brought you here and tended to your hand."

She looked down at her left hand, meticulously bandaged. Tears filled her eyes and spilled over onto her cheeks. It really did happen. For one brief moment, she had thought all of this had been a dream, or a nightmare. Behind Kyros stood Sophronios, smiling at her. Words would not come, but her expression was thanks enough, and he nodded back. Sarah tried to sit up, but Kyros gently pushed her back down.

"No, you rest. You have been through more in just a few days than any of us have been through in a few years. My wife will stay with you if you require anything. We have posted two guards by your door so that you will not be disturbed."

Too tired to resist, she let herself fall asleep. In her dreams, she relived the last moments with Phlegos just before she let the arrow fly. She would not know this now, but sleep—or rather, Morpheos—would be a conduit through which much knowledge would come. The dream changed, she felt herself walk through a pool of water, and then she stopped moving. An otherworldly bliss overcame her and pushed the pain away, releasing the anguish she had felt, and she felt her body and mind healing itself. Warm waters soothed her and cleansed her wound, renewing her strength and vitality. In this dream state, she left the pool and drifted back to consciousness, but she wanted to stay.

The following morning, she awoke refreshed and slowly stood up. Bread, fruit, and pomegranate juice sat on the table, a welcomed feast after being asleep for so long. Sarah put on the tunic left for her by Kyros' wife, a bright blue cloth trimmed with gold thread, as well as a pair of leather sandals. As she pushed her way into the daylight, she shielded her eyes from the sun's rays until her eyes adjusted. Slightly lightheaded, she leaned for a moment on one of the guards, who held out his arm to support her. Kyros and his wife saw her and rushed over.

"Good morning, Sarah. You are looking well. How do you feel?"

"Better, Kyros, thank you."

"Sarah, we are all indebted to you for your courage."

She simply smiled, not sure how to respond.

"Come walk with me," requested Kyros, extended his hand.

He led her down a path toward the grove of Artemis, through the trees, down into a valley where the path turned to follow the course of a river.

"When you first arrived, I was uncertain as to why you had come, but now I know you were sent by the gods to aid us in our dilemma, and aid us you did. I know you have felt like an outsider here, but I hope you know how much you have become a member of our family even in such a short time."

She embraced him.

"Kyros, I am so sorry about Tithonos."

"Fear not, child, he is walking the fields in Elysium. I am very proud of my son for standing up for what he believed. Now we have other matters to discuss. Hermæa consulted with Poseidon, who wished to repay you for your courage, and he asked us to give you something of great value."

He reached into a small pouch attached to his belt.

"If you remember, when we first discovered the *Tetrastoikeia*, the parchment spoke of a key which would make the enchantment work. This ring, worn by King Euenor, is that key, and I believe this is the treasure that Phlegos wanted. The means to call forth the magic is unknown to us, but it still symbolizes all the goodness that Atlantis represents, so please take this as a token of our thanks. You must be a true daughter of Atlantis."

She wanted to refuse, but his expression would not let her. "I'm speechless. Thank you, Kyros," she replied, gingerly putting the ring on her finger.

"The ring has four gems, each one representing one of the four elements. I thought it a fitting tribute."

Continuing to walk along the path, Sarah absorbed the beauty of the Parthosian countryside. She had had no idea how far the land reached, but it did bring a question to mind.

"Kyros, who were those men that Sophronios brought with him? I know they weren't Parthosians."

"Aye, they were from the city of Olympæa. Sophronios had found a traveler who took him as far as the city, where he implored the city elders to help us. Some of the soldiers have volunteered to stay on and help us rebuild. Phlegos' forces decimated most of our warriors, so we have need of strong, able men to help return Parthos to its original state. Fortunately, the women and children stayed safe in the cave, thanks to Poseidon."

He paused. "Well, we have one more matter to which we must attend. Poseidon has intervened on your behalf, making arrangements for you to return home."

"I'm going home? How is that possible?" she asked, clasping Kyros' hands.

A voice from behind them answered, "I can take you."

She did know what to think when a young man, dressed in a white tunic, wearing both winged sandals and a winged silver helmet, clasping a silver caduceus, stood before her. His feet hovered over the ground, the wings almost invisible.

"Keep us in your thoughts, Sarah," implored Kyros, embracing her one last time.

"But, what about—"

"I will give them your farewells. Worry not. May the gods be with you!"

Hermes took her hand gently, lifting her a few inches from the ground, and proceeded down the path, vanishing in a cloud.

• • •

The next thing she knew, she was sitting in her bathtub, the water still quite hot, steamy curls rising from the surface. Glancing over at the clock, she saw it was only a minute after she had drawn the bath, but it had felt like an eternity. Her left hand had healed, if it had even been hurt at all, but on her finger sat the ring with its four gemstones. She unplugged the stopper and toweled herself dry, watching the swirls of clay spiral down the drain, reminding her of the clay arrowhead she had used to vanquish Phlegos. Somehow she knew this had all been real.

.

# 21—FINDING PEACE

**Radio Sudamérica (Bogotá, Colombia)** "For WPR News, this is Jaime Gonzalez. Colombian drug czar Honorio Miguel Ortiz surrendered to Task Force: Theta operatives this morning at Bogotá International Airport after agents found seventeen kilos of cocaine in ceramic jewelry boxes he had tried to smuggle into the United States. Five of Miguel Ortiz's bodyguards tried to protect their employer, but Theta operatives and local Bogotá police shot three and captured the other two men, leaving the known drug lord vulnerable. Government and Theta operatives revealed that sources close to Miguel Ortiz swore he would be back once he posted bail which authorities estimate will be $15.2 million dollars."

• • •

This won't work, she thought.

Chasing Stymphalian birds around Manhattan wasn't accomplishing anything, Aleta mused. Perched on a marble gargoyle jutting from the Pioneer Bank building, the tallest one on Pine Street, she keenly kept an eye on the group of metallic birds hovering over the financial district of New York City. Of course, traffic had stopped moving hours ago when people first spotted these birds, but they didn't so much see them first, but rather smell them first.

287

Stymphalian birds reek of decaying flesh that sat out in the sun, in Death Valley, for a week.

Normally, to catch a flock of these carnivorous creatures would take a herculean effort, but that hero wasn't around, and Aleta didn't have much time. Soon, rush hour would come, and even more cars and taxicabs would fill the streets, if that were possible. More people meant more food. Needing more time to think of a good plan, Aleta took flight, her white wings flapping rigorously to get her to the right height to where she could zoom past the half dozen birds, distracting them and coaxing them to follow her. The stench just about overpowered her as she soared within striking range, close enough to see the sunlight reflecting off bronze feathers. Screeching loud enough to rattle windows all along Wall Street, the six birds took the bait, following their white-winged prey higher into the near cloudless sky.

"Perfect," Aleta thought. "Not only do I have to get rid of these foul things, I get to have all of Lower Manhattan watch."

With avian bone structure, she had no trouble climbing to great heights, lifting her body into the sky to keep the monsters distracted. Birds have hollow bones, allowing them to keep themselves aloft, and Aleta had become accustomed to managing her body weight over the past few months, flying reconnaissance at night, looking for underworld inhabitants who had entered her world uninvited. Flying over the East River would work for a short while until the birds either tired of flying around or became even more ravenous. The stench of mortals to a Stymphalian bird was quite appetizing, so much so that one bird could eat about ten mortals in one feeding. It was time to change up the strategy.

Climbing higher and higher, she waited until they were following her closely before she dove straight for the river. Timing was crucial if she wanted to catch it just right. Tucking her wings against her body, she headed straight toward the water—a bit disconcerting, especially if she didn't want to kill herself in the process. About ten feet from the surface, she spread the white wings wide, turning her body just enough to skim the water like a skipping stone and heading away from the island. Metal birds weigh considerably more than humans, even humans with wings, and two of the birds couldn't turn fast enough and exploded on impact with the surface, metal feathers flung like shrapnel. Four more to go.

She had another way out, but she dithered on whether or not to use it since it could do much more damage if not done correctly. Only twice had she used her weapon before, and one time she couldn't control it the way she wanted to, so there was one McDonald's in Quincy, Massachusetts that would need to repair its parking lot. Aleta's rationale was, if a Crommyonæan Sow hadn't tried to devour half of Quincy, she wouldn't have had to go to that extreme. Extending her hand, a snakelike thunderbolt came at her beckoning, leaving the weapon in her hand. Like most birds, she had the ability to sense changes in the weather, and this change she would welcome with open wings. Another circular maneuver around the Stymphalians got their attention, and then Aleta took off for the open ocean, hoping they would follow and not sense what she did.

Southeast of Long Island, out over the Atlantic, brewed a storm system large enough to concern people in Pennsylvania, bringing with it a thunderstorm that would be portentous for anything seaborne. Winds picked up velocity the closer she got, and the idea of flying even closer didn't thrill her, but she had no more options. The crew of a fishing trawler, anchored out in open water, couldn't believe what they saw: four gargantuan golden birds that smelled worse than rotten fish chasing a woman with white wings. Aleta stopped for a moment, hovering, just to see where they were, and they were closing in much faster than she thought they could. Amazing things, these mythological monsters, she thought. It made her smile a little at how fitting it was to think that an entrance to Hades could be somewhere in the financial district of Manhattan. Over the city, the temperature was in the mid-80s, but out over the ocean, with a storm sweeping through, the air dropped about ten to fifteen degrees and the winds picked up.

Blanket flashes of lightning above the thunderhead lit her way as sheets of rain descended like silver javelins. Despite the raging wind, Aleta climbed higher until she reached the top of the cloud. Once the Stymphalian birds were in view, she dove headfirst into the anvil of the cumulonimbus, spiraling down toward the water. Dark gray clouds surrounded her, with forks of lightning stabbing through, and it was only a matter of time until she had what she wanted. Moving quickly across the ocean, the storm swelled, echoing thunder ravaging the sky. All of the birds had her in their sight, and she hoped that the storm would do exactly as she knew it would. Pointing the weapon at her prey, she first felt the tingle of electricity in the air through her wings, and strands of living light struck out, making contact with the metal birds. One by one, as lightning hit, each creature exploded, showering the ocean with bronze fragments. The crisis averted for the moment, she did one more pass through the cloud until she knew she had destroyed the birds and headed back to the city.

Landing in an alley near Battery Park, she folded her wings folded behind her, and they withdrew from sight. Once her pulse returned to normal, she found the Dumpster behind which she had hidden her clothes and, back in her business suit, went off to find dinner. Flying always made her appetite rage, burning up so many calories, and she was suddenly hungry for chicken. On the corner of Battery Place and Greenwich Street, she found a quaint French restaurant, ordered a glass of Pinot Noir, and laughed to herself about how she had come to be soaring above the clouds.

• • •

"Are we ready, Jack?" asked Dr. Halston, looking intently through her microscope.

The man she addressed was Dr. Jack Forrester, her partner in genetic research. An average person in all aspects, including stature and appearance, he fostered a deep enmity for Aleta, or Dr. Halston as people knew her at Genetix, because she had done what he could not— succeed. He could never speak to her without gritting his teeth, and scorn shot from his eyes like rabid daggers. Friends in medical school, they both simultaneously worked multiple jobs and studied up until their residencies, when hospitals and medical schools forbid students from holding down any other job. Aleta, having grown up with a veterinarian for a mother, had worked around animals her entire life, so working in animal DNA research was as natural to her as breathing. Jack, on the other hand, chose genetics because he thought it would be lucrative, but any self-respecting scientist knew that money only came after years of signing oneself over into indentured servitude to a genetic research facility, publishing multiple times, and teaching doctoral level courses, things Jack didn't want to do. Also, a certain amount of sexism factored into his feelings, the only aspect of Jack's personality that Aleta could handle because her reputation was global.

If it weren't for Aleta, they would not even have the grants to do their research. Genetix hired them both, back when they were amicable, to be part of a team of geneticists trying to isolate the gene in animals that makes some immune to cancer. Ironically, Jack would prefer to do little and ride someone else's coattails, but at the same time, he wanted fame. Puddles of rainwater weren't as shallow as Jack Forrester was.

"Yes, we are," he replied. "Where's the subject?"

"In the cage. We need to check his blood level for the mutations. You know, if you'd rather not do this…"

"No, it's fine. Besides, someone needs to make sure your calculations are correct."

She ignored his comment. Jack brought the cage over and took out the ferret. With rubber gloves on, he removed one vial of blood, putting it into the centrifuge where it would process for a half hour. Aleta stopped what she was doing, inhaled deeply, and looked up.

"I'll be so happy when this is over," she commented, under her breath. Three days without rest she had been in the lab. After these procedures, she told herself, she would take a few days off. Finding the cancer-inhibiting gene was her priority, though.

Aleta made her way to the counter, poured herself a cup of day-old coffee, and then plopped down on the sofa in the lounge. Jack entered behind her and sat in the chair across from her.

"Are you okay?"

She couldn't tell if he really cared, or he wanted to know she was in some kind of discomfort. He was guilty of schadenfreude on occasion.

"Jack, I'm fine," she snipped, rubbing her eyes.

"Hey, just checking. Since you won't let me help with this part of the process, the least I can do is inquire into your health and well being," he grinned.

She wanted to slap that toothy smile off his face.

"Well, thanks, Jack," Aleta retorted, sipping the stale source of caffeine. "When is the next shipment due in?"

"This afternoon. When do we get our payment for this? We seriously overextended ourselves on this equipment."

"Jack, I know, but we had no choice. We *are* still in this for the human factor, right? We get our money when we show results," she said, putting her feet up on the table and throwing back the rest of her coffee. "Pharmaceutical companies want to know how to proceed."

"Well, listen, it's almost 10:30. How about we run down to the cafeteria for some food? Or are you not eating?" he asked.

"I'm not that hungry," she said, shaking her head.

She returned to the lab while Jack went downstairs. A few minutes without him sniping at her would be a mini-vacation, she thought. Rotating her head to relieve some of the pressure in her neck, she resumed her watch on the slide.

Behind her was the fruit of her labor, with little help from Dr. Forrester—a computer that transferred molecules from one place to another, although primarily used to transfer genetic material from one creature to another. She had written her doctoral thesis on trans-animal genetic transfer, something that few had every tried. With worldwide governmental agencies, like Global Health Initiative, or GHI, leaning so heavily on profit margins and less on humanitarian efforts, she had to put in more time and money of her own just to make herself known in the medical community. With this technology, theoretically, a geneticist could target malignant neoplastic cells and remove them by calibrating the Genetic Transfer Device (GTD), something of a futuristic transporter, and replace the cancer cells with benign ones. Neoplastic cells generate a certain DNA structure that, when targeted can be removed with 99.95% accuracy. They might need a brief dose of chemotherapy or radiation treatment to remove the last .05%, but that also depended on the severity of the illness.

The GTD could also perform simultaneous transfer of matter as well as combining two types of living cells together, merging their DNA signatures into a mutation. That technology might be necessary to strengthen genetic anomalies or correct illnesses due to inbreeding where the species, certain dog species for example, would fail to thrive. Cross-species attempts had not been successful, however. Without some success to show for their work, those who gave them funding would not renew their grants.

At 10:30 p.m., operatives from Task Force: Eta, a UN agency whose sphere of influence was endangered species, brought in their next shipment of animals: two dogs, a fox, and an eagle. Sometimes the operatives delivered medical material or sensitive data, depending on the requesting source. Aleta had just finished dinner, another break in time away from Jack Forrester, and had to check in the shipment.

"Hmm... okay... two golden retrievers, one silver-tipped fox, one white eagle," she said. "A white eagle, eh? How odd. Never heard of that before." Shrugging it off as an albino, she brought the animals into the testing area. Dr. Forrester surreptitiously walked up to Aleta, who was checking the vital signs of the animals. He had pulled this routine one too many times.

"Fell asleep in the lounge again, Jack? You've been gone since lunch."

He mumbled a reply and cataloged the new test subjects. The dogs had a rare blood disease, presumably from the same litter; the fox had a small tumor on his front left leg; the eagle came in as 'infection unknown', not an uncommon classification. From the blood work, the procedure worked for the dogs, which they then sent to a recovery room, but the fox went into cardiac arrest and did not survive. The eagle puzzled Aleta, as she had never known an eagle to have an ailment. The bird seemed fine, but she would run a diagnostic x-ray using the GTD anyway to see what was so 'unknown' about the infection. Aleta encouraged the eagle to step onto her forearm, something she had learned from her mother, and carried it to the right-hand chamber of the GTD. Jack, meanwhile, watched from a safe distance. He constantly wanted to outshine Aleta a bit, so perhaps the grant committee would fund his research instead.

Dr. Halston placed a Petri dish in the left chamber with the intent of transferring some of whatever she did find in the eagle into it for further analysis. Turning the corner from the stockroom, Jack saw Aleta in the chamber and found his chance. Pushing the button that closed the chamber, he smiled as Aleta turned around.

"Jack! Open this door! Damn it, Jack!"

Hesitating for just a moment, he reached down on the console and activated the lock, the click in the chamber sending a chill up her spine. This was no longer a sick joke; he meant to do this. The lever had five distinct settings ranging from x-ray to transfer of cellular clumps up to removal of brain tissue, which was too unstable to remove and then transplant. They had never before tested the final setting, cellular blending. Geneticists the world over found that cellular blending would endanger the animals cellular integrity.

Jack slammed the lever to the highest setting; he would say it was her idea. At the very least, she would be in a vegetative state. Worst case? Well, then he could take over her research, after feigning an appropriate time to grieve, of course. It would be his word against hers, if she could even speak afterwards.

"You always have to have the glory, don't you," he began. "It's always 'Dr. Halston's outstanding research revealed...' or 'Dr. Halston's in-depth study brought to light...' Well, now Dr. Forrester can share in some of that. Don't you think?"

"Jack, if that's what you want, then you can have it. You want my credit? Done! Just get me out of here!" she screamed, her voice slightly muffled by the glass.

"What? Can't hear you. Sorry."

Pounding on the glass, her cries went unacknowledged. She crumbled to the floor of the chamber, praying for a quick death. Her head in her lap, she heard Jack flip the switch to begin the transfer just before he left the lab.

• • •

Two hours later, he returned. The chamber with the eagle was empty, not even a trace of feathers. The doctor's lifeless body lay sprawled out in the other chamber, her clothes tattered, a hazy smoke swirling around. She looked intact, dead, but intact. Feigning horror, he called for security.

"Help me! Please! She wouldn't listen to me! I told her not to do it!"

"Calm down, Dr. Forrester. What happened?" one guard asked, looking around the lab.

"Come quickly!" he exclaimed, taking them to Aleta's lifeless body.

The guards opened the chamber and checked for a pulse. None. No breathing. They attempted CPR multiple times, and after about ten minutes, a faint pulse returned. Dr. Forrester excused himself from the lab before security could question him.

"What.. What happened?"

"You were involved in a laboratory accident, Dr. Halston. Are you all right?" replied one of the guards, "Dr. Forrester was just here, but I guess he had to check on something."

For the moment, Jack Forrester was safe. Temporary amnesia had erased some of her more recent memories. In her haze, Dr. Halston noticed that the eagle was no longer in the chamber, but the glass was broken. Then, she passed out.

The next morning, her eyes gradually focused on a man's face.

"She's coming around, Doctor."

A dark-haired man entered with her chart.

"Good morning, Dr. Halston. How are you feeling?" he asked, thumbing through the chart.

Too tired to speak, she nodded her head. She was fine.

"I'm glad to hear that. You gave us all quite a shock. You were involved in a laboratory experiment. Do you remember what happened?"

She shook her head a little.

As her vision improved, she saw an old friend, Dr. Cooper. Dr. Harris Cooper. She interned with him when she was in training at Genetix. He left the field of genetic research and went back to his previous area, internal medicine.

"Hey Harry," she whispered, "Am I going to live?"

"I hope so. You still owe me a racquetball game," he retorted, checking her IV.

Dr. Cooper made a gesture for others to leave. As the door clicked shut, he sat down beside her.

"You know, your experiments are going to be the death of you someday," he remarked, giggling. "Best we can surmise from the settings on the GTD is that you wanted to try genetic cellular transfer on a human using yourself as the subject. We don't know what the other container held."

Her eyes widened. An eagle, Aleta thought.

Dr. Cooper kept her in the hospital for a week for more tests, despite her protests.

Two nights before the hospital would release her, the night nurse went to wake Aleta to bring her dinner, but she wouldn't wake up. Her monitor showed a steady heart rhythm, but nothing the nurse did roused Aleta, so she paged Dr. Cooper who was also unable to get her to wake up. What they didn't notice was a sandy residue on her eyelids. No matter what they would try, nothing could bring her from this type of sleep, not after Morpheos brought her into a dreamscape. Aleta could hear them, but she was unable to respond, and soon the voices faded.

• • •

"Wake up!" a voice shouted at her, followed by cold water in her face.

"Huh.. what?" Aleta coughed, sitting up abruptly. Looking around, she realized she was in the woods, lying on the ground. Naked.

"Who are you?" demanded a voice, distinctively female. "Why do you trespass our woods?"

After wiping the water from her face, her eyes focused and saw three women wearing armor, and one—the one who had thrown water on her—was waving a sword in her face.

"Have you no voice? Answer me!"

"Sister, perhaps she does not speak our tongue," suggested one of the companions.

Aleta stood up slowly, taking in the whole scene. One of the women removed her cloak and tossed it at her.

"Who am *I*? Who the hell are you? And why are you throwing water on me? Where am I?"

The three women laughed. A sergeant, the one waving the sword, commented, "She certainly is a feisty one. I like her. I am Okypous. This is Eumache and Sinope."

"Aleta. Aleta Halston," she replied, her mind absorbing everything. "Where am I?"

"In the Forest of Artemis, on the outskirts of Olympæa."

Wrapping the cloak around her, Aleta raised an eyebrow at Okypous.

"Excuse me? I'm where?"

"This is a sacred forest to the goddess Artemis, Aleta Halston," snapped Sinope. "You would do best to watch your tone speaking to an Amazon."

Eumache, clearly the most amiable of the group, tried to explain to Aleta, who was still groggy from being awakened so abruptly, where Olympæa was. Eumache escorted Aleta way from the others.

"You seem disoriented, sister. Are you well? Did you drink too much wine and wander into the forest?"

"No, I didn't drink too much wine. I was asleep in my hospital bed, and the next thing I remember was your friend over there throwing water on my face," replied Aleta. She realized she was being bad-tempered, so she took a deep breath and tried a different tack. "Your names sound Greek. Are you Greek? Did I hear that other woman correctly when she called herself an Amazon?"

Finding the questions a bit odd, Eumache replied cautiously, "Yes, Aleta Halston, we are Amazons of the White Eagle tribe. And, yes, we are Greek. Olympæa is on the western side of the country, near Elis. Near the *Mesogeios*."

"By the way, you only have to call me by my first name—Aleta." She realized she didn't really understand some of what Eumache told her, but she decided not to pursue it.

"We should take you to our village and meet our Oracle. My hope is that she may know more about your predicament."

Eumache and her sisters escorted Aleta out of the forest into a clearing where a dozen more Amazons met them. One of the women offered her sandals to Aleta, saying the ground could be quite rough for those who did not know the terrain. For some reason, Aleta started to feel itchy on her back, but she rotated her shoulders under the cloak and it seemed to do the trick. As they walked through the rest of the forest, the sun pierced the canopy, striking the leafy ground, highlighting various parts of the undergrowth. Each woman wore leather armor, but some of them also had metal plating on their cuirass, some showed an eagle from the side, others showed just an eagle head. Eumache wasn't joking when she said they were of the White Eagle tribe, Aleta thought. *My mind must be trying to deal with what happened to me.* All of the women had long hair, either braided down the back or wound above their head, held in place with sticks or crude metal pins, and they all had weapons. The most popular weapon of choice was a dagger, some strapped to a thigh, some to an arm, and only Eumache, Sinope, and Okypous had swords. Something about these women was strangely beautiful, Aleta thought, even though she wouldn't see them winning any contests. It was a natural beauty, the kind one had by living off the land and respecting it. Aleta's mother was such a woman when they lived in Colorado. About thirty minutes passed before they reached another clearing, but this time the trees surrounding it were devoid of branches for the first fifty or so feet. When she looked up, Aleta could see tree houses built onto the larger branches, and some of which incorporated the thick oak trunks. For as far as she could see into the canopy, dwellings sat on various branches, and on one particular oak tree, right in the center, sat the most ornate of them all. These weren't tree houses built for children; these warriors had meant for this construction to last.

Two other women climbed down from this larger dwelling to greet the scouting party. One wore her cloak over her head, hiding her face, and the rest of her body was covered in a strange quilt of feathers, leaves, and flowers—all white—and this conjured the image from Aleta's dream of wearing a similar garment. The other woman, dressed like the others, wore a thin silver band around her head, a simple ornament, but this denoted her station.

"Your Majesty, this is Aleta. We found her unconscious in the Forest of Artemis."

"An outworlder," spoke the shrouded woman. She held out her hands.

Slowly, Aleta placed her hands in the woman's hands.

"*Oikoumene Broteios*," she whispered. "My first. Surely the gods have had a hand in this."

The queen eyed Aleta. "Does she pose a threat?"

"No, Your Majesty," the Oracle replied. "I sense no malice."

"I see. Welcome. My sisters will see that you receive food and water. Oracle, come."

Both women climbed back into the tree gracefully, if one could do such a thing. Eumache brought a tunic for Aleta, and another Amazon brought a basket of apples, pears, and pomegranates as well as a metal cup of water. With the approval of their Oracle, the other Amazons treated Aleta with kindness and acceptance as if four words—'I sense no malice'—were enough to assuage their concerns. Such trust they must place in her judgment. The queen's tone seemed detached, even with her offering the hospitality of her people. A quiet spot at the base of a birch tree provided Aleta with the opportunity to eat, drink, and take everything in as the women performed their daily tasks.

With nothing to do, and with no one really paying much attention to her now, Aleta followed a dirt path through the forest, hoping not to get lost. She really needed to clear her head, though, and taking long walks, as she used to do in Colorado, helped her find peace. Something about the air quality intrigued her—no pollutants. All she could smell were the trees, fragrant honeysuckle somewhere in the distance, and the moist loam of the path. The trail diverged a bit, and now ornamental sticks, clean of their bark, lined the sides. Surely, the Amazons were not doing decorative landscaping, she thought. This had to have meaning. When she looked up, she realized she'd reached the end, and it spilled into a circular grassy area bordered by stones. In the center sat a stone table, so natural looking it actually looked as if it had grown from the earth, with grass fringing the base. Piled in the center were offerings of fruits, flowers, vegetables, and feathers.

"Peaceful place, isn't it? You do know that it happened for a reason," a voice said, as soft as the breeze blowing through the glade. "I know that doesn't make it right, but the Fates see a purpose for everything."

Across the table, a shower of sunbeams drenched a woman who Aleta thought was an Amazon. Her leather tunic, with a braided gold cord at her waist, had no blemishes on it, though, unlike the leather armor she had seen on the others. Auburn hair, braided down her back, was nestled beneath a simple silver ringlet resting on her brow adorned only by one small, silver crescent. Aleta knew exactly what the woman meant.

"You're not one of them. I'm going to take a wild guess and say you're a goddess."

The woman nodded once. "Artemis."

"So, do you know this reason? Does this have something to do with that prophecy?"

Artemis walked over to Aleta's side of the table. "If the Fates wanted us to know why they did things, we would know. I know that doesn't justify it, but even the gods don't have all the answers. Omniscience is a myth, Aleta."

A peace that Aleta had only felt when she lived among the animals her mother took care of at the veterinary hospital emanated from Artemis. Respect the creature, and it will respect you, Aleta's mother used to tell her. It was within this peace that she felt comfortable enough to share what had happened to her in the laboratory, whether Artemis understood or not. With the experience came tears—and rage. A protector of women, the goddess understood what it meant to be violated: Actaeon and Orion had done so in different ways. Artemis would have offered to kill the man who did this to Aleta, but she knew Zeus would never consent for her to leave the *Ge Theôn*, and Aleta would need to find her own path. She would give the mortal woman a gift, something that might assuage her anger and channel it into purpose. Even though Zeus' daughter didn't entirely understand how science worked, being mystical herself, she felt the presence of the something within Aleta, something that would come out eventually. She would... help. Artemis, holding Aleta while she released her pain through tears, reached deep within to trigger that which Jack Forrester had hoped would have killed his colleague. A silver rain fell on them both, and *Artemis Hêmerasia*—she who soothes—caressed this pained woman, reaching inside to give her the peace she needed to reclaim her wholeness once again. Aleta allowed herself to feel the range of emotions: anger, denial, revenge, and despair. As the rain subsided, Artemis helped Aleta to stand up.

"These women hold many things sacred. You can find peace among them for a time, if you wish. I think even Zeus would indulge me that."

Both of them spoke for a short time longer before they took another path out of the glade toward the sea. In Artemis, Aleta found a confidant of sorts. She knew the goddess would never betray her trust; such is the sacred bond women have. Who knew she could have such an unassuming relationship with an immortal, Aleta thought. She had always thought the mythical gods to be aloof, petty, and unkind; at least the stories she had read as a child had painted them as such. Perhaps they could be. Right now, though, she was experiencing a side of Artemis that few ever saw. As they walked further toward the sea, Aleta could smell the salt and the sea grasses, and the gentle hiss of the waves crashing in the distance helped soothe her. This part of the village ended abruptly at cliffs that stood over 300 feet above the water, part of the protection offered to the tribe. Only the queen and a handful of the women had come from the tribe of

Amazons from the river Thermodon, prophecy guiding them to this part of Greece and settle. Artemis chose them to take upon the sacred task of guarding her father's shrine in Olympæa, an honor they had upheld for many generations. Only a handful of Amazons guarded the temple and its grounds at a time, and the duty lasted a year, after which, another group would take over. While not initially a god they would worship, their reverence for Zeus was only surpassed by that for his daughter.

In a barren area by the cliffs about a half mile away, two young Amazon girls played with a child who could be no more than two years old. They rolled a small ball to her, and she attempted to roll it back, but she didn't have the strength yet to do it. Continuing their walk, Aleta watched the girls play, remembering her childhood games back at Steamboat Springs Elementary School, a much simpler time. It surprised her that she could see that far so clearly, but she said nothing to Artemis. Just as the path turned to back toward the tree house village, one of the older girls shouted something, and Aleta turned to see the child go toward the cliff to retrieve the ball, but she tripped on a rock, falling over the cliff edge. Without a second thought, Aleta ran toward the cliff edge, hoping to grab the child, making the distance quicker than she thought she might, but found herself going over the edge. The weirdest sensation came over her, but she just felt the need to keep reaching. Instinct took over, and a pair of white wings extended from her back, helping her to glide downward to the child whose piercing shriek reached into Aleta's soul. Grabbing hold, she cradled the young body against her as her powerful wings flapped back up to the cliff. Her only priority was getting the child to safety.

Once back on the ground, Aleta made sure the child was unharmed. Despite the girl's panic-stricken state, she was fine. A small crowd of Amazons had gathered by the two girls who had told them of Aleta's actions, and seeing the winged woman carrying the child, Sinope ran to them.

"Praise the gods! Is she all right?"

Aleta handed the child over and watched Okypous, this strong warrior, soften into a maternal, sensitive woman. It was hard to believe that not long ago she had waved a sword in Aleta's face. Once they assessed that the child, Euryleia, was indeed well, all attention fell to Aleta for obvious reasons. Artemis remained in the background.

"How did this happen?" asked one of the women.

"You are a chosen of the gods!" exclaimed another.

Not quite ready to answer questions, Aleta told them she just wanted to rest. News of this event had already reached the village where the queen and the Oracle stood waiting amid a throng of chattering warriors, but Aleta insisted. Okypous gave her tree house so that their guest could sleep. It was the least she could do. This time, sleep remedied much, allowing her body and mind to heal a little. Morpheus behaved himself, as he knew he had dreams to give her, since Hypnos, his father, forbade him from interfering with her rest.

• • •

At sunrise, Aleta joined the women for their morning meal, able to tell them a little of what had happened. She knew they were not as knowing as Artemis was about the *Oikoumene Broteios*, so her story boiled down the essential components. The Oracle, despite having her head covered, observed their guest, knowing there was much more to the story that Aleta would never reveal. One Amazon gently tugged a feather to be sure it was real, and Aleta shot her a look. The camaraderie she felt with this tribe of warriors felt normal to her, but she couldn't understand why. After the meal, when the scouting parties were off, the queen and the Oracle pulled Aleta aside in the same clearing where Artemis had appeared the day before.

"Aleta, I know that Okypous has thanked you for saving her daughter, but I wanted to thank you as well. You selflessly put your own life in jeopardy to save the life of one you did not know. You have the gratitude of this tribe, and I wish to honor you by making you our sister."

Aleta didn't have the words. She didn't understand herself why she had saved the child, but she knew it felt right when she did it. With everything she had experienced so far with Danelos, Brandon, and Sarah, and now this, she could now say she believed that her destiny tied into something noble, even if she didn't really know what it was.

"When this tribe first came to this region, our blessed patron, Artemis, put into our keeping a weapon that we could give to a worthy warrior. While many of my sisters have fought and died preserving Zeus' shrine, it is for your self-sacrificing act that I wish to honor you with this."

From the forest came Eumache, carrying a long, shrouded object.

"Artemis told our people that whoever was to receive this would be entered into our sisterhood for all time."

Eumache unfolded the leather binding to reveal a silver javelin.

"Take this into your keeping. My Oracle tells me you will have need of it, although she didn't tell me why."

Taking the weapon with two hands from her new sister, Aleta felt a pulse of power travel through it. Rumbles of distant thunder caused the Oracle to reach out and grab hold of the javelin.

"Artemis be praised! She is the bearer. The true bearer."

"Oracle?" the queen asked. "What do you mean?"

"I can now speak of the gift this weapon possesses. When Artemis charged me to keep this weapon, she told me it had the ability to call forth a great power, one that

306

could vanquish our enemies, if the true bearer came forth to claim it. None of our sisters was she."

"What power?" asked the queen. "You kept this knowledge from me?"

A voice from the woods responded, "At my bidding."

Showered in sunlight, as she was when Aleta saw her, Zeus' daughter entered the clearing. All genuflected at her presence, including Aleta, who did so more out of what the goddess did for her.

"When your sisterhood first came to this part of Greece as part of the prophecy, I asked Zeus to prepare a weapon for the one among you who could protect his shrine like no other. My father has never really been able to resist my requests. He playfully offered me a thunderbolt stipulating that if I could find a way to give it to your people, I could have it. Surely, a thunderbolt by itself would incinerate anyone who touched it, so I asked Hephæstos to forge a javelin of silver Earthsteel to house it. To make sure that not just anyone could use it, for fear it might fall into an enemy's hands, I ensorcelled it so that only a true member of the tribe, a true *Aetos Dios*—Eagle of Zeus—who had acted in valor and selflessness, could harness the power. The Fates have selected Aleta to be such a recipient."

Silence shrouded the queen and her Oracle.

"She who wields *Nephoskizetes*, the Cloudsplitter, can call upon *Keraunos Dios*, the Thunderbolt of Zeus. Aleta, when you need it, reach toward the heavens, willing it to you. The weapon will come. When you no longer need it, throw it back to the heavens, who will keep it until you need it once more."

Always wanting to test reality, into the sky Aleta threw the javelin, transforming into a bolt of lightning and dissipating. Reaching her hand skyward, the bolt meandered through the sky to her hand, materializing as the javelin.

"I must tell you something else," the goddess continued. "You are one with the white eagle now. Before the Great War, the first *Aetos Dios* came forth to bear Zeus' lighting to him from the forge of the Cyclopes, carrying the bolts in his great talons. In much the same way, you are another *Aetos Dios*."

The Oracle took Aleta's hands.

"May the gods bless and keep you, child. As you look into my eyes, know that you always have a place among us."

With that, she removed her hood, and Aleta gasped. The Oracle bore a striking resemblance to her grandmother, at least how she looked in pictures when she was young. Aleta saw in the woman's eyes a connection to something beyond this moment, but at the same time, she knew she had always been a part of this sisterhood at some level. She knew she would rejoin her friends and family soon, and she hoped to be able to remember all of this. As surreal as it was now, she knew deep in her soul that this was a part of who she would become.

Artemis faded into a mist without a word, leaving the four women to walk back to the village with much to ponder. That evening, during the evening meal, Aleta couldn't take her eyes off the Oracle, who sat in the shadows beneath the trees. Maybe someday she would get the answers she sought, but for the moment, she was satisfied. One of the last thoughts she had before she went to sleep that night was, when she returned home, how would she explain the wings?

• • •

"She's coming around," a man's voice uttered. It was Dr. Cooper. "Aleta, are you okay? You've been out for about two hours."

Emerging from the fog of sleep, Aleta smiled at her colleague and took his hand.

"I'll be okay," she whispered. She wondered why no one had said anything about the huge white wings, but she didn't feel them on her back. Well, she thought, as dreams go, it was a good one at least.

Once Dr. Cooper was sure she would be fine, he ordered some food for her, and let her wake up fully. She noticed a folded piece of paper in her left hand. It read,

"*Aetos Dios*—your wings will come when you need to soar."

She smiled.

# 22—EYE IN THE SKY

**WPAC (Vancouver)** "For WPR News, this is Sylvia Shepherd. Cetologists from Task Force: Mu rescued a pod of bottlenose dolphins from a fishing net off the coast of Vancouver Island yesterday according to sources at the Pacific Cetaceous Institute. The net, an experimental project produced by the fishing conglomerate Oceanis in conjunction with PCI, was supposed to generate an electrical pulse to keep animals like dolphins and whales away while luring in fish like salmon and tuna. Oceanis, the world's largest fishing cartel, declined to comment, but PCI will be suing for breach of contract."

• • •

Wrestling a khimæra in the Boston Common wasn't what Brandon expected to be doing on a Saturday morning, but there he was, channeling the strength of Taurus, the Bull, keeping the fire-breather away from populated areas. If Bostonians were anything, they were a stubborn lot, Brandon said to himself, since his warnings to stay away went largely unheeded. Standing thirty feet tall, the khimæra's leonine body took up as much room as a school bus, dwarfing the Swan Boats in the Public Garden. The trick to keeping the monster subdued was to avoid the tail, a serpent whose mouth spewed caustic venom. If that weren't enough, both the lion's head and the goat's head jutting from the lion's back breathed fire. With half of the Public Garden singed beyond repair, Brandon had given up hope of saving the other half—his main task was to take this son of Ekhidna down... hard.

He could feel his grip loosening a bit, so he brought out the endurance of Aries, the Ram, to augment his taurian strength, praying to any god who could hear him just to let him flip the three-headed beast on its back. Bucking hard, the khimæra knocked Brandon off, sending him into the lagoon. Concentration was the key, according to Gyges. Lose that, and you lose the connection. His mind had wandered while he was channeling two signs, something he had never done before, and he wouldn't make that mistake again. Sagittarius gave him speed, something he needed to channel before his quarry could enter the Boston T station at Park Street in front of the State House. Once in the tunnels, the khimæra would have a captive food source, and Brandon couldn't allow that to happen. Plus, the considerable body would destroy the subway tunnels, collapsing the streets above, not to mention igniting the methane gas in the sewers. A flaming hiccup could take out half a city block.

He liked tapping into Sagittarius, since he could run like a centaur, but it wore him out faster. Just as a lion's paw stepped down the first steps, Brandon used the combined grip he took from Cancer and Scorpio to latch onto a back leg and pull, tossing his adversary over his shoulder onto Tremont Street. Momentarily dazing the underworld dweller, Brandon leaped over a Yellow Cab parked outside the Orpheum Theater, lifted it over his head, and brought it crashing down on the lion's jaw. A burst of flame shot from the lion's mouth, hitting Brandon squarely in the chest, but the amulet's protection kicked in to keep its bearer safe. Now it was Brandon's turn to be stunned. He noticed that people had started to take him seriously by moving off the street and into the buildings. No matter what he had to do, he'd sworn to keep them safe. In effect, it was three against one, if he counted each head as a separate obstacle. The khimæra had started back to the subway entrance, but Brandon wanted to even the odds, so he leaped onto the hindquarters, channeling the agility from Pisces, and used the bull's strength again to grab the tail. Leaning up against the back of the goat head, he pulled hard, ultimately removing the snake from the body. The lion's roar shook the Theater District, breaking windows, outdoing any opera singer for miles. One down, two to go, Brandon thought.

Charging wildly around, the now two-headed beast ripped trees out with its teeth, and led a rampage down toward Charles Street, and Brandon had an idea. A memory surfaced, and he thought of a hero who had bested the khimæra once, but now he had to figure out a way to make his plan work. Conventional weapons couldn't kill the monster, so he needed one thing to do it. While he ran interference between the lion's mouth and a few passersby who ran for cover, he saw what might work. Leading the khimæra toward the street, Brandon pulled a manhole cover, using all the strength he could summon, spun around a few times, releasing it like a discus. As he had anticipated, the lion breathed fire at the metal object, melting it, but it found its target in the throat of the lion. Molten metal trickled down its gullet, killing it from the inside. Unable to roar, the lion shook its head, hoping to dislodge the obstruction, but it was too late. Falling over, the great beast eventually stopped moving, its body melting into the asphalt.

Cheers from some of the windows above the street, as well as from people who managed to stay clear, buffeted Brandon, but it snapped him out of his exhaustion long enough to wave at a few happy Beantowners. Bruised and scratched, he half-heartedly smiled, heading down the stairs to the T station. Riding the Red Line to Downtown Crossing, he'd eventually get off at the Malden stop. Riding the train felt like the city was embracing him, since he had ridden these trains his whole life. With his head against the window, he allowed himself the luxury of his mind wandering back to when he became the cosmic zookeeper.

• • •

Summer in the White Mountains of New Hampshire brought out the adventurer in Brandon as well as fond memories of his childhood when he and his parents would travel to these mountains every summer to camp out. Not far from Boston, the mountains were less than three hours away, and Brandon always parked at the ranger station and walked the mile and a half to the trailhead. Inexperienced hikers and campers alike who parked at trailheads sometimes found their cars broken into or stolen, a lesson Brandon had never actually experienced, but some of his friends had. Having spent summers in this area, he and his family had befriended the rangers over the years, so they didn't mind when he parked his Nissan hybrid next to the station.

Tourists and native New Englanders overran most of the well-traveled trails during June and July, so he liked to hike White Bear, a trail hardly used by everyday hikers since the terrain was a little less family friendly, but it provided some of the most eye-catching vistas in the whole state. One of the rangers showed Brandon the trail when he was in high school, and he'd always made sure to hike it at least half a dozen times during the summer months, and once or twice in the fall when the foliage transformed the mountains into a patchwork quilt of burnt orange, rich sienna, and poppy red. Starting just before sunrise, Brandon took his "path less traveled," knowing he could make it to his campsite by late afternoon.

313

A zoologist, he had augmented his schooling by taking outdoor safety classes in the event he should come across a bear, wolf, or other 'tenant of the mountain' he called them. Brandon spent much of his high school and college years promoting earth awareness, environmental cleanliness, and wilderness safety, so being in these mountains felt like a second home. He had spent a few years in Africa, observing lion pride behaviors and migratory patterns of antelope, as well travelling the United States on grants to explore ways of maintaining the populations of endangered species while not compromising their habitats. Some of his friends often joked that he would save the life of an animal before a person, and they weren't that far from reality. He believed, like the Native Americans, that people didn't really own any land, but rather borrowed it for a while, and animals were the true inhabitants. At midday, he rested, munching on a granola bar. The majesty of the earth never ceased to impress him, and the mountains always seemed to be alive, just sleeping. He knew it was corny, but he didn't care.

Most campsites in the White Mountains had been marked by the New Hampshire Park Service so rangers could track who went where, but Brandon had his own place to go, and most of the rangers knew where to find him if necessary. He also knew that campgrounds registered with the state had cameras watching them from the trees, a "safety precaution", according to park officials, put up by the Department of Fish and Wildlife allegedly to protect the animals. Brandon, and most people, knew better. Jutting out a little from the side of the mountain, a rocky shelf on the north side gave him the most expansive view. Setting up camp, he let the panorama capture him, and he settled in to read for while. He'd hike down to his favorite lake later, after it got a little cooler, but now he just needed to relax.

After dinner, which consisted of tomato soup and vegan macaroni and 'cheese', he lie back to look at the night sky, something he couldn't do as well at home with all the streetlights and the distant glow from the highway. This sky now looked like dark blue velvet with pinpricks to let in light from behind. His eyes traveled from star to star, landing occasionally on Scorpio, Lyra, and Cygnus— summer constellations. Chains of light connected in his mind, and he reached a hand up, dreamily hoping he could actually touch one. Pulling his fleece blanket up under his arms, he laced his hands behind his head to watch the night sky. Eventually, he succumbed to sleep, the gift that heals and brings Morpheos out to play.

• • •

A cold breeze woke him. It was still night, but something was different. His blanket was gone. And his tent. And all his belongings. He looked around, but the night obscured his vision, and he heard nothing but the wind, so whoever it was that stole his equipment had to be long gone. Something else wasn't right either, but he couldn't figure it out. Get your bearings, Brandon, he thought. The landscape wasn't the same, he concluded. But how? He checked the sky. Constellations were there, but not the ones he had seen. Brisk night wind prompted him to find warmth, but he didn't know where to go. Starlight was enough to see by, barely, so he tried to head down the mountain a bit to see if he could find anything. Even the path he had taken down the mountain earlier was gone. This definitely wasn't the same place, he concluded. He checked his watch, but it showed 10:14 p.m. Not possible. He had been watching the sky around that time, so if he had slept, it would have to be later. Wouldn't it? One of the first rules about camping alone was not to panic. Not the easiest thing to do when you have no earthly clue where you are.

Half an hour later, according to his estimate, he stumbled on a cave, but maybe almost fell into was more like it. Brandon wasn't sure what amazed him more, the fact that he had found a cave, or that the opening was about fifty feet tall. In either case, he was relieved. He wasn't certain, but there was a faint light from inside, enough to let his eyes barely see the walls. Turning a corner, he saw that the cave opened up into a much larger chamber, doubling in height. A wave of heat washed over him, and pungent smoke rose to the ceiling. At least he wouldn't die of hypothermia. Three blocks stood in the center of the cavern and, leaning against them were sledgehammers, or were they? Just beyond the blocks, the heat grew exponentially, and he saw the maw of raging fire in the wall itself. What was this place, and how did he get here? His questions would have to wait because something was coming. Metal shields hanging on the stone clanged against the soot-stained walls as the rhythmic sound continued, and Brandon could swear it was footsteps. Emerging from another opening next to the fire was a giant, with more arms than could be counted, standing about as tall as the ceiling. Then another giant. Then a third. Brandon flattened himself on the far side of a block, the pounding in his head no longer footsteps but his heart. A shadow covered him, and he instinctively looked up to see one hundred eyes staring at him, glowing red like the embers of the fire.

He wasn't sure what finally motivated him to move, but he ran to the opening of the cave, not caring at that precise moment if that creature was behind him. Just shy of the entrance, he almost ran into a short, old man whose long white beard tapered to a point and brushed the floor, holding a tall, gnarled staff.

"You can't stay here!" Brandon shouted. He tried to move the man, but he couldn't.

In a voice as old as the earth itself, the man said, "I *am* here."

"Something is coming. I don't know what it is, and you're not safe!"

It was at that point Brandon realized nothing was coming after him.

"Come inside, mortal," replied the man as he shuffled back into the cave.

Resigning himself to Fate, he followed the man into the heart of the cave where he saw all three giants sleeping in the corner. As Brandon looked closer, he saw that each giant had dozens of heads, every one snoring.

Against the far wall, the old man sat on a worn woolen blanket, its edges eaten by time.

"Who are you?" Brandon uttered. "And, better question. Who are they?"

The old man told him his name was Smolikas, and those slumbering in the corner were Hekatonkheires, the hundred-handed sons of Gaea and Ouranos. Brandon introduced himself, explaining how he had come to be in the cavern, and Smolikas' wrinkled face smiled slightly.

"Morpheos dost enjoy bringing mortals here through the dreamscape." His laughed sounded like sandpaper on stone.

"Why do you live in this cavern with these… giants?" Brandon asked, gesturing.

"I do not live in this cavern, mortal. I am this cavern, and this mountain. I am an *Ourea*, a son of Gaea. Each mountain has its own *Ourea*. We *are* the mountain. All but one of us."

Smolikas wove together the story of how Gaea birthed the mountains—the *Ourea*—and each mountain housed its namesake, a primordial one who took the form of an ancient, bearded man who did more than just guard and protect it: he *was* it. Only one mountain had a female protector. Bringing Brandon to the cavern entrance, he

317

pointed toward the east to where the tallest mountain stood. Gaea's sister, Olympeia, was the only *Ourea* to be female, and Olympos was her form.

After the visit from Ananke and seeing the Delphic Oracle, it wasn't unfathomable that he could be in the presence of another immortal, Brandon considered. He just wanted to know why Morpheos brought him here, to this place of all places to go. Smolikas asked his guest to talk about himself; the *Protogenos* hadn't talked with anyone except for three forge-workers for thousands of years, ever since they arrived when Demetrios freed them.

"My formal schooling is in animal studies, and I've loved them since I was a child. I'd bring home lost cats and dogs, even a snake or two, just to keep them from cars running them over or being killed in some other way. Animals have intrigued me almost more than people do, and when I went to college, I majored in zoology with a minor in cultural anthropology, not really giving much thought to an actual career. My major course of study allowed me to travel to African savannas and watch the mating patterns of aardwolves or the feeding activity of Nile crocodiles. I've seen tropical rainforests and deserts, the tundra and taiga regions of Siberia, and the tidal pools of the Gulf of Mexico. Right now, I work with Northeastern University on a research grant to find funding to make certain habitats protected against poaching and killing of endangered species. A career goal now would be a zoologist working with a zoo or animal preserve."

Being as old as the earth itself, Smolikas could grasp the finer points without understanding some of the details. Brandon's garrulous nature emerged when he was excited about something or nervous.

"One of my high school projects was to organize students to pick up the litter all over the Boston area. Initially, ten people joined, but by the time I graduated, over a hundred had taken up the cause. Just one planet we get. Keeping her free from trash is the least we could do, and everything we do helps."

As he spoke, Smolikas warmed to the idea that mortals, at least this one, regarded Gaea as a valuable entity, not a cosmic dung pile. Brandon relayed with passion ideas that had been popular back during the Heroic Age when Humankind had greater respect for Gaea and the gods.

"I must ask. What brought thee to seek solace in the mountains?"

"Respect for the natural world. If people made the effort to reconnect with nature, I think we would see less war, strife, and prejudice," replied Brandon. "I must sound ridiculous."

"On the contrary, young man. Thou dost make an old mountain proud," Smolikas responded, touching Brandon's shoulder. "And that is not easy to do. Gyges!"

Smolikas wanted one of the Hekatonkheires to retrieve something to give to Brandon, something the old mountain truly believed belonged to one such as him. Drowsily, the many-handed one brought an obsidian box over.

"Through our conversation, I have learned more from thee than I have from any of the immortals who have visited over the millennia, even Zeus. Thy regard for the stars in the sky, the animals in thy care, and the earth of whom thou dost speak with reverence coalesce into one ideal. This… is for thee."

The box contained a silver Earthsteel disk, the one Demetrios had put into the care of the Hekatonkheires.

"Over the many eons, the gods have hung stars in the remains of Ouranos, the heavens, to remind all of creation of many things, not the least of which is the nobility and dignity of heroes. Just after Gaea brought him into existence, the Sky Father forged this amulet in the First Fires of Khaos, embedding within it the *Ophthalmos*

319

*Ouranos*—the Eye of Ouranos. As constellations appeared, the Eye took the grandest ones into its care, evidenced by the twelve gems, even after Kronos castrated his father, releasing his essence to Khaos. These twelve constellations form the *Zodiakos kuklos*, a circle of animals, and I offer this to you. You will be the Keeper of the Twelve."

A flash of memory—the horoscope. Brushing his fingers over the gems, Brandon felt their power, tracing the symbols one by one.

"The Zodiac," he whispered. As he touched each one, he could see them in his mind.

Smolikas spoke them aloud. "*Krios*, the Ram. *Tavros*, the Bull. *Didimoi*, the Twins. *Karkinos*, the Crab. *Leon*, the Lion. *Parthenos*, the Virgin. *Zugos*, the Scales. *Skorpios*, the Scorpion. *Toksotis*, the Centaur. *Aigokeros*, the Sea goat. *Udrokoeus*, the Waterbearer. *Ikhthyes*, the Fish."

"I know them by different names, but I could see them so vividly."

"As *Protogenos*, I pass along this, my brother's amulet, to thee. Through thy mind, and the Eye of Ouranos, realize thy destiny, Brandon. Remember, too, that names have power. Invoke them only when necessary."

The old mountain put the amulet around Brandon's neck. Ancient magic traveled through him like mild electricity, and Smolikas escorted him to the cave entrance, since he could go no further, and gave him directions back to where he had appeared. Thanking the immortal for his hospitality, Brandon left, his hand never leaving the amulet. He saw the sky differently again, this time more like a collection of animals in need of protection, and he made a silent promise to do such a thing. Staring back up at the heavens, he wondered about

Ouranos, the sky, and why Kronos had to defeat him, but before he could ponder it too long, he fell asleep.

• • •

Sometime during the rest of the night, he opened his eyes, and he could tell from the stars that he was back in New Hampshire. Still wrapped in his fleece blanket, he checked to see whether it had been a dream. The silver amulet still rested on his chest, glistening in the scattered starlight. For the first time, he not only felt like a kindred spirit to the earth, but to the sky as well.

# 23—EARTHBOUND

WNN (Washington, D.C.) "For WPR News, this is Anthony Mason. Members of the Church of Heaven protested the hiring of a gay teacher at Millsborough High School yesterday morning, blocking traffic while holding up signs that said, 'Gays Shouldn't Teach.' Community members, teachers, and students rallied in front of the building, showing support for Adam Ebersol, a teacher for twelve years, who said, 'I appreciate the show of support from the school and the community and hoped to dispel the misconceptions promoted by those unwilling to learn.' A riot broke out shortly after several church members wrote obscene graffiti on the school, and local police called in Task Force: Tau to assist. Pastor Jay Paulsen of the Church of Heaven refused to comment."

• • •

"Is it just me, or are we fighting against the tide?" Brandon asked, his feet up on Danelos' coffee table. "I mean, we kill one khimæra, and three hydras show up somewhere else."

Sarah came out of the kitchen, chewing a bagel. "The problem is that we end up racing around based on what's on the news. Seems awfully futile to me."

"Has anyone seen Dan? He asked us to meet him at his place, and he's not here," Brandon said, swigging his protein drink.

"When he called, he told me where the key was and said he'd be back shortly. He had to run an errand."

Two months had passed since they started traveling all over Gaea to stop the underworld from infesting humanity, but they could only go where Danelos had been, since he could only open a portal to a place he had seen. Thankfully, due to his work with Boston University, he had been to conferences and gone on digs all over the world. That, however, wouldn't help them if they had to go to South Africa or Papua New Guinea. Aleta arrived after a morning of shopping, something she hadn't had much time to do. Wound up on triple grande no foam skinny caramel mocha lattes, extra hot, she related her entire morning before Brandon had to stop her.

"Ease up, okay?" he laughed. "You're going to give yourself an aneurism if you're not careful."

"Hey, just sharing. So, where's our host?"

At the same time, Brandon and Sarah said, "Soon."

"All right then," Aleta replied, taking a swig of her third latte.

Across the city, Danelos had to wrap up some business at the university before he could meet the others, but he had something else to do unrelated to school. Pulling the sword from his shoulder harness, only visible when he removed the blade, he used the sunlight from his window to open a portal to Arkadeia in the one place he knew his father would be.

"Am I that predictable?" Apollo asked, knowing Danelos was behind him. He had just finished settling a boundary dispute with a few farmers who debated where their land actually sat since two maps showed two possibilities.

"Somewhat," he laughed. "I did come for a reason, though."

He explained that, with so many underworld monsters slipping into his world through points where their two worlds connected, he and the others couldn't be pre-emptive about where to look or couldn't warn communities in advance.

"There's also the added problem that I haven't been everywhere on the planet, so the vision isn't quite so boundless. Can you help?"

"Possibly. I still have friends in the *Oikoumene Broteios*. I do have someone you could contact, and he should be able to assist you... a little."

"You sound skeptical."

"It means that you might have to make some compromises."

"I think we can do that," Dan replied.

"It also means you would have to tell people about what you can do. So far, the mystical side of your gifts blurs your identity from others. If you reveal your powers, you lose your anonymity. Are you willing to do that?"

Danelos hadn't really thought much about that. He knew it was always a possibility, but being so new to this, he was always more concerned with getting the job done. Apollo told him a little more about his life with Alkinoë, or Allison, as Dan would know her. 'Paul Fairmont' had worked for the Greco-European Alliance as their ambassador when he first arrived. As the United Nations Task Force Division grew, he maintained contact with the directors, each one having a special file just for him. Paul Fairmont exerted some "influence" on the calibrating of the division over the years, and became friends with Nigel Caldwell, associate director of the Task Force division. Nigel needed help removing Albert Helmig, the executive director, whom Nigel believed was taking bribes from corporations to offer protection through various task forces. Knowing something about finding truth, Paul executed a search of emails, extracting encoded messages, ultimately implicating Helmig. At the subsequent board meeting, Nigel took the position of director and told Paul that not only would he rededicate the division to align with its original intent, but made it clear that Paul would have an ally.

"So, you're saying I should just contact this Nigel Caldwell."

"Give him this," responded Apollo, handing Danelos a gold drachma imprinted with a sun stamped into it. "Tell him your father would like to call in a favor."

• • •

"There you are!" said Aleta. "Where the hell have you been?"

"How long have you been here?" Danelos asked, putting his bag near the door.

"Long enough, mister." With her head cocked and a hand on her hip, Danelos couldn't help but laugh.

"Sorry. But I have news."

He didn't want them to miss a detail, so he told them the same story his father had told him as well as the proposal.

Brandon sat up. "You want us to tell the world about what we do? Do you realize how much attention we'll get?"

"Hold on a sec. If we do this right, it'll make our task that much easier. Look, I grant you that I don't like the idea of working for the Task Force Division any more than you guys, but what other choice do we have?" Danelos said.

"What's in it for us?"

"I don't know all the details, Sarah. Why don't we talk to Nigel and see what he can do for us. He'll keep this to himself. My father trusts him."

Danelos had told them about his first experience in Arkadeia right after he returned, and after all they had experienced themselves, it didn't surprise them. Knowing that he was the son of Apollo, and that he had become whole again after reclaiming his original soul, didn't seem all that far-fetched, actually.

Aleta remembered how four words could be so telling, lingering on 'My father trusts him'. "I say we talk to this Nigel," Aleta said.

"Aleta's good to go. You two?"

Sarah looked at Brandon and shrugged. He nodded.

"Okay, chief. We're in. When do we go?" Brandon said.

"Let me make a call," said Danelos, pulling out his phone.

• • •

Two days later, Nigel Caldwell stepped out of a cab in front of Danelos' brownstone. In his late sixties, Nigel looked like one would think an operative for an expansive organization might look in his charcoal gray suit and slick, black hair, his sideburns faded to gray. Danelos thought it best to meet him without the others first, this way Nigel would feel more comfortable. He'd get the others there once he had had the chance to talk a bit.

"So, how is your father?" Nigel asked, taking a cup of Earl Grey tea from Danelos.

"He's well. Thanks for asking."

Okay, pleasantries aside, he thought. It was strange for him to think that Apollo had a mortal guise and that others knew about it. He wondered, though, how much Nigel actually knew.

"Did it surprise you to know that my father was, shall we say, connected?"

Nigel smirked, "Of course. At first." His British accent just completed the secret agent image Danelos had in his mind. He couldn't help it.

326

"Well, he seems to think you can help us. I told you about our concerns on the phone, so what do you think?"

"I've given it some thought, and I'd really like to talk about it with the others, too. Any chance they can join us?"

"Definitely."

Danelos stood in front of the window, removed *Thyroros* and cut a slice into the air, creating a portal into The Beanery where the others had been waiting. As they stepped into Danelos' living room, Nigel sat frozen.

His only response was, "Well. How convenient."

After introductions, Nigel gave them the plan he had in mind.

"We register your group as a task force," he began. "But, we'll have to explain what you do. Dan explained to me that you stop, shall we say, otherworldly creatures from doing harm to the mortal populace. Does that about sum it up?"

Four nods were followed by "Uh huh."

Danelos said, "Nigel, I think we've made peace with the idea that we have a job to do, and we can't worry about who knows what. Besides, our gifts blur our identities enough that no one, mortal anyway, could see who we really are. Under the circumstances, even if our identities come out, it doesn't change what we have to do. So, what's next?"

"You sign your charter which gives you jurisdiction over your area of expertise. I doubt anyone would want to infringe upon it, anyway. Once you have that in place, you have access to our computers, technology, transportation, etc. There's one other thing. You'd have to report in with progress on your missions, and you'd have to be available twenty four seven. And, considering how 'connected' you are, I'll push this through without the requisite background checks."

"That last part we do already," Aleta said. "Report in? If I'm otherwise engaged with a fire-breathing dragon, I'm supposed to call?"

"Uh, well, you would have to radio in before your mission and after. Wait, you fight dragons? Nevermind. The less I know right now, the better."

Nigel preferred when Paul told him little. That wouldn't be the case here, he feared.

"Each operative wears a small transmitter somewhere on his person," he continued, looking at Sarah and Aleta. "Or hers. It's unobtrusive. All you do is speak into it. I think you'll find that it will help you stay in touch with each other as well. If you're addressing each other, you would use your codenames first."

Some debate began about the necessity of codenames, but Nigel explained that the only way to register a private connection with another agent would be to use the codename first, then speak. Otherwise, anyone listening could hear. Normally, it wouldn't matter, since some task force groups overlapped their assistance, but in the case of this group, he didn't want to put other 'mortals' in harm's way. Brandon would finally get to be the superhero he had fantasized about as a boy, codename and all.

"Tell you what. You decide on your own names. Just give them to me, and I'll enter them into our operative database."

Working under the premise that these four wouldn't be joining forces with other groups, Nigel told them they didn't have to wear regulation uniforms. Danelos concurred, explaining that it made it easier to fit in if they could wear their own clothes, plus they had their own protection. Aleta, Sarah, and Brandon weren't entirely convinced, although certainly intrigued. A visit to the TF Boston headquarters on Ashburton Place might help, Nigel suggested, so they could see how the computers could help them, but they would have to find someone to work Mission Ops, some who spoke "myth".

"Nigel, you pick someone you trust. One way or the other, we'll be made public, so it really doesn't matter," Danelos said. "We can always train this person in what we're up against."

Brandon added, "Ideally, it should be someone who knows his underworld monsters and won't wet himself easily."

Danelos glared at him. "Anyway, let us know when you decide that. We'll give you the names tomorrow."

With Nigel's departure, the four had much to talk about, mostly to reassure each other that everything would be fine, even though they couldn't guarantee that. Sarah wanted to get the codenames out of the way so they could focus on figuring out the rest of the prophecy. No matter what happened with the Task Force division, they would have to decipher the Oracle's words. Brandon's was easy; he chose *Zodiak*, with a 'k' just to be different, he said. Sarah chose *Aether*, the spirit that bound the *Tetrastoikeia* together. Aleta knew right away—*Aetos*, eagle. Finally, Danelos realized it was his job to lead the team, since they deferred to him anyway. He was their protector, as well as the protector of Gaea and Arkadeia, so he chose the most logical name—*Aegis*.

Visiting the local Task Force division turned out to be the best way to harden their resolve in joining: sleek architectural design, modern meeting classic, marble floors and stainless steel elevators—everything to amplify the image of this organization and give it the presence necessary to impress. And that it did. Nigel met them the next morning, providing each with a black leather portfolio with all the necessary paperwork they would need to benefit from the technology and resources available to them. As in most public places, they needed to have their scans, palm and retinal, as well as swipe their ID card, issued to all people, in the front door. The four couldn't have been more stunned if Zeus' thunderbolt had hit them square in the face. They had all grown up in Boston, but they never even knew this place existed. Whenever people spoke about the UN Task Forces, most assumed it was from New York, and maybe that's what the UN wanted people to think, too.

Upstairs, in a conference room on the tenth floor overlooking the city, specifically the Boston Common and Public Gardens, a place Brandon had been not too long ago, Nigel introduced them to Quinn, their Mission Ops person. Sarah and the others expected he would look like a typical computer nerd—glasses, pocket protector, shirt buttoned to his neck—but that couldn't have been further from reality. The other extreme one might have expected from a government operative would be a Navy SEAL build, muscles on top of muscles, with a crew cut and square jaw, or perhaps that was just Danelos' impression. Actually, Quinn was the average college student, T-shirt and jeans, with one distinguishing feature: he had no arms.

"How does he...," Danelos whispered to Nigel.

Quinn smiled. "Voice commands, sometimes one or two words. Don't worry, chief. I've got you covered."

"No need to worry about Mr. Hawthorne, Dan. He's been with us for some time now. Just give him whatever info he needs, and he'll get you where you need to be," added Nigel.

"I've brought you some resources, Mr. Hawthorne, but..."

"Dan, right? Call me Quinn. You can just leave that stuff with me, and I'll make sure to take care of it."

Nigel's phone rang, so he left the five to get acquainted..

"So," Quinn started, "Why don't we head down to the cafeteria so I can get some coffee, and you guys get me up to speed. Cool?"

330

A few hours and many cups of caffeine later, Quinn felt as if he had a grasp of the situation. If he didn't, he reassured the others, he would let them know. All Task Force operatives, no matter how high or low-ranked, were strictly on a "need to know" basis. Aleta and the others felt more comfortable once they knew how everything worked, too. Quinn would monitor the 'field', as he called it, just another name for Earth. When something would come up, he'd radio them, give them specs on the creature— location, size, proximity to civilians, etc.—and then send Danelos a few visuals of the area, just so he could use his sword to get there.

"I'll make sure they're panoramics, Dan, so you can get a wider view. I noticed you carry a touch screen phone, so you can pull them up there. For the rest of you, if you don't know where you're going, every city has a TF office with a few helicopters, ground transport, and access to local airports. Just give them your codename, and you're good to go. Speaking of, what are your names?"

He vocally input the information into the main database, then winked and smiled. Must be the caffeine, Aleta thought. No one's this upbeat. Their visit came to a close back at Quinn's station.

"Okay, guys, let me look over the materials you left, and I'll get with you as soon as I see something. We'd received reports of the other disturbances you've encountered, but you were there before we could completely assess the scene, so even if I'm not ready, we'll still let you know. Also, the more info you can give me, the better I can help you."

Just as they were leaving, Quinn had to ask one more question.

"Hey, every division has a designation. Alpha, Gamma, etc. Zeta, Lambda, and Xi are available."

The four shared a glance, nodded silently, and Danelos replied, "Gaea."

# 24—THE RETURN THRESHOLD

**NUR (Amsterdam)** "For WPR News, this is Gabriël Ockerman. Proceedings begin today for former Angolan prime minister Mattan Corribe, on counts of genocide and ethnic cleansing over the past decade. Task Force: Omicron officials, who had investigated Corribe for years, brought clear evidence of these atrocities into the International Criminal Court, stating, "he had slowly poisoned water sources and farm animals over the past ten years, bringing about the deaths of over 550,000 members of the Bumanda tribe. Corribe claims they have "been a pustule on Angolan society since the middle of the 19th century." Omicron sources continue to compile evidence that, they say, will have Corribe spending the rest of this lifetime, and possibly the next, in prison."

• • •

Quinn caught on quickly to the dispatching, learning how to distinguish a hydra from a dragon: hydras, he learned, spewed venom whereas dragons usually breathed fire—certainly an important distinction to make when defeating them. Similarly, Danelos and his group had gotten used to using their codenames when in the field, something that took a few weeks of adjustment. One

332

feature of that communication they liked was being able to have a four-way call, basically, so each could offer input, especially if someone had particular experience with that creature. At Mission Ops, Quinn also kept track of what kinds of creatures they had engaged as well as how often they had engaged them. A disturbing piece of information they discovered was that these spawn of the underworld were emerging faster as the weeks passed. Since they couldn't find the connecting points between the *Ge Theôn* and the *Oikoumene Broteios*, they had no way of predicting where to go next. Reconnaissance of the areas post-attack revealed nothing about a portal to the House of Hades, as Danelos called it, and he knew of one thing he could try.

His memory of the place he needed to go, although quite vivid, made him hesitate. Venturing again could be problematic, but it might be the only way to a solution. He radioed to Quinn that he would be out of the 'field' for a little while, but that didn't register. Danelos rephrased it as 'off world,' and Quinn just shrugged. Although he was able to grasp what Task Force: Gaea had to do because he had seen empirical data, he was a man of science, so 'off world' or out of the 'field' seemed like impossibilities. The last time Danelos saw this place, he was on a quest, and she was helpful. Would she be again? This time, he would go prepared, knowing what he would have to do. He wondered if she would remember him.

Entering the underworld was always risky; one never knew what could be waiting in the precise spot he needed to go. To minimize the risk, he entered through a sword-portal a little further away. He didn't see her until he was almost near her niche, and she looked the same.

"The son of Apollo returns. I know why thou hast come this time."

"Hello Ekhidna."

333

She had curled her lower body around the same stone pillar he remembered, the end of her tail waving back and forth fluidly. Danelos drew *Thyroros*, just to show he was serious. This was no social call.

"No need for that, my child. No need," she hissed.

"Insurance, daughter of Gaea. You say you know why I've come."

"Demetrios, my destiny is to bring challenges for heroes into this world. I no longer need Typhon to father my brood. Imprisonment beneath Mt. Aetna has kept him from me. Perhaps…"

Danelos laughed. No one had called him Demetrios since he had reclaimed his original soul.

"I free Typhon, you help me? Is that what you were going to say?"

Ekhidna's expression softened into something of a smile, serpent-like and mischievous.

"No deal. You know we're killing your offspring, and we'll keep doing it. The mortal world has no means to protect itself, and soon we may have no choice but to stop this from the source." His expression hardened into something of a smile, confident and resolute.

"Succeed in your quest, godling. Perhaps when destiny rewrites itself, I no longer bring my beautiful children into existence. Or, perhaps I populate Gaea. As thou hast said, dispatching me would end thy trials."

He looked at the sword. "Yes, I know. But, I'm not certain that killing you would change anything about the Scales. So, what do you say? For old time, mother of monsters, how about you stop producing offspring."

"Thou hast thy destiny, and I have mine. By fulfilling thine, thou canst possibly prevent mine. Of course, thy success could be thy unraveling."

He hadn't thought about that.

"Long ago, I gave up any hope for a life of my own. Zeus wanted me to be his heir once, but that was not my fate. As you say, duty binds the lives of my companions and me to a higher purpose. Interfere at your peril."

A serpent's laugh slithered from her mouth. "Thou didst suckle at my breasts once, Arkadeian prince. Come. Seek solace and peace in my embrace. By the time thou dost return, it may be too late. Thy journey will be for naught."

Time did move differently in the underworld, that he remembered, but wasn't about to stay. Now that she proved to be a threat, he didn't trust her. He said all he came to say, and she would not cease, nor could he really expect her to do so. Even if she could tell him where the portals lay, she wouldn't have. Of course, he could travel to the *Ge Theôn* and seek out Hades, but that would take up time that they just didn't have. It was worth a try, he reasoned. Out of a pouch at his waist, he removed a small black orb and unsheathed the sword.

"I would cover your eyes if I were you, drakæna. This orb contains my means of departure, flames from the First Fires, the only ones that can burn here."

Crushing the orb, he released the fire, using it to trigger the sword's power. Once he was back home, he knew his next task would be to prepare for battle. Ekhidna's point that fixing the Scales could change his existence stuck with him, but what other choice did he have? Allow her offspring to roam the planet, feasting on mortals? No. He had lived a life both with the gods and without them, with family and friends in both worlds over the course of his reality. His father had told him that prophecy created rules, and one must adhere to them or else the penalty would be weighty.

He stank of the underworld. A hot shower would cleanse his body, but what could cleanse his mind, he wondered.

Danelos had just finished getting dressed when his communicator buzzed. Quinn had already sent the others to investigate. When he asked what the disturbance was, Quinn replied, "Gorgons and then some."

• • •

The Task Force division used aeronautical machines that not even the military of any country of the world possessed. Almost all prototypes, they flew faster than any aircraft, making it from New York to Alaska in a few hours. Not bound by international aviation law, these planes, helicopters, and stealth craft traveled above normal air traffic patterns, allowing them to fly at speeds close to the sound barrier. Sarah, Brandon, and Aleta boarded the *Sabretooth*, an Excelsior class stealth plane with laser technology sophisticated enough to knock a fly out of the air from the stratosphere. Rarely did they have to use that weapon, but the United Nations wanted to prepare itself for any contingency. Flying from Boston to Indianapolis took less than an hour, letting them down two blocks away from the Soldiers' and Sailors' Monument, where authorities reported the disturbance. Hovering around the obelisk-like monument, two gorgons with brass wings had already turned dozens of people who had no idea what a gorgon was to stone, and panic in the streets didn't help. Sarah ran into Monument Circle via N. Meridian Street, and she immediately threw up an earthen wall around the perimeter to keep more people away. So many stone statues of those unfortunate enough to gaze at a gorgon lay crumbled on the street without any hope for resurrection, and she couldn't do anything to help them. *Apoleies polemou*—casualties of war—Acastus would have told her.

From above, another flying body entered the milieu, and she flew into one of the gorgons, knocking it back. Her wings, of white feathers instead of brass, brought her above her prey, and she reached toward the sky, a lone, meandering thunderbolt depositing her silver javelin in her hand. While Aleta assaulted them from above, Sarah threw

336

balls of water from the fountain at the base of the monument at the shrieking gorgons, trying to distract them from human vision as well as knocking them from the sky. Even with her power over the earth element, she didn't know if she could really contain a flying beast like this. Flashes of lightning responded to Aleta's call, disorienting her two adversaries, but they recovered quickly.

"Aether, come in."

"Kind of busy, Zodiak," Sarah replied, hurling water. She wore an earpiece that contained a microphone.

"Me, too. This Hesperian drakon's certainly no picnic here. Aegis wanted me to remind you not to look those things in the eye."

"Yep, knew that already. Have to go. Aether out."

Late afternoon sun glinted off the brass wings of the gorgons, sometimes making it hard to pinpoint where they were, so Sarah just threw larger water balls. Eventually, the fountain ran dry, so she substituted with small whirlwinds instead. Unfortunately, the change in wind currents affected Aleta's ability to stay aloft, too, and she had to settle on the top of the earth wall. As soon as she had her bearings, she heard Sarah's voice.

"Aetos, look out!"

• • •

Unlike a hydra, whose heads have to be cauterized once severed or they grow back twofold, one can chop off or impale a Hesperian drakon's heads, but the problem is that they have one hundred of them. Brandon had managed to channel Cancer enough to pinch off a few heads, but that tended to anger the others—sort of like swatting a few bees; eventually, it angers the hive. Tapping into the Zodiac forced him to use more of his mind than his body, actually. Thus far, he had managed to keep any of the drakon's heads from biting him, but he didn't think he could avoid a bite or two forever. Drakon venom immobilizes the victim, and then each head rips a piece of the prey apart. It's a painful death, to be sure. Now, he seemed to be able to keep the heads away from him as he stood on the far side of the Depew Memorial Fountain, and he had a tree trunk he had ripped from the sidewalk to use as a club. With it being a more open space, civilians had no place to hide and watch, so Brandon was lucky he didn't have to protect people while trying to subdue or kill the beast. The statue in the middle of the fountain created a barrier between the heads and him, but that barrier vanished when a few heads bit into the base of the statue. From experience, he knew that drakons were not particularly intelligent, so Brandon's best chance of defeating it was to put it on the defensive. Taking strength from Taurus, Leo, and Scorpio, more than he usually had, he launched the tree trunk so hard that it not only shattered against the scaly body, but it also pushed the legs back away from the fountain. Now if he could only get to the underbelly, he could do some damage.

Thirty feet tall, this drakon's roaring and hissing would intimidate most people, but now Brandon was just annoyed. Without warning, the heads turned to face a group of curious teenagers who thought they could take a few souvenir photos from a safe distance. Much to their chagrin, they didn't know how quickly a drakon could move. Even at their fastest, all the teens couldn't outrun it, and Brandon's first priority was to save lives. Closing the distance faster than one would think a creature of that size and girth could, the heads reached forward, readying themselves to snatch up one of the smaller children.

Adrenaline mixed with fear prompted Brandon to start running toward the drakon, and as he was channeling Sagittarius, he felt himself moving faster, but his footsteps seemed different. As soon as he was ahead of the serpentine heads, he snatched up the two closest teenagers, throwing them on his back. Wait. On his back? He had been so intent on using Sagittarius' strength and stamina that he didn't think about what had happened to him. The teens safely out of harm's way across the street, Brandon looked down to find that his lower torso and legs were that of a horse, but his upper body remained a man. Not only had he channeled the archer's abilities, but he had also become the centaur itself, and it felt completely natural to him. Through his hooves, he felt the drakon approaching, and when he turned to see, his left hand was holding a bow. Over his right shoulder, he could feel a quiver, and it had arrows. This had never happened before. He had never transformed into one of the signs. With the drakon soon to be upon him, he thought of a way he could stop it, but it was risky. Around the circumference of the fountain grew boxwood hedges about six feet tall, and he galloped toward them hoping to time this just right.

• • •

White River State Park, housed at a bend in that river, normally had throngs of locals and out-of-state visitors alike seeking attractions like the Indianapolis Zoo and the White River Gardens. Boats traveled on the waters, some miniature cruise vessels that offered meals and entertainment, some paddleboats for small groups. Most who spent time at the zoo could see anything from African lions to anacondas, black swans to clownfish, green herons to harbor seals, but what most didn't expect to see would be a sea creature seventy feet tall, with six long necks bearing canine heads, each filled with multiple rows of teeth. That would be Scylla, a daughter of Keto, and one of the most hideous creatures spawned since the Hekatonkheires. Odysseus sailed between one and Charybdis, the whirlpool who sucked in and spewed forth water three times a day. Scylla had positioned herself in the middle of the river bend, just north of the Old Washington Street Bridge, and she was hungry. How she got into the river without people knowing would remain a mystery, unless the entrance to the underworld was

339

somewhere under the White River. As Danelos arrived, Scylla had already taken two people in a toothy maw each, shaking them to cut them in two. One head reached over and bit down on the half of one man sticking out of another canine snout. Screams from the bridge caught Danelos' attention, and he ran down to it telling people to find cover. The creature's girth took up about a third of the river, and boats floating toward her made every attempt to turn around. Some succeeded, but many did not. Swift and merciless, her doglike heads snapped down to the bridge and the boats, snatching up what or whomever she could.

*Thyroros* unsheathed, Danelos jumped onto one of the heads as it lunged for him, holding onto the scaly ears. With one slice, he severed the head and sent it crashing into the water, green blood spewing on the bridge like a geyser. A quick leap and somersault midair, and he was back on the bridge, ready for more. Free of pedestrians, the bridge vibrated as a few heads of Scylla roared at Danelos while the others reached to the bank for more to eat. Anything within reach of those gaping, fanged jaws became food: pigeons, a stray balloon from the zoo, and even trashing floating down the river. He wanted to send this thing to another place through a portal, but since she didn't move, it would be impossible to do. While he considered his options, he neglected to see one of her heads moving toward him from the left until it blindsided him, knocking him into the water. His mobility compromised, he took the opportunity to check out the body of the beast underwater for any weakness.

Scylla had embedded herself in the riverbed, her talons gouging through the earth. Similar to a Venus Flytrap, he thought. Shimmering above the water, one of the heads spied him swimming around, and then plunged beneath the surface, pinning him down. She pulled back to engulf him, and she would have, too, except for something distracting her from above. Making his way to the surface, he leaped from the water, landing on the bridge to see a news helicopter hovering dangerously close. Waving it away had no effect. As he predicted, two of Scylla's heads ripped apart the helicopter, snatching the falling pilot and reporter from the air before they could hit the water. Shredded, the carcass of the helicopter plunged into the river. This gave him an idea. One last scan of the bridge and the riverbank showed no people—finally, they'd been smart.

"Quinn!" he shouted into his communicator, "Send a TF-27 to my coordinates in five minutes. Tell the pilot to keep a half-mile radius. Aegis out."

Slicing through into another realm, he jumped through the portal into a place he had nearly forgotten about—his armory on Arkadeia.

• • •

Aleta looked up just in time to see a brass-winged gorgon flying straight for her, and without thinking, met her gaze. Sarah watched in horror as Aleta's body stiffened first and then took on a gray, stony texture. Her javelin remained silver, caught in her hardened grip. The gorgon snatched up the solidified woman in her talons, flew higher and dropped it, but Sarah stopped her friend from crashing to the ground with a small whirlwind, setting her down gently. A dome of earth grew around Aleta, shielding her from further gorgon attacks.

"Aegis! Zodiak! Aetos is down!"

Both gorgons squawked to drown out the distress call, but it was too late. Only Brandon would receive the call. Sarah clenched her fists, raising a wall around her, spikes protruding from the top and walls. Within the cylinder, the winds spun around so fast that the gorgons didn't have time to maneuver away. Fury fueled Sarah now. In her mind, she reached out to fire, and her heightened emotions tapped into an even greater power that she had before. About five miles away, in the Crown Hill Cemetery, an eternal flame in the Field of Valor appeared in her head. Her eyes looked like balls of fire beneath glass, and soon a plume of flame leaped over the stone wall, becoming part of the whirlwind. It wouldn't be enough to destroy the gorgons, but it would keep them occupied. Using three elements, Sarah felt connected for the first time, as if she had breached an internal barrier.

She shouted over the din into her microphone.

• • •

Building up speed, Brandon galloped up to the boxwood and, pushing off with his hind legs, leaped over it. Turning to face the hedge, he nocked three arrows, tightening the bowstring until it creaked. Silver Earthsteel arrows with fletchings of blue eagle feathers at the ready, Brandon felt the earth shake harder as the Hesperian drakon lumbered toward him. He saw the heads first, but then the creature tried to leap over the hedges, as he had, exposing its underbelly. Two volleys, three arrows each, jutted from the drakon's body within seconds, and the heads flailed, shrieking. Soon, though the scaly body slowed and fell forward, crushing the hedge, driving the arrows in deeper. As the last head hit the ground, scales and skin decomposed, melting into gelatinous ooze.

"Zodiak! Aegis!" came over the communicator.

• • •

Jumping back through the portal onto the bridge, Danelos saw and heard the TF-27 approaching.

"This is Aegis. Fly directly over the target no lower than 100 feet. No lower!"

"Roger that, Aegis," the pilot replied.

Danelos pulled a black cord from off his shoulder, an Earthsteel hook on one end, and spun it around, waiting for the right moment. As if out of nowhere, the black helicopter descended, leveling off at the height Danelos specified. As each of Scylla's heads tried to reach it, they were just shy of the landing skids. Frustrated, the she-beast used all of her heads to snap up, but the futility of snapping at air made her angry. With all heads up in the air, Danelos tossed the hook, and the cord wrapped itself around the necks until the barb caught on the cord itself. Using another hook, he caught the landing skid.

"Aegis here. Take up the slack. Go!"

Eventually, the cording bound all of Scylla's heads together, stretching out her necks. She pulled, but only managed to move the helicopter a little as she lost her advantage.

"Pull all you want! That cord's made with the hair of the Titan Atlas. Nothing can break it!" he shouted, more for himself, since he didn't think Scylla could understand him anyway.

"Keep it taut!" he instructed the pilot. "Lift! Lift!"

Not able to pull the creature from the riverbed, he hoped the helicopter could at least raise enough of it up to expose the sensitive spot where the necks met the body. Danelos retrieved the rotor from the fallen copter and hurled it. An eerie ripping noise as the necks popped off the body filled the air, and green blood pulsed forth, bubbling as it hit the river. Backlash from pulling on the heads took the helicopter off balance, but the pilot flew off, the severed heads of Scylla disintegrating, the ooze dripping until nothing remained but the cord hanging from the landing skid.

"Aegis to TF-27. Thanks. Give me the location of the others."

• • •

"Open the wall! I can't get through!" shouted Brandon over his communicator.

Sarah let him in, and then she released her hold on the wind and fire. She'd kept the gorgons at bay and didn't even feel tired. As long as she kept her tie to the earth, the earth replenished her strength. Good to know for the future. Both gorgons descended toward the two,

343

screeching, their brass wings tucked against them. Before they could get close enough, Brandon closed his eyes and trusted his instincts. Two arrows flew from his bow, landing with a thud in the chest of each she-creature, and they crashed by the fountain.

Before they could recover, he embedded more arrows into them, but that wouldn't kill them. Above them, Sarah heard a whistling sound and took a defensive pose, but landing near them was Danelos who had climbed the earth wall. *Thyroros* came down, decapitating the gorgons, acidic blood etching the ground where it poured out. When he saw Brandon, Danelos did a double take, but then smiled.

"It's a good look for you," he laughed. "Where's Aleta?"

Sarah removed the earth dome to show what looked like a statue of their friend, and Danelos turned around, muttering Greek curses under his breath.

"What can we do?" she asked. Brandon resumed complete human form and put his arm around her.

A few seconds passed, and Sarah said, "Look at that!"

Slowly, the rough stone softened, revealing Aleta's darker skin, and her white wings regained their plumage. Brandon helped her up.

"Dan, look," Brandon said.

When Danelos saw his fallen friend recovering, his expression softened. "Thank the gods."

Aleta assured them she would be fine and threw the javelin skyward. No longer in need of her wings, they vanished from sight, and Sarah put her arm around her as they went to debrief with Quinn and Nigel. Task Force: Epsilon would handle clean up and civil engineering, restoring the city to its original state as best they could, and they would have their hands full over the next months.

# 25—BALANCE

**WNYX (New York)** "For WPR News, this is Geoff Berger. Random earthquakes across the globe have gotten the attention of Task Force: Xi seismologists who have noticed fluctuations and tremors along small fault lines but also in places where no fault lines exist. Ranging from 5.0 to 8.9 on the Richter scale, these quakes are unrelated to any seismic activity monitored by Xi scientists. Dr. Raymond Virtu, lead seismologist for this investigation, wants to predict where these quakes will strike next, but the data collected thus far does not lend itself to such inquiries."

• • •

"I think the prophecy's been pretty clear so far," Sarah stated. "The part I'm not clear on is "*Lead day's darkness to finds its path. Let spirit restore balance without wrath. Four for Gaea, four must be, for being lacks uncertainty*.""

Quinn wasn't usually present when the four talked about the prophecy, but they had all just finished debriefing. All the talk of gods and monsters intrigued him, having heard so little about them until he had met this group. Like most people in the *Oikoumene Broteios*, Quinn's knowledge of Olympian gods and such came from myths and legends passed down, but unknown to him,

345

these gods never lived in his world. When the gods moved the second selves, a byproduct of two looms, these people brought only their memories and knowledge of the gods, Titans, monsters, and heroes. All the marble monuments and temples built in ancient times served only as a reminder of those no longer among them, not a marker of past worship. To think that these gods actually existed, even in some other place, was almost more than he could wrap his head around.

"I'm done with chasing Ekhidna's and Keto's kids around the globe," Brandon chimed in. "I mean, I'll do what I have to do, but shouldn't we figure out how to 'lead day's darkness', and all that?"

Aleta had to add her two cents. "Day's darkness. Shadow? How do we go about leading shadows down paths? What would that leash even look like?"

As usual, her comments always dipped into sarcasm, but she wasn't wrong. How did one lead darkness?

Spending months fighting otherworldly creatures, actually sitting down to have a conversation felt so liberating, even if it was 'business'. Sarah had put more time into her pottery, getting some pieces into art shows and local galleries, and Aleta spent the past months getting rid of Jack Forrester. Suspicion of foul play was all the board of trustees at Genetix really needed to dismiss him. Northeastern University wanted to expand their zoology department, and Brandon needed more flexible hours, so he took a position as an academic advisor in the department. A temporary change, it gave him to chance to set his own hours; being assistant zoologist didn't. Archaeological lectures became the mainstay of Dan's time, since he had been able to hire a few assistants to catalogue new artifacts.

In his own private world, Danelos heard everything they said, but he had other concerns. His conversation with Ekhidna raised the point about fulfilling destiny. After that, would they exist? In another incarnation? At all? It's hard to fight for something when you don't know if you'll even be around to appreciate it. He was the only one among them who had lived among the gods, had even seen Mount Olympos, and knew firsthand what the underworld looked like. Could his father, a god himself, allow his son's existence to go unknown? Would the gods be immune to such a thing? Apollo and the others knew the Scales had been destroyed, but they never made mention of having lived another way. Could they, too, be hesitant about restoring an order that they never knew? Too much to ponder, and he could get lost in his own musings.

"The *Protogenos* Hemera embodies day," he said, still not entirely in the conversation. "Her mother is Nyx, the night. They pass one another in the heavens."

"Isn't Nyx the one who got us into this?"

"Be careful, Aleta. Get her attention, and she might have a bone to pick with you, too," Brandon joked, but somewhere in his heart he knew that could be true.

Figuring out that 'day's darkness' was Nyx seemed too easy to them, but sometimes, Danelos pointed out, figuring out a prophecy simply required knowledge of context. Once the prophecy's content became clear, he added, fulfilling it tended to take much more effort. Apollo had mentioned to him that they would have to put the pieces of the Scales back together for this to right itself. Sometimes a hero's journey would have to embody the impossible to learn what he or she truly could do. How to let spirit restore balance without wrath puzzled him. It just seemed that they would have to go up against Nyx to restore the Scales, but they would have to be strong in spirit to do it. It wasn't becoming any clearer. The rest of the prophecy would have to wait. They had to find Nyx and get her to tell them where she put the pieces of the Scales.

• • •

No one, mortal or immortal, descended into the underworld without carefully thinking about the consequences. Ancient beings took refuge there, some older than the gods. Some parts existed solely for the spirits of the dead, while other parts went untouched, fear of the unknown and oblivion being deterrents. Danelos remembered that Nyx passed Hemera in Tartaros, a part of the underworld largely untraveled, just as Hemera returned from the heavens, having brought day to the world. To Tartaros they would have to go. *Thyroros* couldn't open a portal there, as Tartaros had actually been a *Protogenos*, a bottomless, living pit within the dark realm, although now he was more of an empty shell since he relinquished his life energy when Hades took over. Regardless, they would travel the path that Apollo had taken, as had Danelos— living as Demetrios.

Aleta told Quinn they would be 'off the grid' for a while, and they didn't know when they'd be returning. Frankly, she didn't know if they'd return or even if the world as they knew it would be the same at all. If it were merely a question of only putting their lives in danger, they could make peace with themselves, but when you don't know if you'll even come out of this experience as part of the cosmos, how do you prepare for that?

They traveled to Arkadeia to see Apollo, since he had wanted to see them off on the journey. Danelos asked that no one else know what they were about to do since he didn't want to worry the people. While he might live in another realm, these were still his people, and he hoped they would come out of this. The hardest decision he made was not saying anything to his mother. She of all people would understand, but she was still his mother. She might have wanted to return to the *Ge Theôn*, but she couldn't, as it would mean her death. She had given up her immortality, an integral part of her existence as queen of Arkadeia. The sun god stood in the Hall of Tribunals, not the throne room, since he didn't want anyone to wander into the chamber unannounced. Among him stood a few others, some Danelos and his friends recognized, like Athene and Artemis, but others they did not. One among the crowd, standing behind the others, kindled anger.

"Why is Ares here?" Danelos said. "I thought he couldn't be here."

"He asked to be here, so I allowed it. He knows that what you do affects all of us. Trust me, I have my eye on him," Apollo said, nodding in the direction of the window where a crow sat, vigilant.

"Welcome to Arkadeia," he announced. "I am Danelos' father, Apollo, although he will always be Demetrios to me."

Danelos rolled his eyes.

"What you do now affects the fate of all, mortal and immortal alike."

While he spoke, he approached each member of the team. Sarah blushed when he spoke to her, gently brushing a hair from her face. She could see Danelos in his eyes. He could see the connection to Gaea in her, he said, and that made him proud. To Aleta, he nodded, and admired her tenacity. He briefly mentioned his experience with Amazons many years ago, and he felt strongly she would bring honor to their tribe. Brandon shook his hand, and Apollo looked into the young man's eyes, seeing intricate connections to many things, and something familiar. With his son, he did something he didn't often do—he embraced him. He said something to him in Ancient Greek, something to the effect of, "You are my shining light, my joy." Zeus had said the same to Apollo when he was just a young boy, too.

"I bless your journey, although I don't know if my blessing holds much weight in the underworld. The gods have faith in you. They truly do."

Danelos leaned into his father.

349

"Do you know the outcome?"

Apollo shook his head. Danelos had thought that perhaps his father knew what would happen, and all they were doing was fulfilling a set plan, bringing it to its logical conclusion each to learn something. Not knowing the outcome meant that whatever change came would definitely affect the gods. That scared him.

Four stallions awaited them at the back of the palace near the stables. As they rode toward the city gates, Danelos looked at the stables behind the royal ones, reflecting on his visit there, meeting the horses of the sun-chariot. It seemed like so long ago. The entrance to the underworld they would take was many miles outside of the city, but they would make it there before nightfall. Aleta, wingless for the moment, reached up to summon her weapon, and now all four were prepared. Or were they.

• • •

Grassy hills, speckled with poplar trees, expanded as far as the horizon, with trickling streams winding through the flora. Early afternoon sun gave them ample light to reach the cave before it would be too difficult to maneuver in the syrupy darkness. Three hours into the ride, Danelos took a side road, not well worn, with good reason—it led to the entrance to the Hades' realm. The dead needed no path; Hermes would take them. The living, however, made the perilous journey without godly interference. Deep into the forest, a mound of earth about eight feet tall sat between two cypress trees, those sacred to Hades. Between the trees a boulder blocked the entrance, marked in Ancient Greek: "Go back!" and "Death awaits you." Danelos dismounted, lifted the two-ton boulder out of the way, exposing the stairs. The stench of rotting flesh and despair flooded their nostrils.

"What is that sound?" Brandon asked, cringing.

"Echoes of the dead asking for mercy," replied Danelos. "Those who do not pass through the gates to

Hades' realm must linger for eternity outside. More than likely, their loved ones didn't put an *obolos* on their tongue as payment for Charon. Souls denied entry become bitter and vindictive, so be aware."

Deep growling, followed by barking, echoed.

"Cerberos," Sarah said. "I fought one of his brothers."

"My father said he was cute as a puppy," Danelos said, hoping to break the tension. "Stay behind me, and whatever you do, don't wander off. Darkness lives, and it feeds on anguish. Best not to feed it."

After they entered, Danelos used the cord of Atlas to pull the stone back into place so unsuspecting people wouldn't get too curious.

"Are we crossing the river?" Aleta asked. "Because I didn't bring my Dramamine."

Danelos chuckled.

Following him was Sarah, then Aleta, and Brandon picked up the rear. Smells of mold and pain filtered through them, growing as they descended the stairs in utter darkness. Danelos remembered this journey, and how much it taxed him, but it was the price he, as well as his friends, had to pay. Unfortunately, the pathways change over time, so even if he had memorized the route, it wouldn't have mattered. It felt as if an hour had passed, but they really had no clue how time moved here. Every once in a while, Danelos felt a presence, but as soon as he tried to pinpoint what it could be, it vanished.

"No light works down here, eh, Dan?"

"Unfortunately, no. But, wait…"

He pulled a small black orb from a pouch at his waist. Crushing it, a small fireball sat in his hand, but the flames were darker than normal, almost gray. Some of the walls and floor showed up, but only to a distance of about three feet. First Fires can cut the darkness, but too much could do damage if not watched very carefully. Their purpose was to create, not illuminate. These flames were a living

351

entity used to forge all their weapons, and even Hephæstos didn't like working with them much.

"Better?" he asked.

"A little. Thanks."

Cerberos' barking grew louder which meant they were nearing the river Akheron. Something didn't feel right, Danelos thought. It almost sounded as if Cerberos were in pain. Eventually, the glow from the river lit up their path a bit more, as Akheron shone with the woe of all those souls who had traveled over him. From a distance, it wouldn't hurt you, but if you actually went into the river, the woe could destroy your soul, if you were alive. As they left the cave and walked toward the river, Cerberos' wailing grew more intense. Charon brought them across, thanks to a few drachmas they remembered to bring, and there they saw the source of the wailing. Someone had caged Cerberos, the feared Hound of Hades. Spirits of the dead couldn't enter the underworld unless they walked through the gates, and someone had closed them. But where were the spirits?

First, Danelos freed the three-headed canine, offering him a piece of cake doused in wine—his favorite treat. Then, all four surveyed the river for any signs of trouble, but they saw nothing. Odd. Passing through the gates, dripping with souls that had wasted away waiting for entry, they were passing through Hades' realm unimpeded by any spirits. Aleta flew Brandon and Sarah across the Fields of Asphodel while Danelos followed on foot until they reached Hades' palace. Black marble adorned it, encrusted with gemstones, glistening in the eerie light of the river. No Skeleton Guard. No one to stop them from entering the throne room. And then, they saw Hades.

Sitting on his throne, he looked almost dead himself, if indeed a god could look as such. He looked up when they approached, but said nothing, and made no attempt to reprimand them for approaching him without a summons.

"Lord Hades, what's happened here?" Danelos asked. "Where are the spirits of the undead?"

In a voice as deep as his own kingdom, he replied, "Gone."

"Gone where?"

Hades sat up. He told them about the incantation that the coven did in the *Oikoumene Broteios* to allow Keto's and Ekhidna's brood to enter from this world. Unknown to him at the time, the catalyst for such godly magic to work was...

"The souls of the underworld. That's how the portals remained open," Danelos deduced. With the life force given off by the souls, even those who had passed into your realm had enough power to attract those monsters."

"They must have entered the underworld from our side and caged Cerberos," added Aleta. "I wonder how?"

Hades replied, "The rivers are gods themselves. Khaos only knows what that coven used to bribe them in the first place."

"How could they do this if you're the ruler of this place?" Sarah asked.

"The *Potamoi* have been here since before I took over the underworld. Combined, they have much more power than I do. As long as the incantation is in effect, the souls of the world's dead will continue to keep those portals open. It is old power. Older than the gods."

While the underworld would not be in peril without spirits, it would weaken Hades over time. Yet another consequence of the shattered Scales. No balance. Zeus' brother knew well the task they had to undertake, and although he couldn't directly help them, he could make their journey a little easier. He waved his hand and they vanished, only to reappear by the edge of Tartaros. Now, they waited.

• • •

Deep within the void, they saw movement. Something light, yet shadow. Hemera. She would only house the brightness of Aether or Light, her brother, when they met at the horizon. She was rising from the pit which meant Nyx would return soon. That presence Danelos had been feeling was there again, but it kept leaving and returning. A faint noise prompted them to look up, and meandering down in serpentine fashion was the one they had come to see. No physical form to touch, her tenebrosity was the living night, that which shielded humankind after Day departed the mortal world. Seeing the four mortals by the pit, she swirled around them, investigating the intrusion. That other presence was getting stronger, too.

"No, we are here to speak with you, *Protogenos*, not fight you."

Danelos heard her in his mind, much like Zeus had so long ago.

"Much time has passed, Dark One, and we came to ask you where the pieces of the *Hieros Zugos* were so we could repair them."

Swirling much faster now, the spidery tendrils of darkness caused the four of them to get closer together. Aleta had her javelin ready, although she didn't know how she would even use it since Nyx had no physical form.

"Yes, I know Zeus ignored you. Do you still harbor such animosity after all this time? Please, we implore you, *Poikileimôn*, Spangle-robed one. Tell us what we seek so that we may finish our quest."

Danelos thought he was doing as the prophecy asked, staying calm, and letting his spirit persuade Nyx. It wasn't working.

"It matters because what you've done is disrupt Fate. My friends and I will find a way to repair the damage, to mend destiny."

Her blackness filled the cavern above and below, as if she were growing all around them. Sarah and Aleta stood back-to-back, waiting for something to happen, and Brandon watched Danelos, ready to protect him if need be. For some reason, Nyx only spoke to him, as if she had some kind of connection to him only. Perhaps, it was the presence of either Apollo or Gaea within him, the parts he embraced, that drew her to him. Brandon's stomach knotted thinking she might just as easily obliterate him with a gesture before he could assuage her hostility. She moved more erratically, as if something he had just said annoyed her. Building intensity, her form spiraled around the chamber until it rushed toward him. Sarah's face immediately changed, and she seemed more assured, more powerful, more... regal. Taking Danelos' hand, she looked at him as if she were seeing him for the first time. His expression changed as well, a soft smile expanding. They both turned toward the writhing mass of dark above them just as Nyx was about to strike Danelos. Her assault never landed on him. If she had had a face, they would have seen astonishment. Aleta and Brandon were about step forward when a voice came from Danelos, a voice they had never heard before, but a voice they knew at some level. Pervasive calmness resonated from him and Sarah, a peace almost intoxicating.

"*I can no longer be silent. Hold, sister, stay thy anger. This one's heart is true and speaks not for himself, but for the cosmos. Let go of thy rancor against the son of Rhea, and heed his plea.*"

Nyx's black form entered Brandon, one who was already acquainted with the heavens. She spoke through his mouth, but the words and tone were hers.

"*Now dost thou speak? Lo, all these eons, thou hast remained silent, detached, unaware of the insolence cast upon me by Kronos' pup!*"

The voice through Danelos replied, "*My destiny was to sustain Rhea's brood, nurture them through my being, so that they might bring honor to my sister. What is thy destiny?"*

Agape at this exchange, Aleta had no choice but to observe. Since no harm came to her friends, she resisted using the power of the javelin. Besides, she had no idea if Zeus' thunderbolt could reach Tartaros.

Nyx replied, *"Blanket the world in darkness, cloaking all, preparing all for Hypnos and Morpheos. That, sister, is my destiny, my purpose."*

Aleta was beginning to put the pieces together.

The voice of Danelos continued, *"While Zeus fulfills his destiny as king of gods, thou dost fulfill thine. Guiding him was not thy task, hence why he did not ask. O Night, thou dost scorn Zeus for something he did not have to do."*

Silence.

In her heart, Aleta knew this voice in Danelos. 'Let spirit restore balance without wrath.' After he returned from Arkadeia with his original soul, he spoke about his earlier life as Demetrios, and how, when he traveled the underworld path, she was with him, Olympeia, the *Ourea*, or spirit, of Olympos. If Nyx were to heed her sister's words, she would have done so without wrath. Sarah spoke, but in another voice known by all as well.

*"Sister Nyx, long have I cared for her, our sister who dost speak to thee now. Steadfast, she did what I could not. She did what thou couldst not. Give these four mortals, whose Fate is to fix that which thou didst break, the knowledge they seek. I beseech thee. These four who stand before thee now have given up much. Let their sacrifices not be in vain."*

Gaea. With her connection to the elements, Sarah provided the perfect vessel for Mother Earth. Nyx had now rendered a decision.

*"Once the Hieros Zugos are restored, the cosmos shall become that which it should have been. Thou must accept thy true fate and promise to protect Gaea, Matêr*

*Pantôn, no matter what path Fate giveth thee. No mortal may touch the Scales. I shattered them, and I shall be the one to repair them.*"

That was the last part of the prophecy: four for Gaea, four must be, for being lacks uncertainty. With that, she left Brandon's body; Gaea and Olympeia did the same to Sarah and Danelos. In a flash, they stood in the adyton, that sacred inner place where once the Scales resided, by Gaea's grace. Blackness of Nyx coalesced, bringing fragments from across the globe, and the four friends watched as each piece joined another, a cosmic puzzle, one that balanced all. Holding hands, their last thoughts before the final piece was in place were about each other, and how much meaning they had given to each other, and questions: what would change? What would remain?

Then, obscurity.

# 26—THE MORE THINGS CHANGE

2008 C.E.

Sunrise over the Charles River always made him happy, rays of light dancing on the water, highlighting the crew teams as they glided with perfect precision. From his balcony, he could admire them, their athletic bodies moving their shells like a fine tuned machine. He had to finish his *Boston Globe* before he left for work, since he never had time, teaching five archaeology classes this semester. If that weren't enough, he'd just started dating Jason, one of Dr. Aleta Halston's interns at Genomics, her genetic research consortium. She thought Jason would be the perfect match, especially since he liked to run, a hobby that Dan had just started a few months earlier, but he did it for fun, not competitively. When he realized the time, he cleared his breakfast plate from the balcony, tossed the newspaper on the coffee table, and went to grab a shower, but his roommate was still using the bathroom.

"Hey, Brandon, I have to get ready for work. You almost done?"

No answer. He poked his head in, and Brandon was still showering.

"Will you be done soon? I have to go."

"Two minutes. Promise. Get the shower in your own bathroom fixed and we won't have to share one. Hey, did you call Jason back? He left a message on your cell phone. I heard it ring a half hour ago I think."

"Thanks. I'm counting two minutes."

After he put his coffee cup in the sink, he glanced down at the manila file folders on the dining room table. One labeled 'Prophecy'. Another labeled 'Titans'. He'd read them later.

"I have to remember to tell Quinn not to label them in Braille. She always does that," he said aloud.

Checking his cell phone, he saw the call from Jason, and he missed one from Neil Crawford, the Task Force director his father knew who was well aware of the special nature of their Gaea division. Before he could call either one back, Sarah called to let him know about her art show that weekend and told him to bring Jason.

Dan finished getting ready for work, asking Brandon to call Quinn later to see when the next meeting would be since he wouldn't have time. With a mouth full of oatmeal, Brandon acknowledged his roommate, but he was more interested in the crossword puzzle. Dan always started them, but never finished them, leaving the weirdest words blank just to mess with him.

"Seven letter word for a mythological equine creature. That's easy. Centaur."

Just before Brandon left for the zoo, someone knocked on the door.

"Oh, hey, Mrs. Fairmont, Dan just left."

"That's okay. I need to speak you anyway. May I come in?"

Brandon noticed her hair seemed haphazardly clipped behind her head. Normally, she styled it. Some blond strands hung loosely around her face. He knew something wasn't right. She wouldn't even look him in the face, but she tried not to be too obvious about it.

"Is something wrong? Is it Dan's father?"

She looked around the living room as if she wanted to find something.

"Come sit. You're not okay. What is it?"

Hanging on the wall in the corner was Dan's sword, next to which hung Brandon's silver amulet. Mrs. Fairmont looked at one then the other.

"With my husband being away, well… you know what I mean, I've had some time to think, and I… I need to tell you something, but I'm not sure how to say it."

Brandon fidgeted a little. He liked Dan's mother, but not like that. How was he going handle this? Would he tell Dan? This wasn't how he wanted to start the day.

"Just say it, Mrs. Fairmont. Whatever it is, it'll be okay." He wished he believed that.

"Alkinoë, please. Or Allison. Either one is fine," she replied, slowly wringing her hands in her lap.

"Okay, sure thing. Alkinoë." This wasn't going to go well, he thought.

How was he going to react when she told him? Should he reciprocate? No, he'd have to let her down easy. After all, Dan was his roommate. They were like brothers.

"I need you to know, Brandon… I'm your birth mother."

# EPILOGUE

Gaea's *adyton*. For an impenetrable sacred vault, it had seen more visitors than it was ever intended. One of those unanswerable questions.

In the middle of this cave, two concave stone discs hovered horizontally, each the size of a small mountain, rising and falling to the pull of Order and Chaos. On a ledge perched just above sat Phoebos Apollo, eyes shut in silent meditation. The fact that the sun god found solace in the dark hadn't lost its irony.

After a deep breath, he opened his eyes, staring down at the monstrosity that determined the behavior of the cosmos, listening to the barest movement of air as the pans adjusted themselves.

"I remember," he uttered. "I remember it all."

It would seem at first that he was speaking to the *Hieros Zugos*, or perhaps the underworld itself, but in fact, he spoke to one who had taken on the custodial guardianship of the scales.

"I remember my life prior to the scales' destruction, and after their absence rewrote history... I remember how I was in both times. And, I know that now, after the

361

Scales' restoration, righting that which needed correction, I am different yet again.

"Then you are the only one who does remember, son of Zeus."

"But, why, Themis? Why am I the only one?"

The blindfolded goddess of Justice had no answer.

"When I told you of my time as a mortal man, did you remember none of that?"

"I did not. As god of truth, I take you at your word, but that which you described to me, your penance and its consequences, I knew not."

Like an algae bloom, silence grew again for a time, the scales swishing, filling the void, only to be splintered once more.

"The *Moirae* tell me they, too, remember nothing of that thread of mine, but my time spent as a man taught me much. It changed me. Dear Ios of Trapæzos taught me how to accept my mortality simply by living. I understood how sickness and death or living life to the fullest could give existence depth and meaning.

"I never did return to Themiskyra to see how Queen Otari responded to my presence in her city of Amazons, or whether Danaë ever really spoke much of my actions as an envoy. I gained an appreciation for diplomacy from these women, the alleged 'man-haters'.

"Finding Alkinoë made my soul cry out with joy, sometimes making me weep like a child. She keeps me grounded, Themis, yet challenges me constantly.

"Being human, since it is so much more than being mortal... well, the gods should know what that feels like. Olympos might be better off for it.

Silence again. Themis floated at the height of the ledge on which Apollo sat.

"When you spoke of your penance, you mentioned another reason why Zeus wanted you away from Olympos, stripped of your power."

Apollo stood. He knew she would bring that up.

"I can speak of it now, to you. The reason why Zeus forsook all others and devoted himself to Hera was not altogether out of rediscovering monogamy. He had committed his own odious act, one whose consequences have yet to happen. Even the rewriting of the cosmos cannot erase this.

"While it was true that Nyx acted out of anger, it was not solely because Zeus had neglected to take counsel with her. That was the reason she told him, but he knew it was something else.

"After Zeus had seduced her, here in dark Tartaros, had lain with her as he had with so many others, he spurned her, as he had so many others.

"How do you know this?"

"I saw it. I had journeyed to the underworld to speak with Hades, but I wanted to see more of this tenebrous realm. I followed my father when I saw him here in the Underworld and stumbled upon my father in Nyx's embrace, but he saw me before I could leave. Shortly thereafter, he swore to love Hera alone for all time, accusing me of befouling my godhood, cavorting with mortals.

"After the Scales became whole, I thought that perhaps that act had never happened, but it had. Gaea told me so. And now, I fear, that just as we have come back from the brink of madness, we are to be thrust into yet another tangled web of the *Moirae*.

"Why?"

"Because, dearest Themis, *she* is coming. Soon.

"Who?"

"The daughter of Zeus and Nyx. And she isn't happy."

# GALLERY

## ART BY
## MICHAEL HAMLETT

Danelos Fairmont, aka Aegis

Brandon Jeffries, aka Zodiak

Sarah Bishop, aka Aether

Aleta Halston, aka Aetos

## ABOUT THE AUTHOR

David Berger, born in Boston, MA., grew up in Commack, NY and holds a B.A. in English as well as a masters in Secondary Education. He has been a comic book reader since he was a child, channeling his writing toward the fantasy genre.

He currently lives in the Tampa Bay area with his partner Gavi and teaches high school seniors in both the AP English Literature and IB English programs as well as teaching at St. Leo University.

Made in the USA
Charleston, SC
01 November 2012